ESCAPING SANCTUARY

THE BOOK OF EVELYN

CHER L. JONES

Feisty Scholar Publications

www.feistyscholar.com

Escaping Sanctuary: The Book of Evelyn

First Edition
978-1-913619-46-6 (*paperback*) 978-1-913619-48-0 (*eBook*)
Cover designed by Mibl Art
For news and details of upcoming publications from this author visit:
www.cherjones.co.uk

Chapter One

The Book of Evelyn

What do you see when you look at me? I am a killer; there'd be no point denying it. And in all honesty, if I had to, I'd do it again.

Of course, I had my reasons, both when we were children and more recently. Not that the citizens of the Sanctuary ever cared about my motives. I overheard their whispers and caught their stares. They studied and feared me. But then, maybe they were sensible to be cautious. Because the truth is, when cornered, I have no idea of what I'm capable.

Bug says I'm a leader. I'm not. He's confused that with being a fighter. The difference is that one is a choice, and the other is born of necessity. I've been fighting for so long it's become part of the fabric of who I am. I'm not sure I even know how to stop.

I bet you are wondering why I'm asking you this. It's because I lost myself somewhere along the way. I wish I could see myself the way you seem to, Jared. To you, I'm still the little girl who waded into that lake to retrieve your coin. I hate to shatter that illusion, but she's long gone. I did what I had to do. Help was never coming so, in order to protect myself, I learnt to sting.

Not that it made any difference. Despite all the promises I made myself, here I am, asking for their help. I've come full circle, back to the citizens who abandoned me to put my own pieces back together. But it wasn't that easy. Somehow I got them muddled, and the person I've forged is a stranger to me. My edges have become jagged and there are gaps where there were none. Unfortunately for my enemies, the missing pieces are the parts that would have allowed me to show them mercy.

Jared

Jared stepped through the portal, followed by Martin and Seb.

A circle of guardians surrounded them, Millicent at their centre. 'I'm sorry. I kept them back as long as I could.'

'Get down on the floor, all of you!' A guardian jabbed the muzzle of the laser gun into Jared's ribs, creating a hot circle of pain.

'You know me,' Jared said, wriggling onto his belly. 'I'm not a threat.'

The guardian snatched a handful of Jared's hair and shoved his face into the floor. The salt rock was smooth against his cheek, the swooping plane only broken by some crudely scrawled letters scraped into the surface. Jared focused on the letters, trying to calm his nerves through distraction. *Curtis*, he thought to himself, putting them together. *They won't have liked you doing that.* Jared decided he liked this mysterious Curtis already. Jared swore he'd carve his own name right next to it before he left the Sanctuary forever.

'Of course I know who you are,' the guardian said, too close to his ear for comfort. 'We all do. The prodigal son we never wanted back.'

'Get off him, Felix,' Sienna said.

'Stay out of this. Aleksey said—'

'Aleksey said what? I hope you aren't putting words in my mouth.'

Even years later, the familiarity of Aleksey's accent made Jared relax. 'Thank goodness. Can you get this psychopath off me?'

Silence.

'Did you hear me? I've done nothing wrong. I went back to save Seb.'

'That might be so,' Aleksey said. 'But we appear to be missing a few of our citizens. However, let's make you all a little more comfortable while we get to the bottom of this.'

Felix hoisted Jared back to his feet.

'That's better.' Aleksey dusted off Jared's shirt. 'Jared Morgan, I've lost count of the times I've considered what I'd say if we met again. And here you are.'

'What did you decide on?' Jared asked.

'Excuse me?' Aleksey glanced behind him, distracted by the creaking of the door as Marney entered.

'You said you'd considered what you'd say to me. What did you decide on?'

'Well, that changed with my moods.' Aleksey rubbed his stubble. 'Sometimes I wanted to say I'm sorry for what happened to your grandfather. Other times that I wish I'd done more to protect you. But right now, I think I will settle on 'welcome home'.'

Jared's muscles tensed, but he forced a smile. 'Thank you.'

'And I see you've brought some new friends with you.' Aleksey nodded towards Beth and Aaron.

'I'm more concerned about what happened to his old ones,' Marney said. 'Where are Isaac and Luca? And Victor, for that matter?'

'They're dead.' Martin's voice was a whisper. 'They're all dead.'

Marney's eyes widened. 'H-how?'

'It's a long story,' Jared said.

Aleksey squeezed Jared's shoulder. 'And one that there will be plenty of time for you to tell us. For now, I need you to come with me. I think it's best the citizens don't learn of your return just yet. Not until we sort out this mess.'

For an instant, Marney's eyes lingered on Aleksey's hand. 'No, this needs to be handled properly.' She clicked her fingers, and a guardian stepped forward. 'Emma, escort Jared to the cells. Don't let him out of your sight.'

Beth ran towards them. 'Keep your hands off him.'

Aaron followed. 'He's not going anywhere without us.'

'Quite right,' Marney said. 'Round up the guardians and have all three of them taken to the prison. Martin, Seb and Oliver, too.'

'But...' Jared faltered. Teacher and doctor, he'd always viewed Marney as one of the few people he could rely on in the Sanctuary. Now she was calling for his arrest.

'You don't have the authority to tell them what to do,' Aleksey said.

'Fine. Millicent?'

Every eye turned to her. 'Do as Doctor Wallace says,' Millicent said. 'And lock the door to this chamber. I want guardians posted at the door.'

'Why are you doing this?' Jared asked.

Marney ignored him. 'Take them away,' she said to the guardians. 'Don't let anyone near them without my authorisation.' She looked Jared in the eye. 'Just until we get this sorted out. I promise.'

~

Marney

Before the Sanctuary

The students shoved their belongings into their bags before she'd even finished her sentence. Not that Marney blamed them. In truth, she was surprised any of them turned up at all. She'd nearly given the lecture a hard pass herself, and she was paid to be there. 'If you aren't heading out of the city, I suggest you go straight home.'

Most of the student population had abandoned their studies in the wake of the outbreak. She suspected it was some morbid fascination with the topic that kept bringing these few back, the chance to get up close and personal with the virus that was annihilating the population. Or maybe they'd fallen for that old adage; knowledge is power. As if some basic undergraduate understanding of microbiology might protect them from...No, she couldn't think about that. She wouldn't. Not until all of this was over. Then she'd take the time to unpick those nightmarish images from her subconscious and expel them forever.

Or maybe their motives were more straightforward than that. Hers certainly were. It wasn't the money that brought her back to the university every day. It was the little dose of normality that the lectures provided. She would miss it.

'Doctor Wallace.'

Marney looked up to find a man's hand extended uncomfortably close to her face. She didn't accept it and instead took a step back. 'Depends who's asking.' She was very aware of how fast the lecture theatre had emptied, leaving the two of them alone.

'Doctor Stuart, but please, call me Paul.' He suppressed a grin. 'You don't remember me, do you?'

Marney's face flushed. 'Now you mention it, you do look familiar.' It was a lie. She didn't have the foggiest idea who he was.

'We met at the Microbiology and Infectious Disease Conference. I ended up wearing your glass of wine.'

Marney cringed. She'd been the keynote speaker, and nerves always stopped her eating. An empty stomach plus several glasses of wine had not ended well. 'I'm so sorry. Yes, I remember. Vaguely. If it makes you feel any better, you're basically a hero. If you hadn't taken the hit on that glass of wine, then it would have been a three-day hangover instead of two.'

'Oh dear. You did seem quite merry.'

'That's not my usual style, I can assure you. There are colleagues there that I'd grown to consider friends whose calls I'm still dodging after that conference.'

Stuart laughed. 'Maybe a tad dramatic?'

'Nope. I can make new friends, but I'll never live down that humiliation.'

'Well, I think you were charming, even after you knocked the wine over me. You told me all about your girls.'

'Sorry, I tend to get a touch of mentionitis when I've been drinking, and I always swore I'd never become 'that parent'.' A fuzzy memory of a girl with blonde curls on a phone screen surfaced. 'You have a daughter, too, don't you? How is she?'

'Yes, Amy. She's with her mother.' He blurted it out so fast that Marney knew better than to press the topic. Divorced, perhaps. Or maybe work had taken him away. It was one of the reasons she was better off out of it. At least, that's what she told herself.

'I believe my secretary left a message asking you to get back to me?' he said.

'Yes, she did. I'm sorry for not calling. It's just, these are…unusual times.'

'To say the least. I'm surprised you're still giving lectures.'

'Well, I've always loved teaching and wanted to continue as long as the university would allow.'

'And how long will that be?'

'That was my final one.'

'Excellent. Then you'll have some free time. I was hoping to collaborate with you on a project.'

'Not possible, I'm afraid. As I believe I told your assistant, I don't work in research any more. It's not really conducive to raising small children.'

He pasted on a smile that didn't reach his eyes. 'Sometimes, we need to look beyond our personal inconveniences and think of the greater good.'

Marney bristled. 'I don't *need* to do anything.' Shoving the leftover handouts into her bag, she gave him a curt nod. 'Now, if you'll excuse me.'

He held up his palms in surrender. 'Of course not. Please, that came out wrong. I've been working around the clock, so I'm feeling a little punch drunk.'

'No problem,' Marney said, though she ensured the edge in her voice told him that it was, very much, a problem. She slung her bag over her shoulder and moved towards the stairs.

He sidestepped into her path, forcing her to stop in front

of him. 'So, what is your plan?'

'Not that it's any of your business, but I'll be taking my family and getting out of the city. I would advise anybody with that option to do the same.' She weaved around him and headed for the stairs.

'And what about those people who don't have that option? Don't they matter?' He stood with his hands shoved into his pockets, relaxed and casual. It was hard to believe he'd just insinuated that she was abandoning a whole segment of the population to their death.

Marney pivoted on her heel. 'Compared to my family? No, they don't. I gave years of my life to the Centre for Disease Control. When I needed their support, they were nowhere to be found. So, I carved myself a different life out of the mess they left.'

'If it makes you feel any better, I think you did the right thing. The world deserved to know the risks.'

When she had published her paper, warning that the last outbreak of the virus was just a precursor and that the government should prepare for a more virulent strain, she'd been vilified, labelled a scaremonger, and with her reputation in tatters, she'd been forced to quit. She didn't find any of those same people at her door, ready to apologise, when the strain she predicted decimated the population.

'Well, hindsight is a beautiful thing,' she said. 'It's a shame nobody bothered to stand up for me at the time.'

'You have every right to be angry, but don't you want to be part of the team that beats this? Marney, we are so close to creating a vaccine. You can rewrite your place in the history books.'

She couldn't resist chuckling. 'I think the virus has done

that for me. Besides, I don't care what the world thinks. Such hubris is for the single and the selfish.' She looked him up and down, making it clear she thought he fell into at least one of those categories.

Stuart huffed out a puff of air. 'You were the top of your field. Once upon a time, you would have—'

'Fairy tales are for children. This is the real world.' She paused at the bottom of the stairs. 'Good luck, Doctor Stuart. I really mean that.'

Her heart pounded as she climbed the steps between the tiered seating. It only began to calm once she was on the opposite side of the door. She resisted the urge to flee the building and instead peered back into the lecture hall.

He was still at the bottom with his mobile held to his ear, no doubt badmouthing her to his colleagues. When and if this passed, her name in the scientific community would be mud. Not for the first time. She couldn't let herself care. If it meant the four of them were alive and together, she could take a bit of criticism. It wasn't as though she was a stranger to it.

Marney waved a silent goodbye to the guard on the security desk and headed to her car.

When they first realised that the virus had resurfaced, stronger than ever, the press had swarmed around the car park. They'd waited for her to emerge from the university building before descending on her in a wave.

Now it looked deserted in comparison. Just a few vehicles remained.

The beaten-up Citroen belonging to Albi, one of the tenured professors, was parked next to her BMW. He'd told her it wasn't bravery or stupidity that kept him turning up every day, it was that he wasn't sure what else he'd do. As a widower with no family to flee with or to, he'd just stayed put. That made her sad, and as they'd stood in the staff break room, her hands encircling a cup of bitter coffee, she'd been a beat from offering him a place at the cabin. They didn't need another mouth to feed or another body to protect, but it seemed the right thing to do.

Thankfully, he saved her that dilemma when he clutched her hand and said, 'Look after that family of yours, Marney. They are precious, above anyone else.' Then he tipped the rest of his drink away and left her with her relief.

The other cars looked vaguely familiar, probably belonging to the skeleton facilities staff working as the university ran down the clock.

Compared to the chaos of the first outbreak, she should have felt reassured. She didn't and clicked down the locks on her car as soon as she got in.

The car was stifling. The back and much of the passenger seat were covered with everything they planned to take to the cabin, blocking the AC vents. She turned it up all the same.

The streets were empty as she drove towards the childminder's house. A lone boy, no more than eight, bounced a basketball against a brick wall with 'No Ball Games!' painted on it in huge white letters.

Marney dithered over the idea of pulling over and telling him to go home. 'Do not make him your problem. Do not make him your problem,' she told herself over and over again.

The traffic light turned red, forcing her to roll to a stop. She toyed with the idea of accelerating through it. It was just habit after all; there were no other cars on the road.

The boy stopped the incessant thudding and walked to the kerb to stare at her. Open-mouthed, he seemed as surprised to see her as she him. His woeful eyes looked larger against his dark skin.

Marney's finger lingered over the button to the electric window. But she pulled her hand away as the lights turned green and drove on. She was grateful for the luggage filling the back window, so she didn't have to watch him disappear into the distance.

The childminder must have heard her pull up, because she was at the door when Marney arrived.

'Hi, Isabelle. Did they behave themselves?'

'Of course. But you know they've gone already?'

'What? Gone where?'

'Your husband picked them up about ten minutes ago.' Isabelle gave a titter of a laugh. 'These things happen with busy parents.'

'No, that's not right. Ben's working today.' He had told her that morning how busy he would be cataloguing the most valuable library books ready for transportation. With the incidence of unpredicted catastrophic weather escalating, they were going to be stored somewhere safe. Ben had lamented over the idea of such treasures being locked away in some underground bunker.

Isabelle rubbed the back of her neck. 'I don't know what to say. I guess his plans changed.'

Despite the heat, a cold sweat began to settle over Marney. 'And you're sure it was him that picked them up?'

The smile dropped from Isabelle's face. 'I'm not in the business of handing people's children over to just anybody.'

'Of course not. As you said, it's probably just crossed wires.'

As soon as the door closed, Marney rummaged through her bag. The lecture handouts escaped and turned cartwheels across Isabelle's yard, but she had no time to chase them. Her mobile was to her ear before she got to the car.

On the first two attempts, she got the 'out of service' dial tone that had become frequent of late. Each time she jabbed the redial button, her panic grew.

On the third attempt, the call connected. It rang only once before Ben answered.

'Marney, I'm sorry.'

Her relief at hearing his voice was wiped away as his words sunk in. 'For what? Where are the girls?'

'With me. Some men stopped me outside the library. They said you were already at their facility. They said you'd agreed to help with the vaccine and that if I wanted the four of us to stay together, then I'd have to get the girls.'

She wanted to yell at him, to ask if he actually thought she'd make that decision without consulting him first. But she knew her anger was misplaced so instead said, 'It's okay. Tell me where you are, and I'll come and get you.'

'I don't know. They put us in the back of a van.'

'Okay.' She pushed away a vision of her daughters, huddled against their father, in the back of a blacked-out vehicle. 'Are you safe?'

'I think so—' The line went dead. Marney stared at the phone as the screen blinked into darkness.

Someone tapped a knuckle against the passenger side window. Marney looked up, expecting to see Isabelle.

Doctor Stuart twirled his finger, signalling her to roll down the window.

She debated her options. Drive off and find the nearest police station, if it was still manned? Pull away and then back over the bastard with her car?

She rolled down her window.

'I didn't want it to be like this,' he said.

'Take me to them.' She kept her eyes fixed forward, certain that if she looked at him, she would lose control and launch herself towards him, snarling and scratching.

She tossed the tote bag that had been sitting on the passenger seat into the back. Underneath, she found Emma's collection of My Little Ponies. Marney swallowed back her tears as she swept them into the footwell. Then she clicked open the doors so he could get in. She tried not to look as he rested his feet on top of Twilight Sparkle and Rainbow Dash.

'Head north,' he said.

~

The Book of Evelyn

I'd be lying if I said I wasn't jealous of you, Jared. You've explored worlds in the years we've been apart. I don't think you can experience all that and not allow it to shape you.

I'm also a different person. But, unlike you, my friend, I'm not sure I've changed for the better. Still, you seem convinced that my story is worth including in your 'Book'. I guess it can't hurt. What's done is done.

Ruth and I didn't get far on the day we were banished. She dragged her trolley case, sprinkles of pink flowers embroidered into its cover, along the uneven path. With every bump, it baulked and twisted, straining her wrist. By the time we got to the road, her brow gleamed with the effort.

'Why don't you just carry it?' I asked.

'Because it's got wheels,' she said. 'It's meant to be pulled.' As if in defiance, it flipped again. She roared at it, kicking out with a ballet pump and doing more damage to her foot than the case. Then she slumped in the gutter, her forehead leant against her knees.

I slumped down next to her. 'So we'll live here then?'

'Yes.'

'Right.' I looked at the hardened soil, tufts of brown grass still sprouting defiantly. 'It's nice.'

She sighed and looked at me. 'I'm still letting you down.'

She was and had been my whole life. But I didn't hold it against her. I learnt when I was small that it was best not to set my expectations of Ruth at 'mother' levels. She'd never quite reached the lofty heights of 'responsible adult', so expecting her to act like one just led to disappointment. I lowered the bar long ago, and she'd never given me reason to raise it.

'At least we're together,' I said.

She reached over and tucked my hair behind my ear. 'You deserve so much more.'

I shook my hair back into my face. 'Then get your butt up, and let's get moving, Ruth.'

She did as I said, wiping her hands on her skinny jeans. 'I'd prefer 'Mum' if you don't mind.'

'Sure thing, Ruth. Let's get moving. Pretty soon the sun is going to be unbearable.' Despite the early hour we'd left, sweat cut a constant path down my back.

'Where too?' Her voice was small, child-like.

I resisted the urge to shake her, to say I'd assumed she had a plan. Instead, I said, 'Let's just keep following the road until we find a sign.'

We'd been travelling just over an hour when Ruth stopped. 'Do you hear that?'

At first, there was nothing. Then I heard the hum of motors. 'Quick, hide.'

I ran to the steel verge at the side of the road. Clumps of dead earth crumbled under my palms as I clambered over the small peak.

When I looked back, Ruth was fussing with the long handle of her case. It clicked back into place, and she tugged it along the dry ground.

She was too late. The buzz of motors turned to a roar as they headed towards us. I sneaked a peak and saw two motorcycles with various cars and vans following behind them.

'Stay out of sight,' Ruth hissed, and I slid down the other side of the bank, crouching low.

My heartbeat mirrored the revs of their engines.

Then they cut out.

'What do you want?' Ruth asked.

'I think you know,' a woman said.

'No!'

The scuffling sound left me digging the half-moons of my fingernails into my palm.

'And you may as well tell the kid to come out,' she added. 'Our scouts spotted the two of you a kilometre back.'

I launched myself over the hill. 'Leave her alone.'

I didn't see the second woman until my rear hit the ground. Looking up at her, I supposed I should have been grateful that pushing me was all she'd done. Her skin rippled with muscles, and I knew she could have snapped me like a twig.

'Nobody's interested in your mama,' she said.

I saw then that the first woman was rifling through Ruth's case.

'You can't just steal our things,' Ruth said.

'I think you'll find I can.' She discarded Ruth's clothes and dresses until she came to the meagre rations provided by Malone and his minions. 'At last, something useful.'

'So you're just going to let us starve?' I asked.

The woman looked me up and down. Then she tossed me a bag of dried fruit.

'Please,' Ruth said. 'That's all we have.'

'No, it's all you *had*.'

'Besides,' her friend said, 'you won't live long enough to need it.'

'Is that right?' I asked. 'Well, come on then. I'm not afraid of you.' My throat constricted as if trying to hold the truth inside, which was that I was terrified.

'She's feisty,' the first woman said to her companion. 'Bug would love her.' She turned to me. 'What do you think? Would you like to be a drone?'

I clenched my fists. 'Been there, done that.'

She chuckled. 'Who knows, you might be his next Queen.'

I tried to back away but forgot about the verge behind me and landed hard on my tailbone. 'If anybody tries to touch me, I swear—'

'Relax,' she added. 'I don't mean like that.'

Her friend's eyebrows bobbed. 'I don't think Bug thinks of *anybody* like that.'

She stared at the tin of beans in her hand as if trying to solve a puzzle on the label. At last, she said, 'That could be an option for the two of you.'

'Anya, we're not supposed to—'

Anya held up a finger to silence her friend. 'I know. But I think he'd want us to make an exception.' She turned back to us. 'We've just left a group called the Colony. They might be willing to take you in.'

'No tha—'

Ruth interrupted me. 'Where is this place?'

Betrayal set my heart pounding again. 'No, you promised—'

'Evie. Hush. Is it nearby?'

'That's the tricky bit. The Colony is more of a 'who' than a 'where'. But last time we saw them, they were to the east. As far as I know, they had no plans to move.'

Ruth and I glanced at each other.

The second woman huffed. 'Dear Lord, you two are as helpless as newborns. The direction of the sunrise. Keep following the road.'

'Ruth, you promised. Just us. No more communities. No more living by other people's rules.'

She ignored me. 'If they're so great, why are you leaving?' *At last*, I thought, *a good question.*

Anya sniggered. 'We're swarming. The group got a little big for our liking. And Bug's. But hey, maybe that will leave room for you two.'

One of the cars behind them tooted its horn.

'We've got to get moving. Good luck, whatever you decide.'

Ruth frowned. Then she looked at me. 'Evie, maybe we should at least consider—'

'No. Absolutely not.' I stuffed my belongings back into my bag. 'I'm heading east, because that's the way we were going anyway. No other reason.'

'Suit yourself, kid,' Anya said over her shoulder. 'But either way, find yourself some shelter fast. There's a storm on the way.'

Ruth clasped my hand. 'I'm sorry. I just think we need to keep our options open.'

I pulled away. 'It's not about options. You're a coward, and just like always, you're looking for somebody to take care of us so you don't have to.'

'That's not...'

Fair? True? I was glad she didn't finish the sentence so I didn't have to list all the evidence to the contrary.

'Fine. Just us.' She draped an arm over my shoulders.

I shrugged it off. 'Let's find some shelter.'

Laura

Jared was dozing when Laura arrived, his head lulled against the cell wall.

'My God, you're really here.'

He woke with a start. 'I didn't hear you come in.'

'From what Millicent has told me, you could use the rest. But I had to see with my own eyes that you are real.'

'Well, obviously.' He looked uncomfortable, his eyes fixed somewhere at her knees.

As much as she wanted to reach through the bars and engulf him in a hug, she stopped herself. 'I didn't think you'd ever come back. I hoped...but why would you? There's nothing left for you here, is there?'

He opened and closed his mouth without answering, and she scolded herself. She'd sworn that, given a second chance, she'd be honest instead of putting him through some ridiculous game of 'guess what's in my head'. Laura took a deep breath. 'What I meant to say was that I had hoped you would come back to see me. I know I haven't earned that kind of loyalty, but...' She left the sentence hanging.

'Okay. Here I am.'

'Exactly. My prayers were answered.'

Jared shuffled on the spot. 'I didn't come back for you. I know that's probably not what you want to hear, but you told me always to be honest.'

In fact, Laura distinctly remembered telling him the opposite, that sometimes honesty was definitely not the best policy. 'That's okay. I'm just happy you're here. But are you happy to be home?'

Jared raised his eyebrows. 'It wasn't exactly a warm welcome.'

'Of course. That was a stupid question. But Jared, you have no idea the amount of good you have done here already. You've released the Sanctuary from the clutches of a tyrant.'

'I just wanted Durand to leave my friends and me alone. Besides,' he said, swooping his hand around the cell, 'the citizens don't seem exactly grateful.'

'They are. They're just afraid to show it. You have no idea how much worse it's got since you left.'

'There was no other way. I'm sorry, I don't mean to be heartless, but the people here acted like sheep. How can they be surprised when they are led to the slaughter?'

Laura stood a little straighter. 'That's not like you.'

'You have no idea what I'm like. The citizens didn't stand up to Durand, and as a result, my friend died.'

'I didn't know—'

'And then they lock us up. Why should I have empathy for a community that has so little for me?' Jared spoke without taking a breath, his face flushed.

'We didn't mean to upset you. Marney was trying to protect you when she put you in here.'

'From what?'

'Things aren't as straightforward as they seem. There is a hidden war raging beneath the surface. I can't tell you any more in case I put you in danger. Not yet, anyway. Will you meet me later? Then I'll tell you everything.'

'I'm not in the position to meet up with anyone right now.'

'You'll be released shortly. Marney assured me they just need a statement, and you'll be free.'

'To leave?'

Laura hesitated. 'The prison, yes. Marney's allocated you your grandfather's old unit. It turns out the citizens were too superstitious to use it after, well, you know.'

'But I'm not free to leave the Sanctuary.'

'Nobody will force you to stay, Jared. But I hoped you might like to, for a little while, at least.' Tears stung her eyes. 'You grew up.'

'It was inevitable.'

'You'd be surprised. I think you were more mature than me from the moment you could talk.'

'That's silly.'

'I know. But it doesn't mean it isn't true.' She forced a smile. 'Anyway, that's all in the past. I'd love you to have dinner with me at our old unit later. Around seven?'

'Has your cooking improved?' The subtlest of grins warmed his face.

'Oh yes. I'm basically a Michelin star chef nowadays,' she lied.

'Hmmm. I'll try. It depends on what time we get out of here. My friends—'

'I understand. Thank you for at least entertaining the idea. I know that being back here can't be easy. I'll see you later, hopefully.' Laura resisted the urge to look back as she walked away. As much as it pained her to see her child locked in a cell, at least he was safe.

She spent the afternoon cursing herself for setting such a late time. It had taken her minutes to mine sweep the unit for any evidence that she wasn't the functioning adult she wanted her son to believe her to be. She'd started dinner far too early, the mac and cheese congealing on the stove. Did

Jared even like that any more, she wondered. He'd travelled through time and seen sights she couldn't even imagine. Perhaps setting down his childhood favourite in front of him would come off as patronising.

Laura got up to scour her cupboards for another option, but a knock at the door stopped her. 'Too late now,' she said under her breath. 'I'm coming!' As she turned the lock, she said, 'You're early. Not that I'm complaining. The pasta is already solidifying like concrete.'

'Evening, Laura.'

Felix and Devon looked back at her.

'Oh. I was expecting my son.'

'Yeah,' Devon said. 'Jared's not coming.'

'What? How do you know that?'

'Because he's still locked up.'

Laura took a sharp intake of breath. 'Why? He was trying to help.'

Devon gave a lopsided grin that Laura would happily slap out of existence. 'Maybe the boy wonder wasn't as innocent in all this as he made out.'

Laura's temper flared. 'That can't be right. Jared would never...'

'It's probably a misunderstanding,' Felix said. 'Anyway, Marney asked us to bring you to the Grand Chamber so we can get things straightened out.'

'Yes, a misunderstanding. That's probably it.' She pulled the unit door closed behind her. 'Is Millicent there too?'

'Yes,' Felix said. 'Aleksey, too.'

'Good.' Laura let herself relax. Millicent had witnessed much of what had happened. Jared would soon be home, and at least she could blame the delay for the inedible food.

The young guardians hung back as they marched towards the Grand Chamber. It made her nervous, and the hair on the back of her neck and arms bristled. 'I know the way.'

'We're going that way anyway,' Devon said.

As they approached the arched door, Laura looked over her shoulder. 'I think I can find it from here.'

'Sure,' Felix said. 'But I have to check a few things with Millicent. You know how difficult she is to pin down.'

'Right.' Laura pushed open the door, bracing herself for what she might find. Empty. The chamber was deserted. 'Where are they?'

'Probably at the back,' Devon said.

'I think they're keeping Jared's return under wraps for now,' Felix added.

A clammy sweat crawled up Laura's back. 'Sounds sensible.'

As they walked towards the office, relief propelled her. A dim light shone from below the door.

'Looks like they started without us. Ladies first.' Devon nudged her forward into the office with far more force than needed.

'Don't touch me. Jared?' Laura called, 'Are you here?' Strong hands encircled her arms and dragged her forward.

'Don't fight,' Felix said.

'Get off me.' She scoured the room. 'Where's my son?'

'Who knows?' Devon said. 'But wherever he is, I'm certain he won't be worrying about you or any of us.'

Laura twisted her body, but they dug their fingers into her flesh. 'I'm warning you,' she said before biting down on Devon's hand.

'Bitch!' He slapped her, and Laura's cheekbone exploded in a blaze of pain and heat.

For a moment, she thought it was the jolt to her head that made the world flicker, like the darkness when she pressed her eyes closed too hard. But it didn't disappear. It danced over the surface of her reality before bursting into a scorching light that burnt her retinas long after she looked away. A portal ripped through the air in front of her.

'I'm sorry.'

Was that real? she thought, straining to look for the source of the voice. She could make out the faintest silhouette on the far side of the portal. Still, Laura was only sure it was really there because Felix nodded in its direction. 'You can't do this to me!' she shouted.

'Goodbye, Laura,' Felix said. 'Best of luck.'

One firm shove, and Laura tumbled through the portal into the unknown.

Marney

Before the Sanctuary

What had she been expecting? A shack, perhaps, with her daughters chained in the corner. Maybe Ben tied spread-eagled on a table, a cloth sack over his head. On the journey to the facility, Marney's imagination had not been kind.

Stuart swiped his key card, and she pushed past him into a corridor painted in a harsh white. If it hadn't been for the shadows of the recessed doors lining each wall, she would have been snow-blind.

'Well, where are they?' She resisted the urge to throw open each door until she found her family as if she were working her way through some deranged advent calendar. 'I won't ask you again.' In truth, she had no idea what the consequences of that thinly veiled threat would be.

But it didn't matter; Stuart shuffled a step or two away from her anyway. 'They're fine.' He swallowed hard.

She made him nervous, she realised. Good.

'The girls were complaining they were hungry, so Ben took them for some food in the dining hall. They're perfectly safe. Let me show you around while we wait.'

'There's no point. I'll be leaving as soon as I have my family.'

He removed his glasses and massaged the bridge of his nose, revealing dark circles below his eyes. 'Okay. But do you mind if we wait in my office instead of the corridor? I have a mountain of work to be getting on with.'

'Really? My heart bleeds for you.'

Still, she followed him as he headed through one of the

doors. The pungent smell of bleach, thick and burning within her nostrils, followed them. Marney didn't mind. After a lifetime of working in laboratories, it had a comforting familiarity.

Stuart slumped into his desk and signalled for her to take the seat opposite. 'It's been a long day.'

'To say the least. So is this where you persuade me to stay?' she asked. The possibilities shuffled through her mind. Bribery, of course, was an option. But Stuart couldn't put enough zeros on a cheque to make her feel comfortable staying in the city. Blackmail, though she didn't think she'd done anything interesting enough to warrant it. As her previous employer had been furious to realise after she blew the whistle on their cover-up, she was honest to a fault.

That brought her back to Ben and the girls.

'Would it be possible for me to change your mind?' he asked.

'No.'

'Then I won't waste both of our time. I had hoped that if you saw the facility and what we have accomplished here, then you might want to be a part of it. But I'm not in the business of taking hostages.'

She arched an eyebrow.

'You're all free to go whenever you like,' he said. 'I can assure you Ben and the girls got into that van of their own volition.'

Marney was relieved to hear it but couldn't resist the opportunity to reprimand him further. 'Not without a few lies guiding their way, though, right?'

Stuart pursed his lips. 'I'll add it to the list.'

'What list?'

'Of things I've done that I'm not proud of in order to bring this nightmare to an end. Anyway, please accept my apologies.'

Marney got the feeling she had been dismissed. He shuffled through the papers on his desk, adorning the odd one with his sweeping signature, without looking up at her.

It was some amateur reverse psychology, and Marney knew it. This knowledge made the rejection she felt even more irritating.

As he had, apparently, decided she was not worth his time, she distracted herself by looking at the pictures on his desk. She recognised one of them. He'd shown it to her at the party after the conference. A little girl, all gappy grin and blonde ringlets, perched on a swing. It was the same one she remembered him showing her at the conference.

Stuart caught her looking at it and picked it up, examining the photo as though it were the first time he'd seen it. He placed the frame back on the desk, turned away from her.

'Sorry. I didn't mean to be nosy.'

'It's not a problem.' He continued reading his papers.

'Is she here in the facility, too?'

'No, as I said, she's with her mother.'

'Oh, yes. Sorry, just making conversation.'

He looked up. 'It's okay; we'll be together again very soon. Once I do what I can to get this mess under control.' He twisted his wedding ring, a habit that Marney remembered from the first time they'd met. She'd found it endearing.

'Where are they?' she asked.

'They're waiting for me in a place called the Sanctuary.'

'The Sanctuary? Hmmm. Sounds a bit too much like a commune to me.'

Stuart laughed. 'Far from it. It's run by scientists. In fact, they have funded a lot of the work I have been doing here. We tried going down the 'Big Pharma' route. It was just too slow. Besides, I needed to know that the vaccine I made would be available to everybody, not just to the rich and powerful.'

'A nice dream.' She admired his ideology but had wasted too many years jumping through funding hoops to share it.

'I intend to make it a reality.'

'Good for you. What is this Sanctuary place then?'

'It's a self-sustaining eco-system below the surface. If we wanted, we could live down there forever. No more extreme weather. No more virus. Once the Earth has had time to repair itself, we can return to the surface.'

'Then why bother staying to fight the virus?'

'Every Goliath needs a David.'

Marney groaned. 'Cheesy.'

His brow knitted. 'I couldn't just disappear into safety without first helping the people I'd be leaving behind.'

Marney blushed, remembering their conversation in the lecture hall. She had been more than prepared to let the rest of the world burn if it meant saving her family.

She changed the subject and nodded towards the certificates lining his wall. 'It doesn't look like you need my help. You're just as qualified, if not more so.'

He shook his head. 'Nobody does their best work in a vacuum.'

'And you actually think you can crack this?'

'I know we can because we have.'

'Excuse me?'

He grinned. 'We've produced a vaccine, and it works. And not just with this strain of flu, Marney. With *every* strain. It's a universal vaccine that works on every type of influenza we have encountered back to 1918 and every modelled mutation we have predicted.'

Marney stumbled over her words. 'That's amazing. What's the survival rate?'

'One hundred percent. Well, in apes, at least. We haven't started human trials yet.'

'Ah. Well, although I applaud your efforts, you've still got some way to go.'

'We've been given the go-ahead to move to phase three. The human trials start tomorrow.'

As far as she knew, no other team had managed to get this close. She felt the familiar tingle of excitement crawl over her skin at the prospect of being a part of it.

He must have sensed this, because he said, 'Perhaps I could show you around the lab on the way to meet your girls?'

She tried to cloak her curiosity in motherly concern. 'Well, they'll be there all day if I don't hurry them along. And we need to get going.'

'Of course.'

Stuart led her down a corridor and stopped outside one of the doors. 'This is just one of six labs we have.' He beeped his pass on the pad, and they stepped into a small room lined with shelves. Reaching up onto one of them, he pulled down a gown and mask.

'The subjects are kept in quarantine pods, but we don't take any chances.'

They began to put on the kit.

'They're not very stylish, I'm afraid,' he said, pulling the hood of the blue gown over his hair.

'I've seen worse,' Marney said, fixing her mask in place.

Stuart swiped his security pass on the second set of doors, and they pushed through into the lab.

A familiar giddiness swept over her as she entered. Marney resisted the urge to run her hand over the smooth metal worktops and clenched her fists at her side to stop herself.

An enclosure, secured with thick glass, dominated one side of the lab. Marney touched her gloved fingertips to the surface and peered in. Several unconscious chimps lay curled on a floor covered in hay.

'Quite the palace they have here.'

'These quarantine units will be cleared out and used for the human participants.'

'I hope you'll give them something better than hay to sleep on.'

'I assure you, we'll make them as comfortable as possible.'

Marney squinted, trying to adjust to the dimmed light of the enclosure. 'The chimps are healthy?'

'They're alive. For now, that's more of a success than we dared hope. The post-mortem will tell us for sure whether there has been any internal damage.'

'It's a shame to kill them.' It was an area of her work that had never sat well with her.

'A necessity, I'm afraid.'

'I know. How long have they been in there?'

'Three days. We delivered the vaccine and then infected them with the virus. Their fevers broke after day two.'

'Three days? You are planning to begin human trials after so little time?'

'This isn't our first set of subjects. Besides, I don't know if you've heard, but this virus has killed more people than the Spanish Flu and the Black Death put together. We don't have time to waste.'

'Ensuring that human trials are safe is far from a waste of time.'

'Marney, you don't think this is something I have considered? The fact is, if we don't act now, there may not be much of a civilisation to save.'

He stopped, and Marney could sense him selecting his words with caution, ordering and reordering his sentences.

'If it helps,' he said, 'the subjects are volunteers.'

'Who would volunteer to be a guinea pig?'

'Those with nothing to lose. Prisoners.'

A hiccup of laughter escaped her, although she saw no humour in what he'd said. 'That's unethical, and you know it. The power differential between the test subjects and the researchers means there is no way they can be making an unbiased choice.'

'It's all been approved. I'll show you the paperwork if you like.'

Marney didn't need to see it. The only thing to outpace the spread of the virus was the fear that preceded it. She'd watched the news with interest as politicians at first tried to reassure and appease the population. But it wasn't long before they too began to disappear from public view, leaving their lackeys to deliver their messages. Marney wondered how many of them would survive the pandemic.

'I admire your work; I really do,' she said. 'But what

you've got here isn't a successful vaccine; it's a good start. I won't be part of injecting that into a human being.'

She waited for his protests but was shocked when he nodded instead.

'I understand. I'll take you to the girls.'

Every corner they turned led them to a corridor that looked a clone of the last.

Marney heard the girls before they came into view, bickering between themselves.

Emma saw her first. 'You're here!'

They both launched themselves at her, clinging to her like limpets.

'Wait until you see the games room,' Jodie said. 'It's got everything.'

At eighteen months younger than her sister, Jodie still stood an inch taller. From her untameable hair to her wiry frame, she was every bit her father.

'I'm sorry, but we don't have time. If we don't leave now, we won't get to the cabin by nightfall.'

'We can stay here,' Emma said. 'Doctor Keller said they have a projector so we can make popcorn and pretend it's a cinema.'

'Did she?' Marney glared at the woman standing behind Ben and noticed her blush. 'Not this time, girls. These people have a lot of work to do, and we would only get in the way.'

'Okay,' Stuart said. 'You're right. I've got a lot to do, so I'll let Doctor Keller show you out if she doesn't mind.'

Keller flashed Marney a broad smile lined with coral lipstick, some of which had escaped onto her teeth. 'Not at all.' She pushed back through the double doors, her charges following.

'Marney. One last thing,' Stuart said before she was through.

Her body tensed, but still, she turned.

'If you change your mind, you know where we are.'

'I won't,' she said and let the door swing shut.

Jared

Jared was late. Still, he didn't imagine his mother would have given up so quickly on the idea of their meeting after all these years.

The curl of his fist was bruised from hammering against the wood by the time Sienna walked past.

'I need your help,' Jared said, falling into step next to her.

'Later.'

'This is important. My mother—'

'Well, this can't wait either.'

'Why?' Jared demanded. 'Where are you going?'

'To see Oliver. I can't let him do this.'

Jared wanted to see him, too, but for very different reasons. He'd spent their imprisoned hours listening to Martin's tale, and he had questions.

'Are you still awake?' Martin had checked regularly from the next cell as he talked.

Of course he had been. But it wasn't a story that you could hear without snatching the odd moment to stare into space, turning the brutality of it over in his head. Eventually, he'd begged a guardian for a pen and paper, not trusting his brain to document every painful detail. But these, he told himself, were the horrors that would shape humanity's future. They could not, would not, be lost.

Jared glanced back in the direction of his mother's unit before asking Sienna, 'Can I come with you?' He would look Oliver in the face and demand to know if Martin's story was true.

'Do what you want,' Sienna said.

'What makes you think they'll even let us through?' Jared asked.

Sienna strode on. 'They'll let me through.'

'Because you're a guardian?'

She stopped. 'Because I'm his fiancé.'

'Oh. I didn't realise you were...so close.'

She chuckled. 'You say that like it matters. Durand decided who married who. We had no choice in it.'

'Durand paired you up?' Such evil was unfathomable to Jared. Durand was a psychopath, there was no doubt, but to betroth Sienna to one of the accomplices to her mother's murder seemed like new depths of cruelty.

'If you want to put it like that.'

'But you're free now. You don't have to marry anyone you don't want to.'

'I guess not.' Her voice was flat, and Jared wondered if she was disappointed.

When they got to the prison, the guard nodded her through, and they entered a tunnel with alcoves carved into the walls. Once, they'd have housed the tableaux that his grandfather had so enjoyed. 'History gives us roots,' he'd told Jared. 'The people of the Sanctuary will need that more than ever.' But they'd cleared out the wax figures, and doors were added, making cells of the space within. He'd found out first-hand that morning that they'd added little else. The cell he'd inhabited was towards the end of the corridor, with Martin's right next door. A bunk and bare rock were all the Durand brothers would have to enjoy now. Jared couldn't find any sympathy for them.

They stopped at the only door with a guard outside. 'Open up,' Sienna said.

'Do you want me to cuff him?' The guardian smirked.

'Don't be an ass, Devon.' Sienna took the keys from him. 'We were raised with Oliver. You know he's not dangerous.'

'But *we* weren't raised with him, were we?' Devon said. 'He was one of the chosen ones. Well, how the mighty have fallen.'

'Would you have swapped with him, given a chance?' Jared asked.

Devin hesitated. 'He got the best of everything. We got the scraps from their table.'

'You didn't answer the question,' Jared said.

Devon ignored him. 'He hasn't spoken since he was brought in. But try if you want.'

Oliver crouched on the floor of the cell. At first, Jared thought he was staring at the floor. Then he realised Oliver was running a finger over letters chiselled into the rock. *Jennifer.*

'Who was she?' Jared asked.

Oliver studied him, perhaps considering whether it was worth breaking his silence over. 'I've no idea,' he said, finally. 'A ghost, maybe.'

Sienna perched on the bunk next to him and placed a hand on his shoulder. 'Ollie?'

He flinched away.

'Don't be like that. I want to help you.'

'Just leave me alone.' Oliver's voice was gravelly. 'I'm guilty, and I deserve what's coming to me.'

'You surrendered peacefully, and you persuaded Martin to do so as well,' Jared said. 'That will count for something.'

'I lived as one of them, and I will be tried as one of them, too.'

'Then so should I be,' Sienna said. 'I was forced to take on the Durand name as much as you were.'

'No. We are nothing alike, Sienna. And don't you ever blame yourself for anything that happened.'

'I don't, and neither should you. They took your eye. They branded me. We were children, stolen from our parents. You're no more guilty than I am.'

Oliver's head snapped up. 'You have no idea who I am, what I've done.'

'Of course I know who—'

'Just go away,' Oliver said. 'Durand is gone, and you owe me nothing. I release you from our engagement. Get on with your life. Be happy.'

'What if I want to be here?' Sienna took a deep breath. 'What if I want to be with you?'

'I'm sorry, that isn't what I want. I don't feel that way about you, and I never have.'

Sienna's cheeks flushed, and she got to her feet. When she reached the cell door, she paused. 'I don't believe you. You loved me once. I wish I knew what happened to change that.'

'You're wrong.' Oliver didn't look at her. 'I never did.'

Sienna's eyes pooled with tears. 'Maybe you're more like Durand than I imagined, because I never thought you could be so cruel, Ollie.' She slammed the cell door behind her.

Oliver bashed the back of his head against the cell wall.

Jared fidgeted, wondering if he should call the guard. 'You're going to hurt yourself.'

'That's the point,' Oliver said, but he stopped anyway. 'You should go after her. She'll need a friend.'

'So do you.' Jared surprised himself. He'd come to voice his disgust, not to befriend Oliver.

'No. I'm getting exactly what I deserve. Karma gets everyone eventually.'

Jared sighed. 'I think perhaps you are as much a victim as a villain. Maybe we are all a little of both. I guess it just depends on who's telling the story.'

Oliver smiled. 'Oh yes. I forgot I was talking to the Sanctuary's most wanted. Jared, I realise we hardly know one another, but would you do something for me?'

'What?'

'Get her out of here. Tonight.'

Jared frowned. 'Why?'

'Because what she hears tomorrow is going to break her heart.'

'I'm sorry, but I can't leave. Not just yet.'

Oliver covered his face with his hands and let out a rumble of frustration. 'I can't do this to her.'

'I think it will probably be a relief for her to know what happened.'

Oliver's jaw slackened. 'Wh...You know?'

'About Sienna's mother?' Jared asked. 'Yes, Martin told me.'

'Then you know why I deserve everything that's coming to me. I could take all of this: prison, the citizens hating me, even a death sentence. What I can't take is how she will look at me when she finds out what I did.'

The Book of Evelyn

The wind whipped the dry earth so that it turned the air jaundiced with sand. It stung our skin, leaving our eyes filled with gritty tears.

'We need to find some shelter,' Ruth said.

I pawed my way through the dimming half-light until Ruth jerked my shoulder. 'Over there.'

A blurred silhouette lay on the horizon. I tried to ask what it was, but sand reached into my mouth and stole my words. I choked up lungfuls of grit but could still feel it crunching between my teeth.

Ruth grabbed my hand and tugged me towards that mysterious smudge. I kept my head down, trying to stop more sand from scraping at my retinas.

'Inside,' she said, although I had no idea where.

Ruth dropped to her knees and crawled forward. I did the same, jagged stones stabbing my flesh.

I shuffled back as far as I could, rucking up piles of dried leaves until my back hit something hard. Reaching round, I ran my hand along smooth knots of bark. 'We're in a tree,' I said to myself.

Despite the howl of the wind still screeching outside, Ruth heard me. 'Just until it calms down.' She sounded apologetic, but I was in awe. I barely remembered what trees were like and had certainly never crouched inside one.

The clouds of tears cleared from my vision, and I looked around the hollow. When I dug my nails into the bark, it fell away in chunks. The earthy smell of fungus shrouded us. 'It's dead.' I couldn't help thinking that if this giant, unwavering even in death, hadn't survived the surface, what hope did Ruth and I have up here all alone?

'It was probably hit by lightning.'

No, I thought, *that wasn't it. The problem was that it was too close to the Sanctuary.* I had no idea how far our former prison spanned. Maybe its insidious tunnels ran right below the very spot on which we cowered. That was it, I was certain. The poison of the place had seeped into the soil, killing the tree from the roots up. I tried to push that thought from my mind and rest while we waited out the storm.

Chapter Two

The Book of Evelyn

We'd set off at first light and not stopped since. Dust from the storm still hung in the air, turning each breath into sandpaper on my lungs. The soles of my feet were bruised, and sweat stung my eyes. I'd like to say it was strength of will that drove us on. Really it was a lack of choice.

I ignored the house on the horizon for the longest time, certain my dehydrated brain was playing a cruel trick on me. But as its burnt orange roof and trampled fences came into focus, I turned to Ruth. 'Do you see that?'

Her eyes were fixed on the road. When she looked up, she stopped as if she'd hit an invisible wall and staggered back a couple of steps. 'Thank God. We're saved.'

'Let's just think for a moment. We don't know if it's empty. Anybody could be in there.'

I heard her swallow as if her dry mouth were already anticipating the water that could be inside.

'We've got to risk it,' she said.

And I knew she was right. With no water and hardly any food, we didn't have a chance of surviving, even if we were spared more sandstorms. 'Okay. But let's take it slow.' We left the road and crossed a field of clumped dead earth. 'Don't you think it's strange that they built this place out here all alone?'

Ruth scanned the area around us. 'You know, I think it was probably a farm of some kind. Look at the fences; they run all around the perimeter.'

That should have made me feel better, a logical reason for the isolation of the house. Instead, despite the heat, it made me shiver. Even there, a place dedicated to life and growth, everything was dead.

As we approached, I saw that the house had fared no better. The paint curled from the walls and lay in flakes on the ground. A jagged crack ran through the only remaining window pane.

'They probably smashed in the earthquake,' Ruth said.

The front door was already ajar, and I nudged it open with my fingertips.

'Hello!' Ruth shouted over my shoulder.

'Are you kidding me?' I stared at her, slack-jawed.

'Sorry, I...'

'Just stay quiet.' Although I knew that if anybody were inside, it was already too late. I listened for a thud on floorboards.

'See, everything is okay,' Ruth said.

I ignored her and stepped inside. It wasn't much cooler in the house. But just having the fierce beating of the sun off my head was bliss.

'Let's stick together,' I said, whispering. 'Look for

anything that could be useful. And keep quiet; we don't know for sure there isn't somebody hiding out, waiting for us.'

'Don't say that,' Ruth said as if denying the possibility might protect us. She sidestepped around me. 'Let me go first.'

I trailed behind her, jumping at every creaking floorboard. Sand invaded each room, seeming to warn us that this haven we'd found was just temporary. Nature could snatch it away any time it pleased.

In the kitchen, we opened every cupboard. Nothing.

'What now?' I asked.

Before Ruth could answer, a lizard, perhaps with the same wish for shelter as us, scuttled across the floor, sending her scrambling back into me.

'I think my heart just stopped,' she said.

'You have a few pounds on the poor thing. I think you could have taken him. Let's look upstairs.'

The rooms up there were much the same. The house had probably been abandoned for years. It made sense; after the Levelling, nothing grew. There didn't seem to be much else to stay there for, out in the middle of nowhere.

In the bathroom, I tried the taps. Not a drop fell. Bone tired, I plonked down on the edge of the bath, head in my hands.

'Move out of the way a minute,' Ruth said.

I did as I was told.

She ran her fingernail along the seam of the bath panel. 'My mother had something like this. It was handy for keeping cleaning supplies in.' Ruth pushed the corner of the panel, and it popped open. 'I knew it.' She peered into the gap, but the way her shoulders slumped told me straight away that she was disappointed.

'What's there?'

'Not much.' She held up a couple of small bottles of water.

'That's something,' I said, snatching one from her hand and taking a huge gulp.

'Go easy,' Ruth said.

'Anything else?'

'A few cans.'

'Of?'

She held them up, each naked of their labels. 'Lucky dip.' She placed it all on the tired laminate of the bathroom floor. 'That's not a lot to survive on.'

'But it's something.'

'I admire your optimism, Evie, but we'll need more.'

'No, I mean, why would anybody leave it here? Wouldn't they take everything they had?'

Ruth frowned. 'Maybe they had too much to carry. Or they forgot it was here.'

We both knew that was ridiculous. After the Levelling, the world just about imploded as the population fought over the scraps. Forgetting supplies, no matter how sparse, wasn't an option.

'I don't think so. Not unless they left in a hurry. Or...'

'Don't say it,' Ruth said, pinching the bridge of her nose.

'Or they hadn't intended to leave at all.'

Jared

It began as a game. Not the most interesting one, Jared realised, but it kept his mind occupied. Each time he spotted another name engraved somewhere in the salt rock, he felt a whisper of victory. He imagined that the thrill was shared by the people who had put them there, carving the letters whilst the guardians weren't looking. *Ian, Esther, Susan.* Jared found them spotted around the tunnel roofs. He reasoned that the names were fake. Nobody would be stupid enough to use their own. But he imagined they had chosen something meaningful. A grandparent long gone, a cherished pet left on the surface, a nod that only those close to them would recognise as belonging to them. He found *Grant* and *Jodie* dotted on the brick arches. *Were any of them caught?* he wondered. *And if so, how were they punished?* Despite the risks, Jared could understand their motives. A little bit of control when you had none could be thrilling; he'd learnt that first-hand. He smiled to himself at this new rebellious side of the citizens.

The game helped a little as he took the claustrophobic twists and turns of the tunnels. Jared intended to return to his mother's unit to find out why she'd stood him up the evening before. Instead, it was Evie's door in front of which he stood. At least, it had been years before. It wasn't as if he expected her to be there, throwing her arms around him and reassuring him her exile had all been a nightmare. So when the door swung open, Jared jumped back.

'Who are you?' A bird-like woman looked him up and down.

'I...'

'I asked who you are.' She took a step towards him.

The anxiety of the last few days threatened to over-whelm him. It frayed Jared's nerves, making him clench his jaw until it pulsed and ached. 'Just leave me alone.'

'Me? You're the one loitering around my unit. Tell me what you are up to, or I'll call the guardians.'

'That won't be necessary, Stacey.' Marney appeared at his side. 'Come on, Jared, let's get you back to your friends.'

Jared twisted from Marney's grasp. 'Get off me.'

'I'm trying to help you.'

'Help me? You had them lock me up.'

Marney followed him as he made his way back down the tunnel. 'For your own good. Please, Jared.'

He changed direction, but she mirrored his path. Growling with frustration, he slumped on the floor against the side of the tunnel. 'Why won't you just leave me alone?'

'Because I have to talk to you.'

That's when he saw it on the wall opposite. *Eliza*. He scooted over, running his finger across the sharp angles of the z. *Curtis, Jennifer, Ian, Esther, Susan, Grant, Jodie, Eliza.* Lists always made him feel better, so he repeated the names to himself.

'Will you please stop saying that?' Marney asked. 'Come away from there.'

Jared blushed, realising he'd been talking out loud. 'Brave people,' he said. 'Even a petty crime like graffiti wouldn't be taken lightly in here.'

'Yes, they were brave. But their crimes weren't graffiti. Some might say they committed no crimes at all. Walk with me?'

Jared dusted himself off. 'No. But you can walk with me if you like.'

Marney frowned. 'I think that's the same thing.'

'Then it shouldn't make any difference to you.' But it did to him. He wouldn't let them choose his path ever again.

'Okay. Where are we going?'

'Back to my grandfather's unit, via the lake.' He didn't know why he chose there. Nostalgia, he supposed. That was where he had gone on his first walk with his grandfather, where he'd met Evie. But it was also where Martin had forced his head under the water until his lungs had burnt. Still, there wasn't a place in the Sanctuary without a shadow cast over it.

'Who were they?' Jared asked.

'I didn't know most of them well. Only...' Marney pressed her hand to her mouth.

'I didn't mean to upset you.'

'It doesn't matter.' She drew in a long wavering breath. 'Those people didn't write their own names. The people left behind did. It's become a tradition, be it one that the Durands hated and did everything they could to stop. But then, why would they want such reminders hanging around? The Durands liked to make people disappear. Any remnants of their life here left behind could be...inconvenient.'

'Oh,' Jared said. 'But it's not like they could wipe them from the citizens' memories.'

'Exactly. Although I'm sure if they could find a way, they would. For some of the families, however, memories weren't enough. Especially when they were banned from discussing the people they'd lost.' Marney swallowed back tears.

Guilt prickled Jared's nerves when he thought back to

his outburst. 'I'm sorry, I didn't think about what you might have been through.' He shuffled through the list in his head, trying to pinpoint which name had upset her, but couldn't.

'There's no reason you would. Besides, you had a right to be angry. But I really was protecting you, Jared. I don't know where anyone's allegiances lie right now. There will be plenty who want to keep the status quo. They won't want things around here to change.'

'What's that got to do with me?'

'The grandson of Edmond Pearse could be viewed as a threat.'

Jared's brow wrinkled in confusion.

Marney gave him a tight smile. 'I don't want to end up scratching your name into one of these walls.'

They reached the entrance to the lake. 'This was always my favourite spot, too. I'm sorry to ruin it for you with bad news. Jared, I need to tell you something.'

'There's no need,' Jared said, staring at the cavern roof sweeping over the lake. In metre-high letters, cut perhaps with a medilaser aimed shakily above, were scrawled five letters. *LAURA*. 'My mother is missing. And someone down here wants everybody to know.'

Marney

Before the Sanctuary

During the first summer in their house, when Marney was pregnant with Emma, they'd had a problem with ants. Every time they picked something up, they'd found ants underneath. The ants got into the bed. They found them scavenging in the kitchen cupboards, crumbs of food hoisted onto their backs. It was when she opened the dresser filled with baby clothes to find them ambling over the pastel pink and sunny yellow material that Marney had lost it.

Ben came home to find her furious, ripping out every piece of furniture and cursing the little creatures. She'd tied a scarf around her face and squirted can after can of insect killer at them.

He'd taken her by the hand and sat her on the bed. 'They're just bugs.'

'Ants aren't really bugs,' she said, lifting her feet onto the bed away from them.

'Trust a microbiologist to get technical on me.' Then he'd sat cross-legged on the floor, looking at the ants.

To her, that scene summed her husband up, sitting patiently, watching a line of ants form.

He'd boiled the kettle and followed them to the bedroom windowsill. It didn't take him long to discover the anthill on the other side.

Marney watched as he poured water over the nest. The ants fled in every direction. Then she burst into tears.

Ben hugged her to him, laughing into her hair, and assured her it was just hormones. But she wasn't sure.

Despite the fact that half an hour before, she'd been enveloping the ants with poison gas, Marney hated to see their home destroyed. She knew it made no sense.

The sight outside the facility reminded her of that line of ants. People abandoned their homes, cramming what they could into their cars. It took a moment before her eyes registered the little faces of two children amongst the bundles of belongings in the jeep closest to her.

Horns blared as drivers tried to pull out into the stagnant traffic filling the street.

'Where did all of these people come from?' Ben asked.

'Taking government advice and staying inside, I guess.' The sarcasm was unfair, and she knew it; fleeing the city had been their plan, too.' This is crazy; the roads were deserted when I arrived.' Marney grabbed Jodie's hand and led her towards the car.

She stopped. Belongings blocked every window. They hadn't left space for the girls because they were going to travel in Ben's car. Stuart and his team had ruined that plan. Marney clicked open the locks and started to drag the bags out.

When she noticed the girls staring at their discarded things, she put on a sing-song voice that sounded hideously fake even to her. 'We'll buy new things. Don't worry.'

The girls scurried inside, and she and Ben secured their belts around them.

'We need our booster seats,' Emma said, ever a stickler for the rules.

Ben clambered into the passenger seat. 'We'll get new seats, too.'

The cars next to them crawled past. Each one ignored

her blinking signal light. In her head, Marney baptised each driver anew: scumbag, dick, asshole. Her hand hovered above the horn. Only the nervous chatter of the girls in the back stopped her.

'Mommy, I want to go home!' Jodie kicked the back of her chair.

Marney could relate. She would love to take her frustration out on something. Or someone. Doctor Stuart, perhaps. 'Soon, baby.'

Just as tears of frustration formed in Marney's eyes, a white-haired woman in a beaten-up Ford flashed her lights.

'Thank you,' Marney mouthed.

Over the next half hour, they inched forward. When Marney looked over her shoulder to her left, she was irritated that they hadn't yet passed the boundary of the facility and thumped the wheel.

'Mommy, what's wrong?' Jodie asked.

'Nothing, baby. Just...just a mosquito.'

Ben squeezed her knee.

In return, she offered a strained smile. 'We're good.'

'Exactly. We're together.' He turned to talk to the girls. 'And we're off on an adventure.'

'The cabin!' The one time they'd managed to take them, the girls loved it. Marney wondered if they'd be quite as enthusiastic about the lack of luxuries if they knew they'd be there for the foreseeable. Especially now that they'd abandoned most of their belongings. A problem for later.

The blinking of a turning light nagged at her peripheral vision. Marney faced forwards, refusing to make eye contact through her closed window with the drivers she pulled up next to, silently begging to be let out. She was ashamed that even when one driver wound down his window, reached over and rapped on her glass, she still didn't look. Marney wondered what the good Samaritan behind them made of that.

'Daddy, that man is making the rude sign,' Emma said.

'Don't look. Why don't you play a game with your sister? Thumb Wars?'

But the squeal of metal on metal made it impossible to ignore. The other driver edged his car along the side of theirs, shunting them off course. Marney heard a crunch as he did it again.

The girls screamed.

'It's okay. It's okay.' Marney grinned at them with gritted teeth. She knew she must have looked deranged, but it was that or join in with their screaming.

The tormented metal of the car's side panel whined as he reversed and smashed into them again.

Marney let go of the wheel, her hands hovering above it as though she could relinquish the decision making by not touching it.

'Out,' Ben barked. 'Get out.'

Ben threw open his door, hitting the car next to him. The occupants stared at them, wide-eyed, too shocked at what they'd witnessed to argue over their paintwork.

Marney clambered over the seat and pulled the girls from the back. She thrust Jodie into Ben's arms and hoisted Emma onto her hip.

'You said I'm too big to be carried,' Emma said.

She wasn't wrong. At nearly eight, it had been a long time since Marney had been able to carry her comfortably.

But she had no desire to tow her behind while they were being chased by some madman. 'Just this once.'

They ran.

Marney looked back to see the driver bashing his fists on his steering wheel. He was hemmed in on one side by belongings and on the other by their car. Still, she took no chances and continued to run.

They didn't stop until he was out of sight. When she tried to put Emma down, the girl wrapped her arms and legs around her.

'It's okay,' Marney said between gasped breaths. 'He's gone now.'

'He was crazy.' Not Ben. A woman's voice. The good Samaritan from the car behind.

'Oh, hi. You didn't need to come with us. We'll be fine.'

'Well, dear, I didn't have much choice, did I?' she said, the slightest smirk lingering on her lips.

'We blocked in your car,' Ben said. 'I'm so sorry. We'll make it right when all of this is over.'

'It was a heap of junk anyway,' she said, waving away his promise. 'I was more concerned with getting away from the lunatic parked next to it.'

Marney blushed. It would have been easy for the woman to berate her instead. Had Marney shown the same courtesy, they wouldn't be here.

'I'm Audrey,' the woman said. Then she leant forward to talk to Emma. 'And who might this be?'

Emma hid her face, pressing it into Marney's hair.

'That's Emma, and I'm Jodie.' A puzzled look crossed Jodie's face before she added, 'And they're Mommy and Daddy.'

Marney could have kissed her, thankful that Jodie's trademark cutesy act had broken the tension.

Audrey laughed. 'Well, it's lovely to meet you all. I'm just wondering what to do now.'

'I guess we're going to head home. We aren't getting out of the city tonight.' Ben looked at Marney for confirmation. She gave a little nod.

'No, I don't think anybody is.' Audrey chewed on her lower lip.

'Are you okay?' Marney asked.

'Yes. It's just I'm not from here. I came in for supplies. My house isn't exactly walking distance.'

Marney and Ben glanced at one another.

'Then you must stay with us,' Marney said when no other solution came to mind.

'I couldn't—'

'We insist,' Ben said.

'In that case, thank you.'

Jodie latched onto Audrey's hand before they'd taken even a few steps. 'We live really close,' she said. 'Only about a hundred miles away.'

'My goodness, that close?' Audrey said with a grin.

'Yep.'

Marney wrestled Emma from her hip and rooted her on the pavement. She still walked so close that Marney was careful not to step on her.

They got to the end of the road when a soldier stretched an arm across their path. Marney was used to the camouflage uniform from her work with the CDC, but she heard Audrey gasp.

'You need to take shelter, folks.' He pointed towards a church across the street.

'We're going home,' Jodie told him, her little fists clenched at her side.

He knelt in front of her. 'Soon enough. Once we get all of this sorted.' Looking up at Marney, he added, 'The city's been quarantined. There have been some...' He glanced down at Jodie. '...some incidents.'

For the second time in less than an hour, Marney wanted to punch Stuart. They'd be out of the city by now if not for him.

'Really, it's fine,' Ben told him. 'We live a forty-minute walk away.'

The soldier's eyes shifted between the girls. 'Not everybody is behaving as well as these two little ladies. All residents are to report to the nearest shelter.' He got up. 'For their own safety.'

Marney looked at the queue of people filing towards the church. Crammed inside, she knew just one infected person would allow the virus to run rampant. They'd left her no choice. 'In which case, perhaps you could escort us back to the facility over there? I'm a microbiologist, and we're working on a vaccine.'

The Book of Evelyn

It was the lights that woke me. Ruth had tried to cover the open window with dusty sheets abandoned in a cupboard. Nature mocked her efforts, stripping them down at the first gust. She'd growled with frustration.

'Just leave it,' I told her, curling up on the thin mattress, trying to ignore the smell of mildew and rot.

She lay down next to me, but, when I finally fell asleep, she was still staring at the ceiling.

When I opened my eyes again, the moonlight flooding in was so much brighter. And Ruth's hand was cupped over my mouth. 'Quiet. We need to hide.'

It was then that I realised it wasn't moonlight that flooded the room but the headlamps of vehicles. They revved their engines.

'They don't know we're here. They can't,' I whispered, trying to reassure myself as much as Ruth. 'They're probably looking for supplies, too.'

'Either way, we can't let them see us. Get under the bed.'

I did as I was told and crawled under the rusted frame, jamming myself into the corner.

But Ruth didn't follow me. Instead, she scrambled on all fours over to the window and grabbed the sheet. Then she pushed it in after me. 'Cover yourself with this.'

'You get in first.'

'No. You're tiny. They won't notice you all the way back there.' She gave me a weak smile. 'Don't worry. I'll find somewhere to hide.' She was gone before I could argue.

In contrast to our own entrance to the house, fearful and each step heavy with caution, the people below burst in.

'Knock knock! Little pigs, little pigs, let me come in.'

'We're already in, you crank.'

I pushed myself back further against the wall, but there was nowhere left to go.

'Come out, come out, wherever you are.'

'You check downstairs. We'll check upstairs.'

The floorboards creaked a warning with every footstep the intruders took. My body wanted to heed it, wanted to run. But to where? Even if I tried, I'd meet them on the landing. Unless I fancied my chances jumping out of the window, of course.

Then the shrill misery of Ruth's cries began. Even their laughter, deep and mocking, did nothing to mask it.

Pounding footfalls had told me she'd escaped. They caught her again just outside the bedroom. I pulled the sheet down enough to see her pumps, turned a dirty pink from the dusty road, lift from the floor.

'What do we have here?'

Clunky boots made their way towards the bed under which I hid, their owner carrying Ruth with him.

'No! Please, no.'

He threw her onto the bed, the springs dipping so low that they jutted against my hip.

'Hush now. It's silly to struggle.'

I cupped my hands over my ears and pressed my knees to my chest.

'Rex, there's no time for that.' A woman's voice. That gave me hope. Later I'd learn how misguided that preconception was.

'Didn't your mother ever tell you it's rude to interrupt?' Rex asked.

'And didn't yours ever tell you it's rude to play with your food? Besides, there were two of them. We still have to find the kid.'

'She's gone already,' Ruth said between sobs. 'She ran out the back door.'

'Well, we'd better catch up with her then. Rex, get that one in the car.'

'Fine,' he said. Then lower, I guess to Ruth, he added, 'To be continued.'

I tried to block out her pleas as he dragged her down the stairs. After they faded, I lay silent and rigid. I didn't move, even when I heard the thud of the car door or the roar of the engines. I counted my breaths, willing them to slow, one to a hundred. Then another hundred. It was only when my muscles began to scream that I allowed myself to move. The faintest creak betrayed me.

The night air hit my sweaty face as the mattress was yanked back.

'There you are, Princess,' she said.

'No!'

She reached under the bed and tried to grab me, but I kicked her away.

I heard the sound of running, and then Rex was back. 'I'll get her.' His fingers looped around my ankle, and she dragged me out.

Then he looped my arms through his, restraining me as he turned me to face the woman.

I spat in her face.

The slightest tic of her jaw betrayed her anger. But when she spoke again, her voice was saccharine. 'Now, now. That's enough of that.' She wiped her face with her sleeve. 'Don't take it too hard, Princess. You lasted longer than most. But they all move eventually.'

Laura

'You can't do this to me!' Laura landed on her knees and jagged stones dug into her flesh even through the thick material of her jeans. She hauled herself to her feet and turned just in time to see the portal close behind her. 'Please!'

'It came from that direction.' A man's voice echoed from just over the hill. 'I'm telling you, it was like sunrise.'

Laura scoured her surroundings for somewhere to hide. She eyed the twisted thorn bushes flanking the road, considering burrowing within.

'Maybe it was a fire set by cockle pickers down on the shore,' another man said.

'No, it was definitely in this direction. And I know the difference between a camp fire and a...I don't know what.'

'It's the middle of the night, Malcolm. Maybe you were dreaming.'

'I'm telling you, I saw—'

Laura froze under their gaze as they appeared over the peak of the hill.

'You there,' one of them said. 'I'm the minister of Dornoch and would like a word.'

Minister. That was all she needed to know. She'd sacrificed all she was willing to false prophets. Dropping back to her knees, Laura scrambled into the thicket. She winced, suppressing yelps as thorns bit into her bare arms.

'Stop there!' Heavy footfalls pounded on the dirt road behind her.

Although Laura couldn't see her pursuers, she could hear cursing, no doubt inspired by brambles hooking onto their flesh.

Laura ploughed on until a branch sliced a path across her scalp and snagged on a clump of her hair. She tried to ignore the thorns shredding the skin of her fingertips as she struggled to free herself. A snapping of branches behind her made her light headed with panic. Perhaps it was the surge of adrenaline, but she barely felt it as she yanked her hair out at the root. When she looked down at the chunk she had torn out, she was horrified to find her palm slick with blood.

With no time to assess her injuries, Laura thrust herself forward through the knot of branches. But instead of the open air she'd hoped for, her skull slammed into something solid, and her world turned black.

Marney

<u>Before the Sanctuary</u>

The slap knocked Stuart's glasses crooked.

'I guess I had that coming. Welcome back.'

Marney spoke through gritted teeth. 'You knew this was going to happen.'

'I knew it was a good possibility.'

'That's all you've got to say? You've trapped us here.'

'I wouldn't insult your intelligence with lies. Yes, there's a chance that if you'd left earlier, you might have beaten the roadblocks. There's also a chance they'd have stopped you, and you'd have been stranded, unable to turn around, with two small children. I hear things are already getting dicey out there.'

Marney thought of the driver who had crashed into them, wild eyes and strings of spittle. 'It wasn't your choice to make.'

'No, it wasn't. If it makes you feel better, I am sorry.'

'You know what? It doesn't.'

'Okay. Well, if we're both being honest, given a do over, I wouldn't change what I did. But I am still sorry. Sorry that we're all in this situation.'

'We're basically prisoners. Are you going to stick us in one of those glass cells next?'

'Marney.' Ben clasped her hand, gently squeezing her fingers. 'Let's just hear him out.'

'Look, you're still free to go,' Stuart said. 'I can arrange for an escort back to your house. We have the security clearance to get past the soldiers.'

Marney considered it. They could scoop up their children from the games room where the guard had taken them and head for home. But what then? Did they have enough supplies to wait it out?

'No,' Ben said. 'We're not taking the girls back out there. Who knows how widespread this madness is?'

In truth, Marney was relieved to have the choice taken from her. She turned to Stuart. 'I guess you have me over a barrel.'

'Please don't think of it like that. We're just making the best of a terrible situation. Let me show you where you will be staying. I'm sure you'd like to get your daughters settled.'

Marney nodded. As much as she'd like to throw his offer back in his face and stomp off into the sunset, the girls had been upset enough. Particularly Emma, who had clung onto Audrey like a wild cat as she tried to leave.

'I would be of no help in a science facility, my love,' Audrey had told her. 'I'm just going to the church over there. Maybe I can make myself useful. This soldier and his friends will take care of me.'

Emma sobbed and wailed as though she were losing an old friend, not somebody she'd just met. Ben picked her up and hugged her to him, partly to stop her from racing across the street.

As Audrey joined the queue of people filing into the church, she'd given a little wave. Marney had to look away, reminding herself that Audrey wouldn't have got out of the city whether she'd helped them or not.

Stuart led them into a games room painted institutional green. She heard the clack of plastic before she saw the girls.

'Are you sure you want to go—' Before the guard could

finish his sentence, Jodie slipped in a red disc and let it fall. 'I guess you do.'

'Four in a row; I win!' Emma said, jabbing her finger at the holes containing her white pieces.

When they approached, the guard stood and saluted.

'I've assigned Sergeant Squires to your family for the duration of your stay,' Stuart said. 'He can help you with anything you need.'

He looked younger than the students she taught, but Marney decided that wasn't necessarily a bad thing. She didn't want to be shadowed by some inflexible relic, determined to make her conform to rules she didn't sign up for.

Ben went over to shake his hand.

Before he could, Jodie ran to him, lip poking out. 'Daddy, she keeps winning. Tell her to stop it.'

'That's not how games work, Sprout.'

'Squires will take you to your quarters so you can get settled. We have an early start.'

'We do?' Marney asked. His orders were already irritating her.

'Yes. The prisoners have arrived. We begin the trials in the morning.'

The Book of Evelyn

As they hauled me from the house, the car headlights ignited. I'd been fooled; they hadn't gone anywhere.

I tried to turn my head from the glare, but Rex's arms were still clamped onto my own. Instead, I screwed my eyes shut.

'It's okay,' the woman said, running a finger down my cheek. 'Don't be scared. This is all for a greater good.'

I risked a peek and saw Ruth with her hands pressed against the car window. When she saw me, she pounded her fist against the glass.

'Rex, get her mother,' the woman said.

'What about this one?' He nodded towards me.

'She won't be any trouble.' She looked into my eyes as she said this, giving me a good look at her face. Below streaks of mud, no doubt used as camouflage, her skin was covered in tattoos. Dots followed the trail of her cheekbones. Two ornate scrolled lines arched over her eyebrows, meeting in the middle like the peak of a crown. 'After all,' she continued, 'where is she going to run to?'

Rex released my arms, and I staggered forward. I turned, sizing up my options for escape. But she'd been right. Cars blocked me on every side.

When Rex returned with Ruth, he pushed her towards me.

'We'll be okay,' she promised, holding me close.

'What are we going to do?' I'm not ashamed to admit I was crying. I was well acquainted with fear. But I don't think I'd known true despair until that moment.

'Your mom's right,' the woman said. 'You'll probably live to see morning. But that isn't really up to me.'

The thwack of car doors closing came from every side, and a group of eight people surrounded us. As I searched their mud-smeared faces, I wondered which of them would decide if I lived or died.

'No,' the woman said, 'It's not up to them. She'll decide.' She nodded towards Ruth.

'Me?'

'Yes. One of you will die tonight. The Pack have been travelling all day, and they're hungry. But you can decide which it will be.'

The world spun. Cannibals. All the horror stories they'd told us in the Sanctuary were true.

'No!' Ruth held me so tight it was as though she wanted to absorb me back into her body where she could protect me.

'I can choose for you if that would help?' the woman asked. 'If it makes a difference, you would buy her time, not freedom.'

Ruth cupped my face in her hands and kissed my forehead. 'Take me.'

The woman nodded. 'You have my resp...' Her brow creased in a frown. 'What...' She clasped her neck and pulled something from it. Then she fell to the floor.

'Cerato?' Rex glared at us. 'What did you do to her?'

I backed away. 'Nothing. I swear.'

From somewhere behind me, I heard a yelp. Then another.

'What's happening?' I asked.

'I don't know, but we have to run.' Ruth leapt over Cerato's slumped body.

I tried to follow, but Rex grabbed my shirt.

'No, you don't.' He flinched. Then his snarl turned to horror as he stared at his leg. A dart protruded from his calf. He let go of me to pull it out and toss it far away.

I took the opportunity to run. Certain that he was following, I stole a glance over my shoulder.

Rex had picked up Cerato's body and was limping towards a car.

I swerved around the corner of the house, not wanting to get trapped inside again. The arid earth crunched below my feet as I raced through the darkness. With the night cloaking me, the further I ran, the more hopeful I began to feel. I even began to consider my next move. Finding Ruth was my first priority. Then somewhere to hide in case the monsters who'd captured us came looking. But neither were to happen, because that's when he grabbed me.

Chapter Three

The Book of Evelyn

I dreamt of ripping flesh and bloody fangs. At first, I thought the voices were a part of those nightmares. But as the fog began to lift, I realised I was lying in the back of a truck, Ruth's arm slung across me. Perhaps she shared my nightmares, because I could make out just one repeated word from her sleepy mumbling – *please*.

The voices that woke me were coming from the people in the cab in front.

'Well, it wasn't your call. It was Bug's.'

'Yeah, because Bug is always right.'

'He's got us this...'

The shuddering of the truck bed drowned out their voices. I pushed Ruth's limp arm from around me and scooted closer.

'You think they'll just accept what we did? They'll make us pay.'

'How will they even know it was us? Stop with the whingeing and cheer u— She's awake.'

Wide eyes stared at me in the rear view mirror. 'You're all right, kid. There's no need to be scared.'

I remembered the last time somebody had said that to me. Was it minutes or hours since Cerato gave Ruth her sick choice? The sky was still ink black, so I couldn't tell.

'Ruth, wake up,' I said, shaking her shoulder.

Her grumbles gave way to panic, and she sprang up onto her haunches. 'Where are we?'

'I don't know, but they're taking us somewhere. We're going to have to jump.'

The silhouette of the landscape undulated, but it was impossible to make out how hard our fall would be. Still, I heaved myself up.

'Wait!' The passenger in the cab twisted around to look at me. 'Just listen. I'm Celine, and this is Dale. We're taking you somewhere you can get checked over, maybe put together a plan about where you'll go.'

'What are you saying?' Dale asked. 'If they want to go, let them. They'll be one less problem for us to worry about. But kid, let me stop the truck first, okay? I'd rather you didn't ruin my paintwork on the way down.'

I felt the rough flakes of rust under my palm and wondered if he was joking.

Dale swung the truck over to the side of the road. Then he tugged up the handbrake.

I studied the portion of his face I could see in the rear view mirror. Crow's feet lined skin baked past bronze and verging on overdone.

In contrast, he seemed to make a point of not looking back. 'I don't have all day.'

'You're an asshole,' Celine told him.

I turned to Ruth. 'Should...should we get out?'

A faint dawn light crept over the horizon. We both looked down the road, one way, then the other. Nothing.

'If it's still there, we'd like to take you up on your offer,' Ruth said. Then she squeezed my hand. 'Just while we figure things out.'

Dale put the truck back into gear. 'Suit yourself.'

Jared

'Where's my mother?' Jared asked.

Marney swiped her fingers back and forwards over the console clutched in her hand. 'I can't locate her. Maybe... maybe it's just a glitch.'

'She visited me yesterday at the prison and asked me to meet her for dinner. But she wasn't here. Or at least she didn't answer her door.' Guilt flushed over him. 'I should have waited. Did you see her yesterday evening?'

'Not since I told her about you. Let's assume she's still in the Sanctuary. The orb is locked away. It's unlikely she's wandered up to the surface, especially not with you here. So it tracks that she must be here somewhere, right?'

'I'm not going to gamble her life on an assumption.'

'No, and I wouldn't ask you to.' Marney hesitated.

'What is it?'

'We need to talk to Aleksey so he can begin the search.'

'Okay. Then let's go.'

'It's just Martin and Oliver's trial starts today. Aleksey will be in the Grand Chamber, along with most of the citizens.'

'I see,' Jared said. 'Well, I don't care who knows that I'm back. Let them talk.'

'You're right. Besides, it will be harder to make you disappear if everyone knows you're here.'

'That was something you were worried about?'

'In this place, it would be foolish to rule the possibility out.'

As they strode to Saint Kinga's Chapel, Jared imagined his own name chiselled into one of the walls. But with his mother gone, he wondered if anyone left behind would care enough to take the risk needed to put it there.

'Here we are. Are you ready?' Marney's palm hovered over the handle.

'I guess so.' But his feet felt like lead.

'You can do this,' Marney said.

'Of course I can.' Jared hoped he managed to cloak his fear with false conviction.

Marney entered first. Jared faltered in the threshold behind her, the citizens' stares crawling over his skin like insects. The excited hum that hung over them turned to gasps as they noticed him.

'Don't worry about them. Come on.' Marney headed towards the mahogany table that stretched across the front of the chamber.

'So much for keeping a low profile,' Aleksey said as they approached.

'This can't wait.' Marney pursed her lips. 'But perhaps it might be better to discuss it in the vestry.' She motioned towards the office at the back.

Aleksey spoke through gritted teeth. 'We are about to start the trial. Once Laura deigns to join us, that is.'

'That's the thing,' Jared said. 'She's missing.'

From where Jared looked down upon him, he could barely see the blue of Aleksey's eyes from beneath his drooping lids. 'That's impossible.'

'What is?' Millicent dropped down into the seat next to him.

'Jared claims his mother is missing,' Aleksey said.

Marney handed him the console. 'Look for yourself. There is no sign of her tracker anywhere in the Sanctuary.'

Aleksey glanced at the screen before handing it to Millicent. 'Maybe she went to the surface.'

'What would possess her to do that?' Millicent scanned each page, stopping to pinch her fingers to zoom in on the odd detail. Finally, she placed it on the table. The chiffon sleeves of her dress swished as she raised her hand to her brow. 'I've had the guardians looking for her. We were expecting her half an hour ago to hear the Durands' case. I assumed she lost track of time whilst catching up with Jared.'

'She wasn't in her unit last night either,' Jared said.

'Will you keep your voice down?' Aleksey said as the crowd behind them began to murmur again.

Jared hadn't realised he'd been shouting, but he lowered his volume all the same. 'If they don't know already, they soon will. Somebody has carved her name into the roof above the lake.'

Circles of red rose on Aleksey's cheeks. 'Have they now? Then I suppose the best thing to do would be to push forward with the trial.'

'What?' Marney didn't seem to care who heard her. 'And leave Laura—'

'Leave her where?' Aleksey asked. 'Millicent already has guardians searching for her. What else is there to do?'

'I...We should...' Jared didn't know how to finish either of those sentences.

'How can you continue with a missing committee member?' Marney asked. 'You'll need three people to break a stalemate.'

Aleksey shook his head. 'Millicent and I are quite capable—'

'Marney, you could stand in,' Millicent said.

'Is that really necessary?' Aleksey asked.

Millicent smiled, but there was something about it that didn't seem quite right to Jared. The way the corners of her eyes remained uncrinkled, maybe. 'As I said, we'll need a third in case we disagree.'

'Fine. Jared, would you please take a seat in the pews.'

A battle between fight or flight raged within him. How could he waste time watching this trial when his mother might be in danger?

'Please, Jared,' Marney said. 'I promise we will do everything we can to find her.'

The citizens slid either way on the benches, making space for him. Still, the air pulsed as though they were magnetised towards him. It was a relief when Martin and Oliver entered the chamber, their hands cuffed in front of them, drawing attention away from him. Two chairs had been placed at the end of the table, past the point where the glossy wood ended, leaving them exposed. The guardian put a hand on either man's shoulder and pushed them down into the seats. Not that they looked likely to resist. The brothers looked as grey and spiritless as their matching tracksuits.

Millicent and Aleksey exchanged frantic whispers until Aleksey truncated the conversation with a snarled, 'Fine.' He turned to the Durands. 'Will the defendants please stand?'

They did as instructed, and the court broke into a fresh wave of murmurs. Aleksey bashed the gavel down harder. 'Silence!'

Side by side, the brothers stood, neither related nor alike, facing row after row of citizens. Both men stared at their shoes. The air around them crackled with tension, making

Jared want to run to the apple green bedroom in his old unit, lock the door and escape from them all.

'Martin and Oliver Durand, you are accused of Unlawful Act Manslaughter by knowingly placing our citizens in danger.'

'Manslaughter? They're murderers!' The voice came from within the crowd, making Jared wonder just how far the details of the last few days had travelled.

'Anybody who cannot control themselves will be removed.' Aleksey punctuated each word with a further whack of his gavel. 'Martin Durand, how do you plead?'

Martin didn't look up. 'My father would have killed me if I'd refused to help. I acted out of self-preservation. I'm not guilty.'

An eruption of contempt filled the court. Aleksey didn't even attempt to quieten the chamber down and instead let it ebb away.

'Oliver Durand,' he said finally, 'how do you plead?'

For the first time, Oliver raised his head, although not to address Aleksey, but to scowl at his brother. 'Oh, we are *both* one hundred percent guilty. We deserve to die.'

~

Marney

Before the Sanctuary

'Let me introduce you to some of the people you'll be working with,' Stuart said. Marney shot him a look, and he added, 'What, you thought we were going to be saving the world alone?'

'No, I...I just hadn't really thought about it.'

He placed a hand on Marney's back to guide her forward, and she shrugged him off.

Stuart walked ahead, leaving her and Ben to exchange a look.

'This is Doctor Meredith Cooper.'

The woman stood and pumped Marney's hand with enthusiasm.

'It's a pleasure to meet you, Doctor Cooper,' Marney said.

'Please, call me Meredith. And really, it will be an honour to work with you.' She turned to Ben and repeated her energetic handshake.

In contrast, the man sitting at the bench opposite didn't even look up.

'Richard, we have visitors,' Meredith said.

He didn't respond.

Stuart cleared his throat. 'Doctor Wakefield, let me introduce you to the newest member of our team.'

The man threw them an irritated glance over the top of his glasses. 'Welcome.'

I'm not exactly thrilled to be here either, Marney thought as he returned to the journal he'd been reading.

Stuart wasn't going to give up so easily. 'Doctor Wallace is an expert in her field. Her work on—'

'Yes, yes, I'm sure.'

'...on virus transmission undoubtedly saved many lives during the first wave of the pandemic.'

Wakefield finally looked at her. 'Oh, you're the one from the news reports.'

Marney resisted the urge to roll her eyes. 'Unfortunately, that's correct.'

'The way they treated you was a travesty. As a colleague, it wasn't easy to watch.'

'It wasn't easy to live through either, but I guess there's no point dwelling on that.' But she did dwell on it. A crack pot. A conspiracy theorist. A liar. They'd called her all of these things. She couldn't deny that they still stung. 'There's nothing to be done about it now.'

'Well, let's hope there is still something we can do,' Wakefield said. 'Or we're all wasting our time here.'

'Exactly,' Stuart said. 'And this is Ben Wallace, Marney's husband.'

Ben raised his eyebrows. 'Proudly so. But I'm also the head librarian at Clark Atlanta University. Although my background is in etymology.'

Wakefield gave a titter of laughter.

'Excuse me?' Marney hated how often Ben was demoted to the role of plus one. He deserved so much more. A spark like his wasn't meant to reside in anybody's shadow. So hearing Wakefield laugh as Ben outlined his CV made her anger flare. 'Do you find something funny?'

'Actually, yes. Together your husband and I make quite the punchline.'

'You're going to have to elaborate,' Marney said.

'Haven't you heard that joke? People who confuse ento-mology and etymology bug me more than words can say.'

'I like that,' Ben said. 'So insects are your specialism?'

'I have a rather eclectic skill set, but yes, I'd say so.'

'And you think they could play a part in getting us out of this mess?'

'Quite possibly. Did you know that bees naturally vacci-nate their eggs by passing pathogens from the pollen through the bloodstream of the Queen?' Wakefield's eyes sparkled behind his lenses. 'Extraordinary creatures.'

Wakefield went from monosyllabic to verbal diarrhoea in the space of a minute. Marney wasn't sure which she preferred. She made a mental note to avoid working with him wherever possible.

'Now the introductions are out of the way, let's get on with the tour,' Stuart said.

Laura

Pain pulsed in Laura's temples. Pulling her knees to her chest, she tried to make herself small, hiding amongst the tree's roots, willing her breathing to quiet.

'Did any of you see where he went?'

'He? It was clearly a woman.'

'No. Did you not see the way he was dressed?'

'It didn't look like any lassie I've ever seen in Dornoch before.'

'Nor me.'

'Well, keep searching and we'll soon find out.'

The voices trailed off in another direction. Still, Laura counted to one hundred, waiting for the slightest noise. Finally she unfurled her body enough so she could look around. She noted that the bushes became less dense in one direction. Squinting, she was sure she could make out a small clearing and headed towards it. Laura relaxed as the groping branches around her thinned.

But her relief was short lived when a calloused hand clamped over her mouth. 'Get off me!' Laura whimpered as she tried to prise the fingers away.

'Quiet, you damned fool. They'll hear us.' The woman's breath was warm at her ear. 'I'm going to take away my hand, and you are going to stay quiet.'

Laura nodded.

The woman let go, her palm poised, ready to slap back over Laura's mouth. 'Good. Now follow me.'

Keeping low, Laura could just make out the woman's head, a silvery moon as she cut a path back into the sea of gorse. Laura followed, not daring to glance behind her. The farther they moved, the sparser the plant life became. Finally, they reached a clearing.

The woman clambered to her feet. 'I'm too old to be crawling round like a bairn.'

'Thank you.' Laura kept her tone hushed. 'I don't know who those men were but—'

'Malcolm Abernathy and his cronies. He's the local minister. But that doesn't make him any less dangerous. More so, I'd say.'

'I couldn't agree more.'

'Why were they chasing you?' She studied Laura with watery blue eyes.

'I'm not sure.'

The woman held Laura's eyes for a beat longer than felt comfortable before she said, 'Well, let's get inside before they see us.' She headed towards a wooden building that leant at a precarious angle. Ivy scaled the walls and coiled against the window panes, perhaps the cause of the roadmap of cracks beneath.

'What is this place?'

The woman shot her a look. 'My house.'

'It's...it's lovely.'

Laura followed her in, scanning the small building for danger.

'You're safe here,' the woman said, as though reading her mind.

'Thank you. I'm Laura.'

'Janet.'

'You live here alone?'

'No.' Janet's brow creased. 'My husband Fergus is...he should be back soon.'

'I see. Just let me catch my breath and I will get out of your way.'

'Where are you headed?'

Tears prickled Laura's eyes. 'You know, I'm really not sure. I didn't exactly plan this.'

Janet patted her hand. 'By the way you speak, I'd say you are mighty far from ho—' Male voices interrupted her. 'Get in the bed.' She pointed towards the hay mattress at the side of the room.

'Excuse me?'

Janet was startled as hammering began on the door. 'Face the wall, and pull the covers up to your chin.'

The hammering picked up in pace. 'Are you in there?'

'Do as you're told,' Janet hissed, shoving Laura towards the bed. To the man on the other side of the door she yelled, 'Where else would I be at this hour?'

Laura dragged the cover over her, the smell of damp wool filling her nostrils.

'Open up!'

'Hold on, I'm coming.' The rusted hinges screeched as Janet opened the door.

'And why are you waking us at this time of night, Malcolm?'

'Us? I thought Helen was helping down at the Begg farm?'

'A good girl like her doesn't like to be away from her ma for too long.'

The creak of the door told Laura that Janet had opened it further. A rectangle of light beat back the shadows above the bed. Laura could feel Malcolm Abernathy's eyes boring into the back of her head.

'Could we talk to her?'

'She may be a good daughter, but she has a sharp tongue, which you will find out for yourself if you wake her. Now, if you would remove your foot from my door, I would bid you goodnight.'

The soft clunk of wood told Laura he had not obliged.

'You've not even asked why we are here in the middle of the night,' Malcolm said.

'Aye, I know the charm us Horne women have over you young men. But I'm afraid we'll entertain none of that nonsense.'

'Stop with your japes, Janet Horne. We're looking for a woman...'

'I knew it soon as I looked at you.'

'...believed to be a witch. It won't surprise you that we decided to check to see if you knew anything.'

'Because you are so concerned for my welfare, I assume.'

'Something like that.'

'And what did this witch look like?'

'Well...I...Dark hair.'

'Dark hair, you say. We'd best round up half the women in the village then.'

'Don't mock me, Janet. This is serious. This is the Lord's work.'

Janet sighed. 'Malcolm Abernathy, unless the person you are looking for is hiding in my bed, I really can't be of any help to you.'

Laura cringed, bracing herself for him to fall upon her.

'Now, if you'll excuse me,' Janet said. 'I have a busy day tomorrow.'

'Tell Helen I was asking after her.'

Janet slammed the door shut, but still added, 'Like hell I will.'

Laura threw back the covers. 'I'm no witch,' she said, her voice a frantic whisper.

'It's none of my business, either way.'

'Aren't you frightened?'

'Of a bag of bones like you? Unlikely. I've more power in my pinky finger. Now, I'm off to bed.' She nodded towards the twisted pile of sheets on the other side of the room. 'You're welcome to stay, although I don't have much to offer but the roof over our head.'

'Thank you.'

Long after Janet's soft snuffles filled the air, Laura lay awake on the hay mattress, trying to make sense of what had happened. Was it only the day before that she'd been in the Sanctuary, excited at the prospect of reuniting with her son? Now she was trapped goodness knows where, leaving him to think she'd abandoned him. She couldn't let that happen. If there was a way to get back, she intended to find it.

The Book of Evelyn

'I want to talk to Bug.' It was the first thing I said as Dale drove us through the massive iron gates.

'Doesn't everybody,' Dale said.

I didn't know how to respond to that. 'So...so you'll take me to him?'

Celine gave me a strained smile. 'Bug isn't accepting visitors right now. I can answer any questions you have.'

'No.' I don't know where I got the nerve. After all, who was I to make demands? 'Take me to him, and he can tell me that himself.'

Dale gave the horn a brief toot, sending a flock of chickens flapping from our path. 'Celine is telling the truth, kid.'

'And he's okay with you talking for him?'

Dale gave a snort of laughter. 'Absolutely. If it means he doesn't have to talk for himself.'

'Dale...' Celine shot him a warning look.

'It's true, and you know it.'

'Let's just get settled,' Ruth said. 'I'm sure we'll meet him soon—'

'No. I'm not getting settled until I know who we're dealing with.'

For the first time, Dale shifted round in his seat to look at me directly. 'Demanding little thing, aren't you?'

I flashed him a grin. 'I've been called worse.'

'Hmmm. Well, Celine is free to take you to him. But it's up to Bug if he wants to speak to you.' Dale pulled the car to a halt outside a looming wooden barn. Then he hopped out without giving us as much as a goodbye.

'Doesn't think much of this Bug person, does he?' Ruth asked.

'Oh, he likes Bug just fine,' Celine said. 'They're brothers.'

I tried to imagine a more obnoxious, bossy version of Dale but found it difficult. 'What's he like?'

'Bug's the only reason we're still alive,' Celine said.

'That's not what I asked.'

She let out a long breath. 'Complicated. He's very complicated. But he's a good man. Okay, if we're doing this, then let's go.' She stopped mid-step. 'It's probably best if it's just Evie.'

'I'm not letting you take her anywhere,' Ruth said. 'Not without me.'

'Okay. But I'm telling you he's more likely to talk one-on-one.'

I hesitated, not thrilled at the idea of being trapped alone with a strange man. 'I'll be fine.'

'I...I'm really not sure about this, Evie.'

'Ruth, trust me.'

Before Ruth could argue further, Celine waved over a woman tending a vegetable patch nearby. 'Kayleigh, show Ruth to the dorm room, please. The two of them can set up in Anya's section.' Ruth followed, casting looks back at me as she went.

Celine led me across a vast field dotted with rectangular boxes. 'What are they?'

'Hives.'

'As in bee hives? I thought all the bees were dead.'

'They were. They basically still are, except for the hives we've got here. But Bug's working on that. As I said, he is one of the reasons we're still alive.'

We walked in silence, and the awkwardness of it left me searching for something else to say. 'Who's Anya?'

'Sorry?'

'You told Ruth that we could take her bunk. So whoever she is, I guess she's not here any more.' I don't know why I was trying to be so diplomatic. As you know, I'm usually pretty direct. What I really wanted to know was whether Anya was dead. And if so, was one of them responsible?

'No, she's not. I believe you met her already out on the road.'

I thought the name sounded familiar. 'She was one of the women who robbed us?' I spluttered my disgust. 'So this is the Colony? They are part of your group.'

'They were. They've swarmed.'

'That's what they said as well. Swarmed. What does that mean?'

'It's the way of things here. When the group gets too big, it breaks off and creates its own colony. We're still friendly.'

'Anya and her buddies seemed anything but friendly.'

Celine laughed. 'Yes, they have some very different ideas from the rest of us. Which is probably why Bug selected them for swarming.' Celine climbed the steps of a wooden building before hammering her fist against the door. 'But Anya is a decent woman. If she hadn't radioed us, telling us the Pack were hunting you, you'd be dead now.'

'The Pack? Is that what they call themselves?'

'Yeah. And each of them have a nickname based on dinosaurs from different eras.'

I couldn't help it; a snigger escaped. 'What are they, five?'

Celine grasped my wrist and looked into my eyes. 'You haven't seen a fraction of what they are capable of. It's no joking matter.'

'I understand. Really, I do.'

She realised she was clutching my wrist. 'Sorry. I get a little fired up whenever they crash back into our orbit. They aren't good people. In fact, they're barely people at all any more.' She turned back to the door. 'Will you open up, already?'

My throat was scratchy and dry at the thought of what might have happened to us. 'Thank you for saving us.'

'It wasn't my call.'

'Still, thank you.'

'You're welcome.' She beat her fist so hard I wouldn't have been surprised to see bloody knuckles. 'Bug, if you don't answer, I'm coming in anyway.'

'Go away!'

'Not happening, I'm afraid. One of our new guests is demanding to see you.' Celine threw open the door.

Bug didn't look up as Celine nudged me forward. 'Did she? Well, I guess I've no choice then.' Bug took off his magnifying glasses and put on his spectacles, the lenses so thick I could see the red veins surrounding his irises. 'You'll have to wait until I've finished this before I can talk.' He nodded to Celine. 'You can go.'

Celine rolled her eyes. 'Good luck.'

Bug seemed to remember the tweezers he held, poised so close to his nose that they almost touched. 'Give me a moment,' he said, running a tiny paintbrush over the pincered creature wriggling before him.

'What is it?' I asked.

'Apis mellifera. Or, to you, a bee. And it's not an 'it' but a 'she'.' He dropped the bee onto his palm, and it scuttled up to his fingers.

'Aren't you worried she will sting you?'

'Not at all. My logic is, treat her like the lady she is, and you'll be just fine.'

I huffed. 'A little sexist, don't you think?'

'Not at all. Before the Levelling, there would be on average thirty thousand bees in a hive. But the number of males in that number would be down in the hundreds. The females would gather the food, look after the young, and protect the hive. Without them, the bee colony would die. The way I see it, if you think being called a 'lady' is an insult, then you're probably underestimating what they're capable of. Being a lady demands respect.'

I was sure I was dealing with a crackpot, so I just said, 'Okay then.' I should have left it there. But I never was very good at holding my tongue. 'What you're doing to her doesn't look like a respectful way to treat a lady.'

He sighed. 'A necessary evil. I've been trying to train my assistant to help care for the bees. But she's proven...' He paused. '...lacking when it comes to identifying the Queen, so I'm marking her. It won't do her any harm.' He stretched out his hand to me so I could see the tiny green spot on the top of her head. Then he dropped her into a container and screwed on the lid. I tried to ignore the faint tapping as she flew against the inside of the jar over and over. 'What is it I can do for you?' Bug asked.

'I...' In truth, I didn't know. Even if I could persuade Ruth to leave, where would we go? Besides, I didn't want to leave yet either. Not while the horror of the previous night was so fresh. Not without a plan. So, I tried to buy a little time. 'Do they call you Bug because you're a beekeeper?'

'Bees aren't bugs. Bugs have piercing mouth parts that suck the life from things.' His deadpan face cracked into a snorting laugh. For the first time, I saw a mild resemblance to his brother. 'Don't worry. That isn't where the name comes from either. I was a curious child, asked too many questions.'

'And?'

'My family said it bugged them. After a while, it became my nickname. Anyway, it seems a little unfair that you know my name, but I don't know yours.'

'Evie.'

'Short for Evelyn?'

'Yes.'

'Hmm. Well, that's very...sweet.'

'What? You don't like my name?'

'I like it just fine. But did you know that Evelyn is Hebrew for 'life'? With a name like that, especially in this dying world, who would want to be cut down to little Evie?'

I'd never really thought about it. After all, what's in a name? I wavered between being pleased he thought it was special and annoyed at his presumption.

'Anyway, Evelyn, I need to get Her Majesty back to her hive. Did you have anything else to say?'

'Yes.' The words tumbled from me. 'I'm not a prisoner. Ruth and I will leave whenever we see fit.'

Bug cocked his head. 'I couldn't have said it better myself.'

~

Marney

<u>Before the Sanctuary</u>

Marney expected orange jumpsuits. Instead, the men all wore the same drab grey scrubs. 'What did they do?'

Stuart sniffed. 'What haven't they done? The less you know, the better. At least now they can be of service to society.'

'They're still human, you know.' She wasn't sure if she actually felt indignation on their behalf, or she had just picked the stance that would contradict Stuart.

'I guess that depends on your definition. Personally, I think you need to demonstrate humanity to earn that title.'

He walked towards the line of men. 'Welcome. Firstly, thank you for volunteering to take part in these trials.'

Although it was Stuart who spoke, she could feel eyes boring into her. She turned to find the oldest of the four prisoners smirking. Marney crossed her arms over her chest and tried to focus on what Stuart was saying.

'Without human trials, a working vaccine wouldn't be poss—'

'We get early release, right? For helping, I mean.' When the prisoner reached up to scratch his shaved head, Marney noticed the card suits tattooed on his knuckles. The ink had bled into the skin around, making them barely recognisable.

'Absolutely,' Stuart said.

'Will we be locked up?' a squat man at the end of the line asked. He was as wide as he was tall, but Marney could see by the bulges below his scrubs that it was pure muscle.

'We will conform to the same rules that you had in your

institution with the exception of yard time, for obvious reasons. But we have a well-stocked recreation room.'

Marney's skin crawled at the thought of them touching the same games as her girls. How quickly her charity had melted away.

'This is safe, right?' The young man, who to Marney appeared little more than a boy, asked in a strained staccato, suggesting just how recent puberty was for him. Or maybe he was simply nervous. Who could blame him?

'All trials contain risks,' Stuart said. 'But so far, the participants have reacted well.'

Marney's eyebrows shot up as Stuart glazed over the fact that the other participants were chimps.

The boy nodded. 'Will we be able to talk to our families while we are here?'

'I'm afraid not. All contact with the outside world is restricted for the duration of the trial.'

'Why?' Marney asked.

Stuart poked his tongue into his cheek and dragged in an exasperated breath. 'We'll discuss this later.'

Marney understood his annoyance. They should be presenting a united front, but she wanted that boy to be able to talk to his mother. In this new reality where she had so little control, it felt important.

To the prisoners, he spoke softly. 'I understand how you feel. But we can't risk any misinformation getting out. People are desperate, and the last thing we want is a surge of flu victims landing on us, thinking we have a cure. We'll release any findings at the right time.'

'Oh, I wouldn't tell them anything,' the boy said. 'I'm not even really sure where I am.'

'The answer is no. For now, at least. Are there any more questions before we leave you to settle in?'

Marney scanned their faces and was startled to see the man on the end staring at her. His grin widened at her discomfort.

'No? Then we'll leave you to it,' Stuart said.

Marney followed him out of the door. When she turned for a final look, the men were whispering amongst themselves. All except her admirer, who gave a little wave.

An hour later, the first prisoner perched on the trolley in front of her. The boy. She'd cursed to herself when they'd led him in. They couldn't have eased her in with...with who? She didn't want to experiment on anybody. But certainly not on a kid.

Marney fastened the Velcro on the blood pressure cuff.

'Will it hurt?' The machine whirred and tightened around his arm.

'This? Not at all. Didn't you ever have a physical?'

'No. But I meant what comes after.' The sides of his mouth tugged down, and he looked even younger.

She was embarrassed to realise she didn't even know his name and glanced at his file. Thomas Wells.

'Tom, I'll do my best to make it as painless as possible.'

'Thank you,' he said. 'Can I ask you a favour?'

'Sure.'

'Call me Thomas. My mother hated the name Tom. She said if she'd wanted a cat instead of a son, she'd have visited a shelter.' He laughed, but Marney noticed that his eyes glistened at the mention of his mother.

'Of course.' She hesitated, telling herself to keep her nose out. 'Did you get to see much of her? Before, I mean?'

'No.' He picked at the skin around his thumb, avoiding her eye. 'She died years before I went to prison. I was still just a kid.'

Marney cursed herself for raising it, as if he didn't have enough to feel glum about. 'Sorry, I shouldn't have asked.'

'It's okay. It's nice to have someone to talk to.'

'Well, you're all done here.' She nodded to Squires.

The keys on his hip jangled as he approached.

Thomas hopped down from the table, and Squires put his cuffs back on.

'Thanks, Doctor...'

'Call me Marney.'

'Thanks, Marney.'

Stuart entered as they left. 'How did it go?'

'Fine. It's just sad. He's so young.'

'Even the young can be evil.'

'Evil? Really?' Marney said. 'You're supposed to be a scientist.'

'He's a rapist.'

Marney opened and closed her mouth wordlessly. Finally she said, 'Oh. I had no idea.'

'No reason you should have. They come in all shapes and sizes. Just don't fall for his act.'

~

The Book of Evelyn

Celine gave me the side eye as I slurped down my soup without breathing. 'Sorry. I'm starving.'

'Don't mind me.' She spooned in another mouthful.

'Did you save all of these people?' Ruth asked.

'Some of them. Others found us and asked to join. We try not to turn anyone away, as long as they can contribute in some way. And, of course, some were with Bug from the beginning.'

'He created this place?' I asked.

'I suppose. But we all play our part in keeping it going.' She hesitated. 'At the end of the day, this is just a place, a scorched patch of earth we're trying to bring back to life. It's the people that make it what it is. A community.'

Ruth put down her spoon and pushed her bowl away. 'I couldn't help but notice that there are so many more women here than men.'

I swallowed down a comment about her not liking the competition. I'll admit it – even after all of her apologies, even after all the times I'd told her to forget it, I was still angry.

'That isn't by design,' Celine said. 'It's just how things have worked out.'

'So he's not some...? Well, you know,' Ruth asked.

Celine remained silent.

Ruth shuffled uncomfortably. 'You hear about these men who gather together vulnerable women for...' Ruth glanced at me and then looked away. 'I don't know. Forget I said anything.'

'Bug isn't some crazy cult leader, if that's what you mean.'

'No...I...I just wondered.'

'The leaders in our last place...' I said, throwing Ruth a lifeline. 'They weren't always kind. I guess we're both a little wary now.'

Celine nodded. 'You aren't the only one to experience something like that. And I include myself in that statement. But you have nothing to worry about. Bug's a good man. Grumpy as hell and with the people skills of a paperweight, but a good man all the same.' Celine scraped the last of the soup from her bowl and dropped her spoon with a clang. 'In truth, I think Bug would be just as happy by himself. But he's always been a sucker for a charity case. And that's what we all were, at the beginning at least.' She got up from the table. 'I still have work to do. After dinner, you two should get some rest. You start your work duty tomorrow.'

'I told you, we aren't staying,' I said. 'We just need a few days, and we'll get out of your way.'

'Oh, I know, but if you are using our resources and eating our food, you can work for it while you're here.'

'Sounds fair.' Then I added, 'You know, maybe it's not a coincidence that so many women found their way here. Maybe we were just never given enough credit for how strong we really are. Even by one another.'

Celine chuckled. 'I like that.'

I should have done as Celine instructed and gone back to the dorm. But the sun hadn't even set, and I was too curious to sleep.

'I won't go far,' I told Ruth.

She massaged her temples. 'I'm too tired to argue. Please, just keep out of trouble.'

'You too.' I flashed her a smile that I didn't even pretend was genuine.

I passed several other dormitories as I circled the camp, keeping close to the buildings. A babble of voices drifted from inside, but I wasn't tempted to go in. When it came to meeting new people, I was rusty. Besides, I'd never found it easy to fit in with regular types. I always found I gravitated towards the quirkier sort. But then you would know all about that.

As I approached the building where I'd met Bug, I saw a lone figure clothed in white wandering between the beehives. They stopped and lifted something from the wooden box. Puffs of smoke rose above them, and they pulled something from within the hive. They slid it back into place and replaced the top.

Then the figure marched towards me. As they approached, I saw that it wasn't just their body that was swathed in white cloth but their face, too.

I looked back towards the dorms, wondering if I should scarper before they reached me. Certain I was about to get a ticking off from Bug or one of his assistants, I was already stating my case by the time they reached me.

'I didn't mean to—'

Before I could finish, the person pulled off their hood, leaving me speechless.

'Didn't mean to what?' she asked. 'Spy on me?'

A teenage girl, not much older than me, cocked her head, waiting for my response. When I said nothing, she huffed and started walking away.

'I'm sorry,' I called. 'I've just arrived, and I was just scoping the place out.'

She stopped and turned. 'Some of us don't appreciate being watched.'

'Yeah, I get that. I really didn't mean to make you uncomfortable.'

She studied me. 'All righty then. Just don't let it happen again.'

'I won't.'

'Oh,' she called over her shoulder. 'My name is Riley, by the way.'

That was it. That was how I met my first real friend in the Colony. You may be wondering why I'm bothering to tell you. But that moment, in that field with its crunchy grass, meeting that snarky, wild-haired girl is important to my story. Because what we had, our friendship, was real. I didn't want her to die.

Some would say I've said that too many times before. *One death*, they would say, *is unfortunate. However, when you need both hands to keep count of the lives lost, somebody has to take responsibility.* But you know the background to my story, and I hope you'll give me the benefit of the doubt.

Chapter Four

The Book of Evelyn

I was assigned to the gardening work group. Not that I had a clue what I was doing. Although that wasn't really my fault as I'd spent the last chunk of my life hiding below the earth and the rest watching it wither and die.

Michelle, the team leader, patted the soil down over the seedling. 'Now we wait.'

'What's the point? I didn't think anything grew any more.'

'You're right about that. This earth isn't fit for growing much that's edible. Most of what we eat is grown inside.' Michelle nodded towards the greenhouses dotted across the surrounding fields. 'But we don't have enough of anything to make that a long-term solution. Not when our community seems to be continually growing.'

A pang of guilt flushed my cheeks. I hadn't thought about how my stay would affect the Colony. I'd spent the past few days declaring my wish to leave, when in reality, our staying would mean stretching their rations to two extra mouths. 'Enough of what exactly?'

'Building resources, for one. The plastic sheeting we need for the greenhouses isn't just lying around. Nor is the piping for the irrigation system.'

'I guess not.'

'But don't you let that concern you. Believe me, when it's time to worry, I'll let you know.'

'Isn't this just a waste of time, then?'

'Maybe not. Bug's been cooking up some new concoctions that he hopes will give the plants a fighting chance outside the greenhouses. And if there's something I've learnt about Bug over the years, it's that when he wants to achieve something, he's usually stubborn enough to get it done.'

'Like this place.'

'Oh yes. None of us would be here without Bug.'

'So people keep telling me.'

'Well, I mean that in every sense. Bug didn't just build this place; he handpicked every resident. Have you met any of the other teenagers yet?'

'Just one. She seemed kind of...frosty.'

Michelle laughed. 'You must mean Riley.'

'That's right. Wow, she really does have a rep.'

'No. Well, a little. But there are only a few teenagers here, and she seemed the most likely candidate. She's a nice girl when she's not snarling. It would be good for you to make a frie—'

'Oh, we're not staying.'

'I know. I know. You told me already. But it can't hurt to have a few friendly faces around while you're here.'

'Is she some kind of beekeeper?'

'Not 'some kind'. Riley *is* a beekeeper.'

'That's...kind of a weird job for a teenage girl.'

'If Bug is to be believed, and he is, it's the most important job here. He selects the beekeepers himself. It's the only part of job allocation he gets involved in. Riley was Anya's apprentice until she swarmed. Now it's all on her.'

'That's a lot of responsibility for someone our age.'

'To say the least,' Michelle said. 'If our bees don't survive, then none of this is sustainable. We're just running out the clock until the end. So, with that much pressure, we all try and cut Riley some slack for being a bit of an arse.'

'Then why give such an important job to a teenager?' I asked.

'You'd have to ask Bug that. But everybody here has to play their part if we're going to survive.'

'Well, I'll try to be useful, at least while I'm here.'

Michelle wiped her hands on her jeans, leaving muddy trails across the denim. 'Oh, you will be useful. There's no question about that. We don't have the resources to keep anybody who isn't.'

I'm embarrassed to admit I hadn't considered that they might not want me. The realisation sent panic bubbling through me.

I searched my brain for something to say, and somewhere from its depths came a fact you once told me. 'Did you know that plants look green because they only need red and blue light to grow? They reflect the green because they don't need it.'

'I didn't. So you're a scientist.'

She sounded impressed, and for a moment, I was

tempted to lie. 'No. I just had a friend who was. He liked to tell me about these things, whether I asked or not.'

Maybe I should have left out that part. But don't take it personally, Jared. If there was one thing I missed about the Sanctuary, it was the few friends I'd made. Particularly you.

Besides, Michelle didn't seem to notice my little barb. 'Now, he sounds like a useful guy to have around.'

'He was. Is. I hope he found some happiness there, even if I couldn't.'

Michelle studied me for so long that I began to cringe.

Finally, she said, 'Maybe that just wasn't the right fit for you. Perhaps this could be if you gave it a chance.'

I didn't answer her because I didn't want her to think I'd agreed to anything. But a tingle of hope danced over me.

That should have been my first warning. Good things don't happen to me. And when trouble finally caught up with me, as it always did, that hope would just make reality all the more crushing.

~

Laura

'You'd best tell me what you've done with my mother.'

Laura woke to the sting of a blade pressed to her throat. 'Please, I haven't done anything wrong.'

'No? Well, you're here sleeping like a bairn in my bed, and my ma's nowhere to be seen.'

'Maybe...she just went out.' Laura edged herself into a sitting position, waves of the woman's dark hair falling onto her face and chest.

'There's nowhere for miles around.' However, her voice wavered as if she couldn't rule it out.

'Maybe she went looking for your father. She said she was expecting him.'

'My pa has been dead since I were a babby.' She got up from where she was crouched next to the bed. 'She's wandered off again.'

'I'm sure she'll be back soon.' Laura rubbed the sore spot on her throat. 'You must be Helen.'

'She's been talking about me then.'

'A little. Your mother is very proud of you.'

Helen sniffed. 'You didn't tell me who you are.'

'I'm Laura. A friend of your mother.'

Helen's eyebrows arched. 'My mother doesn't have any friends.'

'No? Well, she was kind enough to give me a bed for the night.'

'Aye. My bed. Most generous of her.'

Laura felt heat in her cheeks. 'Sorry, I'll get out of your way.'

The chilly morning air flooded the shack as the door was thrown open. 'I see you two have met,' Janet said.

'Where have you been so early?' Helen asked.

'I've been telling the bees about our visitor.'

'The bees?' Laura asked.

Helen pinned her with a stare, telling her in no uncertain terms to keep out of their business.

'Of course.' Janet went to the fireplace and began positioning tinder. 'You have to tell the bees about all the comings and goings of the house, lest they take offence and abandon you.'

Helen tutted. 'They did just that years ago, you old fool. Don't you remember? You tangled with the Clark boys when they stole our seed. The next morning all our skeps were smashed, and the bees were gone. The honey, too.'

Janet's hands hovered for a moment before going back to work. 'No...I can hear them. You can hear them too, can't you, Laura?'

Laura strained to listen. 'I'm sorry but—'

'I am so tired of this,' Helen said, throwing her hands in the air. 'I tell you what, bring us the honey, Ma. I've done a day's work already and could do with—'

'I should go,' Laura said. 'It was kind of you to let me stay.'

'Don't hurry yourself,' Helen said. 'You can watch over this mad old coot for me. You're welcome to my bed. I won't be needing it tonight.'

'And where is it you think you're off to?' Janet asked.

'I'm going to cut peat.' Helen hesitated. 'Fion has asked me to ride up in his cart with him.'

Janet's face flushed red. 'Over my putrid rotting corpse, you will.'

'Aye, that can be arranged.'

Janet followed her out of the door. 'Don't you walk away from me, girly. I'm your ma, and you will listen when I speak.'

'Why should I when you want nothing good for me?'

'What idiot talk is that? Of course I want good for you. Which is why I am telling you that you are far too good for Fion or any man for a hundred miles around here.'

Helen held up a hand. The knuckles were bloated and gnarled, the fingers twisted into a claw. 'This says otherwise.'

Janet waved her away. 'If a man can't see past a little thing like that, then he's not worth thinking on.'

'That's for me to decide. Fion has a plough, Ma. He said he would help us work the fields.'

'Because he wants to take what is your birthright.'

'And what good is the land to me, to us, if all we can grow are weeds? Maybe Fion wouldn't be as poor a match as you think. He's promised to look after us both once we're married.'

'We don't need him. This farm was blessed until the famine.'

'That was before I was even born, Ma.'

'This land feeds us, clothes us.'

'Barely. We don't have the right tools or the money to—'

The sound of horse hooves stopped them.

'That's Fion now. Be nice to him, Ma. He might be our only hope of surviving another winter in this place.'

'I've survived fifteen winters without a man to help me.'

'And where has that got us? I've eaten only a handful of

oats in two days. I can't go on like this.' Helen turned to the approaching man, who bounced upon a horse-drawn cart.

'Good morning, ladies. Janet.'

Helen smiled at him. Janet spat on the floor.

'I don't believe we've met,' Fion said, nodding at Laura.

'Laura is a family friend. I was just telling Ma how kind you are to take me to cut peat. We'd have been in for a cold couple of weeks without it.'

'No doubt he'll expect plenty in return,' Janet said.

'Don't be like that,' Fion said. 'I've been good to this family.'

'Because you want my land,' Janet said. 'Tell me, are you even interested in my wee girl here, or is it just the deeds you're after?'

Fion's face darkened. 'Is that the kind of man you think I am?'

'Ignore her,' Helen said, clambering up into the cart. 'Laura, I'll be gone until tomorrow night. Can you stay around that long to keep an eye on her?"

'I'm not a bairn,' Janet said.

'Yes,' Laura said, despite Janet's protests, because there was nowhere else for her to go.

Fion chuckled. 'It seems these two think you could do with a little swaddling.'

Janet glared at him. 'I wouldn't mock me if I were you.'

Fion's face split in a grin. 'Is that right? Going to curse me again, are you, Janet?'

'Don't encourage her,' Helen said.

Janet puffed out her chest. 'I could if I wanted. I could turn your crops to dust and sour your milk while it's still in the udder.'

'Aye, because you're a witch. Isn't that right, Janet?' He pressed his lips together to suppress a laugh.

Janet lifted her chin high. 'What I am or am not is nothing to do with you.'

'You've lost your mind, Janet Horne. Helen shouldn't suffer because of you.' He whipped his horse's flank, and it walked a wide circle before setting off towards the road.

'I'll be back tomorrow night,' Helen yelled over her shoulder, but she didn't look back.

Marney

<u>Before the Sanctuary</u>

The skin on the prisoner's knuckles was white as he gripped the arms of the chair. It made the shapes tattooed onto them even more prominent.

He caught Marney looking. 'The card suits remind me life is a gamble.'

Stuart injected him with the vaccine. 'Personally, I prefer to play it safe.'

'How's that working out for you, doc?'

'A fair point,' Stuart said. 'As well as for anyone nowadays, I guess.'

'Exactly.' He rubbed the top of his arm where the needle pierced his skin. 'Lucky for the rest of you, I'm more willing to take risks than most.'

Marney was relieved he was compliant. She'd battled enough for one day. The four members of the team had met that morning.

'It's too soon,' Wakefield said.

'How long would you have us wait?' Stuart asked. 'Until there's nobody left to save?'

'Don't act like you want this more than me,' Wakefield said. 'I've dedicated years of my life to finding this vaccine, as you well know. I just don't think a few more days will—'

'They would make a difference,' Marney said. 'You haven't seen what it's like out there. People are desperate.'

Stuart offered her a thankful smile. 'Meredith? What do you think?'

'I...I don't want anyone else to die.'

'Exactly my point,' Wakefield said.

Meredith kept her eyes trained on Stuart. 'Let's try it.'

Wakefield didn't flounce out. There was no slamming of doors. He simply said, 'Democracy is the worst form of government.'

Marney was glad to have been chosen to help administer it. At least it showed she had the courage of her convictions. Still, her hand shook as she delivered that first injection.

The prisoner watched, bemused. 'Don't be nervous, Doc. This isn't the first trial I've volunteered in.'

Marney smiled her thanks. 'Well, you're all done for now.'

As he got to his feet, the prisoner began to sway.

'Are you okay?' Marney asked, sweeping in to steady him.

'Yeah, I just got up too...' He clasped the top of Marney's arm, digging his fingers into her flesh.

'Get off,' she said, prying his hand away.

'I can't...' He reached his cuffed hands to his throat and began to claw at his skin. The bracelets on the handcuffs jangled as his desperation grew.

'He can't breathe.' Stuart ran to one of the medicine cupboards and returned with a syringe of epinephrine. 'Help me get him on the floor.'

The air whistled from the prisoner's constricted throat. Stuart stabbed the needle into his thigh.

Marney grabbed his hand. 'You're okay. Keep looking at me. You're okay.'

He craned his neck as he tried to plead for help, his chest shuddering as he wheezed out panicked breaths.

'Go get another shot of epinephrine,' she told Stuart. 'It's not working.'

Stuart ran back to the cabinet, reading and discarding boxes. 'I'll get one from the other lab.'

The prisoner's eyes shrank within the puffy purple skin of his swelling face. He tugged at her blouse as he struggled to tell her something.

'Don't try to speak. He'll be back any second.'

At first, she thought he was following her instructions. The muscles in his face relaxed, and he slumped back onto the floor. It was when the painful rattle of his breathing stopped that Marney realised he was gone.

Stuart skidded onto his knees and stabbed the needle into the prisoner's leg.

'He's dead,' Marney said. Her voice sounded hollow even to her.

'We could try resuscitating him.'

They both looked at his bloated face and knew it was useless.

'Marney.'

She was aware Stuart was talking to her but couldn't find the strength to answer.

'Marney, look at me.' She did as he said. 'He went into anaphylactic shock. There was just no time to help him.'

Realising she was still holding the prisoner's hand, Marney dropped it and flinched away.

'It's all right,' Stuart said. 'I'm going to have one of the guards help me move him. Will you be okay getting back to your quarters?'

'No, I can't leave. There will be paperwork to fill in. The

prison will want to know what happened to him. Oh God, his poor family.'

'Marney, listen to me. I will fill in all of the forms. Some casualties were to be expected.'

'Casualties.' She whispered the word to herself as she stared at the froth spilling from the man's mouth and coating his cheek.

'So you will be okay getting back?'

Marney cleared her throat. 'Um, yes. I'm sorry. It's just I've just always been a lab rat. I've never seen anybody...' She let her sentence drift off.

'Just go home and get some rest.'

'Yes.' Her legs wobbled beneath her, but she managed to stand. 'Yes, I think I will.'

She headed for the door but paused. 'What was his name?'

Stuart pulled his chart from the end of the table and read. 'Jerome Kelly.'

'Okay,' she said. 'I wish I'd asked him.'

'Me too.'

Marney didn't remember navigating the corridors back to her quarters. When she threw open the door, Ben greeted her with a frown. 'You're early.'

'Am I?' She had begun to lose time in the closed ecosystem of the facility. 'Where are the girls?'

'In bed.' He dropped the spoon into the side of the pan he was stirring. 'Are you okay?'

She hated crying in front of him or anybody else. Such strong emotions were frowned upon when she was growing up. But she couldn't help it.

'No, I'm not.' She dissolved into tears.

'Hey, talk to me.' Ben came around the kitchen counter, his arms raised to her.

She didn't go to him, though. Instead, she went to the bedroom the girls shared.

Marney smoothed Jodie's wild hair.

'Mommy,' Jodie said, waking at her touch. 'Mommy, why are you crying?'

She climbed onto Marney's lap, followed by her sister.

'I'm sorry I woke you,' Marney said. She pulled them closer, breathing in the smell of soap and sleep. The familiarity of it brought more tears, and her shoulders began to heave.

'Don't cry, Mommy.' Emma's voice wobbled as she cupped her mother's face in her hands.

'Marney, you're scaring them,' Ben said, though she could tell by the strain in his voice that he was afraid, too. She couldn't help it; the tears wouldn't stop.

The Book of Evelyn

I'd be enough waiting for Ruth for what felt like ages. I finally stomped from the dormitory, intent on finding her. That didn't take long. She was leaning against the wooden planks of the dorm wall, chatting to Dale.

It's not like I'd caught them kissing. In a way, that would have been better. Then I could have confronted Ruth and demanded she pack it in. I would have reminded her that she'd promised to focus on our future. I didn't factor Dale, or any other man, into that.

It was that ridiculous cackle she gave when Dale said something I didn't hear. The way she put her hand on his chest and let it linger there. I stormed back into the dorm and threw myself down on my bunk.

Only the shoulder height partition offered me any privacy from the rest of the dorm. I didn't care. I beat my fists against the thin mattress and let out a growl of frustration.

Riley's head popped up like a meerkat's from the other side. 'What's got into you?'

'Sorry.'

'No, don't be. Your feral side is a big improvement.' She navigated round the partition and flopped down on the bed next to me. 'I find it very relatable.'

'In that case…' I let out a high-pitched scream.

Grumbles came from somewhere in the dorm. 'Will you please shut up.'

We broke into fits of giggles.

When we calmed down, Riley asked, 'Better?'

'I think so.'

'Alrighty then. So do you want to tell me what happened?'

'No, you wouldn't understand.'

'Okay.'

'It's just…I don't understand why my mother always has to have a man around. It's never ended well. For either of us.'

Compared to the laughter of a moment before, the silence that hung between us felt heavy. 'Yeah, I've been there. Who is her poison of choice, then?'

'Dale.'

Riley snorted. 'That guy is a complete ass.'

'I don't know. He did save us. Maybe she feels like she owes him something.'

'Ugh. And I can guess what that is.'

'No. I mean, this isn't about Dale. Not really.'

'Of course it is. My mother told me the smartest thing I'd ever do is learn to live without a man.'

'She wasn't with your dad then?' I asked.

'Unfortunately, he took until death do us part literally.' Her eyes glistened, and I wished I could hit rewind on our conversation.

I was relieved when Riley broke into a grin. 'Wait here. There's something I want to show you.' Seconds later, she launched herself back round the partition so fast that her shoes squeaked. She tossed me a book. 'Here, I marked a page you might like.'

I looked at the cover. 'A Societal Analysis of the Bee Colony by Doctor Richard Wakefield.' Catchy title.'

'Just read it.'

I ran my finger along the top right-hand corner of the book until I found a turned over page. Not that she really needed to mark it. The spine was broken, and the book opened right to her selected page. Clearly, she read this part a lot.

'I think you'll get a kick out of this,' Riley said.

I began to read. 'Drone bees, which are all male, do not have an obvious role in the colony beyond mating with the Queen. They do not forage or collect pollen, yet are provided with shelter and food by the worker bees.' Is this supposed to make me feel better?'

Riley lay down on the bed and turned over onto her back, her arms behind her head. 'Keep reading.'

'Fine. 'This seemingly easy lifestyle is to be balanced with the...the brutal death that they will likely endure. If they are selected from the mating swarm by the Queen, their barbed reproductive organs are ripped from their body, killing them."

'See, that's a little more like it, isn't it?' She smiled at the ceiling, so she didn't notice the wide eyes I viewed her through. 'Bees have it right.'

I read to the end of the page. 'Those that fail to mate with the Queen do not fare much better. When winter approaches and food is short, the worker bees stop feeding the drones. Once they are weak enough to be forcibly removed from the hive by the smaller female worker bees, they are left to starve or freeze to death.' Wow. I mean...that's intense.'

'Oh, lighten up. Nobody is going to evict Dale. Or rip off his stinger.' She winked at me.

'You have kind of a wicked sense of humour, don't you?'

'Oh, I have a wicked everything.'

Intrigued and wary in equal measure, I wasn't sure what

to say. I flicked to a random diagram of a bee and feigned interest.

'Borrow the book if you like,' Riley said. 'I've read it cover to cover. Bug made sure of that.'

'I don't...'

'You may as well. There's not much else to do around here. And who knows, learn enough, and maybe I could take you out to the hives sometime. As long as you aren't scared?'

'Maybe I am,' I said. 'But being afraid has never stopped me before.'

'I think I'm going to like being friends with you.'

Those were her words. I feel guilty even telling you them after what I did. But that's the thing with betrayal, isn't it? It can't come from an enemy.

Excerpt from <u>*A Societal Analysis of the Bee Colony*</u> <u>by Doctor Richard Wakefield</u>

<u>Colony versus Hive</u>

A novice beekeeper may use the terms hive and colony interchangeably. The reality is that they are very different. A hive is a structure, sometimes man-made, where the colony resides. Scout worker bees select it as an appropriate base. This could be anything from a tree to a crevice. It is also changeable as circumstances dictate.

The colony, however, comprises subgroups of the bee population, including the Queen, workers, drones and larvae. If the hive is the house, then the colony is the family that chooses to make it their home.

Wakefield, R. (2025) *A Societal Analysis of the Bee Colony*. Third edition. London: Feisty Scholar Publications.

Cher L. Jones

forewing
hamuli
ocelli
compound eye
antennae
hindwing
spiracle
mandibles
spindle hair
proboscis
legs
abdomen
thorax
head

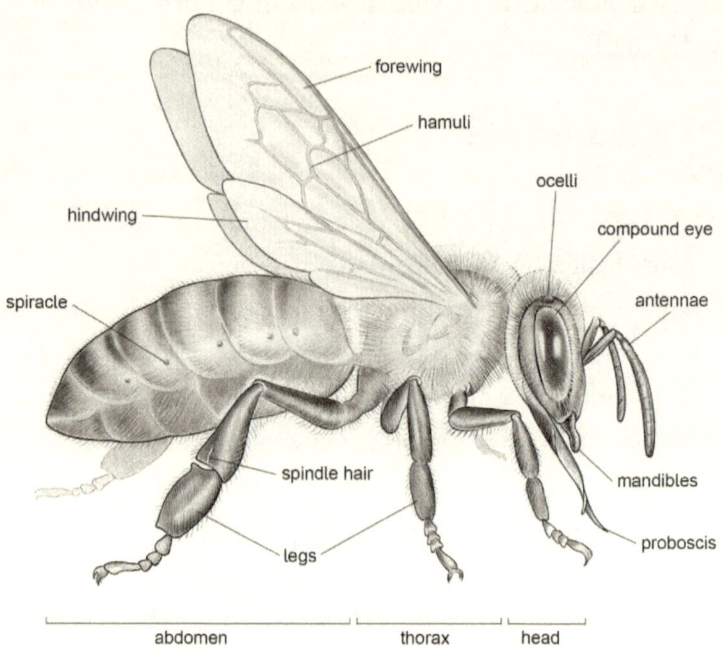

Marney

<u>Before the Sanctuary</u>

'The data shows Jerome was just an anomaly. We can continue with the trials right now if we want.' Stuart's words suggested that he did want to continue, but his bloodshot eyes told another story.

'You do what you like,' Marney said. 'But I haven't seen my kids in nearly twenty-four hours.'

When she got to her quarters, all was silent. 'Hello?' She pushed open the bedroom doors, but Ben and the girls were nowhere to be found. 'So much for the welcome wagon.' The games room had become one of the girls' favourite haunts since they'd arrived, so she decided to try there.

Jodie's giggle floated down the corridor to greet her as she approached.

'I'll play the winner,' Marney said, expecting to see both girls sitting at the table.

Although, as she entered the games room, she realised Thomas sat opposite Jodie. Previously she had thought of him as just a boy, but all charity she had felt evaporated when she saw him with her child.

Marney flew towards them. 'Get away from her!' She cradled Jodie's head to her chest.

Thomas sprang from the seat, knocking over the plastic stand and scattering the discs across the table. 'I'm sorry. She asked me to play.'

'Well, she doesn't get to decide that. Do you hear me?'

'Marney, they were just playing. I was right here the

whole time.' Ben lounged on a bean bag at the other end of the room, Emma curled on his lap. 'And Squires is here, too.'

The young guard stood with his hand to his holster, hesitating over whether there was a threat he should be addressing. 'Ben said it was fine for them to share the room as long as they were properly supervised.'

Emma clutched a book. 'Mommy, what's wrong?'

'Nothing. I'm just tired. Everything's fine.' She pulled Jodie towards her hip. Then she turned to Thomas and lowered her voice. 'Stay away from my children. You have no business talking to them.'

Thomas held his hands out, palms open. 'I'm sorry. I just...'

'Just what?'

'I guess I just thought you were different.' Thomas looked at Squires. 'Can you take me back to my cell?'

Squires dithered. 'Doctor Wallace, is that okay with you? The guard that brought him here was called away.'

'You'll get no complaint from me.'

As Squires led Thomas away, Marney questioned her actions.

But not for long, because as she doubted whether she was being reasonable, Ben jumped on the chance to clarify matters for her. 'It's not like you to be so judgemental. I think you dropped your principles somewhere back in the lab.'

'You don't know what he did.'

'Do you? The details, I mean.'

Marney hesitated. 'I know enough. Can we please feed the girls so we can all get to bed?'

The family dinner she'd craved became a nuked microwave meal for the girls and a row for her and Ben. His liberal disgust still rang in her ears as she tried to sleep. He'd preached second chances and redemption. She didn't care. On paper at least, she was all for fresh starts. But let someone else risk *their* children.

So despite her exhaustion, Marney stared at the ceiling until her alarm sounded. The practicalities of sharing the facility with a group of convicted criminals weren't something she'd considered when she had agreed to stay.

Breakfast was just as frosty. Finally, Marney caved and broke the silence. 'Look, I'm sorry, okay? I know you'd never put the girls in a situation where they could be in danger.

'Even if he intended to hurt us, which I don't believe for a second, there was a guard right there.'

'I know. You were right,' Marney said. 'I'm a terrible 'not in my backyard' hypocrite.'

'I wouldn't go that far,' Ben said, kissing her forehead.

'I'll do better.' It was a lie. If she had her way, the girls and the prisoners would live completely parallel lives. But Ben was thawing, and she didn't want to jeopardise that.

So that morning, Marney found herself simultaneously rehearsing what she would say to Thomas and preparing the vaccine when the guard entered. 'I've got the prisoner here for you.'

'Thanks. I actually wanted to talk to—' Marney gasped. 'What the hell happened to you?'

Thomas' eyes bulged purple, dwarfing the brown irises within. A cut spanned the bridge of his nose, patches of dry blood caking it.

'One of the other prisoners decided that I'm a paedophile.' He glared at her, making it clear where he thought the blame for that lay.

Marney's throat felt tight. 'Are you?'

He stared, aghast. 'Of course not. The girl I was locked up over was fifteen.'

'You just said it yourself. Girl. Underage.' She snapped on a pair of rubber gloves.

'Oh, here we go, another middle-class know it all, judging me before they know any of the facts. I was seventeen, and I'd known her most of my life. We were in love. Still are, I guess, if she made it.' He fell quiet.

Guilt prickled Marney's skin. 'It's none of my business. I shouldn't have asked.' She gathered together cotton pads and antiseptic, ready to clean his wounds.

'Oh, you made it your business with your little performance yesterday. Your husband said it was okay, you know?'

'I know he did.'

'But you still don't want me around your daughter?'

Marney considered lying but realised there was no point. 'That's right.'

She dabbed at the cut on his nose with a moist cotton pad. 'Don't take it personally. I don't want any of you near them.'

'That's a hard thing not to take personally, but I'll try. Do you believe me about Cara?'

'Cara?'

'My girlfriend. You must have read my file if you know what I'm in for.'

Marney hadn't. She didn't think hearing the details would help her care for any of them. Instead, she decided to assume the worst and hope for the best. 'I guess so. But those laws are there for a reason.'

'Yeah, but we were young and in love. My lawyer said it

would never have come to court if her parents hadn't pushed for it.'

Marney wondered what she would do in that situation. What if one of her children brought home a boy, or girl, of whom she disapproved? Would she see that person in prison to keep them from her child? Marney didn't think so. But then she couldn't rule it out either.

'Didn't you ever do something stupid at my age?' Thomas asked.

Marney could give him an impressive list but chose not to. Instead, she busied herself with covering the cut above his eye with a butterfly stitch.

Her face was an inch from his when he asked, 'Where did it come from?'

There was only one 'it' to which he could be referring. The virus. 'Animals, probably. Birds, most likely.'

'No, that's not what I mean. I guess I'm asking 'why?''

'Pure bad luck. If you're after an answer any more meaningful than that, then I'm afraid you're asking the wrong person. I don't believe God, or Allah or any other deity did this. I think it was just shitty luck.'

'Okay.' His brow was knitted into a frown.

'What do you think?'

He sniffed. 'I'm not educated enough to give my opinion on much of anything.'

'Go on. Everyone has a right to an opinion.'

'All right. I guess I think that this was the chance for the world to reset itself. All of the craziness that's been rumbling along over the last few years couldn't go on as it was. My mother would have said it was God intervening to teach us a lesson.'

'And do you believe it was God?'

'I hope not. If he is willing to do this to nice families like yours, he must have some whole new level of hell waiting for me.'

'Well, I wouldn't know anything about that.' She stepped on the pedal of the waste bin and dropped the rubbish inside.

'You're going to give me the injection now, right?' He stared at his shoes. 'The one that killed Jerome.'

'You know about that?'

'We all do. The vaccine killed him.'

'No,' Marney said. 'Well yes, but he was allergic to one of the chemicals. The chances of one of you also having that reaction is minuscule. All the same, we've run your bloods, and you are all fine.'

He met her eye. 'You would say that.'

'Trust me. Besides, you're all done for today. I can't give you the vaccine while you're healing; we need your immune system to be functioning normally.' She gave Squires the nod to take him back to his cell. Thomas hopped down from the gurney.

'Which prisoner was it that hurt you?' She didn't want to get involved but thought it sensible to know.

'O'Neil. The guy's a psycho.'

'Well, if I played a role in what happened, I am sorry.'

'Thanks. And I guess I might have done the same in your situation.'

The icy shell she had been cultivating for the last twelve hours began to melt, and she wracked her brain for a crumb of comfort to throw him. 'This isn't forever, you know.' Her words felt clumsy, but she was bolstered by the way his slumped shoulders straightened. 'One day, this will be a cautionary tale you use to get your kids back in line.'

'I hope so,' he said. Then he grinned at her, exposing a chipped incisor. 'We've just got to save the world first, and then I can go home to Cara.'

'That's right,' Marney agreed. 'Easy peasy.' But she couldn't shake the feeling that he'd made a liar of her again.

~

Jared

Marney gave a heavy sigh. 'I appreciate how upsetting that must have been to share, Seb.'

Jared questioned the magnitude of such an understatement. Seb didn't look upset; he looked wrung out by his grief, as if a phantom had drained the colour and joy from his face. Jared pictured it squeezing Seb's lungs, leaving him snatching his breath between swallowed sobs.

'Isaac was my best friend,' Seb said. 'I can't imagine a future without him.'

In a way, Jared envied him. Not the loss, of course. But the way he shared his grief so openly. Although Jared knew that his own despair over Nell was just as consuming, he forced it below the surface, willing himself not to break down. *Not here*, he told himself. *Not in front of them*. But eventually it would come out, he knew that. It would wheedle a path beneath the veneer he projected until it found a weakness, then it would burst out, fracturing any sense of well-being he'd pieced together.

'We are so sorry for your loss,' Millicent said. 'You are free to go, Seb.'

Aleksey cleared his throat. 'Actually, I have one last question.'

Seb froze in an awkward stance between being seated and standing. He hovered there for a second, before slumping back into the chair.

'I was just wondering,' Aleksey said, 'if you saw which of the Durand boys pushed you?'

'Excuse me?'

'You said you were shoved through the portal. Was it by Martin, Luca or Oliver?'

'It wasn't any of them,' Seb said. 'Victor Durand pushed me.'

'I see.' Aleksey scribbled something on the pad in front of him. 'Thank you. You are excused.'

The shadows on Seb's sunken features darkened further. 'But his sons helped him. They made sure I couldn't fight back.'

'They threatened you?' Aleksey asked. 'Hurt you?'

'No, but they would have done, given the opportunity. That was clear. Don't you believe me?'

'No, Seb, that isn't what he meant,' Marney said, shooting Aleksey a brief scowl. 'We just need to ensure we have all the facts straight. Isn't that right, Aleksey?'

'Of course. I meant no offence. Perhaps we should move onto our next witness. Jared Morgan, could you take the stand please?'

Despite knowing he would be called, Jared's throat still constricted. He was certain that when he took the seat Seb had just vacated, his mouth would open and release just a squeak of air.

'Jared, did you hear me?' Aleksey asked.

'It's okay.' Marney nodded, beaming him a smile that looked too large for her face. 'A few questions and you'll be done.'

Done. That word got him moving, because once he'd given his evidence, the search for his mother could begin.

As Jared shuffled to the desk, he could feel the eyes of the citizens boring into him. It was a long time since he had cared what the people of the Sanctuary thought. However, as row upon row of citizens stared back at him, his pulse began to race and he could hear it beating in his ears.

'Can you tell us, in your own words, what brought you back to the Sanctuary?' Marney asked.

He could, easily, because his every waking moment, and many of his sleeping ones, were plagued with memories of what happened. Jared's words tumbled over one another as he relayed the events that had knocked his life off course. The fire, Nell's capture and death, Luca's threat, Treblinka, Isaac's murder, Luca's demise, Durand's arrest; he told them it all.

Marney seized the gap he left to catch his breath. 'Let me stop you there. That was a lot of information to take in at once.'

Jared was tempted to explain that keeping to the facts was the only way he'd survive this testimony. If he went into details, told them how every agonising moment of Nell's death was branded into his brain, he'd likely implode. Instead, he said, 'You asked.'

'I did. Thank you.'

Aleksey tilted his head. 'Just to clarify, you and your friends travelled to Rome of your own volition?'

Jared wondered why that mattered. 'That's correct.'

Aleksey checked his notes. 'To make arrangements for some kind of show.'

'Yes. It's how we've earned a living these last few years, allowing tourists from other timelines to experience historical events.'

'How very...industrious of you.'

'Thank you,' Jared said, but he could tell by the way Aleksey's eyebrows bobbed that he'd missed some hidden meaning in his words.

'If I have this right, Luca Durand followed you to carry out the orders of his adoptive father.'

'That's right.'

'So, I'm not sure how Martin and Oliver are implicated in this at all.'

Jared opened and closed his mouth, but no counter argument materialised.

Aleksey, picking up momentum, continued with his point. 'Just like it could also be argued that they were just witnesses to Seb's exile.'

Millicent rapped her nails on the desk to get Aleksey's attention. 'I was there, too, remember.'

'So you were,' Aleksey said. 'And as a fellow *witness* to this atrocity, do you feel you could have done more to stop Victor Durand?'

Millicent shrank back into her chair. 'I had no power over him.'

'Exactly. I don't think we can—'

'No!' Oliver faced the committee. 'I won't let you do this. I won't let you justify what we did.'

Martin tugged at his arm. 'Ollie, sit down.'

Oliver shook him off. 'You know what his plan is, Martin. Victor still has followers here. And who better to take up his mantle than his two *innocent* sons.'

'I don't think—'

'You're not stupid. Aleksey wants to use us to keep power over the Sanctuary. We're no use to him if we're exiled or dead.'

'That's slanderous,' Aleksey said. 'I would never—'

'We killed someone.' Oliver's words left Aleksey open

mouthed, mid-sentence.

'I don't think now is the time to share new information like that.'

'Go on,' Marney said.

'It was an accident, I suppose.' Oliver scanned the crowd, and Jared didn't need to look to know it was Sienna that his gaze landed on. 'She was just supposed to be exiled. But the portal closed while she was still between worlds. We never intended for her to die.'

Aleksey waved a shaky hand. 'These are new charg—'

'Who?' Marney asked. 'Who died?'

Oliver's face crumpled. 'I can't.' The chamber was so silent that all Jared could hear was Oliver's rasping breaths as he tried to calm himself.

Martin got to his feet and squeezed Oliver's shoulder. 'It's okay. Do you want me to say it?'

Oliver shook his head. 'The woman who died, the woman we killed, was Stephanie Hiatt.'

Gasps and cries bounced off every salt rock surface, forcing Jared to cover his ears. But he didn't need to hear to tell what Oliver mouthed next. 'I'm so sorry, Sienna.'

The Book of Evelyn

Life in the Colony was efficient. There's no better word I can think of to describe it. Riley spent most of her time tending to the hives. But she wasn't the only one dedicated to her job. Each person knew their place, a cog in a well-oiled machine. Which is fine, until you find that you're the spare part. Surplus to requirements. I'd try to help, I really would. But dishes were swept away before I could clear them. Plants were pruned while I was still figuring out what they were. It's not like the residents were unfriendly. There were no bitchy cliques or spiteful initiations. I was just an outsider. So I went to discuss it with the biggest misfit I knew.

'I don't fit in here,' I said.

'Me neither,' Bug said. 'Shall we run away?'

'You're mocking me.'

'What makes you say that?'

'You're the leader. It's no big deal if you don't fit in. They have to respect you. Or you might make them leave.'

'I can't *make* the Colony do anything.'

'Not even Anya and co?'

Bug considered this. 'The Colony was getting too big. They understood that. And Anya is strong and perfectly capable of looking after her own hive.'

'You don't know what it's like to be asked to leave a place you thought was your home. Even if you never fitted in. I don't expect you to understand.'

'Then why are you here?' Bug asked. 'I'm hardly Doctor Phil.'

I looked at him blankly.

'Oprah? I guess you're too young. Or I'm old. What I mean to say is, I'm hardly the type people go to for advice.'

I shrugged. 'You're the smartest person I know.'

'A man far wiser than I once said that intelligence is the art of getting what we want without making unnecessary enemies on the way.'

'Right there,' I said. 'That's a smart thing to say. And I'm not sure I understood a word of it.'

Bug laughed. 'That's all I'm doing here, muddling my way through like the rest of you. You know, when Dale and I were kids, I had a conversation very similar to this one with our mother. Socialising always came so easily to Dale. Me, however...I swear, if there was a way to embarrass myself, or him, I'd find it.'

'What did your mother tell you?' I asked.

'That when I stopped trying to be like everyone else and learnt to celebrate my individuality, I'd find friends just like me.'

'Did it work?'

'No. I was lonely and miserable as sin. But then, I never really nailed that whole accepting myself thing.'

'Well, this has been useful.'

'There's another way you could look at it. Perhaps someone who doesn't fit into a group is meant to lead it.'

'Someone like you, sure. But I'm no leader. I think I'll stick to your mother's 'find your tribe' idea.'

Bug smirked. 'Suit yourself.'

My own mother had given me similar advice. But then, Ruth had always found making friends easy. I suppose she was what you'd call charming. On my first day of school, she told me to look for somebody who might be into the same things as me. But while the other girls wore backpacks with fairies and ponies on, I walked in clutching my Simpsons lunchbox.

However, I can't deny now that her advice was sound, because eventually I managed to find someone in the Colony with a common interest. It just happened to be our dislike of Dale.

'I told you, we are not a delivery service. A supply run is for e-ssen-tials.' Dale sounded out each syllable as though she were stupid.

'Do not talk to me like I'm an imbecile, you intolerable sack of cow dung.'

'I've got better things to do than listen to your nonsense, Pearl.'

'You do? Does your brother's rear need kissing? Run along then.'

It wasn't so much what she said, but how her crude words conflicted with her polished looks. Her age was hard to place. I'd have guessed in her sixties, but even after we became friends, I'd never have dared ask her. Yet there wasn't a grey hair on her unnaturally plum head. Her nails were manicured to perfection, making me hide my own broken ones behind my back.

'Is there some reason you're staring at me?' she asked.

I jumped, as she glared at me over lowered sunglasses. 'No. I just like how you handled Dale.'

'That man is the reason God gave us a middle finger. I'm Pearl. And you are the daughter of Dale's latest squeeze.'

'I prefer Evi...Evelyn, if you don't mind.'

'Evievelyn, huh? Quite the mouthful.'

'No, just Evelyn. And for the record, I'm not exactly thrilled about Ruth and Dale trading saliva.'

Pearl wrinkled her nose. 'I could have lived my whole life without that image.'

'Trust me, so could I.'

So that was how I made my second friend in the Colony, a sarcastic curmudgeon who was old enough to be my grandmother. Why am I telling you this? Because whilst she might be remembered for her foul mouth and sharp tongue, nobody in the Colony could deny that they'd all be dead without Pearl.

Chapter Five

<u>Excerpt from *A Societal Analysis of the Bee Colony*</u>

<u>Honey Bee Drift</u>

It is a widespread misunderstanding that alien bees entering a hive will inevitably be met with hostility. It is common, especially when hives are positioned close together, for honey bees to drift into neighbouring hives both accidentally and intentionally. In such situations, it is the job of the guard bees to distinguish whether this is a migrating bee or one with the more sinister motive of stealing honey. The guard bee demonstrates admirable detective skills and can gauge merely by factors such as flight pattern and speed the bee's intentions. A bee judged as suspicious will be stung and killed before it even has a chance to enter the hive.

Wakefield, R. (2025) *A Societal Analysis of the Bee Colony*. Third edition. London: Feisty Scholar Publications.

The Book of Evelyn

'E avesdropping is a nasty habit,' I said, loud enough to make Riley jump. 'Dinner service is over you know. No second helpings.'

'Quiet, they'll hear us.' She tugged me below the window of the canteen. 'Look. You aren't the newbie any more.'

Inside, I could just make out two figures surrounded by a group of Colony members. Celine and Michelle were closest to the window, each perched on the edge of a table.

'I can't see anything through Dale's fat head.' Riley risked peering a little higher. 'Why does he need to wear that stupid cap every second of the day?'

'It covers more of his face, so I'm all for it.'

She pouted her lips. 'Your mother seems to like his face.'

'Shut up.' But I couldn't deny it. Ruth spent more time in Dale's unit than in the dorm with me. It was only a matter of time before she moved in with him. That's how my mother operated. She was insidious.

It was a woman's voice that drifted over to the open window. I strained to hear what she was saying. 'I'm only alive because of Fiona. If she hadn't helped me escape, then I'd be dead, too.'

'I'm so sorry you had to go through that.' Celine's words caught in her throat.

'We all are,' Dale said. 'You are free to rest here for tonight, then we will give you what provisions we can spare for your journey.'

Michelle sprang to her feet. 'You can't be serious. We aren't sending them out there to be slaughtered.'

'In case you didn't notice, we aren't exactly flush with resources,' Dale said. 'We can't take in every waif and stray.'

'I can work,' the woman said. 'Let me work.'

'I'm sorry, but we just don't have—'

'Who made you boss?' Celine asked. 'You don't get to decide who stays and goes, who lives and dies.'

'Fine,' Dale said. 'Let's put it to a vote.'

'No.'

'Wow,' Riley whispered. 'That's Bug. He actually left his unit.'

'This isn't up for debate,' Bug said. 'I'll decide.'

'That's how things work around here nowadays is it?' Dale asked. 'Your way or the highway.'

'No. Nothing's changed. That's how it's always been,' Bug said. 'Franklin put it best. Democracy is two wolves and a lamb voting over what to have for lunch. It. Doesn't. Work.'

Dale threw himself down into a nearby chair. 'Do what you want.'

'I intend to.' Bug began asking the women questions I imagine were standard for potential colonists. Unless, of course, like me you claimed not to want to stay. Where did they come from? What skills did they have? Predictable. Only, I couldn't focus on their answers because when Dale huffed onto the chair, he had cleared my view.

'I know her!' The woman's auburn hair was a greasy mess and her face was streaked with dirt and tears, but she was unmistakable. 'That's my friend's mother!' I darted for the door.

'Are you insane?' Riley called after me. 'We aren't even supposed to be out of the dorm.'

I didn't care. 'Susan!' I burst into the canteen. 'I'm so

happy to see you.' I turned to Bug. 'She can help us. Susan's a doctor. Please let her stay.'

Susan gave a nervous laugh. 'I'm not a doctor, and my name isn't Susan. It's Gabriela.'

I pulled up short, just a step away from throwing my arms around her 'What are you talking about? Don't you recognise me, Susan? It's me, Evie.'

Her brow knotted. 'Please,' she said to Bug. 'I'm telling you the truth. My name is Gabriela.'

'You see where charity has got us?' I heard the click of Dale's gun before I saw it. He held it pointed directly at Susan. 'She's clearly one of the Pack, lying her way in here.'

'No.' Susan held shaky hands in front of her face, as though she could somehow stop a bullet. 'I promise I'll tell you everything.'

None of us had been watching the other woman. I'd forgotten she was even there. It was only Bug's whimper of panic that alerted us to his plight.

'Put the gun down,' she said to Dale, a knife pressed to Bug's throat.

'Fiona, you don't need to do this,' Bug said, his Adam's apple bobbing dangerously close to her blade as he talked.

'Oh I do,' she said. 'Cerato has a message for you. You took what's hers and she doesn't take kindly to people stealing from her.'

'People aren't possessions to be owned,' Bug said.

'Then give her the choice. Save yourselves and let me take her back to the Pack.'

'I can't do that,' Bug said. 'It wouldn't be right.'

'Then you know Cerato will come for you.' Fiona

pressed the knife closer to his throat, making Bug flinch. 'Is she worth sacrificing all of this for?'

Bug didn't have the chance to answer. Susan grabbed Fiona's arm and pulled it away from Bug's neck. 'Drop it,' she said, trying to pry Fiona's fingers from the handle.

'Stay out of this.' Fiona jerked the knife back towards them and Susan yelped. A gunshot tore through the air and both women tumbled to the floor. They lay motionless.

Paralysed by fear and confusion, I tried to piece together how, in moments, I'd gone from rejoicing to find a friendly face from my past to looking down at her unconscious body. 'Is she dead?'

Dale pressed the barrel of his gun into Fiona's back. She didn't move. 'This one is. I'm not sure about her friend.'

Whimpering from below Fiona's body told us Susan was alive. Michelle and Celine dragged Fiona off her. Susan rolled over, her hands raised in submission. 'Please, she tricked me. I thought she saved me, not that she was using me as a cover to get in here.' Susan looked directly at me. 'I've told so many lies, and I'm truly sorry for that. Evie did know me as Susan Cole. But my real name is Gabriela Campbell. My husband Lewis was murdered by the Pack, and I am begging the Colony for protection.'

~

Marney

<u>Before the Sanctuary</u>

It wasn't revenge that made her select O'Neil. After all, she didn't really know Thomas. It was justice. O'Neil had temporarily taken Thomas out of the trial with the beating he'd delivered and Marney had played a part in that. Using him as the replacement subject seemed only right. Not that it mattered. They'd all be selected in the end and, should they need them, she was sure the army would find more participants. Still, guilt pricked her nerves as she punctured his skin. If it hurt, he didn't show it.

'What's your name?' It was just a pleasantry. Marney knew before she'd even picked out his file, swearing she wouldn't let another man die in her care without knowing something so basic. She recited their names to herself: Carter, O'Neil and Wells. Still, she couldn't think of anything else to say and the silence was torturous.

'O'Neil.'

'I see. Just the one name. Like Madonna or Prince.' If he got the reference, he didn't respond.

Marney lifted his chart from the end of the gurney. She'd read it over and over before he'd arrived, as though it could somehow prevent another death. She wished she had such power. Still, she pretended she was reading his name for the first time.

'Michael O'Neil. Is that Irish? My father—'

'No offence, lady, but let's save the chatter.'

'Okay. I was just being friendly.'

'If you're fishing for friends amongst us lot then you're making a mistake. We're sharks, every one of us, and we bite.'

Marney held his gaze. 'Is that a threat?'

'No. It's a warning.'

'Fine. We'll stick to the business at hand then. You'll be monitored for twenty-four hours to ensure you have no adverse effects from the vaccine. The next stage will be exposure to the virus.'

'How long until we know if it's worked? Or is it a matter of timing how long it takes me to die?'

Marney's mouth was dry, and her words stuck to her tongue. 'We've had promising results in previous participants.'

'Human participants?'

'No. All previous trials have been on apes.' The ethical considerations of her work had been drummed into her over a course of years, so lying wasn't an option, even if it would be a kindness.

'Very comforting. How long before we know if it's been successful?'

'Without the vaccine, most people die within twenty-four hours of exposure.'

'And with it?'

'Well, that's what we aim to find out. You'll remain in quarantine for a week after exposure, but if you make it that far, we'll consider it a success.'

'Got it. Survive for a week. I can do that.'

Marney hoped for all their sakes that he was right.

'Anything else?' he asked. 'Can I go?'

'Sure.' Marney nodded for the guard to lead him off.

Checking her watch, she swore under her breath. She

tore off her plastic apron and gloves and stuffed them in the bin.

'Sorry, I can't talk; I'm late,' she called as she passed Doctor Keller in the hall.

By the time she got home, her family had left without her. Marney pulled on a pair of jeans and T-shirt and headed for the conference room.

It didn't take long for her to locate the girls. Emma was silhouetted against the light of the projector as she bobbed up out of her seat like a meerkat. Ben looped his arm around her and pulled her back into her seat.

Marney slumped down in the chair next to her.

Jodie leant over her father. 'See, Mommy, didn't I say it was like a real cinema?'

'You sure did,' Marney said, looking at the semicircle of folding chairs and rickety projector. 'I can't wait.'

The film started. As her eyes adjusted to the dimmed light, Marney noticed a familiar figure a couple of seats from them. Thomas gave a discreet wave.

Ben put his mouth close to her ear. 'Leave it. He has as much right to enjoy the film as we do.'

'I didn't say a word,' Marney said through clenched teeth.

She tried to watch the cartoon characters dancing around the screen. Her reprieve came fast in the form of an alarm.

'The things you'll do to get out of watching Disney,' Ben said.

The lights came up. One of the guards passed them on his way to cuff Thomas.

'What's the alarm for?' Ben asked.

'Lockdown. For everyone, I'm afraid. Back to your quarters.

Marney stared at the wall, the projected figures ghost-like in the bright light. It was only then that she felt someone watching her.

O'Neil sat at the end of the row. When the guard approached, he held up his wrists compliantly and the guard fastened his cuffs.

'I'll get the stuff together and catch up with you,' Ben said.

'Come on girls.' She held their hands. Although she didn't relish the idea of leading them so close to O'Neil, it was the only way out.

Marney felt a tug on her arm when Emma stopped. 'Hello,' Jodie said, her head cocked to the side.

O'Neil didn't answer.

'Come on. Don't bother him,' Marney said, trying to haul her away.

Jodie dug in her heels. 'I'm Jodie.'

O'Neil looked back, dead pan. Then he lurched towards her. 'Boo!'

Jodie squealed and wrapped herself around her mother. Emma buried her face into Marney's hip on the other side.

O'Neil jerked with laughter.

'I'll thank you not to scare my children.' She hoped the crackle of fear in her voice wasn't as obvious as it was in her head.

O'Neil waved her away. 'If they don't want to be scared then they should stay away from monsters.'

'Leave the good doctor alone,' Squires said as he hoisted him to his feet.

Marney risked one last glance at O'Neil as he was led away. He smiled at her and snapped his teeth together like the chomping of a shark.

~

<u>Laura</u>

'Janet!' Laura yelled into the spring morning, but the wind stole her voice. 'Where are you?'

She cursed herself for agreeing to this. Getting home should be her priority, not chasing around some strange woman. She had planned to spend the afternoon retracing her steps back to where they'd stranded her. Instead, she was spending goodness knows how long searching for Janet.

Laura squinted her eyes against the light reflected from the glittering sea. There Janet was, up to her thighs in the water, her skirts pooled around her like weeds.

Laura dug her heels into the sandy slope to stop herself from slipping and made her way down to the shore. She stopped at the edge, the waves kissing the toes of her ballet pumps.

'You should get out,' Laura said. 'It's still much too cold to swim.'

If Janet heard, she ignored her. 'Some people think bees don't cross water, but that's nonsense. It was one of my favourite routes. Silvery wings and peppery bodies, darting over the cold water; we were magnificent.' Janet swooshed her hands through the water, and droplets showered Laura. 'And if we got tired, we could call the wind and ride it like a faithful mare.' She let out a long breath. 'I miss those days.'

Laura tried to make sense of what she was saying but decided there was none to be made. 'Come in now. Please.'

'Of course, there were some that tried to stop us. Fat fish with 'o's for mouths would burst through the surface and try to snatch us from the air.' Janet giggled. 'We were much too fast. Nothing and nobody in this place could catch us.'

Laura kicked off her shoes and waded in. 'It sounds like a nice dream.'

Janet turned to Laura, her smile fading behind a cloud of sadness. 'I wasn't caught, you know? Never. I chose this life, fool that I am. Do you have children, Laura?'

'One. A son. Jared,' Laura said, clasping Janet's bicep and trying to guide her from the water.

'Then you know what it's like to have your wings clipped.'

'Yes.' As bad as it made her feel, Laura always felt she'd signed over her autonomy when she became a mother. Even in the days after Jared left, a part of her was in constant panic – both that she'd lost him forever and, if she was honest with herself, that she hadn't. The unknown tortured her. How could she rebuild her life and learn who she was without him when she didn't know if he was really gone?

'I loved Helen's father,' Janet said. 'But once he planted his seed in me, I grew roots, pinning me to this worthless ground. I'd love to tear myself free. To fly again.' Janet looked down at her legs. 'Look at us, wet through and freezing. With no peat for the fire, we shall never get warm. I'll find you something of Helen's to change into.'

'Thank you.' Laura reached out her hand. 'Let's get you home.'

'I do love Helen, you know,' Janet said. 'But I wouldn't have chosen this life for either of us.'

'Yes,' Laura said. 'I completely understand.'

The Book of Evelyn

The next chapter in Susan's story began much the same as mine, frogmarched from the Sanctuary at David's command. I suppose the key difference was that I wanted to leave. And I was taking all the family I had left with me. It must have been awful leaving Luca behind. But her pain was only beginning.

'After they shoved us out into that barren wasteland, I stood there for the longest time. It's family that gives you direction in life and, other than Lewis, what remained of mine was lost to me down in the depths of the Sanctuary.'

'Lewis? Not Robert then,' I said.

'No. Robert Cole was an architect with far more impressive credentials than Lewis ever achieved. I think that was part of the appeal to him; as Robert Cole, Lewis would get the respect he'd always craved.

'But it wasn't our idea. My brother Glen came up with the plan. He spent his days ferrying the rich to the Sanctuary. 'Why should they get to be safe when you are stuck up here just trying to stay alive?' he asked. Notice how he said 'you' and not 'I'. That was Glen. He basically raised me. I was always his priority.'

'As sweet as that sounds,' Dale said, 'skip to the part where you ended up impersonating the Coles.'

'I don't know what happened to them. I like to think that...Never mind, that would just be a story to make myself feel better. I knew by taking their places we were likely condemning them to death. I won't make excuses other than to say it was them or us. I chose us.'

'Could you not have reasoned with the Sanctuary leaders?' Celine asked. 'Begged them to let you in? Your brother must have known people who work—'

'No,' Bug said. 'They wouldn't have granted her entry.'

Dale rolled his eyes. 'And you know that from personal experience, do you?'

'Yes. Actually, I do.'

'Don't think you and I won't discuss that more later, Bug.' Dale fixed him with a cold stare. But I need to take this one headache at a time. So, Gabriela, Susan, whatever your name is. If you were willing to do such terrible things to get into the Sanctuary, why did you leave?'

'I had no choice. One of the founders, David Malone, knew our secret and was blackmailing us.'

Bug sniffed. 'Ironic but not unexpected. And after you left?'

'We weren't out a day before the Pack found us. They locked me in a makeshift cage made of metal grates.' Susan, or I suppose I should say Gabriela, hooked her fingers into the air as though she could still feel the bars. 'They kept me there for days with no food or water. They only let me out when he wanted...when it pleased them.'

I thought back to the bedroom in that deserted house and the way Rex had tossed Ruth on the bed. There was no need for Gabriela to elaborate.

'Then, on the third day, Fiona brought me some food, and we got talking. I'd given up hope by then, so when she said she'd help me escape, I didn't believe her. But she was true to her word. One night, after the camp fell silent, there she was, unlocking the padlock with shaking hands. Every step I took away from them, I expected to be dragged back.' Gabriela looked over at Fiona's body. 'Now I realise it was all a plan to get her in here.'

'Is your husband still with them?' Celine asked.

'No, not really.' She picked at the skin around her nails.

'What kind of an answer is that?' Dale said.

Gabriela looked him dead in the eyes. 'I'm pretty sure they ate him.' Her words were like a slap to me, but when Dale barely reacted, Gabriela's top lip curled. 'You already know they're cannibals.'

Michelle sighed. 'We've seen evidence to suggest so. Remnants of human bones left in the ashes of their campfires. Bodies abandoned but with pieces missing.'

'Why didn't you kill them?' Gabriela clenched her fist to her mouth. 'If you'd done the right thing, then Lewis would still be here.'

'We don't kill people,' Bug said.

'They aren't people. Do you want to know how deranged they are? That day Fiona brought me food, I couldn't believe they'd be generous enough to share their meat with a prisoner.' She cupped her hands over her face and sobbed.

My stomach wrenched, and bile burnt my throat. Were the Pack really evil enough to feed her husband to her?

Celine placed a hand on her shoulder. 'I'm so sorry. But you're safe now.'

'Hang on a minute,' Dale said. 'I feel bad for her, I really do. But even if we put aside the matter of her stealing some poor woman's identity and possibly being an accessory to murder, we still don't have the resources to keep her.'

'I won't turn her away,' Bug said.

Dale shoved his seat back, so the legs scraped along the

tiled floor with a shriek. 'If my opinion is worthless, what the point of me being here?' he said as he stormed off.

'Evelyn, would you please show Gabriela to the dorm?' Bug said.

Gabriela got to her feet. 'That's it; I can stay?'

'For now.'

I walked a pace in front of Gabriela as I led her away. It was like she read my mind when she said, 'You can't even look at me, can you?'

'It's not that,' I lied. 'I was just wondering why you left Luca behind.'

'His real name is George.' Gabriela smiled. "G' was kind of a family thing. Glen, Gabriela and George. I hadn't wanted to change my surname when I married Lewis, so a name beginning with G was a compromise to keep some-thing of my side alive.'

'He didn't look like a George.'

'No, I suppose he didn't. It was just a silly tradition. And to answer your question, I had no choice. David wouldn't let him leave with us.'

'Oh.'

'Would you have done the same in our situation? Stolen the Coles' identities, I mean.'

I gave it some thought. I was yet to recognise the waning moon of my integrity. If she asked me again today, I couldn't deny that I would do whatever it would take to survive.

Gabriela must have taken my hesitation as denial because she said. 'I guess not. You were always a good girl. I pray you're never put in a predicament where you have to decide whether to sacrifice innocent lives for your own.'

But Gabriela needn't have worried, because when such a situation arose only months later, I didn't even hesitate.

Jared

The citizen grabbed Jared's hand. 'We're here for you, Jared. If your mother is somewhere in the Sanctuary, we'll find her.'

The knotted brow and downturned mouth told him the woman felt sympathy for him. What he wasn't sure of was why, as he didn't think he'd met her before in his life. But he decided it didn't matter either way. They needed all the help they could get. 'Thank you.'

She squeezed his fingers, grinding his knuckles together. 'Everyone has been talking about how happy they are to have you home.'

'They have?'

She had no time to answer as Beth stepped between them. 'I'm going to have to steal Jared away.'

'I have no idea who that was,' Jared said. 'But apparently she's thrilled to see me.'

'She's not the only one. You're all anybody wants to talk to me about. And here you had us believing all this time you were a pariah.'

'Hmmm.' They could coat their words with all the niceties they wanted, but Jared still couldn't wait to make his escape.

'Don't worry about it,' Beth said. 'If it means we get more help to find your mother, let them be as fake as they want. Where's Aaron?'

'He's joined a search party already.'

'And where shall we start?'

Jared knew she'd meant her question literally, but that was the very question he'd been asking himself. With hundreds of kilometres of tunnel to search, what hope was there? 'This way, I guess.'

Seb fell into step next to them. 'Hey, Jared. Do you mind if I talk to you about something while we search?'

'You know,' Beth said, 'Aaron probably has the right idea about us splitting up. We can make sure there's no funny business.'

'No, let's—'

But Beth was already walking away. 'I'll catch up with you later.'

Seb and Jared walked in silence. Jared knew Seb was waiting for him to ask what he wanted. But as sorry as he felt for Seb, Jared didn't want to know. The last thing he needed was more demands on his time.

However, Seb decided to forgo an invitation. 'You can't let them get away with it. At the very least, Martin needs to pay for what happened to Isaac.'

'You say that like I have any power,' Jared said.

'You do. Don't you see? With your grandfather and mother gone, the citizens will look to you for leadership.'

'Me?' Jared couldn't help but laugh. 'I'm no leader.'

'Of course you are. In fact, I'd say you were born to it.'

'You've got me confused with somebody who wants the job. I plan to make sure my mother is okay, and get out of here.'

'How lovely to have that option.'

Guilt prodded at Jared's conscience. 'I can't save everyone.'

'But don't you see, you can. If you don't want to lead in the Sanctuary, take the citizens somewhere else in time. Let them start again with you as their leader.'

'No. We can't really know the effect such a big change to a timeline would make.'

Seb stopped in his tracks. 'If you leave again, Aleksey will try to seize power.'

'Is that so bad? There are worse options.'

'Maybe. But a great deal of the hatred for the Durands was directed at him as well. They won't let him take control. Not without a fight.'

'They?'

'The resistance. Jared, I've been asked to pass on a message to you. If you decide to stay, they'll support you. If you stay, they'll follow you wherever you choose to lead us.'

~

Marney

Before the Sanctuary

Marney stood on the threshold of her quarters. 'This is ridiculous; it's been hours. I want to speak to Stuart.'

'I'm sorry, mam, but he's said that everyone needs to stay in their rooms.' Squires scanned the hallway, no doubt hoping to find someone with more authority to handle her.

'So you said, but you didn't give me a reason.'

'For your safety.'

'For my safety? You do realise I am one of the leaders on this project? If something dangerous is happening, then I should be out there.'

'I'm just following orders.' His tone was pained.

Ben appeared at her elbow. 'Leave him be and come inside.'

She waved a finger to quieten him; no doubt they'd have words about that later.

'And if I just walk past you, are you going to try and restrain me?' she asked.

'No, of course not,' Squires said.

'Okay then.' She stepped around him into the corridor.

Ben gave a disapproving shake of his head. 'Do what you want.' Then he closed the door.

Marney turned to Squires. 'Well, if you were asked to keep me safe, maybe you could escort me to Stuart.'

Squires massaged his brow. 'Fine.' He led her to the prison block, where technicians swathed in plastic overalls milled around. Masks covered their noses and mouths.

'Oh no. Has one of the subjects died?'

She looked at the glass cubicles in which the prisoners spent most of their time. Michael O'Neil and Thomas Wells stood with their palms to the glass, watching the commotion.

'Where's Carter?' she asked.

When nobody answered her, she went to his cell. He was huddled at the back, his arms looped around his knees, his face buried against them. All three prisoners were accounted for.

She tried to stop one of the technicians. 'Could somebody explain what's going on?' He rushed past her without answering.

In the middle of the corridor, something was covered with a white sheet. Marney stepped towards it.

'Doctor, please don't,' Squires said.

Marney ignored him. She held her hand an inch from the sheet when somebody grabbed her wrist.

'What are you doing?' Stuart said. 'Get away from there.'

'If I'm a part of this, then I need to know everything.'

'Yes, and I intended to tell you everything later. Now isn't the time.'

'What's under there?'

They locked eyes, neither looking away.

'All right,' Stuart said. 'You want to see?' He dragged the sheet back, exposing the body. The burst veins in the whites of the man's eyes told of his fight for oxygen. Black tears trailed down his cheeks.

'Oh my God. Is that a guard? But...' Her mind raced with the implications. 'That means the infection is inside the facility?'

'No. Not necessarily. It means this guard was on a

supply run and was infected. If we clean the areas he's been in, we can prevent it spreading.'

Marney looked at the technicians around her, cloaked in their suits, and had never felt more vulnerable. She stared at the flesh on her bare wrist where Stuart had grabbed her.

'Don't panic. I just got here. I've not touched a thing.'

'You should have told me.' Marney backed away until she hit something solid. She jumped away when Thomas slapped his palms against the glass.

'Doc, is that what's going to happen to us?' His voice was strangled, the tension pinching his vocal cords. 'Please, nobody will tell us anything.'

'I'm sorry,' she said. 'I have to go.' She turned and ran.

Ben was reading on the sofa when she burst through the door. 'That was quick.'

'Start packing. We're leaving.'

'Excuse me? I'm going to need more information than that.'

'Just do it, Ben.' She went to the bathroom and turned on the shower. Then she stripped off her clothes and stuffed them in the hamper.

She began scrubbing the arm Stuart had touched. Her skin began to welt in protest. She turned the temperature up as high as she could bear and stood beneath the stream. The water scalded her back and she whimpered when it ran over her scalp. Then she wrapped herself in a stiff towel and went to dress.

Ben plonked on the bed. 'Are you going to talk to me?'

'The virus is in the facility. One of the guards is dead.'

'Oh. That's sad.'

'Sad? Ben it's terrifying. We need to leave.'

'What would you tell me if it were me panicking now?'

She sighed. 'I could do without the amateur therapy.'

'Indulge me.'

'I'd say precautions have been taken. I'd say that it's out there anyway so our odds are better with one case in here.'

'Exactly.'

'I still don't like being shut in with it.'

'That might be preferable to being shut out there with it.' His voice wavered. 'You're so consumed with the vaccine you've not heard what's been going on. The emergency broadcasts, what titbits of information I can get from the guards – it's terrifying. What's left of the population is tearing itself apart.'

She stared at the angry skin on her wrist. 'What are you saying?'

'I'm saying there is no way around this. We'll have to go through it like everyone else.'

Chapter Six

Excerpt from *A Societal Analysis of the Bee Colony*

A Life of Servitude

After 21 days, a worker bee will leave her larval state and emerge from its cell. This new adult bee will immediately be thrust into a life of servitude. Her first three days will be spent cleaning the freshly vacated cells in preparation for the Queen's next brood.

A shift in her hormones initiates the nursing phase of her life cycle, where she spends several days feeding the larvae with royal jelly.

The third phase of her life involves around a week of construction, building cells to store the hive's food within.

Finally she reaches the most dangerous part of her life cycle, becoming a forager. Only older bees fulfil this role, as risking the lives of the young could endanger the stability of the hive.

If she survives these dangerous missions, there is no cosy retirement waiting for her at the end. A honey bee approaching the end of her life will, where possible, die outside the hive, sparing her sisters the job of disposing of her body.

Wakefield, R. (2025) *A Societal Analysis of the Bee Colony*. Third edition. London: Feisty Scholar Publications.

The Book of Evelyn

During that first year with the Colony, they encouraged me to try out different roles. The garden was hard work, but it was satisfying to see my effort transformed into food. It pleased me to contribute something worthwhile.

The kitchen was less appealing. Somehow I managed to irritate the colonists working there with my very presence. No matter where I positioned myself, I got in their way. They clucked and flapped at me, until I gave in and sloped off.

It was after Susan's…I mean Gabriela's arrival that I found something I was really good at, a vocation I'm sure none of my benefactors expected me to explore. I discovered that I was an excellent thief. Once I saw how Gabriela slotted into their way of life, that she was clearly going nowhere and fitted in far better than I, I assumed my time at the Colony was drawing to an end. It's not as if I'd put much effort into establishing roots in the Colony before Gabriela's arrival, but still she was the catalyst to my life of crime. She knew my darkest secret, and I didn't plan to hang around for her to share it. However, my great escape was going to require resources.

I began pilfering anything useful I could get my hands on. Small tools from the greenhouse, a knife from the kitchen; they were all squirrelled away amongst my things.

But I knew I was pushing my luck when I saw the door to the infirmary ajar. The doctor, Beverly, had treated me kindly when she examined me on my second day. 'It's just a check up. But I can see already that you're in good shape.'

Remembering her encouraging smile may have pricked my conscience, but it didn't stop me creeping inside. I half expected Beverly to be waiting, shaking her head. 'I knew you couldn't be trusted. I knew you could never be one of us.'

But the infirmary was empty. I went straight to the supply cupboard and began cherry picking the things we might need on our onward journey. I rifled through the drawers and found a carrier bag. Then I stuffed my haul inside and headed towards the door. I froze when the light clicked on, as though keeping perfectly still might make me invisible.

'What do we have here?' It was Pearl, the woman with the plum hair and smart mouth.

'It's not what it...No, that's a lie, it's exactly what it looks like.'

'I see. You're stealing.'

'Yes.'

'Might I ask why?'

'I can't stay here. But it's not safe out there. I just wanted a few things in case we get hurt.'

'Makes sense. Let me take a look.' Pearl took the bag from me. 'Bandages and paracetamol. Hmmm. Let's hope the worst you suffer is a sprained wrist or a headache.'

'I'm sorry. Please don't tell anybody. I'll put it back.'

'Tell anyone? Why would I? This place is Doctor Beverly's problem, not mine.'

'Really? Thank you.'

Pearl ran her finger along a shelf, reading the labels on the bottles. 'Ohh,' she said, twisting open a cap and shaking a pill into her palm. Scooping it into her mouth, she gulped it down.

'How do you swallow those things dry?'

'With practice,' she said, before taking another.

'I guess we're both stealing medication.'

'I prefer the term 'liberating'.' She continued scanning the shelves. 'You'll definitely need these.' A pot rattled as she dropped it into my bag. 'Antibiotics could save you if you get an infection. But let's avoid it getting that far.' She reached for a bottle of ethanol and added it.

'Won't they notice it's gone?'

'Probably not. Beverly doesn't have much of a system and she's a trusting soul, the fool.'

I blushed. 'Why are you doing this?'

'Because I want you to live. I'd ask you the same question; you're safe here so why leave?'

I don't know why I told her the truth. Perhaps she was my litmus paper, testing the reaction of the group. 'The new woman, Gabriela, knows things about me that I'd rather keep secret.'

Pearl scoffed. 'You don't think the other colonists have secrets? I would bet everyone here has done things they'd rather forget in order to survive.'

'Like murder?'

She looked me up and down. 'Probably. The world has changed. There are no laws stopping people taking what they want. Doing what they want. We have to protect ourselves.'

'It was self-defence.'

'There we are then. The only person you need to justify it to is yourself. So before you run off, perhaps you need to consider whether you've punished yourself enough.'

I know now she was right. But at the time my guilt was a

festering wound I couldn't stop probing. 'I'll give it some thought.'

She passed me the bag. 'You do that.'

Laura

'Open the door!'

'Helen?' Janet scrambled from the bed. 'I thought you were—'

'Just hurry up, will you.'

Janet raised the bar, and Helen tumbled through. 'What's wrong?' Janet held her daughter by the shoulders, scanning her for harm. Grasping her chin, she turned Helen's face first one way, then the other. 'What happened to you?'

'Nothing...I...' Helen disintegrated into sobs. 'Ma, it was awful.'

Laura poured a glass of water from the jug and handed it to the crying woman. 'Did he hurt you?' Considering the red welt marring one of Helen's cheekbones, Laura felt foolish asking.

'He meant...' Helen took a steadying breath. 'He meant to take what wasn't offered.

'I'll kill him,' Janet said. 'Worse than that, I'll curse him, make that little worm of his shrivel up and drop off.'

'Ma, stop talking like that.'

'Drink some water,' Laura said. 'It will make you feel better.'

Helen gulped it down. 'Besides, if anybody is going to kill him, it will be me. It took me hours to get back here, looking to see if he was following the whole way.'

'Was he?' Laura's eyes shot to the door.

'He'll be in no rush. Won't be able to after I lodged my knee deep in his privates.'

'Good girl.' Janet kissed Helen on the top of her head.

'I'm sorry, Ma, for the terrible things I said. I just can't see a way out that doesn't involve marriage.'

'Don't speak of it any more. You're home now and safe. He'll not risk coming here with me to deal with.'

Three slow thuds pounded upon the door.

The women froze, staring at one another wide-eyed. 'Well, it looks like he's made a liar of me,' Janet said.

'Janet, Helen, open up.'

'That's not Fion,' Helen said. But even to Laura, the voice sounded familiar.

'I know you're in there.' Another three thumps echoed through the house.

'This eejit again.' Janet muttered under her breath as she went to answer. 'Malcolm Abernathy, if you could leave my door on its hinges, it would be much appreciated.' Her hand hesitated over the board barring the door before flinging it wide. 'I take it Fion sent you.'

'Aye, that he did.' Malcolm looked past Janet into the house, straight at Laura. 'Do I know you?'

'Sure you do,' Janet said. 'She's my cousin's girl.'

'You have a cousin?'

'Distant. Did Fion tell you what he tried to do to my Helen?'

'No.'

'Of course he didn't.' Helen's upper lip jumped in a snarl. 'Acting like an animal, he was. Had to fight him off me.'

'Just look at her cheek,' Laura said.

'Aye, I see someone has given you quite a whack. But the way he tells it, he caught you stealing from him. Says you cut peat from his land and gave no payment.'

'That's a lie!' Helen was at her mother's side in seconds. 'Fion offered that peat to me. Not that I got it anyway; I had to get away from him so fast.'

'That's not how he tells it. He said you turned wild, attacked him.'

'And of course you believe him,' Helen said.

'That's not all he said. Janet, have you been cursing people again?'

'I...just a turn of phrase.'

'So you didn't threaten to poison his crops and cattle?'

'Not exactly.'

The minister rubbed the bridge of his nose. 'You have to stop speaking like that, Janet. There are those round here who would burn you for less.'

'Nobody has been convicted of being a witch in years.'

'Let's not risk changing that,' Malcolm said. 'Maybe Helen could apologise and stop this nonsense going any further.'

'Apologise?' Janet's voice started small, but the anger it was laced with was still clear. 'Apologise for what? He tried to force himself upon her, and she defended herself. There's no shame in that.'

'Fine.' Malcolm sighed. 'Just stay away from Fion. Both of you.'

Janet closed the door behind him. 'That lying toad, I swear I will—'

'Ma, stop! No more curses. No more spells. You heard what the minister said. They'll burn you as a witch.'

'I *am* a witch.'

Helen growled in frustration. 'Not this again. You're old,

and you don't have much more than a few dried beans where your senses used to be.'

'You doubt me, child?' All the anger left Janet's voice. 'You question if I could really soar above the trees and escape this place?'

Helen took her hand. 'I know you want to. We both do. But that doesn't make it real.'

Janet pulled her hand away. 'No. You're your father's daughter. Your feet are made of stone, just like his. Looking to the sky would terrify the likes of you.'

Helen grasped her hand again and this time refused to let go. 'Maybe we're not as similar as you'd like. But I still love you. I miss my ma. I wish you'd come back to me.'

Marney
<u>Before the Sanctuary</u>

'What if I've changed my mind?' Thomas asked. He looked younger than ever.

'About the vaccine?' Marney swabbed the skin on his bicep.

'Yeah.'

'Well, then I would let you go back to your cell.'

'And then back to prison?' The fading bruises still shadowed his eyes.

'Probably, yes. But the fact is we need a vaccine because without it we're all dead.'

'Did...did O'Neil and Carter make it?'

Marney frowned. 'It's been over twenty-four hours and they look normal.'

'That would be a first for them.'

Marney suppressed a laugh. 'Surely you've seen them in the rec room?'

'No. I thought you might be hiding it from me. Maybe you thought it was best not to let me know I'm the last man standing.'

'I can assure you they are doing fine. We need to run more tests to ensure the vaccine is acting as predicted before we expose them to the virus, but it looks promising.'

'Okay. I guess I'll have to take your word for it.'

Marney turned to the guard. She didn't recognise him, and she wondered if he'd been selected to replace the one who died. This made an image of the dead guard's bulging eyes flash to her mind, and she pushed it back below the surface. No wonder the boy was terrified.

'Could you fetch O'Neil from his cell?' she asked.

'There's nobody else to stay with him.' The guard nodded towards Thomas.

'We'll be fine,' Marney assured him. 'He's cuffed.'

'Doctor Stuart wouldn't like—'

'Doctor Stuart isn't running the lab this afternoon. I am. Now go and get him please.'

'Suit yourself.'

After the guard had gone, she patted Thomas' hand. 'I'll run the checks on O'Neil. You can see for yourself he's absolutely fine. Then we'll inject the vaccine, if you're still willing.'

'Thank you.'

Marney returned the vaccine to the tray and began to prepare the equipment she'd need for O'Neil's physical. 'Are they providing much for you guys to do while you're in the cells?'

Marney's head jolted backwards as she was yanked by her ponytail. She reached up to prise it free and felt thin wrists in metal cuffs 'Thomas? Let go of me.'

'I'm not going to hurt you,' he said.

'You *are* hurting me.' She tried to dig her fingernails into his flesh, but her gloves declawed her.

Thomas must have felt it all the same because he jerked her head back again. 'Stop that.'

'If you're planning to use me to escape, there's no need. I told you, the trial is voluntary.'

'I'm not trying to escape.' He bent her over the gurney. The metal frame smashed against her stomach, knocking the wind from her.

'What are you doing?'

'If I'm going in the same way as that guard, I'm going to have a bit of fun first.'

'No!' She shoved her body away from the bed. Her buttocks pressed against him in the process, and she felt the swell of his erection.

Thomas pinned her back down and tugged at the waistband of her scrubs.

'No. Stop.' She tried to kick back at him, but he pushed her down with his bodyweight.

'Just keep still.'

'What are you doing?' It was the guard.

Please, Marney thought. *Please help me.*

The pressure from behind disappeared, and she yanked up her trousers.

'Get on the ground,' the guard ordered.

Thomas didn't listen. He ran at him, barging him against the wall. Despite his cuffs, he still managed to grip his hands around the guard's throat.

As the guard turned from red to purple, Marney looked around the room for a weapon. Anything potentially dangerous was locked from the prisoners' reach. She was debating using the metal tray to batter him around the head when she saw O'Neil loitering in the doorway. Their eyes met, and she scooted into the space below the gurney, wondering how she'd fight off both of them. O'Neil put a finger to his lips as he stepped into the lab.

The guard stopped fighting, but Thomas didn't let go. So intent was he on squeezing the last of the life from the unconscious man that he didn't notice O'Neil behind him.

O'Neil lifted his cuffed hands over Thomas' head and

ensnared his throat. The guard dropped to the floor as Thomas fought to free himself.

O'Neil was taking no chances. He heaved Thomas to the metal refrigerator. The thud of his skull, over and over, against the heavy door made Marney's stomach churn. After the third time, the surface was coated with blood and hair.

Marney covered her ears and closed her eyes. Still, she could hear the incessant thump as O'Neil continued.

When it finally stopped, she found him standing over her. His thinning hair was stuck to his face with sweat. She tried to push herself further away from him, but already her back was against the wall.

Perhaps it was pity that made him back away towards the door. Once there, he slid down the frame and slumped there panting.

'I told you,' he said between snatched breaths. 'If you don't want to be scared, then don't hang around monsters.'

The Book of Evelyn

It wasn't a surprise. From the moment I'd seen them flirting, I knew Ruth would wheedle her way into both Dale's unit and his bed.

'Leave me here then,' I said, my jaw clenched so hard I could feel a muscle in it ticcing.

'Never,' she said. 'I told Dale as soon as he suggested it that we come as a package. We both go, or neither of us go.'

'Then I choose the second option.'

'Sorry?'

'Neither of us will go. We'll stay in the dorm together.'

'I...' She clearly hadn't been expecting that. 'It's not that simple.'

'It sounds pretty straight forward to me.'

Ruth leant in closer. 'Evie.'

'Evelyn.'

'Evelyn. This place is fit to burst, and we were last in.'

'I see. So to avoid being first out, you plan to make yourself indispensable.'

'My only plan is to build a life here with Dale. And you. If you keep making it abundantly clear that you don't want to be here, why should they inconvenience themselves by allowing us to stay?'

I stomped off into the fields, mostly because I was furious with her, but also because I didn't want her to see that I knew she had a point.

Usually walking around the grounds of the Colony cheered me up. Bug was a genius; none of us could deny that. The Colony was an island of green floating amongst scorched earth. I didn't know how he managed it. Michelle used terms I hadn't heard before. Irrigation systems, soaker hoses, tap roots, drought tolerance. Somehow they all mixed together to form a field of green with daisies dotted throughout. He'd breathed life back into it.

But that day, nothing was going to lift my mood. I still think there is nothing so frustrating as watching someone you love repeating the same old pattern and being helpless to stop it; even if their choices ruin your life as well.

So when I saw a shifting of shapes in the woods beyond, I almost walked on. Curiosity got the better of me, and I headed towards the Colony boundary. I was a few steps away when I realised that it wasn't an animal as I'd suspected, but a child.

I blinked against the harsh morning light, certain I was hallucinating. It would have taken me just a minute to sprint back to the dormitory and fetch a gaggle of colonists, all eager to confirm I was losing the last shred of my sanity. But then, they already thought me weird, and I didn't want to do anything to compound that belief. Still, I couldn't deny the tiny figure I saw silhouetted between the trees. I squinted to get a better look. With twig-like limbs and a face so filthy I could barely see the skin beneath, it was difficult to place his age.

'Hello? Are you lost?' I called, but he melted into the shadows of the rotting trunk. 'You don't need to be afraid of me. My name's Evelyn.'

There must have been something in my tone that sounded plausible because he peeked from behind the tree. 'I'm not supposed to be here. You won't tell on me, will you?'

I took a step towards him. 'No. You can trust me. Are you alone?'

'*Right now* I am. But my family are nearby.' He looked over my shoulder towards the huddled buildings behind me. 'Is that where you live?'

'For now. You know, it's not safe to be out there alone.'

The boy puffed out his chest. 'I'm not scared.'

'I'm sure you're not.' I went right up to the fence and hooked my fingers through the wire. 'But you should be. There are monsters out there.' You probably think me cruel, but I'd met them, and I didn't want that tiny scrap of a child falling into their clutches.

'You're just saying that.' But he couldn't hide the gulp he took.

'I wish I were. What's your name?'

'Cory.'

'Well, Cory, I'm completely serious. Do you want to know how I'm so sure?'

Cory tilted his head, as he gave it some thought. *Sensible boy*, I thought. *Ignorance is bliss.* I miss the days when I was naive to such horrors.

'All right,' he said.

'I know because they tried to eat me.'

He frowned before breaking into a grin. 'Nah, you're just saying that. Besides, my family would kill them if they touched me.'

I bent down so I was looking him straight in the eyes. 'Maybe they would. Maybe they'd make them pay. But you'd still be dead, eaten up and digesting in a monster's belly.'

Cory backed away. 'You aren't very nice.'

I bit my tongue, resisting the urge to call him back, to tell him it was all a joke. I was softer back then. Time has allowed me to compartmentalise such things into a box labelled 'Necessary Evil'. Silent, I watched him disappear into the forest.

Even then, I wasn't sure I believed in God. And, if I did, we weren't exactly on speaking terms anyway. Still, that didn't stop me saying a little prayer that Cory got back safely to his family.

~

Jared

I don't want to know, Jared thought. *It's none of my business.* But he had that pegged as a lie before his foot hit the first step. Aleksey was up to something, and he had to know what.

The tunnel he'd followed Aleksey down wasn't familiar to him. That wasn't what bothered him; there must have been countless unexplored tunnels in the Sanctuary. After all, he'd loved exploring them himself. It was the fact that Aleksey was heading down it, the man he'd only ever seen shuffle between the Grand Chamber, the dining hall and his unit.

When they'd approached the staircase, Jared considered calling after him, faking a cheery wave, and asking him where he was going. Something inside, a tic in Alexey's jaw and a tightening in his temples, told him not to. Instead, Jared followed his descent into the darkness.

Only, after a few footfalls gingerly placed in Aleksey's wake, he found it wasn't so dark any more. An eerie amber light glowed from beneath. The walls of the staircase were lit by deep orange lamps that dragged their shadows out before them. Jared kept back, watching as Aleksey disappeared around the spiral.

When he reached the last step, Aleksey was nowhere to be seen. Jared found himself on a wide platform, a fence encircling it. He edged forward and peered over. He'd expected something like the platform at the entrance to the Sanctuary, which hung above the oblivion where Martin's mother had plunged to her death. Jared often found his mind wandering to that drop since hearing Martin's story. He'd come to think of that boundary like teeth, encircling a mouth that swallowed her up.

Instead, there was a hive of activity below. Men and women hewed at the solid chunks of halite. Thin and pale, their sinewy muscles heaved as they swung their pick axes above their heads or chiselled at the rock.

One of them stopped, dropping to his knees. A guardian approached and bent to speak to him. Jared couldn't hear what was said, but the shaking of the man's head was clear. The guardian slapped him, and Jared flinched in sympathy. Still, the man did not move.

Another guardian approached, gun in hand. He jabbed it against the man's ribs, causing him to sprawl on the floor, muscles contorting. The guardian nudged him with his foot. What they did next brought bile to Jared's throat; they looked at one another and laughed. Then they took one of the man's arms each and hauled him to his feet. Jared thought that they would take him away to receive medical attention. Instead, they handed him his axe and waited for him to return to work. He swayed, but after a few moments, he raised his tool again.

'They work until they die.'

Jared's heart jumped to his throat. He turned to see a guardian.

'It's Felix, isn't it?'

Felix ignored the question. 'I'm not sure what they do with the bodies. I imagine they drag them into some abandoned tunnel and leave them to rot.'

'Who are those people?' Jared asked.

'Nobody and nothing. Once they were citizens. But they made their choice.'

'Choice?'

'You're working for the good of the Sanctuary, or...' He nodded to the workers below. 'You're working for the good of the Sanctuary. Not much of a choice, I know. Yet some still insist on making lives hard for themselves.'

'They're being kept here like slaves?'

'There's no 'like' about it. We couldn't let them leave. The likes of David Malone were fools to think banishment was an acceptable punishment. You have to see how vulnerable that left the Sanctuary. They might have told the dregs of humanity on the surface our location. That isn't a risk we're prepared to take anymore.'

'This is barbaric.' Jared bristled at the thought of all the lost relatives. How many citizens had family members that they assumed were taking their chances on the surface? 'Nobody has a right to do this to another human being.'

'Why not? There has to be a system. Some are born to lead, others to work.' Felix lunged at him, shoving Jared against the barrier.

'Get off me!' The railing dug into his spine as Jared was forced backwards over it. He heard the gasps of the people as they gathered below him.

'You'll be a lesson for them,' Felix said. 'The boy who escaped the Sanctuary will die in its bowels.'

'Please, Felix...' Jared kicked out at him as his feet lifted from the floor.

Felix's nose was millimetres from his face. 'I won't let you ruin this for me. I've earned my place—'

Kristoff appeared behind Felix and yanked him away. 'What are you doing?'

Jared teetered, and gravity almost dragged him down,

but he managed to right himself. Crouching on the wooden floor, he tried to calm his racing heart.

'You were going to kill him. I saw...' Kristoff paused. 'What is this? Who are those people?'

Felix growled. 'You should have kept your nose out.'

A sickening thud echoed as Kristoff's head struck the wall. He slid down it, unconscious.

'You see what you made me do?' Felix said. Then he charged.

Jared had no time to think, for which later he was thankful. Else, he doubted he'd have had the stomach for what he did next. Grabbing Felix by the arm, Jared pivoted and launched him with all his strength over the barrier. Felix fell head first. The screams of the people below dulled the crash of his landing.

～

Marney
<u>Before the Sanctuary</u>

Marney couldn't look O'Neil in the face as she prepared the syringe. 'Thank you, by the way. I know you didn't have to save me.'

O'Neil ignored her comment. She'd have wondered if he'd heard her at all through the plastic shield of her hazmat suit, but he'd robotically followed her instructions from the moment she'd entered his cell. That was the limit of the response he'd given her.

'The guard is going to make a full recovery,' she added. 'I'm lucky I wasn't fired for taking such a stupid risk, but it could have been a lot worse, if not for you.' She knew she was babbling but she couldn't bear the silence. 'Why did you save me?'

'Why wouldn't I? Besides, the guy was a pervert; I didn't like the way he was looking at that girl of yours. The world is better off without him.'

Bile rose in her chest to think of Thomas looking at Emma or Jodie in that way. In the spaces between hugging her and berating her, Stuart had told her the truth. Cara, the girl Thomas painted as his childhood sweetheart, had been ten years old. Only a couple of years older than Jodie. The day he took her was the first day they'd met. It was also the last time anyone saw Cara alive. He refused to tell them where her body was hidden.

They had found his journal in his cell, detailing his plan. Stuart told her that she hadn't been his primary target; that was one of her daughters. Marney couldn't bring herself to read the details. 'Burn it,' she'd told Stuart. 'I can't bear to think that those sick thoughts are still in the world.'

'Sorry,' he'd said. 'A prisoner can't die in our care without an investigation. It's evidence.'

She'd spent the night fretting over whether she could go through with the trial. Despite O'Neil's nonchalant manner, the dark rings around his eyes suggested he might have done the same.

Marney flicked the syringe. 'This will only sting for a second.'

In return O'Neil gave an almost imperceptible shrug.

This reaction was a far cry from Carter's. He'd sobbed when she'd administered the virus and made her promise that, if it came to it, she would tell his family that he'd died helping to save them.

O'Neil drew in a deep breath. *This is it*, Marney thought. *This is when he'll break down.*

'Do you think they'll give us a parade? If this works, I mean.' His voice was calm, level, as if he'd just asked whether it was likely to rain tomorrow.

Marney found it more unnerving than Carter's sobbing.

'I don't know. Maybe once you've finished your sentence.'

'I'm in for life. Murder.'

Marney could tell he wanted a reaction. Her heart thumped but she kept her hand steady as she wiped away the spot of blood that formed on his bicep. 'Then I imagine a parade would be difficult. Although I'm sure they'll think of some kind of reward.'

'Do you?' His scathing tone told her he disagreed.

It was her turn to ignore him. 'You're infected now, so

until the quarantine period is up, we won't be able to enter. All provisions will be passed via the hatch.'

'How long until I know if it's worked?'

'It's hard to tell. In all noted cases of infection, within twenty-four hours...' She let her sentence drift off.

'The patient is dead,' he finished.

'Yes. But the vaccine has shown good results.'

'Tell that to Jerome.'

'That was an allergic reaction. A one off. You tolerated the vaccine well.'

'I guess I better hope my luck holds out.'

She covered his hand with her own gloved one. 'I'll be hoping for the same.'

O'Neil pulled his hand away. 'Bye, doc.'

'I meant what I said. Thank you.' Marney closed the glass door of the cell.

O'Neil nodded, then lay down on his bunk and rolled over to face the wall.

The Book of Evelyn

It wasn't the first time that I'd seen a man die, and the last was by my hand. It's nothing like you think it will be. Not that I believe you've given it much thought. I sincerely hope you've never had to.

When I killed my stepfather, the knife met bone, and we both stopped, suspended in time and disbelief. Years of abuse, and he had the audacity to look confused. Sorry, that's enough said about that. I'm not sure how I got onto that topic anyway.

But yes, the day Dale's team returned from the supply run amid a crescendo of tooting horns, every member of the Colony ran out to meet them.

Pearl reached them first. 'Put pressure on his wound.' Then she guided the colonists as they lifted the injured man from the back of the truck. 'Where's Bev?'

'Michelle's gone to fetch her.' A map of dried blood splattered Dale's ashen skin.

'She'd better get a move on,' Pearl said. 'I think there's more of his blood on you than is left in his veins.' I was in awe at how my snarky friend, who somehow made her every move in the Colony into a battle, orchestrated the people around her. She barked instructions, and everyone, including Dale, obeyed without question. I salivated at the thought of such control.

'Get him up on the bed,' Pearl said as she shone a penlight in his eyes.

Bev slammed through the door. 'Is he still with us?'

'A stubborn sod like Sullivan won't be going anywhere without a fight,' Pearl said.

I watched in awe as they worked on him. They were incredible. Suctioning blood, ripping bandages, placing stitches, they worked tirelessly. He died anyway.

It wasn't like the movies. Neither of them 'called it'. They just exchanged a look, and Pearl patted the back of Sullivan's hand. 'What happened to him?'

'The Pack,' Dale said.

Pearl's head jerked up. 'They found us?'

'I don't think so. It was just bad luck that our paths crossed.'

'Where's Porter?' Bev asked.

Dale's eyes flitted over to me, and I knew he was debating how much to say in my presence. 'They took him.' I knew what that meant. There was no need to sugarcoat it. They were going to eat him.

It was only then that Pearl noticed me. 'You shouldn't be in here, Evelyn.'

'But, I...'

'Don't argue with me, girl.'

I backed out of the surgery, and directly into Bug. 'How is he?'

'Dead,' I said.

He nodded. 'I better go see his family.'

'Bug,' I said. 'I'm going to stay in the Colony. I mean, if that's okay with you?'

'It's always been okay with me. But ask yourself, 'why?''

'What do you mean?'

'Being here is a choice. And that choice should reflect your hopes for a future here. Not fear of what's out there.'

'I won't lie to you,' I said. 'I'm terrified. But I do want a life here.'

'Then you'd better consider what you can offer. Everybody needs a role here.' His words weren't exactly welcoming, but I like to think I saw the hint of a smile.

I sat on the steps outside, mulling over his words.

'You're still here.' Pearl eased herself onto one of the porch chairs.

I knew she didn't just mean outside the infirmary. 'A wise woman told me I had to forgive myself. I'm going to hang around here for a while and work on it.'

'That sounds like a sensible plan.'

'I'll bring back the things I took. It makes sense now. Why you were arguing with Dale, I mean.'

She scrunched up her nose. 'It does?'

'Yes. You're a doctor. You needed medical supplies.'

'I needed hair dye. And I *was* a doctor. I've been retired since before that blasted asteroid hit.'

'You're allowed to retire here?'

'Allegedly. As long as you keep making yourself useful.'

'Well, that looked a lot like doctoring in there.'

'That, my dear, is called lending a hand.'

'Maybe...Have you ever considered taking on an apprentice?'

'You mean you?'

I blushed. 'Why not?'

'I've been there and done that. Bev is the doctor now. If you want to learn, talk to her.'

'It's probably not a good idea, anyway,' I said. 'I've never liked the sight of blood.'

'Probably not then,' Pearl said. 'It's no great loss, believe me. If you save your patient, the masses shrug it off because it's just what you do. If you lose them, they question whether you did enough. It's a thankless job. And the odds are always stacked against you, especially nowadays.'

'Then why did you do it?'

'Me? I'm a drama whore, dear. Given my time again, I'd probably be something like a firefighter instead.'

'They'd never let you wear those heels.'

'Fair point. Look, speak to Bev if you want. But give it some thought first. Once you've chosen your place in the Colony, it's hard to escape it.' She sighed. 'No matter how often you tell them you're retired.'

Chapter Seven

Excerpt from *A Societal Analysis of the Bee Colony*

Absconding

Whereas swarming is a healthy behaviour for a colony that has grown too large, it must not be confused with absconding. Bees, including the Queen, will sometimes abandon a hive completely. Any young bees who are unable to fly will be left behind. This behaviour is caused by threats such as parasites and predators. It may also result from environmental factors such as lack of ventilation. As a bee keeper, it is your responsibility to eliminate as many of these threats as possible in order to ensure your colony thrives.

Wakefield, R. (2025) *A Societal Analysis of the Bee Colony*. Third edition. London: Feisty Scholar Publications.

The Book of Evelyn

Time in the Colony was strange. Days, weeks, and months melted together without me either noticing or caring. Despite this, my life ran like clockwork, waking at sunrise and tackling my list of chores and falling into bed when the light disappeared. Seasons dictated whether we were ploughing the fields, sprinkling seed, or worrying over our paltry crops, but I couldn't have told you the date if you asked. What I mean to say is, it feels both impossible that it has been years since we last met and as if I have lived a whole other life since then. Does that make any sense?

What little free time I had revolved around Riley. We became inseparable. I trailed after her as she wandered between the hives in the apiary. I'd kept my distance at first, claiming to be sensible rather than afraid. But as I witnessed the confidence with which she unpacked the covers of the hive to reveal the honey laden frames within, my curiosity grew.

Shrouded in the same beekeeping outfit, I hung at her elbow. 'When do we extract the honey?'

'We don't.'

Honey leeched from the edges of the wax-layered frame as she slid it back into place. 'Then what's the point if we don't get to eat it?' I was going to add that I'd never tried honey, but considering that until recently I thought bees were extinct, it seemed a moot point.

She smirked at me. 'Did you think they were making the honey for us?'

'No. I didn't really think about it at all, to be honest.'

'Yeah, well, Bug said that's one of the reasons we got to where we are today – arrogant humans assuming nature is there to serve us.'

'Probably,' I said. 'That and the massive asteroid that smashed into Earth.'

'That too. No, the bees aren't making honey for us, or for fun; it's to store for the winter months.'

I stared up at the cloudless sky. 'Looks pretty sunny.'

'In temperature, maybe. But, I don't know if you've noticed, but there isn't exactly a wealth of plant life round here.'

'I guess not.'

'Did you finish the book?'

'Nearly.'

'Well, spoiler alert. If this world is ever going to be habitable again, the bees need to survive. So hands off the honey, okay?'

It was a side to Riley I rarely saw when we were outside the apiary. She could take or leave the rest of the Colony. If she cared about any person who lived there, she didn't show it. But the bees, they were different. And if she thought they were important, I decided that I did, too. Because *she* was important to me.

Something on the other side of the fence caught my eye. 'It's him! The boy is back. I told you I wasn't crazy.'

'I didn't say you were.' That was true, but she'd barely reacted when I'd told her of the small child wandering the perimeter of the Colony. I guess I'd drawn my own assumptions. 'It happens. This is the only patch of land for miles with any hope of growing anything. Sometimes survivors try their luck in the hope of foraging something near the fence.'

'Why don't they ask to join us?'

'I guess they have their own gig going on. This life isn't for everyone.'

From subterranean life in the Sanctuary to wandering the desert, I couldn't think of a single scenario that existed any more that rivalled the Colony. Curiosity propelled me in his direction.

Cory didn't back away, which surprised me after I'd done my best to scare him last time. In fact, he seemed to be waiting for me. 'I told you, it's too dangerous for a boy your age to be out there alone,' I said.

'I'm not a baby. I'm nearly eleven. Besides, I'm not scared.'

That surprised me. I wouldn't have put him at more than seven or eight. 'I'm sure you're very brave. But sometimes it's smart to be afraid.'

He reached into his pocket and pulled out a scrunched up piece of paper. 'What is your name again?'

'Evelyn.'

He stared down at the paper, and I could see his lips moving as he tried to sound out the letters.

'Do you want me to read that for you?'

He pressed the note to his chest and took a step back.

'Just hold it up. I won't take it from you.'

Cory smoothed out the paper and held it in front of me. The handwriting was pretty and looped, the 'I' dotted with a heart. *Riley*. My breath caught in my chest. 'You see that girl over there, that's Riley. Do you want me to give it to her?'

Cory shook his head. 'I'm only supposed to hand it to her. Nobody else.'

'Okay.' I trotted off towards her. 'Riley, the kid – he's got a note for you.'

'For me?' She dropped the smoker to the floor and headed in his direction. 'My friend said you have something for me.'

'Maybe. What was your nickname when you were little?'

'Smiley.' Riley glanced at me. 'They were being sarcastic.'

'Clearly.'

The boy rolled up the note and poked it through the fence. Riley plucked it out. 'Thank you.'

'I've got to go now,' he said.

'Wait just a minute.' Riley flatted the note in her palm.

'I can't. I'm supposed to go straight back.' Cory disappeared into the forest.

'How will I find you?' she called after him. But he was gone.

'What does it say?'

Riley hesitated. 'Can you keep a secret?'

'Of course.'

She handed me the note. *I haven't forgotten you, little sister.*

'She's alive. Rhiannon's alive.'

'You didn't tell me you had a sister.'

'I haven't seen her in so long.' She beamed. 'I need to think.'

I have to admit, I felt more than a little jealous as she wandered off without me. I suppose I was happy for her. But how easily I'd been forgotten. With nothing else to do, I wandered off towards the garden.

'There you are,' Michelle said. 'Bug wants to see you.'

'Why?'

'Well, as I'm not telepathic, you'll have to ask him that.'

'But...Have I done something wrong?'

'Will you stop asking me stupid questions and shoo.' She gave her rake a prod in my direction. 'And give him an update on the new fertilisers while you are there.'

I knocked on the door but heard nothing from inside. I banged harder, my knuckles chafing. When I was still met with only silence, I pushed the door open.

Bug was at his desk, staring down a microscope. He didn't even acknowledge my presence.

'You called for me?'

Nothing.

'Um...Michelle wanted me to tell you that the new fertiliser is working well.'

Bug let out a puff of air. 'She's failing.'

'Who is?'

'The Queen.'

My first thought was that the Queen bee must have died. My second thought was how devastated Riley would be. I wanted to explain, should have explained, that whatever happened couldn't have been her fault. Instead, I asked, 'What will we do?'

He looked up at me. 'We?' A smile played on his lips. 'We hope that they rear another. If not, then we'll try to requeen the hive ourselves.'

'Oh.' It wasn't quite the catastrophe I feared.

'Did you know that researchers from the University of Illinois once placed barcodes on bees to see just how much they interact?'

'No, I definitely did not know that.'

'Hmmm. Well, they did. Tiny little barcodes like you used to find in shops.'

'Why?'

'Good question!' He seemed genuinely pleased I'd asked. 'To track their movements in order to see which individuals they performed trophallaxis with most often.'

'Tro-pha...'

'Trophallaxis – mouth-to-mouth liquid food transfer.'

'That's revolting.'

'On the contrary, it's very efficient. But that's not my point. Choi and the rest of that team found that the bees favoured some individuals over others. And if bees were all identical with no individual characters that just wouldn't happen.'

'I still don't get you.'

'They formed relationships, built bonds, just like us. More care and attention was given to those they deemed worthy.'

His eyes sparkled, and I knew he was expecting me to read something into his words. When I said nothing, he added, 'Just like you, Evelyn. It appears you have been making friends, too.'

'I guess. I've been helping Michelle in the garden.'

'And Riley.'

'Yes, Riley has been showing me the ropes in the apiary. The hives are pretty cool.'

'*Cool.*' Bug grunted, and even as he turned his attention back to the bee, I could see he had deflated. My reply disappointed him. I don't know why it was so important to me, but I wanted him to look at me with that sparkle again.

'I've been reading your book.'

'My book?'

'The one you lent Riley. I've nearly finished it. I hope that's okay. She said she didn't need it any more.'

Bug's lips were pressed together in a thin line. 'Did she? And what do you make of it so far? Has it inspired you to become a beekeeper?'

'You already have one of those.'

'Yes, I suppose I do.'

Something in the dish below the microscope caught my eye. 'The Queen, she's alive.'

Bug looked from the dish and back to me. 'Yes, of course she is.'

'But...but you said she was...'

'Failing. I said she was failing. A colony needs a strong Queen, or it will die. If a Queen becomes unproductive because she's sick or old, it's better to replace her or risk losing the whole colony.'

'Replace?'

Bug nodded. 'Replace.' We both knew what that meant.

'So the old Queen is killed? That seems kind of brutal.'

'It's a necessary evil and not one that I take pleasure in.'

'Couldn't you just leave her in there?'

Bug laughed, but it didn't reach his eyes. 'Wouldn't that be a happy ending. But the truth is, they wouldn't live happily ever after. Just like us and most other living things on this planet, she'd fight to survive. And I doubt the new Queen would stand a chance.'

❧

Marney

<u>Before the Sanctuary</u>

Marney had watched them via the video feed over the last few days. Every morning she told herself that she would go down and see them in person, but there always seemed a valid excuse. Tests to run, vaccine to synthesise, all legitimate reasons and all rubbish. With the risk they were taking, and after what O'Neil did for her, the least she could do was stand on the other side of the glass and look them in the eye.

Still, she held her vigil, eating and sleeping in Stuart's office. The only respite she allowed herself was half an hour to put the girls to bed.

Marney watched as the men tossed and turned and sweated and retched. And then they were still. Her breath caught in her chest, uncertain if they were dead or their fevers had broken.

It was when Carter rolled onto his back, eyes open and lucid, that they knew they'd done it.

'Could somebody get me something to eat?' he'd asked.

She threw her arms around Stuart. 'This is it. The vaccine works.'

Stuart patted her on the back before stepping away, apparently made awkward by her embrace. 'We'll have to keep them in quarantine, but it looks good.'

'Good? A bit of an understatement, don't you think?'

'It's amazing. I just think we need to hold off on the celebrations for now.' He glanced at his watch. 'They're resting peacefully enough. Why don't you go and see those beautiful girls of yours? Maybe eat a meal with them. Take a shower.'

Marney laughed. 'You're smelling pretty ripe yourself.'

'We'll handle the next stage in shifts. At least if you take a break first you might get to see the girls before they go to bed.'

Marney nearly crashed into Doctor Wakefield as she headed to her quarters. 'Richard, did you hear?'

'Yes.' He didn't smile. In fact, he looked positively miserable.

Marney fended off her irritation. 'Don't you see, all that sacrifice will be worth it.'

'I guess that's a matter of perspective,' he said.

This again, Marney thought. It wasn't as if she didn't feel bad about Jerome. She didn't need Wakefield making her feel worse. 'I know,' she said. 'But it's for the greater good.'

Wakefield's eyebrows bobbed. 'So I'm told. Well, I'm off to see the expendable few.'

'Don't act like I'm the enemy,' Marney said. 'We're a team. Let's celebrate this moment.'

Wakefield pursed his lips. 'I'll send them your regards.'

Marney tried to push aside her annoyance at Wakefield's attitude as she reached her quarters. Pecking the girls on the forehead, she led Ben by the hand to the bedroom.

'We've done it.' She covered her mouth to suppress a giddy laugh. 'The vaccine works.'

'I knew you would,' he said, folding her into his arms. 'What now?'

'Now we eat. I have to get back to the lab soon.'

Ben kissed her on the end of the nose like he used to do when they started dating. 'I'm proud of you.'

Marney felt lighter than she had done in years as she chatted to her family over dinner. Still, her mind kept drifting back to the vaccine. She hoped Wakefield hadn't already told O'Neil and Carter the news. She wanted to be there.

'Go on,' Ben said.

'Sorry?'

'You are itching to get back to work.'

'Actually, I was thinking how great it will be to tell the participants we've been successful.'

'They've earned that moment,' Ben said. *'You've* earned it.'

'Thank you,' she said, abandoning her half-finished plate and heading for the door.

When she strode into the quarantine area, O'Neil was standing at the glass. She grinned at him, expecting it to be returned full beam. Instead, he frowned.

Carter was nowhere to be seen. She walked right up to the glass, searching, as though he could find some way to secret himself away in the tiny cell.

Marney turned to Squires, who clicked his computer mouse, deep in thought. She suspected he was playing solitaire. 'Where's Carter?' she asked.

'Doctor Stuart took him to the lab,' he said, as though chiding her for forgetting such an important fact.

'He didn't say anything to me.'

'I don't know what to say to you. You know as much as I do.'

Marney marched to the lab, irritation bubbling within. Different scenarios played out in her mind. Perhaps when she got there the president would be on video phone. Stuart would present Carter to her, the first ever survivor of the virus. Marney imagined the president's reaction, the promises of rewards.

Marney's jaw ticked as she mulled over the nerve of the man; this discovery belonged to them all. The four of them should be announcing it together. Although she might not have been involved since the beginning, she'd poured her heart and soul into it since then. She rehearsed the tongue lashing she'd give him.

What Marney did not anticipate was pushing the door open to find Carter spreadeagled on an operating table. She didn't need to get closer to realise he was dead.

Marney wasn't sure how long she stood there. Stuart held his scalpel poised over Carter's open skull. 'I'll be right back,' he said to Wakefield, who was organising the instrument tray.

Stuart walked towards her. 'Marney, listen to me.'

'The vaccine failed?'

'No, nothing's changed. It's a success, we think.'

'Nothing's changed?' She blinked at him, trying to process what he was telling her. 'But you've killed him. He volunteered to help, and you murdered him.'

'I had no choice. We have to investigate every avenue, explore every possible limitation of the vaccine. We don't have enough time to wait and see if it's caused damage elsewhere.'

'Wakefield knew?' She thought back to his reaction in the corridor. How crass he must have found her celebrations, knowing that a man was about to lose his life. 'Why tell him and not me? If you are so certain this is the right thing to do, why aren't Meredith and I in there with you?'

'Because Richard has more of a stomach for this stuff, Marney. He may dig in his heels, but he knows sometimes there's just no choice.'

When she didn't reply, he added: 'Carter would have died in prison anyway. At least this way his life meant something.'

'That wasn't your decision to make.'

'Yes, it was.'

She backed away through the double doors. 'You're a monster.'

Stuart followed her. 'Maybe.' The emotion drained from his face. 'But I made myself one so you wouldn't have to. Go back to your family and leave me to make the tough calls.'

Marney watched in stunned silence as he turned and shoved through the double doors, leaving them swinging on their hinges.

'O'Neil,' she said, snapping back to her senses. Once Stuart finished with Carter, he'd be next. Marney ran, only forcing herself to slow down as she neared the quarantine area. She prayed that Stuart hadn't messaged ahead, ordering the guards to keep her out.

'Did you find him?' Squires asked.

She didn't answer. Instead she walked to the cell door.

'Doc? I asked if you found him?'

'I found them,' she said. But it wasn't to Squires she spoke.

O'Neil approached the glass.

'Carter's dead. Stuart killed him. He's autopsying him right now.'

'Jesus,' Squires said, still thinking she was talking to him. 'Do you think you should be saying that in front of ...'

He didn't finish the sentence, as though by not saying his name O'Neil wouldn't realise that they were talking about him.

'What do you want me to do?' Marney asked O'Neil.

'Do?'

'Shall I open the cell and let you escape?'

'Hey! Don't even joke about that, Doctor Wallace,' Squires said. 'He's still quarantined.'

Marney ignored him. 'What do you want me to do?' Her hand rested on the handle.

'You're going to kill us all,' Squires said. Marney heard his steps retreating down the hall.

'I want...' O'Neil stared at the floor around him, as though searching for an answer to her question. 'I want you to get away from that door and leave me be.'

Marney released a sob. 'You're sure?'

'I knew I wasn't leaving this place alive. It might not be the way I thought I'd go, but I'm ready.'

'I mean it, you know? I'll set you free.'

O'Neil dropped onto the bed. 'I know. But I don't deserve it. Now go back to your children, Doctor.'

∽

Jared

Jared tried not to look at Felix as they descended the staircase into the pit below, but it was not something he could help. His eyes drifted to Felix's broken body, which lay on the salt rock, limbs at jagged angles, splintered bones puncturing his skin.

'I don't understand,' Kristoff said, still groggy. 'Who are all these people?'

'Citizens who tried to stand up for themselves.' Jared scanned the workers, hoping to find his mother peering back at him.

A flock of guardians gathered around Felix's body. Hearing the unfamiliar voices, they sprang to their feet, hands on their holsters.

Kristoff was quicker. 'Don't bother,' he said, pointing his gun at them. 'We didn't come alone. There are reinforcements above us with the order to shoot if you try anything.'

He was convincing; Jared had to give him that. So much so that he found his gaze following theirs to the platform above.

The guardians relaxed, dropping their hands to their sides.

'Devon?' Kristoff said. 'What is all of this?'

Devon stepped from the back of the group. 'Nothing to concern you. We are following orders.'

A familiar voice rumbled from a nearby tunnel. 'As you should be.' Aleksey stepped out of the shadows. 'Would you like to explain to me what happened to Felix?' Aleksey checked Felix's pulse before closing his eyes.

'He tried to kill me.' Jared said.

Kristoff nodded. 'It's true. I saw it all.'

'Did you?' Aleksey viewed him from narrow eyes. 'And what, may I ask, are you both doing here?'

Jared hesitated, not wanting to admit he had followed him. 'I knew you were up to something. All these people... you have no right to keep them prisoner.'

'What prisoners?' Aleksey asked. 'Every man and woman here is free to leave whenever they wish.'

'That's a lie.' Jared looked at the miners, waiting for one of them to back him up. 'Him.' He pointed at the man he'd seen tasered by the guardians. 'They tortured him, then dragged him back to work before he could even stand properly.'

'Is that true?' Aleksey asked him.

'No,' the man said, not meeting Jared's eye. 'To my knowledge, every person in this mine, including me, is here of their own free will.'

'You don't need to lie for th—'

'Doctor Hiatt?' Kristoff stepped closer to him. 'It *is* you.'

Doctor Hiatt flinched at the sound of his name. 'Just leave me alone.'

'You can head back to your dorm,' Aleksey told him. 'In fact, let's all take a break early today. You've earned a rest. The Sanctuary, as always, thanks you for your service.' The men filed into the tunnels.

'Something isn't right,' Jared said. 'They're frightened of you.'

Aleksey sighed. 'That's not true. They're afraid of this place failing, that their families will be forced up into that wasteland.'

'How did they come to be working down here?' Kristoff

asked. 'I thought Doctor Hiatt headed to the surface with his wife.'

That name resonated somewhere in the back of Jared's head. Where had he heard it?

'Where the other Doctor Hiatt is, I have no idea,' Aleksey said. 'Her husband chose to stay and do his duty. He, at least, knows something of loyalty.'

That's when the cogs in Jared's brain began to turn and spat out the answer. Outside Saint Kinga's Chapel, when they'd been listening to Oliver and Sienna, Oliver had called her Miss Hiatt. That man was her father.

'Did you think there would be no consequences to the Pearse family's great escape?' Aleksey asked. 'People got restless and decided they'd try their chance on the surface. So when systems began to deteriorate, we didn't have the expertise to fix them. The people enlisted down here are looking for gas and minerals that could be useful to the Sanctuary.'

'Enlisted or conscripted?' Jared asked.

'You heard what he said; they want to be here.' Aleksey signalled towards Felix, and two guardians lifted his body. 'Now, if you'll excuse me, it appears I have another one of your messes to clean up.'

The Book of Evelyn

The forest surrounding the Colony was haunted; that they all agreed on. We listened to the stories by the campfire, shadows flickering across our faces.

Dale loomed over the fire pit. 'During the day, you'll be all right. But go in at night, and you'll never be seen again.'

'Is that so?' Pearl said. 'Don't fancy a midnight stroll, Dale? You can test that theory for us.'

He ignored her. 'It starts with whispering in the treetops. Some say it starts with the rustling of leaves. You try to reason that that's all it is. But what leaves? The trees are all long dead. Before you know it, voices are filling your head, screeching at you to run while you can.'

I spied Ruth on the other side of the fire, leant forward and hanging on his every word. That gave me the motivation I needed to ruin his tale.

'And how exactly would you know that?' I asked. 'I mean, if you're never seen again, how could you tell anyone?'

Dale hesitated. 'Well...There must have been a few survivors...' His eyes lit up, and I could see the flames reflected in them. 'Old William, for one. He told me he'd heard them.'

Pearl snorted. 'The same William who told me a phantom child was wandering the Colony's perimeter?'

I felt the heat of the glare Riley shot me before I saw it. My orders were received and understood; I stayed silent.

'Who are the ghosts?' Ruth asked. 'Or I suppose I should ask who were they?'

'That depends on who's telling the story,' Dale said. 'Most believe they were killed in the Warsaw uprising during World War II. Brave men, murdered and still seeking justice.'

'Or revenge,' Riley said.

Michelle took a swig of some fermented concoction she'd been experimenting with in the greenhouse. She winced and passed it on to Celine. 'Have you heard of the Treasurer? No? Well, there's a salt mine close to here, and legend has it that there was a demon stalking the tunnel. His name was the Treasurer.'

Ruth and I locked eyes for a fleeting moment, but neither of us spoke up. Besides, it wasn't so far-fetched. I'd met plenty of demons in the Sanctuary, just none by that name.

'A demon in the woods,' Celine said. 'Not exactly original.'

'You're jumping to conclusions. The Treasurer wasn't evil. In fact, he helped the miners. From finding wealth to navigating their way around the tunnels, they put good luck down to him. And then, there was his most important job.'

'What was that?' I asked.

'When accidents happened, as they inevitably do in a mine, it was the Treasurer who guided the lost souls to the surface and into the light.'

Pearl sniffed the bottle as it reached her, flinched away, but took a glug anyway. 'I suspect this story is about to take a tragic turn.'

'It wouldn't be much of a ghost story if it didn't,' Michelle said. 'The mine closed, and the demon moved on. Or was called home. Or evaporated into a puff of smoke. Whatever demons do when their purpose is fulfilled.'

Dale chuckled. 'Yeah, I heard he bought a condo in Florida.'

'Hilarious. Anyway, years later, the mine reopened as a museum. Some say that after the meteorite hit, survivors fled down there. Some of them might even be down there to this day, scurrying around the tunnels in the dark.'

I pressed my lips together to suppress a smirk. Michelle's story didn't match my experience of dinner schedules and sermons.

'Aren't you forgetting the haunted woods?' Dale asked.

'Oh yes. Well, naturally, the survivors down there eventually die. There's no escaping death, even in the bowels of the earth. But without the Treasurer guiding their souls to the afterlife, they are trapped here. Those who make it to the surface end up wandering the woods, tormented, looking for a way into the light.'

I hadn't intended to say anything, so when the words popped out, they shocked me. 'What if they don't deserve the light, or heaven, or whatever you want to call it?'

Michelle studied me for a second before adding, 'Then I guess they're already exactly where they deserve to be.'

That might be the case, I thought, *but what about the living that they choose to haunt? Do they deserve it?*

So when I found Riley sneaking towards the boundary of the Colony the next night, it was thoughts of my stepfather that played on my mind. *Could he be out there waiting for me?* I thought.

'You know,' Riley said, 'After the sperm donor took my mother away from me, I used to send messages to her phone all the time. Nothing deep. Just the usual. I love you. I miss you. I hope Dad is rotting in hell.'

'Did it help?'

'I think so. You know...No, forget it.'

'Go on,' I said. 'Tell me.'

Riley's cheeks were tinted pink, but she continued. 'I almost convinced myself that she was receiving them. Do you remember those little ticks that used to go onto messages when they'd been read?'

I'd been too young to own a phone when the Levelling happened, but I nodded anyway.

'Yeah, well, I thought that was her. That is until I found her phone in my sister Rhiannon's bedside cabinet. When I asked her about it, she said she kept the phone charged so I could talk to mum if I wanted. Although she'd prefer it if I went to her.'

'I'm sorry.'

'Don't be. It was a long time ago.' She talked over my condolences without missing a beat, clearly not wanting to discuss the matter any further. 'It was for the best finding that phone. It gave me closure. And besides, after that, if I felt sad or worried, I went to my sister. She became my world, and I hers. That's why I need to find her, Evelyn.'

'Are you just planning to wander around out there?'

'That boy can't have travelled far on foot. She must be close. You have to understand how much this means to me. Isn't there anybody left from your old life you'd like to speak to?' Riley took my silence as a sign that I was upset. 'Just ignore me. You know me well enough by now to know I chat rubbish. Verbal diarrhoea, that's what my sister used to call it.'

'No, you're right. I did have a few friends left in the Sanctuary. But I'm not sure the people in charge would even let me speak to them.' Then I saw it, a bottle poking up from the grass. It inspired me. 'But maybe I could write a note and tell them I'm okay. Perhaps one of the guardians will take pity on me and pass it on.'

Riley beamed. 'It's all coming together.'

I picked up the bottle, wiping off the dirt from the lime label with my sleeve. 'Perfect.'

'I wouldn't say that. The plastic they covered this world with will still be around when we're dust.'

'You know what I mean. Hopefully, this will stand out enough for one of the guardians to see it.'

That's how my first note came about, Jared. I kept it simple, imagining you, Luca or Martin breathing a sigh of relief as you read it.

I am safe. I miss you. Evelyn.

The rest wasn't hard. It turns out Riley had mastered the art of escaping the Colony. 'As long as you go when the watch tower lookouts are changing shift, you can jump the fence,' she explained. 'Not that I think they'd stop us. But I'd rather avoid the questions.'

'What then?'

'We move fast,' Riley said. 'We don't want to be outside for long if there is any chance the Pack is about.'

Just their mention gave me goosebumps. 'Have you ever dealt with them?'

'No, but I'd like to after what they did to you,' Riley said.

'Promise me something?'

'Sure.'

'If you see them, run as fast as you can in the other direction.'

I expected Riley to argue, to give a show of bravado. But she nodded, and my tension eased.

We set out as the sun crested the horizon. It didn't take

more than half a day to get there and back; the Sanctuary was unnervingly close, and we searched the area for Rhiannon as we went.

When we got to that familiar barbed wire fence, I tossed the bright green bottle over. I knew it was unrealistic to think one of you would find it. Or even that if somebody else did, they'd have the empathy to pass it along. It didn't really matter. For my own sanity, I had to say goodbye.

Laura

'You promise we'll get what we need and get out again,' Laura said.

Janet waved at a passing woman, who scurried into a shop. 'Yes, yes. I already said that.'

'I'm sorry. I just have to get back to my son. I can't do anything to risk that.'

'Like starving?' Helen asked. 'Because if we don't get some supplies, that's what will happen.'

'You're right. Please don't think I'm not grateful.'

'You save your thanks until we've got something to show for our trip.'

'Can I at least carry the basket for you?' Laura asked.

Helen shifted it into the crook of her elbow, away from her weak hand. 'You don't think I'm capable?'

'That's not what I meant. I just want to help.'

Janet took the basket from her daughter and handed it to Laura. 'You're too proud sometimes, my girl.'

The basket was hefty, and Laura wondered if she'd soon regret her offer. 'What's in this?'

'Vegetables to trade mostly,' Helen said. 'And some mending Ma did for the baker in exchange for bre—'

'Janet Horne, I want to talk to you!' Fion stomped towards them. Several townspeople followed, apparently enticed by the prospect of a row.

'I don't have time for your jabber,' Janet said, continuing towards the bakery.

'You will stop and talk, or I swear I'll see you in irons.'

'For what? Wanting better company than you?'

'For striking down my cattle.'

'What nonsense are you talking now?' Helen asked. 'If your cattle are sick, it's because you're too lazy to walk them up the river away from the Patersons' farm. You know they dump all their shite into it.'

'Your mother said she'd kill them. Now they're frothing at the mouth, and I can't get them on their feet.'

'That doesn't mean Janet did anything to them,' Laura said. 'I've been with her the whole time.'

Fion's top lip twitched. 'That means nothing other than that you're probably guilty too.'

Laura took a step back. 'I've done nothing to your cattle.'

'Of course you'd say that. What do we have here?' Fion tugged the basket from Laura's arm and tipped the contents onto the dirt. 'Half rotten carrots and onions. What do you hope to get for that? Certainly nothing worth my cows.'

Helen dropped to her knees and began scooping up the vegetables. 'Your cows are none of our business.' Laura followed suit and began putting them back into the basket.

Fion smirked and leant close, so only Laura and Helen could hear him. 'If you'd been so fast to get to your knees the other night, Helen, all of this ugliness could have been avoided.'

Helen reached out her good hand and squeezed his crotch. 'Is that right?'

Fion yelped. 'Let go. Please!'

'I don't know how you can judge our veg. These tiny turnips wouldn't even be worth sticking in a stew. Let alone anywhere else.' Helen finally let go.

The men behind them chuckled, but none of them as loudly as Janet, who whooped until tears streamed down her face. 'That will teach you to raise your hand to a Horne woman.'

When Fion finally looked up, it wasn't just pain that flushed his cheeks red. 'You'll pay for that.'

'Why?' Helen asked. 'You wanted me to touch them, didn't you? Ma, Laura, let's go.'

'That showed him,' Laura said, looking back at Fion as he stood hunched, puffing out deep breaths.

But Helen looked neither pleased nor proud. She gnawed at her bottom lip. 'I'm an idiot. He means it, you know. If he can think of a way, he'll make us pay.'

'Then let's get out of here.'

'We'll drop this off; then we need to lie low at the house until things calm down.'

'When do you think that will be?'

'I won't be holding my breath. If there's one thing I know about Fion, it's that he holds a grudge.'

The Book of Evelyn

As I already said, I hadn't expected an answer from you. I'd been gone for so long, and I assumed you'd moved on with your life. Little did I know just how far you'd travelled. But still, something drew me back. I even got into the habit of stashing away bottles. The colonists wouldn't have been happy. Any resources were to be shared for the greater good.

As it turned out, I needn't have bothered. On my next visit, I saw the same lime green bottle several metres away. It was just sitting there, propped against a rock. I fumbled with the lid, keen to get at the curled piece of paper inside. It rolled towards the crevice, and I plucked it into my hand before it disappeared.

Don't come back here. It's not safe.

Panic turned my blood to ice. I regretted not asking Riley along, but I knew she wouldn't have approved. 'Don't let something that was supposed to bring closure turn to torture,' she'd warned me. Besides, she was too busy trying to rebuild her family to be concerned with what I was up to.

My body was rigid, ready to be jumped by guardians. I needn't have worried. Nothing had changed. The same strip of lifeless earth encircled the unassuming black building. To the unsuspecting, it looked like an abandoned power terminal of some kind, dead and not worth the trouble of investigating.

In some ways, that bothered me more. What were you enduring, unseen, below the surface? I knew all too well the terror and suffocation of the Sanctuary. But what could I do?

They say that misery loves company. I thought that was the least I could be for you. And so our little ritual began. I'd get away whenever I could, and scribble notes filled with half-truths and exaggerations about how life had changed on the surface. I don't regret that. My intentions were good. In my head, I was helping you build the confidence to break free. Although it was never actually you that I was misleading, was it?

And in return, I got little snippets of life below.

Slavery, not Sanctuary...

Don't forget us...

The citizens want freedom...

Of course, none of the countless notes I read were from you. How gullible I was. My heart always pounded as I unscrewed that lid. I was desperate for updates on your plight. One thing you can be sure of, when I wrote, '*Just hold on. We'll be together again on the surface.*', it wasn't Oliver Durand that I imagined reading it.

Chapter Eight

Excerpt from *A Societal Analysis of the Bee Colony*

Swarming

Factors such as overcrowding and lack of resources may cause a colony to swarm. The existing Queen will split from the group, taking around half of the workers with her, whilst the virgin Queen will remain with the rest of the workers in the existing hive.

This split in the population occurs for the good of the colony, and the two groups appear to stay on good terms. Indeed, research by those such as Seeley and Morse (1977) found that although bees swarm at least 300 meters away, presumably to ensure they are not in competition for food, they seem to favour nest sites close to their parent colonies.

Fascinating research has occurred into how bees choose where to build their new hive. A group of older, more experienced bees head off to find a suitable location. When they return, these scout bees use a special 'waggle dance' to communicate directions to their favoured site. The more desirable the scout believes the location to be, the more times she will perform her dance. This allows more bees to learn the directions, and these bees can then fly off and judge it for themselves.

When they return, their enthusiasm for what they've seen will again be reflected in the number of times they repeat the waggle dance for the rest of the colony. Pretty soon, thousands of bees are voting for their preferred location by dancing the directions.

Wakefield, R. (2025) *A Societal Analysis of the Bee Colony*. Third edition. London: Feisty Scholar Publications.

The Book of Evelyn

On our third day of searching, we found Cory. The landscape was desolate except for a few clumps of dying vegetation. But suddenly, he popped up like a meerkat from its burrow.

I thought he would be afraid of us. I'd certainly given him reason. Instead, he turned our pursuit into a game and headed towards a valley, a decaying forest trailing along its bottom. Cory broke into a sprint, his laughter bouncing around the valley walls.

'Just let him go,' I said. 'His family must be nearby. We'll find them.'

'Not before we have to head back.' Riley stared, forlorn, at the sun as it began to dip below the horizon.

'We'll come out again tomorrow.' I'd wasted so much energy worrying that we'd be caught. In reality, if anybody even noticed we were gone, they didn't bother to mention it. Bug had been true to his word; the Colony was no prison.

'But they might have moved by then.' Her eyes glistened, and she shook her hair in front of her face.

'No. They'll be setting up cam—'

'I am the spider! You are the flies!' Cory's voice boomed from the bottom of the valley.

Riley's brow knitted. 'What was that?'

'You never played 'Spiders and Flies'?'

'I guess not.'

I took a deep breath. 'We're going to catch you!'

'Just you try!' Cory sang back.

'He's in that direction,' I said, leading her further into the valley.

After a few minutes of pushing through hollow twigs, we hadn't heard anything else. 'Maybe we followed an echo,' Riley said.

'Maybe. Let's see if he answers.' I filled my lungs to bursting and yelled, 'We are the spiders!' Nothing.

'I'll try,' Riley said. 'We are the spiders!'

We heard Cory's giggle come from high up on the slope. 'No, you are the flies!'

Riley beamed. 'We're going to catch you!'

'Just you—' Corey's words were cut off by a gut-wrenching shriek. 'Riley! Evelyn! Help me!'

I was already clambering up the valley when Riley snagged the back of my shorts. 'Are you crazy?' she hissed. 'There could be someone up there with him, and if there is, we've already given away exactly where we are.'

She was right, of course. 'Okay. We'll loop back and come at him from the side. He's probably just fallen and hurt himself.'

We zigzagged between the rotting trunks until we found a part of the slope knotted with roots. Clasping them, I pulled myself to the top. I kept my belly to the ground, whilst trying to peer around the tree shielding us.

'What do you see?' Riley asked, scaling the slope behind me.

Cory was a sobbing tangle of flailing limbs. But he wasn't on the floor, nursing a scuffed knee as I'd first suspected. He was hanging in a net, suspended from a branch. 'Let me down. Please!'

'One of the Pack has caught him.' Even from where I lay, I recognised the man below him. Rex pulled out his blade and jabbed it towards the helpless boy. I couldn't hear what

Rex said, but Cory's whimpers intensified. Then he began to scream. 'Riley! Evelyn! Please help me!'

Riley shuffled forward, and a twig snapped under her weight. Rex glared in our direction but must have decided it was nothing, because he went back to tormenting the helpless child, prodding him with his knife.

'Pull me up,' Riley said.

'No. We need to get out of here. They're using him as bait. Don't fall for it.'

'Don't you think I know that?' she said. 'But we can't just leave him.'

'Then he'll kill us, too. We need to get back to the Colony and ask for help.'

Riley buried her face into the crook of her arm as we listened to Cory beg for our help. It felt like a lifetime before his wails turned to whimpers.

'Come on,' I said, slithering back over the valley's edge.

Rex suddenly strode forward, making us both freeze. But it wasn't in our direction. Instead, he walked to the edge of the valley, directly above the place we'd stood, and yelled down, '*I* am the spider. *You* are the flies. And I'm going to get you.'

My voice may have been a whisper, but I spat them from between clenched teeth. 'Just you try.'

Jared

'I...I saw your father.' Jared had been rehearsing what to say, so he cursed himself for blurting it out.

Sienna blinked at him slowly. 'You're seeing ghosts now?'

'No. He's alive.'

'Whatever this is, Jared, it's cruel, so go and play your silly joke—'

'I saw him too,' Kristoff said.

'Wh— where? How?'

Jared wasn't sure how to explain, so he just said, 'I can take you to him. But I don't think we should go alone. Let's ask Marney to come with us.'

Half an hour later, Jared led the party of four along the same winding path he'd taken whilst following Aleksey. He'd relayed the basic facts to Marney; citizens they thought had returned to the surface were working in mines below the Sanctuary. What else could he say when they claimed to be there of their own free will? She hadn't said much, just nodded and agreed to follow them.

'This is it,' Jared said when they reached the platform above the mine.

'Is this the only group?' Marney asked.

'I don't know.' Until that moment, Jared hadn't even considered the idea that there could be other groups of prisoners. Because, no matter what they or Aleksey said, he knew that was what they were. They might not be shackled, but something must have forced them to stay.

Sienna headed for the stairs. 'I'm going to find my father.'

They followed her into the depths.

She went from prisoner to prisoner. 'Have you seen

Avery Hiatt?' Few answered her, instead staring through puzzled eyes.

Marney grasped her shoulder. 'Calm down, and let's think for a moment.'

Sienna stood in the middle of the group and yelled. 'Dad? Are you here? Dad?'

'Will you keep your noise down?' Aleksey must have been standing under the platform watching them the whole time. *Always skulking in the shadows*, Jared thought. It was starting to dawn on him just how wrong he'd got his grandfather's old friend.

'Where is Doctor Hiatt?' Jared asked.

'As you saw for yourself earlier, he wasn't feeling well,' Aleksey said. 'We took him to the dorm to rest.'

'Take us there,' Marney said.

The side of Aleksey's mouth twitched, and he forced a smile. 'With pleasure.'

They all fell into step behind Aleksey, except for Marney, who still stared at the men around them.

'Are you coming or not?' Aleksey asked.

'Be honest with me,' Marney said. 'Is Richard Wakefield down here?'

Aleksey scrunched his nose. 'Who?'

'The man that arrived with my family.'

'Oh!' Recognition lit Aleksey's eyes. 'I haven't seen him since the day he left. It was David who took against him. He said he'd dealt with Wakefield before, and he was unstable. Trust me, if he were here, I'd tell you.'

At that moment, Jared couldn't think of anyone he trusted less. But Marney nodded, and they followed Aleksey into a tunnel.

The smell was the first thing to hit him. Body odour and damp filled the air so completely that it felt almost viscous in Jared's mouth.

Aleksey flicked on the light, and groans went up around the dorm.

Jared frowned. 'Are they all sick? Why aren't they working?'

'Aren't you a little tyrant?' Aleksey chuckled. 'We operate a hot racking system here.'

'What's that?' Sienna asked.

'Two men are allocated to each bunk. While one works, the other sleeps.'

Jared grimaced.

'It's an efficient way of working,' Aleksey said. 'But we have some spare beds through here for the sick.'

He led them into a room no bigger than the living area of the unit Jared used to share with his mother. Aleksey pointed to the one inhabited bunk. 'There's your father, Sienna. Safe and sound.'

Sienna ran to him. 'Dad.' He didn't move. 'Wake up,' she said, giving him a gentle shake.

'Sienna?' Doctor Hiatt turned. 'Are you real?'

Sienna gasped. 'Dad, you're so skinny.'

That's an understatement, Jared thought. The man's wrist, as he reached to cup Sienna's face, was twig thin.

'You shouldn't be here,' Doctor Hiatt said.

Sienna pulled away. 'I thought you were dead, and that's all you can say.'

Doctor Hiatt didn't seem to hear her. 'Your mother isn't here, is she? I don't want her to see me like this.' He ran his fingers through his hair as if that would draw attention away from his sunken cheekbones and chapped lips.

'Mother?' Sienna took a deep breath. 'Dad, she's dead.'

'What? Why would you say such a terrible thing?'

'It's true,' Sienna said. 'I'm so sorry. I'll explain more once we get you somewhere safe.'

Jared looked away as Doctor Hiatt's face crumpled. 'No. You're lying. Take it back.'

'Dad...'

'I said take it back!'

Sienna hugged him to her. 'I wish I could.'

Marney glared at Aleksey. 'You didn't tell him.'

'I didn't think he'd ever find out,' Aleksey said. 'I wanted to spare him the pain.'

'Well, you failed miserably there.'

Sienna cradled his face. 'Can you walk? Jared, help me get him up.'

As Jared reached for him, Doctor Hiatt shuffled away, rucking up the stained sheets of his bed. 'No, I made a deal. I work down here, and my family get to stay in the Sanctuary.'

Jared scowled at Aleksey. 'You made him a slave.'

'Don't be ridiculous! The Hiatts were criminals. We showed mercy.'

Sienna sprang to her feet, jaw jutting out. 'Mercy? What kind of mercy is this?'

'They were inciting rebellion,' Aleksey said. 'Durand wanted to expel them. I offered them an alternative. Down here, your father has made a difference, helped the Sanctuary thrive.'

Tears still streamed down Doctor Hiatt's face. 'You said

if I agreed to work down here, then my wife would be forgiven, that she and Sienna would be taken care of.'

'I am sorry,' Aleksey said. 'I had every intention of fulfilling that agreement. Durand was an evil man.'

Sienna slapped him with such force Aleksey's head snapped back.

'I had nothing to do with what happened to your mother,' Aleksey said.

'Maybe not,' Sienna said. 'But you were happy for me to lose both parents. You knew they'd taken my mother, and you still couldn't find the compassion to leave me my father?'

Marney
<u>Before the Sanctuary</u>

Sleep hadn't salved Marney's anger. In fact, she'd spent the majority of the night lying there, planning what she would say to the rest of the research group. She'd been wide awake when her alarm sounded. Ben rolled over and pressed snooze. He was still snoring as she dressed.

'The girls will be up soon,' she said, pulling back the blanket. All she got in return was a thumbs up as he pulled the covers back over his head.

Marney hammered on the office door. 'Stuart, open up and face me.' She stopped banging and listened. Nothing. 'I know you're in there.' It was a lie, but she'd looked in all the usual places.

She'd bumped into Meredith while searching the lab. 'Did you know what they were going to do?' Marney asked.

'I had an inkling,' Meredith said.

'And you didn't think to stop them? Or at least tell me so I could?'

Marney always found Meredith annoyingly optimistic. Her general attitude was so saccharine-sweet it made Marney's teeth hurt. So what Meredith said next shocked her. 'Their deaths were an acceptable sacrifice, Marney. Besides, think of the good they did. Maybe it went some way to make up for their crimes.'

'They were people! Flawed, yes. But their worth didn't boil down to a profit and loss of their sins.'

Meredith sighed. 'Don't put words in my mouth. None of us wanted it to end like that. If there were a way to avoid it, we would have done. But every second costs more lives. So save the righteous indignation, please.'

Marney stormed out, but Meredith's words rang in her ears. If they had put it to a vote and hers had been the decider, would she have changed things? She liked to think so, but if she weighed O'Neil against her family, she doubted there would have been much competition.

There were only so many places to go in the facility, and she'd been to each of them twice. So Marney figured Stuart must be hunkered down in his office or his quarters.

She tried his quarters first. The door was unlocked, and she wasn't ashamed to admit she let herself in. When she saw no sign of him, Marney decided she wanted him to know she'd been in there, to feel his space had been violated. She took his pictures – a copy of his daughter on the swing, a woman in a scarlet dress with her head back laughing – and slapped them face down on his dresser. It wasn't enough, so she ran her hand along the top of his bookshelf. A vase crashed to the floor. A statuette, declaring some award or other in the field of virology, bounced on the tiles and broke in two. *That's more like it*, she thought. *You don't deserve awards.*

But Marney wasn't satisfied. When she'd found him with Carter the day before, shock robbed her of all eloquence. Before she left the facility, which she intended to do as soon as possible, she wanted to express her disgust to his face. Marney smashed her fist on the door again.

Squires lingered at the end of the corridor, wary of coming closer after their earlier run-in. 'Doctor Wallace, I don't think he's in.' Uncertainty mixed with fear puckered his brow. After all, he'd thought she would open O'Neil's cell door and unleash the virus on them all. Inspiring such panic made her feel oddly powerful.

Marney turned to Squires. 'Open the door, and we'll find out whether he's inside.'

'I can't do that.'

'It's my research in there too, and I'm giving you an order,' she said.

'No, I mean, I really can't. I don't have a key.'

'But you know who does?'

He nodded.

'Then go and get it.'

He trotted off to find one.

The delay calmed her anger somewhat, and Marney rested her forehead against the cool wood. 'Look, I guess I can understand why you did what you did,' she said through the door. 'I disagree with it, but I can understand. But I at least deserved to be told beforehand.'

There was still no movement from behind the door. Marney slammed down her fist on the surface. 'Will you just talk to me?'

'Doctor.' Squires stood behind her with a bunch of keys in his hand. She stepped aside to let him in.

The office was empty. 'See,' Squires said.

'I...Where else could he be?'

They heard a thud from the cupboard at the side of the room. For a fleeting second, Marney imagined Stuart crouched inside it. But that wasn't his style. As much as she'd disliked his recent actions, Stuart was never a coward.

Marney strode over to the cupboard and yanked open

the door. Stuart was inside. But not hiding as she'd imagined. He was slumped with a belt tight around his neck. The other end was jagged, snapped under his weight, causing the noise that had caught their attention. From the bruised colouring of his face, she guessed he'd been there all night.

'Dear God!' Squires held his hand over his mouth as he gagged and raced from the room.

In contrast, Marney couldn't move. She couldn't react at all.

The man she'd held such boiling rage for seconds before stared up at her through haemorrhaged eyes. A bloody foam covered his clenched jaw, and Marney realised that if she searched around the bottom of the cupboard, she'd probably find a severed piece of his tongue.

'You didn't need to do this,' she told him.

His balled fists drew her eyes down, and she realised he'd soiled himself.

Marney scanned the room for something to cover him. She saw his jacket hung on the back of his chair and went to fetch it.

Her name caught her eye, printed in bold capitals at the top of the piece of paper.

MARNEY,

I'm sorry for what I said to you earlier. I didn't do this monstrous thing so you wouldn't have to. I decided without you because I thought you would try and talk me out of it. But we just don't have the luxury of either time or morality.

The reality is that many more will die before enough vaccine can be produced. And we all know that when something is in such short supply, it will likely only benefit the rich and the elite. So I have sent the vaccine details to a larger facility where it can be synthesised at a faster rate. I hope you will not take this as a slight, but I have asked Meredith to oversee this process. I know that before I hijacked your life, you intended to find a safer, happier place for your children. We both know that's not a lab.

So, to the question at hand: why have I ended it like this? You have no reason to feel guilty. This is nothing to do with our crossed words. It isn't even the lives I took, although they weigh heavily on my conscience.

The answer is simple. This was always my plan. The virus took my family from me. They've been dead for nearly a year now. I hope you don't see my pretence as a betrayal, but it felt good to imagine they were waiting for me. I suppose they are, if you believe all of that, which I do. I pray that God will forgive my cowardice, but my only purpose in being here this last year was to stop the virus that took them from me. I've climbed over more bodies than I care to remember to achieve that.

But history may forgive me yet, because, if there is a hierarchy of evil, I am far from the top. There's something that you need to know, Marney. Something I should have been honest about from the start. This virus didn't evolve. It didn't mutate. Powerful men created it with self-preservation as their primary objective. That seems ironic now, considering many of them are included in the death toll. Those left enlisted me to help clean up their mess, as if I had the power to scrub away the blots they've put on their souls. I won't tell you their names. Such unprincipled devils would kill you if they found out you know the truth.

But there is a ray of hope for you. Although my family are not there, the Sanctuary does exist. I believe it will soon be the only safe place left for your children. In the top drawer of my desk, you will find all the details you will need to get you and your family safely there. My tickets and passes should grant you safe passage to Poland. Given my actions today, the Sanctuary will now be short of a virologist, and you need to persuade them you can fill that spot. I've vouched for you and given full credit for your role in the vaccine development. However, your admittance is not assured. I'm sorry, it just isn't in my power. But if you want my advice, do not take 'no' for an answer. Your children's lives depend on it.

This is where those famous morals of yours may be tested. You will find another file in there about the founder of the Sanctuary, Edmond Pearse. There are details inside that he will not want anybody else to find out. Use them, Marney. Make sure he stamps your application personally and makes your life there as comfortable as possible. He owes it to you.

Good luck, my friend. Look after those little girls.
Paul Stuart

The Book of Evelyn

The sun had all but disappeared as we reached the woods around the Colony. I stopped short.

'What are you doing? Keep running.' Riley looked from me to the dense trees in front of us. 'Is this about Dale's stupid ghost story?'

I didn't want to admit it, but it was true. Although I willed my pounding heart to slow, fear drove it as much as exhaustion.

Riley squeezed my hand. 'If there are any evil spirits in there, they'll have to deal with me. I'm not scared.'

She'd never had the misfortune of meeting my stepfather, but I appreciated the sentiment. 'Okay, let's go.' Branches lashed my skin as we ploughed through the woods. We didn't even bother with the usual spot where we hopped the fence. Instead, we ran straight for the gate and rattled it frantically.

'Kayleigh, let us in!' Riley waved up at the blonde in the watch tower, who could have only been a few years older than me.

'What the hell are you two doing out there?'

'We'll explain everything,' Riley said. 'Just open the gate first.'

Kayleigh raised her hand as though she were about to slap it down upon a button but froze with it in mid-air. 'Is somebody following you?'

'Yes, now open the damn gate!' My voice was shrill, almost unrecognisable even to me.

'I don't...I'm not sure.'

'What's going on?' Celine appeared on the other side of the bars.

'Please,' Riley said. 'We ran into one of the Pack. They might be behind us.'

Celine took a step back. 'You shouldn't go out there on your own. It's not safe.'

'Lesson learnt,' I said. 'We'll take whatever punishment you want; just open the gate.'

Celine looked behind her, perhaps hoping to find someone who outranked her to swoop in and make the decision. 'Okay. Kayleigh, open the gate.'

It clunked into life, and Riley and I squeezed through the gap as soon as it was wide enough. When we were on the other side, we yelled for Kayleigh to close it.

'Screaming at me won't make it move any faster.'

'Can you see anyone from up there?' Celine asked.

Kayleigh picked up a pair of binoculars and scoured the Colony's perimeter. 'Nobody.'

Celine deflated with relief. 'All right. Let's get Bug and Dale and decide what we will do. For a start, we'll have to get more people on watch. Maybe put some patrols along the boundary.'

'I'm sorry,' I said. 'We didn't think—'

'No, you didn't.' Celine's eyes were fiery. 'For most of us, this place is the first safety we've known in a long time. If you've ruined that...' She took a huge breath and let it out in a long stream. 'Don't make me regret saving you.'

It felt like she'd thumped me. 'Please don't say that.'

'Besides, it was my idea,' Riley said.

'And you should know better,' Celine said. 'You know the Pack has forced us to move before. And now you might have led them straight to our door.' She ran her fingers through her hair. 'Please God, I can't start all over again.'

I wracked my brain for something I could say to make it right. 'But we don't even know if he followed us. We didn't see him.'

'Let's hope not. Wait for me in the canteen while I fetch Bug and Dale.'

Maybe they were letting us stew, but it felt like an eternity before the three of them appeared. Either way, my feelings were still smarting from Celine's tongue-lashing.

'You told me we were free to leave,' I said, pleading my case before Bug opened his mouth.

'I did. But not that you could come and go as you pleased. You have to understand that every time you cross paths with another survivor, you risk leading them back to the Colony.'

'I realise that now.'

'We should make arrangements,' Bug said, 'in case we need to move.'

'Is...is that necessary?' Celine asked, her voice breaking.

'We can't take the chance.'

'Calm down, little brother,' Dale said. 'From what we can tell, no harm has been done, so let's not jump the gun. I've arranged extra patrols. Every watchtower is manned. In fact, maybe a stint up there will give these two some time to think.'

'Thank you.' I was simultaneously relieved and suspicious of Dale's attitude. 'And I will go up there every night for the rest of my days if I can make this right.'

'Well, that's a tad extreme.'

'But...'

Dale sighed. 'But what?'

'But we haven't told you everything. There was another survivor out there, a little boy. Rex caught him.'

'I see,' said Dale. 'That's a shame.'

I blinked at him, wide-eyed. 'A shame? You know what they'll do to him.'

'We do,' Bug said. 'But we can't put the Colony at risk by going after them.'

'You did for me.' I caught Celine's eye, and she looked away.

'We'd hoped to get to you before they did,' Dale said. 'A rescue mission was never part of the plan. It was a one-off.'

'So make an exception for him, too.'

'I'm sorry.' Dale shook his head. 'I hope the kid finds peace and he finds it quickly. But we can't get involved.' He planted a hand on Bug's back, guiding him out. I knew what Dale was up to; he didn't want to risk me changing Bug's mind.

I was so shocked at the way things had unfolded that it was only then I registered Celine staring at me. 'I shouldn't have said what I did. I could never regret saving you.' She headed for the door but paused before going through it. 'I'm sorry about your friend.'

~

Laura

Janet huffed. 'If you're just going to drop my linens in the dirt, you may as well leave me to it.'

Laura looked down and saw the bottom of the sheet she was holding pooled on the floor. 'I'm sorry. I'm not being very helpful.'

'Aye, you're all right. Were you thinking about your wee boy?'

'Yes, but he isn't so wee any more.'

Janet picked a peg from her apron and fixed the corner Laura was holding to the washing line. 'They'll always be wee to their mothers. You say he was supposed to come for you? Did he not say when?'

'It's complicated.'

Janet sniffed. 'And you don't think the likes of me would understand?'

'I don't mean that at all. It's just...I'm not sure he even knows where I am. If anyone can find me, it's him. But we weren't always on such great terms.'

'Ah, now that's something I know a lot about. Squabbling with Helen is a daily occurrence for me. But would you like my advice?'

'Please.'

'Don't wait for him. You go to him first and tell him you're sorry. Us Horne women know a lot about stubbornness. But not when it comes to that.' She patted Laura's hand. 'We're quick to snap but quicker to apologise.'

'If I get the opportunity, I will.'

But Janet wasn't looking at her any more. 'Who is...? Agnes?'

Laura followed the direction of Janet's frown to find a woman stomping across the nearby field towards them. She was thickset, and her neck was muscular under her lace collar. 'Who is it?'

'Agnes McCalister. She owns the neighbouring farm. But I don't think in all my years of living here she has ever visited us.'

'Janet!' Agnes puffed out winded breaths. 'May I have a word?'

'Sure you can. I'd offer you something to eat, but...'

Agnes waved away the offer. 'I can't stop.' She eyed Laura, perhaps weighing up if it was safe to talk in front of her. 'Have you heard what's been happening in town?'

Janet continued to peg out her washing. 'You know me, Agnes; I try to avoid all that as much as possible.'

Agnes grabbed her by the crook of the elbow. 'Avoid it? Word is that you're the cause of it all.'

Helen appeared at the door to the house. 'And what is it they're accusing my poor ma of this time?'

Janet shrugged the woman off. 'Just ignore her, Helen.' Picking up her basket, she headed for the house.

Agnes followed her. 'You've brought this storm upon us, and you'll be the one to fix it.'

Stepping between them, Helen put her palm on the woman's chest. 'What are you talking about?'

'The townspeople have gone mad, accusing one another of witchcraft.'

'That's no business of ours.' Despite the steel in her words, Laura saw how Helen paled.

'She started this with her talk of curses.'

Helen stepped towards Agnes, teeth bared. 'She's a batty old woman. Not a witch.'

'Well, the damage is done. They've pointed the finger at my John. I swear to God, if they take him, I'll burn this whole place to the ground.'

Helen shoved her away. 'Get off our land.'

Agnes raised a wavering finger at her. 'Confess that you're a liar, Janet Horne, and end this madness.'

'Confess to what?' Janet's wrinkled face creased further as she looked from Helen to Laura. 'What is it they think I said?'

'Don't act innocent,' Agnes said.' I've heard your wicked words myself. Tell them you lied. Or tell them you acted alone. I don't care. But either way, this has to end.' Agnes stormed back towards the field.

'Helen? Have I said the wrong thing?' Janet's voice was a whisper.

'Always, Ma. But don't you be worrying about it. Everything will be fine.'

Laura prayed she was right.

The Book of Evelyn

I walked to Bug's unit, anxiety battling with hope in my gut. He'd barely spoken to me since the day Cory was taken. It wasn't for lack of effort on my part. But every door knock, every awkward hello, went unanswered. I hadn't realised how good the warmth of his favour felt until it was gone.

When I reached his unit, I was surprised to find Riley inside. 'You wanted to see me?' I asked. Considering he'd asked for us, Bug did a fine job of pretending we weren't there. Instead, he studied a shabby map that had been folded and unfolded so many times that its creases had split. I frowned at Riley, who shrugged in return.

We stood in silence as he traced a finger along a path we couldn't see and circled something with a flourish. 'You girls have become very close,' he finally said. 'And Evelyn, I know how much you have enjoyed learning about beekeeping.'

'Riley's a great teacher.'

'No doubt. But there is only enough work for one. A colony doesn't need two Queens.' His tone was clipped, and he didn't meet my eye.

'I've kept up with all my chores in the garden. You can ask Michelle.'

'It wasn't a criticism – just a fact. You have become a talented apiarist. It would be a shame to waste that.' He looked up and gave us his full attention for the first time. 'Petra, down in the most southerly Colony, has sustained an injury.'

'Is she okay?' Riley asked.

'She will be. But such falls are going to get more common

with her age. She needs help. Which is why it's time for one of you to swarm.'

Swarm. The word swirled around my head, and with each rotation, the weight of its meaning grew. I'd be leaving. Riley wouldn't be coming with me. We'd likely never see one another again.

'What? No.' I hadn't realised how desperate I was to stay until that point. 'I promise—'

'And it's going to be you, Riley.' Perhaps he thought delivering the news fast, without fuss, was kinder.

Riley still looked devastated. 'This is my home. You can't make me leave.'

'Considering you have more experience, and you already know members of Colony 3, you are the logical choice,' Bug said. 'That must be clear.'

'It's nothing to do with that, and you know it.' Riley's chin trembled, and I wanted to hug her. 'You don't want to split up your idiot brother and her mother.'

Bug rubbed his brow. 'That's got nothing to do with this.'

'But what about the fact that I don't want to leave? Those are my hives. I've been in charge of them for the last two years. And you just want me to desert them?'

'Evelyn and I will take care—'

'I'll go,' I said. 'Riley's right. She was here first. It should be me.'

'This is neither a debate nor a democracy. You have five days before you will leave with the next supply run, Riley. I'm sure you will be very happy in Colony 3.'

Riley's lip quivered. 'Both of you can go to hell.' She slammed the door, rattling the equipment on Bug's desk.

When I didn't follow her, Bug gave me a sheepish look. 'Did you want something?'

'I don't understand you sometimes.'

'That's because you are ignorant of the bigger picture. I'm being cruel to be kind.'

'If there was any kindness there, it was hidden well.'

I chased after my friend and found her sitting cross-legged in the apiary, ripping up clumps of grass and daisies and throwing them.

I covered her hand with my own. 'They're for your bees, remember.'

'They're not my bees, though, are they?'

'Please, don't be like this.'

'Like what? Hurt? Betrayed? Tell me, have you planned to take my place since the beginning, or did you only recently decide to stab me in the back?'

'I had nothing to do with this!'

'Liar!' She snarled the accusation at me. 'You know what, you're welcome to them. The bees, the colonists, all of them. I have family out there. I have people who care about me.'

'I care.'

'Get away from me.' But it was she who got up to leave. 'I know when I'm beaten. All hail Queen Evelyn.' She looked me up and down with a sneer. 'I never want to see you again.'

Chapter Nine

Excerpt from *A Societal Analysis of the Bee Colony*

Colony Collapse Disorder

Colony Collapse Disorder (CCD) is characterised by the abandonment of the Queen, nurse and young bees by their worker relatives. With no obvious cause, otherwise healthy hives are deserted, leaving the bees that are ill equipped to forage behind to starve. No one factor can be pinpointed as the cause for CCD and it is thought likely to be a combination of stressors such as pesticides, lack of genetic diversity and poor nutrition. Whatever the cause, the rate at which these pollinators are disappearing should set off alarm bells for every member of our society.

Wakefield, R. (2025) *A Societal Analysis of the Bee Colony*. Third edition. London: Feisty Scholar Publications.

The Book of Evelyn

Riley avoided me at every opportunity after that. At first, I tried to follow her to state my case. It was no use. As soon as she saw me, she would storm out.

'What do I do?' I asked Pearl.

'Absolutely nothing.'

'But she's my friend. What am I supposed to do, never talk to her again? I can't do that.'

'Sure you can. Never argue with a fool. She'll drag you down to her level and beat you with experience.'

'It's just a misunderstanding,' I said. 'She's not a fool.'

'Well, she's sure acting like one. But if you are set on patching things up with her, just give her some space.'

So that's what I did. I stopped trailing after Riley, begging her to listen. I didn't loiter around her dorm, hoping to reason with her. So we still weren't speaking on the day the earth split in two.

'Do you feel that?' I'd been working in the garden with Michelle when a rumbling sensation travelled up through my feet.

She dusted off her hands. 'I don't feel—'

There was a snap, and the ground before us split into a cavernous yawn.

Michelle dropped to her knees and peered inside. 'Dear Lord, what is that?' The earth groaned, and she pushed herself backwards just in time to see our wheelbarrow fall into the cavity. It didn't stop there. The fracture travelled across the field, pulling our paltry crops into its depths. We chased it, shouting for the colonists to get out of its way. But it easily outpaced us, and we followed it towards the apiary.

Riley was leaving the field as it rushed past her feet. 'Evelyn, what's going on?'

'It's sucking everything down inside.'

Before I could stop her, she sprinted back into the apiary. Michelle and I followed. When we reached her, Riley clung to one of the hive boxes as it teetered on the edge.

I tried to help, ignoring the bees as they swatted at my bare hands. Michelle hopped over to the other side and pushed. It didn't budge. Not until, that is, the gap widened. It dragged Riley and me forwards. Digging our heels in, we gave one last heave.

'It's no good,' I said. 'We need to let go.'

'No!'

I was still clinging to her shirt when the ground gave way. The hive plummeted, shattering as it bounced off the sides. We fell to the ground in a heap.

'Are you okay?' Michelle asked.

I wasn't. My heart was beating out of my chest, and I wanted to cry. 'Yes,' I replied.

Riley stared down into the depths.

'You could have been killed!' I yelled. Then I hugged her.

The colonists soon made their way over to us, some to assess the damage, others just magnetised by the excitement.

Bug paced along the edge of the ravine. 'There must have been a weakness in the ground.'

Michelle's eyebrows knitted. 'You don't say.'

'The Vistula River used to flow through here. I guess it

formed an underground cavern after it dried up. I never imagined this could happen.'

'What now?' Riley asked.

'You aren't going to make us move again, are you?' Michelle asked.

'No, we can't,' Riley said, a little too fast. 'They'll never find us.'

Bug frowned. 'The other colonies? They know the deal. We focus on the good of our own people. But I don't think it's come to that just yet. We might be able to use this...' He flapped a hand towards the hole. '...to our advantage. There could be water down there.'

'But it's not safe,' I said. 'What about the apiary?'

Bug scanned the area. 'We move the hives. It won't be easy, but it's possible.'

Bees were vacating the chasm. They zigzagged an angry path around us before darting away.

'Please, Riley.' I nodded towards the gathering crowd. 'For the Colony.'

'No. They don't deserve my help. ' She turned towards the apiary. 'But I'll do it for *my* colony. At least they know how to be loyal to one another.'

Like that, Riley and I stopped being rivals and became a team again. Rebuilding the friendship took a little longer.

Marney
<u>Before the Sanctuary</u>

The file was clear on this point; the human race had been warned. Marney flicked through one article after another about the 'population bomb', snipped from newspapers and journals and slipped within flimsy layers of manilla. The message in each of them was both consistent and urgent; act now, or the human race will become the catalyst for its own destruction.

None of this was new to her. For decades scientists had yelled this message from every metaphorical rooftop. Over-consumption paired with rising populations was at the root of every environmental issue the planet suffered. But then, of course, the meteorite struck and fast-forwarded climate change at a catastrophic rate. Governments no longer debated its existence but began to work together to find a solution.

Too little, too late. Earth began to self-destruct, and for the first time, population numbers declined. But not fast enough for some. Not when the competition for resources was so ferocious.

Marney wasn't sure she had the energy to read any more when a handwritten report caught her eye. With curly handwriting full of sweeping loops, she wouldn't have been surprised if she'd found an 'I' dotted with a heart. It was an emergency dispatch incident report detailing an anonymous telephone call. A virus would be released in Franklin, Georgia, and somebody needed to stop it from happening. At the bottom, in capital letters and double underlined, was written

'HOAX?' Only it wasn't. Franklin gave them patient zero, plus hundreds more.

Marney flicked over and found a map with coloured spots detailing the outbreak sites. They'd baffled scientists at the time, including her. It wasn't airborne, but the sites were far apart. Viruses didn't have legs, so how was it travelling across the country in such a haphazard manner? It was clear to her now.

The following few pages confirmed it. Minutes of meetings, incident reports and mission reviews all led her to an inescapable conclusion. When the Earth began to self-destruct, and resources were scarce, an unnamed few decided that sharing was no longer an option. Neither was sacrificing the lifestyle to which they were accustomed by rationing. Their solution? Population control with a targeted virus. The intention was to wipe out the most disadvantaged areas, killing off the poor and leaving the wealthy to claim the remaining resources. Nature, it seemed, laughed at their plans. Because the virus broke loose and came for them, came for everyone.

'Here, take this.' Marney was startled by Wakefield's voice. He held a tissue in front of her face.

It was only then that she realised tears streamed down her face. 'Thank you. I guess it's all got too much today.' She tried not to look at the cupboard where she'd found Stuart's body. The guards had taken him away, but it was as though she could still feel him watching her through those bulging eyes.

'I can relate.' Wakefield nodded to the paper strewn across the floor. 'You found *the* files.'

'Stuart told me I could look.'

'I thought he should have told you from the start. That way, you'd know what you were dealing with and could decide if the human race was worth saving.'

'It's true then? The virus was manufactured.'

'Yep. They sacrificed whole segments of the population so that they didn't have to struggle. We weren't even talking about survival at that point. The men who created this thing, they already had enough squirrelled away.'

'Did you meet any of them?'

'I think so. Just one. I don't know for sure, but I don't think he was financing our work here out of the goodness of his heart; he didn't seem the charitable type.'

'Did you not share your suspicions?'

'Of course. But when I did, I was told to shut up if I didn't want my career to be over.' His eyes widened. 'I'm sorry. I guess I'm not as brave as you.'

'Don't worry about it. Besides, it isn't over. They basically kidnapped me to get me here.'

Wakefield laughed. 'You are in demand.'

Marney stared at the map. 'All these people.'

'Meant nothing to them,' Wakefield added. He pointed to the folder with 'Edmond Pearse' printed neatly on the label. 'That one's new.'

'That's...something different.' She pushed the folder behind her. 'Just some notes Stuart put together for me.'

'Paul knew Edmond Pearse?'

'I think every scientist has at least heard of him. I used to be quite in awe of his work myself. Anyway, he's created some kind of bunker. Stuart told me to go there.' She frowned. 'What's your plan after this?'

'I don't really know. I hadn't imagined getting this far.'

'Come with us,' Marney said. 'Stuart told me it would be our best chance for survival.'

'Well, weren't you the teacher's pet? It doesn't sound like he gave much thought to me.'

'He probably assumed I would tell you. They will need both of our skills if this virus mutates. Are you in?'

Wakefield nodded. 'Nothing is keeping me here.'

Jared

Marney and Millicent waited at the table in Saint Kinga's Chapel. Jared lingered at the side, adrenaline keeping him on his feet.

'Thank you for coming, Aleksey.' Millicent spoke through clenched teeth. 'I'm sure we'll be able to get this cleared up quickly.'

Aleksey puffed out his chest. 'Let's hope so because I don't have time to waste with silly games.'

'Of course, you're a busy man,' Millicent said. 'But we need your help to understand what has been happening.'

'Do you?' The sneer in Aleksey's voice was unmistakable.

'Yes. It's clear you think the miners were a necessary evil, but...'

'How convenient to be able to take the moral high ground yet reap the rewards,' Aleksey growled. 'Don't act like you didn't know what was going on. The committee were informed years ago that life here was not sustainable unless we found an alternative fuel source.'

Millicent's mouth dropped open, and she turned to Marney. 'I swear to you, I didn't know.'

'Liar. And what of him?' Aleksey asked, pointing to Jared. 'Am I to be judged by a child? And one that abandoned his community at that?'

'I'm no child,' Jared said. 'Besides, from what I saw down there, you're no man.'

Aleksey scoffed. 'This is a joke. I saved you all, and you deign to sit in judgment on me.'

'Saved us?' Marney asked, incredulous. 'How can you think—'

'Easily. That's exactly what I did. Do you know what sent Julian Manning crazy? Guilt.'

Jared had been just a child, but he could still remember as clearly as if it were yesterday the way Julian's particles had bounced around the chamber. 'He was unwell; that wasn't his fault.'

'No, *that* wasn't. But Julian designed the air filtration system that was supposed to keep us alive. It didn't take a genius to work out that cutting corners to save time wasn't safe. His design wasn't fit for purpose; that was clear right from the start. It was always going to fail eventually. And that's exactly what happened.'

'What do you mean?' Millicent asked. 'The air is fine.'

'Because of me. Edmond turned a blind eye to Julian's failings and cobbled together a quick fix. Then he disappeared, leaving me to deal with the fall out.'

'My grandfather was a great man.'

'I thought so once, too. Until he left me to clean up his mess. The system was supposed to be self-sustaining. When it failed, we had to look for a fuel source to run it. That forced me to make difficult decisions. I had to act. It has always been the same, living in the shadow of the great Edmond Pearse. He gets the glory. I manage the aftermath.'

'No,' Marney said. 'There must have been other options.'

'Oh, there were. Tell me, which death would you have preferred? Dying on the surface or slowly suffocating?'

Jared looked from one woman to the other. 'That can't be true.' It had been a small solace to him that his grandfather's work had at least saved a fragment of humanity. But if what

Aleksey said was true, he'd abandoned them in little more than a tomb.

'It is.' Aleksey released a long breath. 'I didn't want any of this, you know. But sometimes the difficult decisions, the ones that keep you up at night, are also the correct ones. I think if Edmond were here, he'd have done the same. You know I had no choice. Which brings me to my next question; what exactly are the charges against me?'

'Let's just calm things down,' Millicent said. 'Nobody said anything about charges.'

'Of course you didn't.' Aleksey smirked. 'Because there are none to answer. Every man down there agreed to the arrangement. Victor Durand endorsed it completely. As unpalatable as you might find it, I had no choice. Now, if you'll excuse me, we are midway through a trial if you remember. I have arrangements to make.'

'Aleksey, please wait a moment.' Marney spread her hands on the table and drew in a deep breath. 'We appreciate your efforts. It's all just come as a bit of a shock. But now that we understand what you've been contending with, we could help.'

Aleksey stooped so he was looking Marney directly in the face. 'Do I look like an idiot?'

'No, you look like a man who has far too much weight placed upon him. I had no idea we were in such dire straits.'

Nausea churned Jared's stomach. 'You can't seriously—'

Millicent cut him off. 'We can't assess the situation when we only have half the facts and none of the context.'

'At last, some reason.' Aleksey straightened up. 'What did you have in mind?'

'Let's bring the mines out into the open, make them a legitimate option for workers within the Sanctuary.'

'And how would we do that?' Aleksey asked.

'We'll start with honesty,' Marney said. 'How many mines are there?'

Aleksey hesitated. 'Three.'

'Three?' Marney echoed.

'That's right. I don't oversee them by myself. I have guardians to help with that.' He shot Jared a withering look. 'For instance, Felix ensured the smooth running of the mine you found.'

'Will you show us around the other two?' Millicent asked. 'If we can assess the conditions there, make sure the miners are treated humanely, it would reassure our citizens.'

'Fine. But it's a trek. We'll have to take a cart. Meet me in the west cavern at seven a.m. We'll have to get there and back before the trial recommences.' With all Aleksey had done, it pained Jared to see that he was still calling the shots. 'Now, if you'll excuse me, it's been a tiring day.'

Jared waited until Aleksey left the chapel before he turned on the two women. 'That was it? That was him paying for his evil...' Words failed him, and he got up to leave.

Marney clasped his wrist. 'Don't you see that we have to be smart about this?'

'And that's what you're doing by letting him get away with it? Being smart?'

'Yes. Once we know where the other mines are and who else was part of this scheme, believe me, Aleksey will get what he deserves.'

'What if he was telling the truth?' Jared asked. 'What if one or both of you knew all along?'

Millicent's mouth dropped into a little 'o'. 'Do you really believe that of us?'

'I don't know what to believe any more. So before you even try and argue, I'm going with you tomorrow.'

Marney shook her head. 'I don't think that's a good idea.'

'I asked for neither your opinion nor your permission. If my mother is in one of those mines, I *will* bring her home.'

'I understand how you feel,' Marney said. 'You aren't the first to lose a loved one down here, and I doubt you'll be the last. So come if you must.'

Millicent's eyes widened. 'You can't be—'

Marney held up a hand to silence her. 'Be there promptly in the morning and don't tell anybody else about this.'

Jared kept his promise, so he was bemused when the following day, he found himself filing through the tunnel with at least fifty other citizens.

He spotted Millicent on the other side of the crowd. 'Why are all these people here?'

Millicent swept her silk shawl over her shoulder. 'Word somehow got out.'

'It wasn't me.'

'My dear boy, I never suggested it was. Keeping a secret in this place is impossible.'

'What do they want?'

'The same as you. They're hoping for a miracle, that their loved ones might be returned to them.'

'I can't imagine it,' Jared said. 'My mother has been missing only a few days, but the worry has been torturous.

Some of these people might have been missing their relatives for years. It's the uncertainty that's the worst. Maybe...maybe it was a kindness to let Sienna think her father was dead.'

'Perhaps. Sometimes I think it is a blessing that I only have myself to worry about here. I never thought it would pay off being an independent old shrew like me.'

'Right.'

Millicent laughed. 'Please, don't feel obliged to correct me.'

Jared frowned. 'Did I say the wrong thing?'

'No, you are as authentically you as ever. Don't ever change.'

Confused, Jared said, 'Okay.'

'Besides, you can flatter me all you like, you're still not coming with us.'

Jared's hackles raised. 'I told you...'

'I know, but look at all these people. I can't show favouritism. I promise, if Laura is—'

'I'm not arguing with you. If you try and leave me behind, I swear I will round up these people and lead them right down that track behind you.'

'Then I guess you leave me no choice.' Millicent clambered into the cart and arranged the purple material of her skirt.

The crowd behind them dulled to a murmur, and Jared looked over his shoulder to see Aleksey stalking towards them.

'Have you seen Marney this morning? She should be here by now,' Aleksey asked, ignoring that he was late, too.

'I'll do a lap and see if she's here,' Jared said, happy to be out of Aleksey's orbit for as long as possible.

'If she doesn't get here soon, we'll have to go without her,' Millicent said. 'This crowd is getting tetchy. It won't be long before they stop requesting and start demanding answers.'

Jared made a wide arc around the gathering citizens. He wasn't sure he recognised their faces, but they certainly knew him, as his name was uttered and repeated throughout the chamber. So it was a relief when he saw a familiar face.

'Can I talk to you for a minute, please?' Seb beckoned him into a nearby tunnel.

Jared followed him so far into its depths that he feared he wouldn't get back to the cart in time. 'Is everything okay?'

The last thing Jared saw before his sight fragmented into shards of white hot pain was Seb's fist.

'I'm sorry,' Jared heard Seb say, before the darkness pulled him under.

The Book of Evelyn

It took two days to move the hives. To be honest, it was a relief; busy work to take our minds off Riley's impending departure. We shuffled towards the site of the new apiary, a hive suspended between us.

'Do you know many people in Colony 3?' I asked.

'I know all of the original swarm. Although, I imagine they've taken in some new members by now. Petra is bossy but nice.'

'By the sounds of it, you'll only be working with her for a short time.'

'I wouldn't be so sure about that. She'll be as reluctant to hand over her bees as me.' We set the hive down, and Riley ran a palm over the box.

'I am sorry. You have to believe that I had no idea Bug would do this.'

'I do believe you. That doesn't mean that it doesn't hurt.'

'I know.'

'What if Rhiannon comes here looking for me?' Riley's voice caught in her throat.

'Then I'll tell her where you are, and she'll come to find you. Are you all packed? Have you said all your goodbyes?'

'I guess. I don't have a lot to pack. And it's not like I put down many roots here. That's pretty pathetic, isn't it? I've spent almost half my life here, and you're my best friend.' Her eyes were watery when they met mine. 'You're the only goodbye that I care about.'

I pulled her to me. 'We will see one another again, won't we?'

When I let her go, she swiped the tears from her face with her sleeve. 'I hope so. It's time I got moving.'

Dale was driving her to Colony 3. When Riley and I headed to his truck, he was already loading up the surplus supplies he planned to trade with the other group. 'Are you ready? I want to be back before dark.'

'As I'll ever be.' Riley gave me one last hug. 'Don't take any of his crap while I'm gone, you hear me?'

'Never.' I watched the horizon long after the truck disappeared behind it.

I was sitting on the porch of Pearl's unit when Dale's truck pulled back into the gate. The engine's thrum still hung in the air as he raced towards Bug's workshop. I'd have ignored him except for the fact that Riley trailed behind him.

'She came back.'

'Clearly,' Pearl said. 'Let's find out why.'

Dale was already relaying the facts to Bug when we entered. 'Completely empty. The whole Colony has disappeared.'

Bug paled. 'And there was no obvious reason?'

'Nothing.'

'Everything, including the apiary and all the equipment, looked fine,' Riley said. 'But the Colony was gone.'

'Can we raise a Queen from our hives?' I asked. 'If we can transplant it into the—'

'Evelyn, we aren't talking about the bees,' Bug said. 'We mean the people. The residents of Colony 3 have vanished.'

~

Laura

They heard the crowd long before they were close enough to see them. 'Who's that?' Laura asked, but if she was honest with herself, she knew.

Helen peeked from the window before jabbing a finger in Janet's direction. 'You stay inside.'

Laura followed her. 'You know those people?'

'Unfortunately.'

Laura, too, recognised one of the women at the front. Agnes headed straight for them. 'None of us wanted it to come to this, Helen.'

'Whilst it's very neighbourly of you, it's not a good time for visitors. We were just sitting down to supper.'

A man spat on the floor in front of them. 'You know why we're here.'

'I can honestly say I have no clue, John.'

'Send out your mother, and we'll let you get back to your meal.'

A mirthless laugh escaped Laura. 'You think we could eat whilst you do goodness knows what to that poor woman.'

'What you choose to do is up to you,' John said. 'But she's coming with us. Now, get out of our way.'

The group surged towards them.

'This is our house!' Helen's voice was shrill and all but drowned out by the crowd. 'Get back.'

John shoved past her, and the others followed. Seconds later, they appeared, dragging Janet between them.

'Girls, help me!' Her fingertips brushed Laura's as she was propelled forward on the wave of people.

'Where are you taking her?' Helen weaved between the

people, trying to reach her mother. 'Are you taking her to the prison?'

But Laura knew that couldn't be true. It was the shore they were heading towards.

'Stay out of this, girl!' John slapped Helen hard around the face. The jolt snapped her head backwards, and she tumbled to the ground. 'I mean it!' While she lay defence-less, he booted her hard in the chest.

Laura looked back at her friend, curled in the foetal position. Torn between stopping and helping her and following Janet, she chose the latter, knowing it was what Helen would want. 'Please, let her go!' Laura grabbed John's sleeve.

'This has to be done. We have to end this before it goes any further.' There was a soggy crunch as he drove his elbow into Laura's nose. She collapsed to the floor, her sight dissolving into hot white flashes of pain. She didn't know how long she lay there before she willed herself to roll onto her knees.

'Where are they?' Helen was beside her, still clutching her ribs. 'Laura! Answer me! Where did they take my mother?'

Blood was dripping down the back of Laura's throat and she spluttered a mouthful of it into the sand. 'I don't know.' Just ahead of the puddle, black in the moonlight, she saw their footprints. In the middle, Janet's feet had left twin trails as she'd been pulled along. 'There! Look!' Laura scrambled to her feet, and they raced to catch them.

When they reached them, Agnes and John were already up to their waists in the water. The rest of them waited on the shore, silent. Janet was nowhere to be seen.

Helen launched herself at the closest woman. 'Where is she? What have you done with her?'

She looked back, wide-eyed and terrified. Then she pointed a finger towards Agnes and John.

'Oh God,' Laura said. 'She's under the water. They're drowning her.' Laura and Helen sprinted into the surf.

'Stay back,' John said. 'It's the only way to know for sure.'

Helen plunged her hands into the water and pulled her mother's head to the surface. Janet vomited a lungful of seawater. 'I've got you, Ma.'

But their relief was short-lived as several of the spectators waded in and grasped Helen by the shoulders. 'Let me go!' Janet disappeared back into the inky depths.

Laura dived under. It was impossible to see, the water stinging her eyes and leaving her flailing around in the darkness. When she'd all but given up hope, she felt a twig-like arm. To her horror, Laura realised Janet was bound, arm to foot. She pulled her towards the surface.

'Stop this,' she begged as Agnes and John splashed towards them.

'I will not die because of that old witch!' John lunged, arms outstretched.

'Enough!' A voice from the beach brought everyone to a standstill. 'What is the meaning of this?' Malcolm's cheeks were flushed with rage.

'They mean to murder my ma!' Helen helped Laura hoist Janet towards the shore.

'This madness needs to stop,' John said. 'If we prove she's not a witch, then we know it's all lies.'

'And if she is?'

John gulped. 'If that happens, which I don't think it will,

then they'll have to investigate properly. No more of this spiteful finger pointing.'

'I will have none of this hysteria in my ward. Do you hear me? Back to your homes, the lot of you!' The crowd began to disperse into the night.

Helen picked at the knots binding her sobbing mother. 'You stupid woman; do you see what you've done?' Still, once she was free, Helen folded Janet into her arms.

'Thank you, Malcolm,' Laura said.

'They shouldn't have done that.' Malcolm stopped, a few steps from his horse, and turned back to them. 'Still, you can be assured, justice will be done.' By the way he glared down at the embracing women, Laura knew that he meant it as a threat.

The Book of Evelyn

The mystery of Colony 3 spread throughout our community. Nobody could understand why they would abandon their home, equipment and all. But that didn't stop us from speculating.

'An extreme threat would make them move,' Pearl said. 'This isn't the original site of Colony 1, you know. Or even the second. Keeping the inhabitants alive is what matters.'

'That makes no sense. Why wouldn't they take the equipment with them? Or radio to tell us?'

'I have no idea.' But that was a lie, and we both knew it. There was one very plausible reason they hadn't been in contact. The Pack had found Colony 3, and they were all dead.

As for Riley, whenever I talked to her, it was like walking on eggshells. 'You must be relieved that you don't have to go.'

'Relieved that my friends are missing or dead?'

'No, I mean...You'll get to stay here with me.'

'In a place where I'm not wanted. Great.'

She came to find me later that evening. 'I'm leaving, Evelyn.'

'Is Bug making you go to one of the other colonies?'

'No. I'm going to find my sister. Don't you see, there isn't a place for me here any more?'

Guilt swept over my skin like probing fingers. It may not have been my idea to take her place, but I hadn't fought it. If I'm honest with myself, I only said what I did next on the assumption she'd argue with me. I never imagined she'd agree. 'Then I'll go with you.'

'You'd do that for me?'

'Of course.'

She threw her arms around me. 'You just wait; you'll be like a third sister to us.'

Looking at her beaming face, how could I take it back? Like that, I'd agreed to leave the Colony.

As I packed my bag, I told myself it was just short-term. I'd help Riley find Rhiannon, and then I'd return, telling her that she belonged with her family and me with mine.

I was surprised to find that I really did want to be with Ruth. I realised, as I said what could have been my final goodnight to her, that the discontent I'd felt with our new life was of my making. A scab had formed over my heart, and I refused to stop picking at it. Daily, hourly even, I reminded myself that people were not to be trusted. And the more I reminded myself, the more that scab would itch. So I'd rip it off, draw fresh blood. An accusation tossed at Ruth, a refusal to follow an instruction from Dale, it was all new pain to confirm what I suspected all along. I did not belong there. If something didn't change then I'd be destined to follow that same pattern of heal, itch, pick forever. Taking Riley's job, guilt free, could be the catalyst I needed.

'It's my fault that I lost her,' Riley said as we crept towards the exit. 'I may have been small, but I remember. Rhiannon asked me to go with her.' Riley hesitated, reluctant to tear open her own scab. 'Bug persuaded me to stay. Said I was too young and that I could go and find her when I was a little older. At least, that's what I tell myself. The truth is, I didn't want to go back out there. I was tired of being thirsty and hungry. Tired of being tired.'

'That's understandable. How did she take it?'

'I don't remember exactly. Just that she wore this huge smile that I knew was fake. She told me she'd come back for me soon. But we've moved three times since then. I guess she couldn't find me.'

I pictured an older version of Riley, turning up at the gates of the original site to find it abandoned. 'That's awful. But that wasn't your...Shouldn't we be heading for the gate?'

Riley smirked. 'Well, Dale took your mother from you. Maybe we should return the favour by taking the thing he loves the most.'

'Himself? There's no way I'm taking him with us.'

'His truck.'

I gave it some thought. What was the worst he could do to us if he found out? Besides, if my plan went as I hoped, he'd get it back soon enough. 'The bodywork is a little rusty, and it makes an annoying droning noise. That sounds like a fair trade for Ruth. I guess I could try and swipe the keys.'

Riley jangled them in front of me. 'I told them I was looking for you. These were just sitting on the table, tempting me. And that's not all I took.' Riley reached into her bag. 'What do you think?' she asked, pulling Dale's baseball cap down over her eyes.

'That nobody will ever think you're him.'

'Sure they will. I'll be sat in his truck, remember.'

For all our bravado, we both slowed our pace as we approached the truck.

'So, which one of us will drive?' Riley asked.

'I think I'd better leave that to you. I don't exactly have a lot of experience.'

'You think I do?' She clambered in and stared down at the pedals. 'Automatics are just big go-karts, right?' Riley jerked the truck forward.

'Are your shoes made of concrete?'

'Feel free to take over.'

I kept my mouth shut.

The gravel crunched under the tyres as she guided us towards the gate.

'Dale drives like a lunatic. They'll know it's not him if you keep going this slow.'

Riley sighed and pushed her foot on the accelerator.

As we neared the gate, she screeched the truck to a stop. 'What now?'

I thought back to the day we'd arrived and the two small, one long toots Dale had given on the horn. I repeated the pattern. Nothing happened.

'What was that?' Riley asked.

'A code. Or at least that's what I thought.' I did it again.

'Shall I just drive?'

'What? Through the gates?'

'Yeah.'

'I'm pretty sure this thing would disintegrate on impact.'

Riley covered her face with her hands for so long that I worried she might be crying. Then she started smashing the wheel in a furious crescendo of honks and squeals.

'All right, Dale, you impatient arse.' The voice came from the lookout post above us. As the gate began to open, I cupped my hand over my mouth, trapping my cry of joy within.

We pulled away, Riley accelerating so fast that my head

was forced back against the seat. Neither of us dared speak for the longest time. But I couldn't help but grin. I felt more excited than I had about anything since I could remember. Winding down my window, I yelled into the night, 'We're coming for you, Rhiannon!'

Chapter Ten

Excerpt from *A Societal Analysis of the Bee Colony*

The Queen

The Queen is the only bee capable of laying fertilised eggs. Although a Queen's life expectancy is approximately five years, she only produces eggs for two or three. Without an egg-laying Queen, who can lay up to two thousand eggs in a single day, the hive is weakened and will eventually die.

Should a hive become 'queenless', the workers can create a new Queen bee. They achieve this by feeding a young larva, which would have been otherwise destined to be a worker bee, a diet of royal jelly. This is only possible up to a certain point before it becomes too old to convert. Without a Queen, the worker bees may lay their own eggs. However, unlike their Queen, worker bees have never performed a mating flight. This means their eggs will be unfertilised and can only produce male drone bees. With no fertilised eggs, the colony will most likely perish.

To increase the chances of creating a viable Queen, the workers will often create more than one. However, this does not lead to an oligarchic government. Reality in the hive is far more brutal. When the first Queen hatches, she will kill any competition with the potential to dethrone her whilst they are still in their cell. She achieves this by stinging them. Unlike worker bees, a Queen's stinger has no barbs, so that she can stab with it as many times as necessary. Should two Queens hatch simultaneously, a royal death match will ensue, with the winner taking the metaphorical crown.

Wakefield, R. (2025) *A Societal Analysis of the Bee Colony*. Third edition. London: Feisty Scholar Publications.

The Book of Evelyn

Riley pulled the bottle away from my lips so that water sloshed down my shirt.

I swiped at the growing wet patch. 'Careful!'

'Sorry, but we need to ration.'

'I know, but you making me spill our water all over myself isn't going to help.'

We drove, just the hum of the engine between us.

'You aren't regretting coming with me, are you?' Riley asked.

'I want you to be happy.' It wasn't exactly an answer, but it was the truth. Besides, leaving Riley settled with her sister was the only way I would ever feel good about taking her job.

'All I'm saying is I can turn around if you've changed your mind.'

We were playing a game of chicken, and we both knew it. All sunlight had disappeared, taking a good portion of our courage with it. But neither of us wanted to be the one who asked to go back. 'No, I'm good.'

'Okay then.'

I rested my temple against the window, each bump in the road making it thud against the pane. I didn't mind. The adrenaline of our escape had dwindled, leaving only the darkening landscape for entertainment. All I could see were the outlines of dying trees silhouetted against the twilight sky.

I watched a star, brighter than the others, in the wing mirror for a while. It was when it fell, rose, and fell again that I realised it wasn't a star but a headlamp mimicking the undulating pattern of the road.

'Riley, they're following us.'

She strained to look over her shoulder, apparently forgetting she had mirrors. 'I don't see anything.'

I tapped the glass of the mirror. 'See that light. I think it's a motorbike.'

As if to confirm my theory, it swerved from left to right.

'Crap.' Riley put her foot on the gas.

'Why would they follow us? What happened to us being free to leave whenever we like?'

'Yeah, but they didn't say we could take Dale's truck with us.'

'Good point. Should we pull over?'

Riley gnawed at her lip. 'No. We keep going.'

I kept my eyes trained on that single light. It seemed to swell in size. 'I think they're getting closer. Can we go any faster?'

Riley shot me a glare, and I didn't ask again.

Even in the dim light, as I looked back in the mirror, I could see it wasn't a motorbike following us but a car with one headlamp out. Soon, it was right behind us. It swerved from side to side, trying to find space to draw up next to us. Riley was hugging the centre of the road, weaving her own jagged path.

'Good, don't let them get in front of us.'

The car hit the back of our truck and metal grated against metal.

Riley's knuckles were white as she gripped the wheel. 'Are they crazy?'

The road widened, and the car scraped along our side until their window was level with ours. I expected to see

Dale scowling. Maybe Ruth would be thin-lipped and furious in the passenger seat.

But it was Rex who waved a gloved hand at me, and I screamed.

Riley's fingers dug into my shoulder. 'What's wrong? Who is that?'

Before I could answer, Rex accelerated past us.

'Look, I think he's lost interest,' Riley said as Rex's car disappeared out of the reach of our headlights. 'Whoever it was, he was just playing mind games.'

'Turn around. We need to go back to the Col—'

Thankfully, Riley's reflexes were good, and she slammed on the brakes. My seatbelt bit at the side of my throat and snapped me back, knocking the wind from me.

Rex's car straddled the road. Our truck had stopped with centimetres to spare, so that, if there hadn't been two windows between us, I would have been able to reach out and rake my fingernails down his face.

'Reverse the truck. Reverse it now!'

Riley did as instructed, turning the wheel to begin a three-point turn. As they neared the edge of the road, the back wheels sank. When she tried to accelerate, they spun uselessly.

'Come on!'

'I'm trying!' she yelled back at me.

I strained to see Rex and immediately wished I hadn't. He ran his tongue over his lips and then cackled silently from behind his window.

'Please, try again,' I begged.

This time the wheels caught, and we made it back over

the hump. As we sped away, I fixed my eyes on Rex's car as it disappeared into the distance.

'Was he a member of the Pack?' Riley asked. 'The one who took Cory?'

Words deserted me.

Riley grabbed my shoulder and shook me. 'Will you calm down and talk to me.'

'I am calm,' I said between gulped breaths. 'Why...why isn't he following us?' I stared at the inky landscape around us, expecting his headlight to blink on at any second. 'We need to get back to the Colony. The rest of the Pack must be close.'

'Evelyn, was that the one who tried to hurt you and your mother?'

I looked at her through wide eyes, wondering how she hadn't recognised him for who he was as soon as she'd seen him. 'Yes. That was the devil.'

~

<u>Marney</u>

<u>Before the Sanctuary</u>

The journey went as Stuart planned. Although the media coverage, before it dwindled to nothing, said all planes were grounded, they soon found themselves soaring towards Poland. It appeared the rich and powerful retained control of the sky even in their apocalyptic reality. When they touched down, they were ushered into first a car and then a bus. They followed instructions, praying that Stuart had known what he was doing.

Even with the addition of Wakefield to their number, it took only minor cajoling to let them aboard. With the odd white lie claiming a clerical error, the exaggeration of the importance of their 'team' to the Sanctuary, they were waved through every checkpoint. At a couple of junctures, she'd had to use her ace card, whispering into the right ears about the vials of the vaccine that she carried locked in her case, ready to replicate once she reached her destination. She left out the fact that it also contained samples of the virus.

'You have a way of making people do as you say, Marney,' Wakefield said.

'She sure does.' Ben shepherded the girls in front of him as they got off the final bus on their journey. They were all exhausted, but if that was their only complaint, Marney was happy. Things could have been so much worse.

'It's just luck,' Marney said. 'I think the guards want to get this over with as much as we do. Being stuck outside right now can't appeal to anybody.'

'Well, thank you,' Wakefield said. 'I wouldn't have

persuaded them alone. I've never been much of a people person.'

'Really?' Marney asked in mock surprise. 'I hadn't noticed.'

The three adults stood shoulder to shoulder, surveying the place they hoped would become their new home.

'Not exactly welcoming, is it?' Ben said, looking up at the barbed wire.

'I don't care if they install a portcullis and a moat if it means we're safe inside,' Marney said. 'Come on, girls. Mommy has some persuading to do.'

The first guard she spoke to didn't respond past a pointed finger. It led them to a looming black building.

'Cosy,' Ben said.

'Is this where we are going to live?' Jodie asked.

'Maybe.' But what Marney was really thinking was, *Please, God, make them let us in.*

They joined a queue. 'Very orderly,' Wakefield said. 'That bodes well.'

Marney stood on tiptoes and saw the guards checking credentials with painful vigilance. 'Yes, but we might have more chance of getting through if they were a little more slapdash.'

'Credentials.' The guard stuck out his hand. Marney placed Stuart's pass on it.

The guard glanced at it. 'I'm going to go out on a limb and say that's not your picture.'

'No, it's a colleague of mine—'

'Next!' the guard yelled over her head.

'Please. Listen to me. Sadly my friend died and—'

'If you don't have the correct credentials, I can't let you in.' He waved for the people behind her to step forward.

'Don't you dare dismiss me like I'm nothing.' Marney jutted out her jaw, hoping she looked braver than she felt. 'I am Doctor Marney Wallace, and I demand—'

'I don't care who you…' The guard stopped talking as another man in the same blue uniform walked towards them.

'Is there a problem?' he asked.

'The lady here won't move. She's holding up the queue.'

'Please,' Marney said. 'I've been sent as a replacement for Doctor Paul Stuart, your virologist. If you let me speak to Edmond Pearse, I can clear all of this up.'

'Caleb, you know the rules as well as I do,' the guard said. 'We can't let anybody through without the correct papers.'

Marney saw that Caleb wasn't looking at her but down at the girls. 'Yes, but it won't take a minute to check with Doctor Pearse.'

The guard huffed. 'Do what you want then. But don't say I didn't warn you. David is going to be pissed.'

'Thank you,' Marney said, edging between the two men. 'He will want to see me.'

'Follow me,' Caleb said.

'Them too.' Marney nodded towards Ben and Richard. 'This is my husband, Ben. And this is Doctor Wakefield, an integral member of my team.'

Caleb shrugged. 'Mind your head and hold onto the rail.' They followed him through the door and down a winding set of stairs.

'Mommy, I don't like it,' Emma said.

Marney wanted to tell her that neither did she. Instead, she grasped her hand tighter.

They reached a platform. Vaulted stone ceilings dwarfed them.

'This way,' Caleb said as they trailed behind him through a tunnel.

'Where are you taking us?' Marney asked.

'To see Doctor Pearse, as you requested.'

Finally, they reached a huge set of doors. Caleb pushed through them. 'Careful on the steps.'

Marney blinked back stars as they stepped into a serene white light. As her surroundings came into focus, her jaw dropped. 'This is beautiful.'

They followed Caleb through an ornate hall carved with religious figures. Their footsteps bounced around the vast space and assaulted them from every angle.

'He's through here.' Caleb thumped on the door at the back of the hall before stepping through. 'Doctor Pearse, I have visitors for you.'

Pearse was hunched over a pile of paperwork. The first thing Marney noticed were the tufts of hair that stuck up, haphazard, at the back of his head. Next were his eyes, a sparkling blue.

He looked at them over the top of his spectacles. 'Is that right?'

Marney swallowed, and her fear slipped down like a stone. 'I'm Marney Wallace. Doctor Paul Stuart sent me. I think there are some things you and I need to discuss.'

Edmond stared at her for so long that she began to fidget. 'Well,' he said finally, 'I guess you'd better sit down.'

The Book of Evelyn

I leant across Riley and tooted the horn over and over. Then I wound down the window, no longer caring whether the guard on the lookout post saw me, and yelled into the night. 'Open up.'

The gates to the Colony lurched open, the hinges groaning as if I'd awoken them in the same way I had the people filing from the nearby dorms.

'I hate to state the obvious,' I said, 'but we are in so much trouble.'

'It was my idea. I'll make sure they know that.'

A small crowd gathered around us. Suddenly they parted, and Dale stormed through.

'You little...' He grabbed the top of my arm, his fingers grinding my flesh against my bones.

'Get your hands off her.' Riley shoved him hard, and he held her back with his other hand.

'Dale!' Ruth followed in his wake through the crowd. 'What are you doing? Let them go.'

Dale froze. 'But she—'

'But nothing. *I* will talk to *my* daughter.' Ruth shot him a glare, silencing him.

'Whatever.' He pushed us both away and made his way back towards his cabin.

'Asshole!' Riley rubbed at her collarbone, a red patch visible over her t-shirt where he had grasped her.

'Are you both okay?' Ruth asked.

I wanted to say no, that the very monsters that haunted my nightmares, that I feared were ready to pounce the moment that we stepped outside, really were there, lurking in the shadows. But I looked at the faces around me, and I couldn't bring myself to say it, to appear vulnerable to them. Instead, I said, 'I'm fine.'

'You scared me, Evie.'

'Evelyn,' I corrected.

'Fine. Evelyn, what did you think you were doing?'

I stared back at the gates as they finally clunked shut, wondering if they would be strong enough to keep out the Pack. 'We went to find Riley's sister.'

'On your own?'

'Would you have helped us?' Riley asked. She eyed the colonists around us. 'Would any of you?'

'Well, you'll never know for sure now.' I hadn't noticed Bug lingering at the periphery of the crowd. 'But I certainly wouldn't have sent you out there unprepared. Have I ever let you down before?'

Shame overwhelmed me. 'I guess not.'

'Our rules are there to keep you safe, not to hold you prisoner,' Bug said. 'But if you were set on this idiotic mission, you should have spoken to me. There were better ways to go about it than stealing from us.'

'I didn't mean...' Mean to what? Steal from them? Seem ungrateful? Because I had done both of those things with zero regard for the Colony. 'I'm sorry.'

'It doesn't matter.' Bug turned away from me. 'We'll discuss your departure in the morning.'

'No! Wait. I saw...I saw Rex. I think they've been watching us.'

Bug stopped in his tracks. When the group broke out into panicked murmurs, he said, 'Be calm. The fences are fortified, and we have lookouts on every tower.'

Michelle stepped forward. 'But if the girls have led the Pack here...If they know where we are...'

I simultaneously wished she'd finish her sentences and was glad that she didn't. 'I'm sorry. I didn't consider the fact we were leading him here.'

Bug cocked his head. 'No, you didn't, did you?' He sighed. 'This changes nothing. We go on as we have always done. The rest of you, back to bed. Evelyn, Riley, come with me.'

Although uninvited, Ruth trailed after us. 'Do you think they've been looking for us? It's been years since we escaped them? Surely they've moved on.'

He pushed open the door to his cabin. 'They hold a grudge. They've found us before, and they'll probably find us again.'

'Then why have I never seen them before?' Riley asked.

Bug rifled through a pile of papers. 'We don't go about scaring children by telling them things they don't need to know.'

I thought about the Sanctuary and the bedtime stories we had grown up hearing. Cannibals that would hunt you down and gobble you up. Only now they weren't stories. I was living it.

'We deserve to know if we're in danger.' Riley leant closer. 'What about my sister? Did you warn her before she left?'

Bug ignored her questions. 'Where is my map?'

'Answer me!' She yelled into his face, and we all froze.

Bug took off his glasses and polished off the bit of spittle that had landed there with the bottom of his t-shirt. 'Yes,

Riley. I warned your sister before she left. The Pack are the very reason we wouldn't let her take you.'

'Wouldn't let her? I thought she agreed to leave me. She told me the plan was to come back for me once she met up with another group.'

'Yes, I think that was her plan. But it wasn't one I would ever allow until you were old enough to decide for yourself, to understand the risks.'

'You had no right to keep us apart.'

Bug pushed his glasses back up his nose. 'I needed to protect you. Riley, your sister is gone. And if I had let you go, you'd be lost to us, too.'

'That's not true. She sent me a note.' Riley pulled the scrunched-up piece of paper from her pocket.

Bug smoothed it out. 'This is a trap. They were trying to lure you to them.'

I couldn't deny that it made sense. The way they were there every time we went looking for Rhiannon; of course they knew. 'Riley, I'm so sorry.'

'No.' Riley shook my hand from her shoulder and backed towards the door. She jabbed a finger towards Bug. 'This is your fault. If you had let us leave together, we could have looked after one another.'

'That's not tr—'

'Murderer!' She spat the word at him and stormed from the cabin.

Bug let out a long wavering breath as he continued to dig through the pile. Finally, he pulled the battered map from the bottom. 'I have to warn the other hives that the Pack are around. Show me where you saw him.'

I traced my finger along the route Riley and I had taken.

'It was here.'

Bug marked the point in pencil.

'I am sorry.' It sounded feeble, but I didn't know what else to say.

When Bug didn't answer, Ruth gave my forearm a gentle squeeze. 'He knows. Come on, we should let him work.'

I didn't think I would sleep that night, but I did. I dreamt somebody was following me, cloaked in a mist. I wasn't frightened. In fact, I wanted to see them. Something told me that they would have an answer for me, that they would have a plan to get us out of the mess we were in. Maybe it was you.

I tried to ignore the voices for the longest time, to persuade myself that it was just Dale and Ruth in the little kitchenette outside my door. But pulling the blanket over my head couldn't hide the fact that the noise was not coming from inside the cabin but from outside my window. Eventually, I threw back the covers and looked.

It appeared that every member of the Colony stood in the field beyond the cabins. I pulled on my jeans and headed out to join them. Shuffling between the people, I tried to piece together what had happened from snatches of their conversations. I needn't have bothered. It was blatantly clear as soon as I got past them.

The cracked wood of the hives lay around the apiary. Not a single structure was intact. I listened for the familiar thrum of the bees behind the shocked murmuring. It was futile. Even if I stood there completely alone, I knew I would hear nothing. They were gone.

~

Jared

Jared woke with a start. The jolt sent pain searing down his neck. Probing the back of his skull, he checked his palm for blood.

'I didn't mean for you to bang your head.' Seb was crouched next to him. 'Are you okay?'

'What do you mean, am I okay? You hit me!'

'I know. Please believe me, if there was some other way...'

'For what? I don't understand.' Jared scanned the tunnel around them. It looked like so many others in the Sanctuary, smooth walls glittering even in the dim light. The difference was that it was deathly silent.

'I dragged you here,' Seb said. 'I couldn't let you get in that cart.'

'You, of all people, should understand. I have to find my mother.'

'I do.' Seb picked up a fragment of salt rock and threw it against the wall. 'But you never would have made it to the mine.'

'What do you mean?'

'Jared, there are people in here who want Aleksey gone.'

'So do I. And I know once the citizens see for themselves—'

'No. The resistance are taking far more direct tactics.'

Unease danced over Jared's skin, giving him the urge to jump to his feet and run. 'Tell me what they have planned.'

'A bomb. It will detonate when his cart passes.'

'That's insane. Murder isn't the way to deal with this.' Jared tried to get up, but his pulse throbbed in his eyeballs, pushing him back to his knees.

'Murder and justice; the resistance wouldn't be the first people in this place to get the two mixed up.'

'You can't agree with what they're doing.'

'Not completely, no. But at least they are *doing something*. And with them in charge, Isaac will get some sort of justice.' Seb held out his hand and pulled Jared to his feet. 'But I couldn't let you become collateral damage. Not after you saved me.'

'I need to stop this.' Even putting one foot in front of the other made the world spin. Jared clutched the wall of the tunnel, trying not to vomit.

'You should stay and rest,' Seb said. 'It's already too late.'

'I have to try.' Jared heaved himself along the tunnel wall. 'Don't try and stop me.'

'I won't,' Seb called after him. 'But please don't tell them I told you, or I'll be next.'

When Jared reached the lit chamber at the other end, he tried to puzzle out where he was. It looked much like the cavern where the Guardian Elite began their orienteering expeditions, but he knew he could be wrong. It had been so long, and they were all nearly identical.

Jared felt the explosion through the wall of the tunnel first, the vibrations travelling through his palms. The air was sucked from the tunnel, pinging his eardrums. His skin stung as chips of stone struck him.

Moving on instinct, Jared headed back towards the tunnel where he'd left Aleksey and Millicent. He was greeted with a wall of rock blocking the tunnel they must have travelled down. Citizens ambled around the chamber, white from dust and shock.

'Why aren't you digging?' Jared asked, trying to pull away a boulder.

Devon crouched against the nearby wall. 'We've tried. There's no shifting all that. Even if we could, they'll be dead by the time we get to them.'

'You don't know that.' Jared wrenched another rock from the pile, but the rubble shifted to fill the gap he'd made.

Marney appeared at his elbow. 'Come away. It's not safe.'

Jared pulled her to him, the anger he'd felt the previous evening forgotten. 'I thought you were with them.'

She shook her head. 'Somebody locked me in my unit. The power was completely dead, too. All I could do was wait.'

Suspicion nagged at him, but he marked it as a problem to be dealt with later. 'Is there another way through? If this tunnel was important enough to have a track, maybe it branches off to other areas. Pull up a map.'

Devon pushed some buttons on his tracking console and handed it over.

'There.' Jared jabbed at the screen. 'We can reach them that way.'

'I'm not going in there,' Devon said. 'It's not safe.'

Marney took the console. 'Give me your torch, too.' She took another from a nearby guardian and handed it to Jared. 'I'll go with you.'

'Are you sure you want to do that?' Devon asked.

'Of course not. But they need our help.'

As they made their way into the tunnel, Jared took a last look at the semi-circle of light behind them. 'Do you think there's any chance they survived?'

'If I'm honest, no.'

'Then why come with me?'

'Because I couldn't let you go alone. Besides, I like to think Millicent would do the same for me.'

Particles of dust danced in their torch beams. They made the air dense, and Jared hacked it from his lungs. 'We must be getting closer.'

They reached the main tunnel a few minutes later. 'It looks clear on this side,' Marney said. 'Maybe we'll be able to reach them.'

Jared hesitated.

'Are you okay?' Marney asked.

'Yes. I guess I'm just a little nervous about what we'll find.'

'Aren't you used to death? If Aleksey is to be believed, you've made it into a spectator sport.'

'The shows are different. There is nothing I could do to change those events, as much as I'd like to.'

'But you still turn them into entertainment.'

'I had to survive somehow. Besides, I don't know those people. However much I disagree with how things are done here, nobody deserves to end their life like this.' Jared navigated his way over a pile of rocks, wobbling as they shifted beneath his feet. He offered Marney his hand so she could do the same.

'Sadly, cave-ins are a reality of living in a mine. We've had a few recently.'

'But it wasn't just a cave-in. A bomb caused it.'

'Who told you that?'

Jared thought what a strange question that was. Not how

he knew or what made him believe that, but who told him. 'Does it matter?'

'Yes. It's a pretty big accusation to make.'

'Well, I believe him.' They reached a mound of rock. 'It doesn't touch the roof of the tunnel. I think I can climb over. You stay on this side in case something goes wrong. Keep your torch on the area above me so I can see what I'm doing. 'Jared started to climb, heaving himself up one boulder at a time. He dug the toes of his shoes into the pile, sending an avalanche of stones down towards Marney. 'Sorry!' Reaching the top, he peered through the gap.

'Can you see anything?' Marney asked.

Jared took his torch from his pocket and shone it into the tunnel beyond. 'Nothing. Aleksey? Millicent?' Grit invaded his mouth. 'Can you hear me?' In return, there was only the patter of falling halite. 'I don't think they made it.'

'Then come down,' Marney said. 'I won't let you risk your life on a pointless rescue miss—'

'Shhh!' Jared wasn't sure he'd actually heard anything more than the rocks settling. But there was something about it. The sound was too rhythmic, too regular. Three short taps, three long, then three short again. SOS. 'Someone is alive back there!' Jared hauled himself over the pinnacle, sending gravel tumbling before him as he slid down the other side. The torch slipped from his grasp and blinked into darkness on the tunnel's floor.

'Are you okay?' Marney called.

'I'm fine. My landing wasn't as graceful as I planned, and I lost my torch.' Jared dropped to his knees and fumbled around, looking for it. Nothing. He crawled further into the tunnel, trying to ignore the biting chips of rock against his skin. Jared's fingers met something metallic. He grabbed for it. As he lifted it, he heard a familiar jingling sound. Millicent's bracelets. 'Millicent, are you hurt? Can you talk?' Jared curled his hands around her cold fingers. 'Millicent?' He felt his way down her wrist to where he knew her head and shoulders must be but found only rock. 'I'm sorry,' he said before gently laying her hand on the floor.

The knocking sound started again with increased urgency. When he headed in its direction, Jared's foot struck something. It rolled until it hit a chunk of salt rock with a tinny ding. He pawed the floor until he found the cylinder of his torch.

Flicking it on, he shone it back at Millicent. Her purple sleeve trailed from beneath jagged slabs. There was no hope.

The regular tapping of SOS had turned to a frantic thump. Jared shone the circle of light on the upturned cart. 'Aleksey, are you under there?' Digging his fingernails under the edge of the cart, Jared heaved. It didn't budge.

Jared searched the ground and found a length of metal from the track. Using it as a lever on a nearby rock, he edged the car up. Aleksey lay underneath, sucking in air like a beached fish.

'I don't know how long I can hold it,' Jared said. 'Can you crawl out?'

'I...I don't know.'

The lever slipped through Jared's sweaty hands. He caught it in time to stop the cart from imprisoning Aleksey again. 'You have to try.'

Aleksey flipped onto his stomach and began to wriggle from below the cart.

'Hurry!' The muscles in Jared's arms screamed at him to let go.

Aleksey dug his fingers into the ground and pulled his legs clear just as the car crashed to the ground. He rolled on his back and lay panting.

Jared waited for him to catch his breath before asking, 'Are you hurt?'

'I think my arm's broken. Probably a few ribs, too. How is Millicent?'

The beam of Jared's torch darted back towards the pile of rocks. 'She didn't make it.'

'Oh God. Who would do this? This wasn't an accident, you know? There was an explosion.'

Jared nodded. 'Can you stand?'

Aleksey clambered to his feet. 'Climbing might be more of an issue.'

'I'll be behind you the whole way.'

'You're a good boy, Jared. I've always said that.'

It took them far longer to reach the top, as Aleksey stopped at regular intervals to catch his breath between pained whimpers. Each time, Jared braced his arms on either side of the ailing man.

'I can't do this,' Aleksey said.

'There's no choice. Nobody else is coming.'

Aleksey fell silent, and for a minute or so, the only sound was the peppered dropping of salt rock fragments. 'I don't have many friends left in the Sanctuary. I'm glad you're home.'

'We aren't friends. But I wouldn't let anyone die if I could prevent it.'

'I admire your honesty.' Aleksey started to climb again.

'It's rare in the Sanctuary nowadays. Jared, have you considered what you'll do next?'

'Find my mother and get out of here.'

'Have you thought about staying?'

'Only in my nightmares.'

'I'm serious, Jared.'

'So am I.'

Aleksey sighed. 'With your support, this place—'

'Let's just focus on getting out of here. I'll go first.' Jared threw his legs over, then yanked Aleksey up after him.

'I was wondering where you had got to.' Marney smiled up at Jared. 'Aleksey, I see you made it out in one piece.'

'Just about. Sorry to disappoint.'

'Don't be like that,' Marney said. 'Is Millicent behind you?'

'She's dead,' Aleksey said.

'No.' Marney cupped her hands over her mouth. 'That's awful. Do you have any idea what caused the accident?'

'Let's call this what it is.' Aleksey's top lip rose in a snarl. 'An assassination.'

~

Laura

Laura looked around, wondering what to pack, but realised that nothing was hers, not even the clothes she stood in. She looked over at Helen, who was sleeping soundly, wedged into the bed next to her mother, and said a silent apology that she wouldn't return the things she took. The women could ill afford to lose anything, even the threadbare dress that Janet had lent her. But if trouble was on the horizon, Laura didn't intend to be there when it arrived. As much as she'd have preferred to have stood with them, she couldn't find her way home if she was locked up or dead.

Helen reached over and swatted her mother, irritated by the snores that Laura had become all too familiar with. 'Will you shut up, Ma,' Helen said before rolling over and adding her own snuffles to the cacophony of noise.

The hinges on the door screeched as Laura opened it, making her grimace. She slipped out of the narrow gap, not risking widening it further.

A breeze blew from the direction of the sea, chilling her through the thin fabric. Laura didn't care. If she hadn't been worried she'd be caught there, she might have even risked a barefoot stroll in the surf. Jared was still small when she'd last seen the ocean, yet the memory was as crisp as if it had happened yesterday. Laura hoped he remembered that too, a day they could cherish before the world fell apart.

A dust cloud caught Laura's attention and interrupted her daydream. It didn't take long for the silhouette of five horses and the men on top of them to come into focus. Laura scrambled back towards the house.

'Stop there, girly!' The man's voice was punctuated by the beating of hooves.

'Janet! Helen!' Laura tripped, tearing a hole in the blue cotton of the borrowed dress. She cursed and dragged herself back to her feet.

'What's with all the yelling?' Helen appeared in the doorway, rubbing her eyes. 'Oh, I see. Well, if you think you can take me, Fion, I could go another round. Get inside, Laura. I'll take care of him.'

But Laura waved her away. 'We're in this together now.'

'Have you got nothing to say to me today, Fion?' Helen called. 'You had plenty to say when you were trying to rip off my dress.'

Fion didn't meet her eye. 'We're not here for you. It's your mother we'd speak to.'

'Really? Are you going to try your luck with an old lady now? Do you have no shame?'

'That's enough,' Malcolm said. 'Where is Janet?'

Laura put her hand on the doorframe, barring the way. 'Resting. She needs it. Or have you so easily forgotten what the villagers tried to do to her last night?'

'They're frightened,' Malcolm said. 'And can you blame them? Her words haven't just brought her character into question, but many of theirs, too. They don't know who to trust.'

'They don't need to fear Janet. She's a good woman.'

'Is that right? Because you seemed to be heading off somewhere when we arrived.'

'I was just seeing what all the noise was about,' Laura said. 'I didn't expect to be chased by five men on horseback.'

Helen sneered at them. 'That sounds about right. You're a bunch of cowards.'

'We aren't here to argue,' Malcolm said. 'How about you be a good girl and wake your ma?'

'First off, I'm no girl. Second, anything you want to say to my elderly mother, you can say to me.'

Malcolm huffed and clicked his fingers at the men behind, and they jumped down from their horses. 'Don't make this more difficult than it has to be.'

Helen backed away into the house. 'What are you talking about?'

One of them grabbed her wrists and dragged her out. 'Come here.'

'Get off her!' Laura sprang towards them, but a second man clasped her around the waist and pulled her away.

'Bring her out,' Malcolm said to the final man.

A petrified squawk flooded Laura with dread. 'Don't you touch me!' Janet bucked and wriggled as she was half carried from her home.

'Janet Horne.' Malcolm jumped down from his horse. 'You are charged with the crime of witchcraft.'

'It's not true!' Helen strained against her captor. 'It's all in her head. Tell them, Ma.'

'I...I don't understand. Where's Fergus? What have you done with him?'

'Listen to me, Ma. Just tell the truth. You made all that cursing business up. You have no powers.'

Janet's confusion seemed to lift. Shaking the man's arm from around her waist, she stood on tip toes so she could look Malcolm in the eye. 'Power. Yes, I have power; and God help you if you lay another hand on these girls or me.'

Laura couldn't tell if it was an act, but Malcolm's jaw dropped. 'Then it's true. Bind her arms and get her up on a horse. She'll confess to everything before this day is through.'

Two of the men wound a rope around her wrists and hauled her onto a horse.

'Please,' Laura said. 'She's just confused.'

Malcolm ignored her plea.

'Fion!' Helen grasped the reins of his horse. 'Don't do this.'

He kicked out so that Helen had to dodge his boot, forcing her to let go. 'Your mother has brought this on herself, Helen. Let the court deal with her now. She's not your problem any more.'

'You scum!' Helen fell to her knees as they rode away.

Laura knelt next to her. 'We'll think of some way to get her back.'

'But she's still in her nightdress. She's going to be so scared and cold.'

Chapter Eleven

Excerpt from *A Societal Analysis of the Bee Colony*

Threats

With their built-in weapon and undeserved reputation for ferocity, it is difficult for some to see bees as vulnerable. The reality is that they are surrounded by threats, not just to the individual but to their very species.

Insectivores such as the skunk will attack a hive, treating the colony inside as an all-you-can-eat buffet. Sucking out the internal juices, they will discard the hard parts of the body. This is a clear sign that your hive has been attacked, and you must take action to prevent further losses.

Threats that are not so easy to spot are parasites and diseases. These can infect not only adult bees but also those still in a larval state. For example, American Foul

Brood (AFB) is caused by a bacterium that kills the larvae whilst still in its brood cell. The bee then decomposes, leaving behind a foul-smelling liquid. Left unchecked, AFB can decimate a bee colony.

The *Varroa Destructor* mite, although minuscule, is another huge threat. Whilst the blood-sucking parasites themselves would have little detrimental effect on the hive, the diseases they carry can be catastrophic. These include the *bee paralysis* and the *deformed wing* viruses. A viral infection would make short work of killing a colony.

Despite the numerous threats facing our honey bee populations, without doubt the single biggest are humans. Destruction of habitat, use of pesticides and climate change are all contributing to dwindling populations. Given that the survival of the human race is reliant on these tiny pollinators, it is clear that we are now becoming the agents of our own annihilation.

Wakefield, R. (2025) *A Societal Analysis of the Bee Colony*. Third edition. London: Feisty Scholar Publications.

The Book of Evelyn

It had to be me who told her; I knew that. She was my best friend.

'No. That can't be true.' She carried on making her bed, her back to me.

'Riley, look at me.'

She did as I asked.

'The hives have been destroyed.'

She stared at me for a moment longer. Then she ran for the door.

I reached the apiary not long after her. But already she was lifting a splintered frame. The fat bodies of dead bees stuck to the rope of leaking honey stretched between the frame and the ground. Riley dropped what was left of her work and sank down next to it.

'I'm so sorry, Riley. You've worked so hard.'

'Who would do this? It makes no sense.'

'I don't know. Maybe it was some freak accident...' I was reaching, and her stony glare told me she knew it.

'This was no accident. Can't you smell it?'

I breathed deeply. There were so many scents I couldn't place, but one cut through them all. The sour bite of vinegar made my nostrils burn.

'Somebody wanted to get rid of them. Those that they didn't manage to kill will never come back. Not while it stinks like this. They'll die without me taking care of them.' She sprang to her feet. 'I bet it was him.'

'Who?' I turned to see Dale marching towards us.

'You girls stay away from there. We've got no clue what they sprayed on the—'

'But you do know, don't you?' Riley took a step towards him.

'What are you talking about?'

'You wanted to get back at us, so you destroyed the hives.'

Dale viewed her through narrow eyes. 'Yeah, that's it. I destroyed years of my brother's...our...work to teach one stuck-up little madam a lesson.'

She opened and closed her mouth wordlessly before she shoved past him. 'Just stay away from me.'

Dale and I were left staring at one another.

'It wasn't me, you know?' he said.

'Yeah, I know. So does she. It's just—'

The clink of metal on metal cut my sentence short. I looked towards the fence, and what I saw brought bile to my throat. Cerato peered through the chain link fence as she ran her blade across the wire. At first, I thought she was trying to cut it. Then, as I noted the lazy way she pulled the knife in zig-zags, I realised we were being summoned.

'You should go back to the cabin,' Dale said.

'Not a chance. I'm not leaving you alone with her, whether she's behind a fence or not.'

As we reached her, Cerato grinned. 'Well, if it isn't my favourite redneck. How are you, Dale? Long time no see.'

She knows his name, I thought. *How could that be possible?*

'I don't have time for your games,' Dale said. 'What do you want?'

Cerato stuck out her lip. 'Rude. First, you all move without telling me where you are going. Then you don't have the courtesy to engage in a little polite conversation.'

'Well, as you can see, we've been the victim of some needless vandalism, so I don't have time for pleasantries.'

'Oh yes, the bees. That's unfortunate.'

'Unfortunate?' A fire had been lit in my belly, and I wanted to scream at her. 'Don't you understand? Those bees were hope that one day life could grow on Earth again.'

'I understand perfectly well, little girl. Probably far better than you do.'

'It was you, wasn't it? You wrecked the hives.'

'Now that's how nasty rumours get started.'

'Just tell us what you want,' Dale said.

She shrugged. 'I'd like to go back to our previous arrangement. Oh, and you need to return what's mine. That seems only fair.'

Dale shook his head. 'Not a chance.'

'Really?' Cerato's voice was a whisper, so I leant a little closer to hear. 'Nobody steals from me, Dale.' Then she stabbed the blade through the wire of the fence.

Despite being a metre away, Dale and I took a simultaneous step back.

Cerato broke into a tinkling laugh. 'Scared you.' She pulled the knife out. 'I mean it, Dale. The girl is mine. I want her back, and I won't take no for an answer.'

The ferocious sun couldn't stop the icy chill that spread over me. The Pack were coming for me.

~

Marney

<u>Entering the Sanctuary</u>

'I'd like to speak to Doctor Wallace alone,' Edmond said.

Ben raised his eyebrows at her. 'I don't think…'

'I'll be fine.'

'Caleb will show you somewhere comfortable you can wait,' Edmond said. After they'd been led out, he turned to Marney. 'You'd better take a seat.'

Marney perched on the chair opposite him. They felt too close with just the narrow table between them.

'So Doctor Stuart sent you in his place? It's rather presumptuous of him—'

'He's dead. Suicide.'

'What? Why would he do such a thing?'

'The virus killed his family.' Marney cleared her throat. 'Stuart had a little girl not much older than mine. He told me in his note that he'd have done it sooner, but he wanted to create a vaccine first.'

'Which he did?'

'Which *we* did. But, yes, Stuart spent a lot of energy trying to fix the evil created by corrupt men.' She let her words hang there, an accusation.

'I'm not like them,' Edmond said. 'I need you to know that.'

'Okay. But didn't someone once say that the greatest failure of all is the failure to act when action is needed?'

'It's not something I'm proud of. Thoroughly ashamed is more like it. But what was I to do? The virus was already out there. If I'd told the world it was concocted in a lab, they'd have torn one another apart.'

'They might have taken more precautions,' Marney said. 'Watching the news, seeing the virus rear its head in a state across the country, they thought they were safe. How were they to know it might be signed, sealed and delivered to their doorstep? Unless, of course, somebody had the guts to warn them.'

'You don't think I wanted to?'

'No,' Marney said. 'I don't.'

'Well, you're wrong. I tried. Do you think I wanted this responsibility?'

'I guess not. So tell me, what did you try?'

Edmond removed his glasses and rubbed the bridge of his nose. 'I first found out from a lab technician where it was developed. She'd already tried contacting the police, anonymously, of course. I can hardly blame her. The kind of men who created this would have had her killed without a second thought.'

'The police didn't listen?' Marney had seen the call log with her own eyes.

'No. They thought it was a hoax. So she came to me. I took it to the government and begged them to warn the public. But their answer was firm. The genie couldn't go back in the bottle. Their efforts would be focused on finding a vaccine.'

'And those responsible?'

'They'd be punished. Later.' Edmond couldn't look at her. They both knew that was rubbish.

'Later? I suppose this end-of-the-world scenario is

working out well for them, then. You can't be held account-able if there's nobody left to judge you.'

'If there is an afterlife, I hope they will get what they're due.'

'Eternal damnation sounds fitting,' Marney said. 'Although, I think they deserved something more immediate to go with it.'

'Yes. Why are you here, Marney?'

'To seek sanctuary, of course.'

'But why did you ask to speak to me specifically?'

Marney squirmed inside. Was he actually going to make her say it out loud? *Blackmail, Doctor Pearse. I'm here to blackmail you.*

'To ask for your help. I have two young girls, and I don't think we can survive up there.'

'I can understand how you feel. I have a daughter,' Pearse said. 'Laura. And a grandson called Jared.'

'Are they here?'

'No. But I hope they'll take up my invitation.' He sighed. 'Even if I give you my stamp of approval, you'll still need to go through a panel before you're accepted. My power here is limited at best.'

'I'll take my chances. I think, once they hear what I have to offer, they will welcome us in.'

'And what is that?'

'In return, I can keep you safe.'

Edmond paused. 'If that's a thinly veiled threat...'

'No. I mean it literally. I have samples of the vaccine with me, and I know how to replicate it. Grant me admission, and I can protect everyone down here.'

Jared

'Are you sure you're well enough to do this?' Marney said. 'You must be in shock.'

'We need to finish this so the citizens can move on.' Aleksey pushed through the door of Saint Kinga's Chapel. 'Besides, I want everyone to see that I'm still alive and kicking.'

'They'll wonder where Millicent is,' Jared said.

'No doubt. That's if the rumour mill hasn't already been turning.'

'Then maybe we should tell them the truth,' Marney said. 'Millicent was a huge part of their lives.'

Aleksey stopped. 'Martin Durand is giving evidence today. One way or another, we will put this whole sorry business behind us. Are you with me, Marney? Or should I start looking for a suitable replacement?'

'Suit yourself.'

'Oh, I will. Now, let's call the first witness.'

Jared was relieved to see Aaron and Beth in the front row.

'Where have you been?' Beth asked, squeezing his hand. 'I've been worried.'

'I'll explain later.'

When the guardians led Kristoff in, he smiled at them.

'You may sit,' Aleksey told him. 'Kristoff, you have known for Durand boys for quite some time, haven't you?'

'Yes. Since back when Oliver was still a Sawyer.'

'You might say you were raised with them?'

'I suppose...' Kristoff faltered. 'No, not really. They were kept apart from us most of the time. We slept in the dorms, ate together in the dining hall, and ran drills together. But Victor Durand kept his three boys close. He claimed we were all one happy family, but we knew the truth.'

'And what was that?' Marney asked.

'Victor Durand would use our bodies as stepping stones if it meant his sons didn't need to get their feet wet.'

A babble broke out in the chapel. 'Quiet!' Having lost his gavel, Aleksey thumped the fist of his good hand down on the table. 'That's speculation, Kristoff. Just stick to the facts.'

'It is a fact. Just look at what happened to Jodie.'

Although it was fleeting, Jared saw Marney's face drop. She composed herself just as quickly. 'My daughter's death is not relevant here.'

'Really? Because I think she's a prime example of what and who Durand would have sacrificed to save his sons. Martin was sick, and Durand told us not to come back without antibiotics. I was there that day, and Luca sent Jodie into that hospital without a thought for her safety.'

Marney stared down at her laced fingers. 'Let's move on, please.'

Kristoff might have been the first, but he wasn't the last guardian to testify that Oliver and Martin gained preferential treatment from Victor Durand. If the witnesses were to be believed, Oliver enjoyed a life of luxury. If Jared hadn't heard Martin's story himself, he might have bought into the narrative of the spoilt rich kid. By the time Martin was called to the stand, Jared was wondering if he'd imagined it.

'Before we start, can I say something?' The quiver in Martin's voice was clear, but still Jared wondered if it was an act. 'Is that allowed?'

'It's your trial,' Marney said. 'If you think it's relevant, then please do.'

'The witnesses from the Guardian Elite, what they said about us being favoured, not having to endure what they did...they were right.'

'Is he trying to get a death sentence?' Aaron whispered.

'I have no idea.' Jared had given up long ago trying to predict Martin's motives.

'Well, that's very honest of you,' Marney said.

'With one exception. Oliver. He wasn't favoured like we were. Far from it.'

Oliver's head snapped up. 'Shut up, Martin. I don't want your help.'

'And I'm not offering it. I just want to tell the truth. Ollie was locked up and starved; Luca even took his eye, all so that he would fall into line. Even then, he tried to reason with us, to make us see the error of our ways. But how do you reason with a madman?'

'Did you at least try?' Marney asked.

'Did *you*?' Martin left the question hanging for a beat. 'Sure, we're grown now, but we were children when he shaped us. You were the adults. You were supposed to protect us.'

'I'm not sure how to answer that,' Marney said. 'But I'd like to try.'

Aleksey cleared his throat. 'You don't owe him or anybody here an explanation.'

'Maybe not. But I think it needs to be said.' Marney took a steadying breath. 'At the beginning, when I saw what Malone and Durand were up to, I tried to stand against them. But I was a lone voice and had no power. Still, I had hope. I thought education was the best antidote to their evil, that you, the children of the Sanctuary, would be enlightened enough to see through them. But they punished me and gagged me, and I let my fear rule me. And I paid a terrible price for that. I watched as my children were conscripted into the Guardian Elite. Jodie paid for my weakness with her life. That regret will haunt me.'

The legs of Aleksey's chair screeched as he pushed it back. 'I think this is a good place to adjourn for lunch.'

'I'm sure you do. But he has a point. Evil prevails when good people stand by and do nothing. However, Martin, our failures do not excuse yours or your father's actions.'

'I know that. I'm not asking to be pardoned. Neither is Oliver. I just want you to understand that if the seeds of evil flourished here, it's the generation before us that tilled the soil.'

Laura

Laura did an awkward half-run to keep pace with Helen. Even Janet's dress, which was slung over Helen's arm, didn't slow her. 'Let's stop and make a plan.'

'I'll tell you what the plan is right now. I'm going to knock heads together until they return my mother.'

'That's an excellent idea. You can spend some quality time with her when you're in the next cell.'

Helen growled. 'And what do you suggest? I need to get her home.'

'I don't know, but I know we need to be smarter than this.'

'It's all my fault.'

'Don't you dare say that. Fion caused this, not you.'

'Maybe what she's been saying all these years is true.' She held up her curled hand. 'If I hadn't been born like this, she'd have been free to go wherever she wanted. Instead, she was weighted down by a lame daughter.'

'Look at me. Do you believe that's true? I doubt Janet would have abandoned her family's land whether she had children or not. Besides, I think you're forgetting the most important point.'

'That she's a mad old bampot?'

'That she loves you.'

Helen swallowed hard. 'I'm pretty fond of her myself.'

'So let's go and talk to them. Calmly.'

Helen nodded but kept up her pace until the prison was in view. Then she paused. 'I recognise that flea-bitten head.' She broke into a run. 'Duncan Murray, I want a word with you.'

Duncan backed away. If the door behind him hadn't been closed, Laura would have considered that a wise move.

Helen clutched his lapels. 'Is she here? Where are they keeping my mother, Duncan?'

Great, Laura thought. At *this rate, I'll be trying to get two of them out of jail.* But she bit her tongue and gave the guard what she hoped was her most pleading look. 'We just want to make sure she's safe.'

Duncan sighed. 'Yes, she's here, but I can't let you through.'

'Why not?' The pitch of Helen's voice matched her rage. 'What is it you think I'm going to do, strap her to my back and ride off into the distance with her?' She barged past him. 'Tell them I overpowered you.'

'No,' Duncan called after her. 'It's because Fion is with her.'

Helen stopped in her tracks. 'And what business is she of his? He's got his revenge on me; isn't that enough?'

Duncan spread his palms. 'That's nothing to do with—'

'Tell me.'

'Ah, Helen, you're going to make trouble for me.' Duncan massaged the skin of his face, giving it a rubbery look. 'Fion is the one who's accused your mother of witchcraft, so he's been tasked with keeping watch.'

'Is that right? Then I'll definitely be needing a word.'

Laura followed her. 'Let me talk to him.'

'I have my own mouth and my own tongue, thank you very much.'

But when they saw Janet, both were left speechless. The only furnishing in her freezing cell was the wooden stool she was perched upon. Still in her night dress, she looked fragile as she swayed upon it. Her teeth chattered, and she wrapped her arms around herself. But as pitiful as she looked, it was the chain around her ankle that made Laura's blood boil. It trailed across the floor, and Fion clutched the other end.

'What. Is. This?' Helen spat every word and somehow made them sound more threatening by doing so in a near whisper.

Fion jumped down from his stool. 'You shouldn't be here.'

'Aye, but I am. I'm here to see you've chained my mother as if she was one of your cows.' Helen lunged towards Fion.

Laura pulled her back. 'Don't give him the satisfaction. He'd love to see you in the cell next to her.'

'Ma, are you well?'

'I'm cold. Have you come to take me home?'

'I don't think we're allowed to right now.' Helen's voice quivered. 'Soon, though.'

Janet slid from her stool and headed towards the bars.

Fion mirrored her, striding towards the cell door. 'You're not supposed to—'

Laura shot him a glare, and he gulped down the last of his sentence.

Reaching through the bars, Janet laced her fingers with Helen's. 'I'm sorry we quarrelled. Can't I just come home now?'

Laura turned to Duncan, who skulked in the doorway. 'How long are you planning to keep her here?'

'It's nothing to do with me. I've just been told to watch the door.'

Fion glowered at him. 'Aye, and you even managed to mess that up.'

'But the magistrate is going to hear her case in the morning,' Duncan added.

'What time?' Laura asked.

'Midday,' Fion said. 'But they won't let you in.'

'We'll see.'

'Can we at least give her this?' Helen held out Janet's dress towards Duncan. 'She'll catch her death in here.'

Duncan pinched the fabric between two fingers and dropped it onto Fion's vacated stool. 'Now, I need you to leave.' He squared his shoulders. 'I mean it.'

Helen squeezed Janet's hand. 'Don't you worry, Ma. I'll be here to speak to the magistrate for you in the morning, I promise.'

~

The Book of Evelyn

Children weren't permitted at the meeting. That was unusual for the Colony. They liked to pretend that every group member had a say, even if it was Bug who ultimately made the decisions.

Not that night, though. I trailed after my mother and Dale, desperate to know what was happening.

'Go back to the cabin, kid. This is for grown-ups only.'

I didn't listen. But when Celine stepped into my path as I tried to enter the dining room, I had no choice.

'It will bore you anyway,' she said. 'Just a bunch of grumpy adults arguing in circles. I wish I didn't have to go.'

Still, I hung by the door, straining to hear. And for the majority of the time, Celine was right. The jeers and grumbles all tumbled into one so that I couldn't make out what they were saying.

That was until Dale intervened. 'Quiet. We aren't going to decide anything like this.'

'Who made you boss, Dale?' I didn't recognise the man's voice, but I instantly liked him.

'Well, we can wait for Bug if you like, but he's in one of his moods, so goodness knows when he might join us.'

'That still doesn't answer my question. You don't have the authority to run this meeting.'

'I'll stand aside for anybody else who wants the job. But right now, somebody needs to take control.'

The low murmur faded.

'I thought not,' Dale said. 'Let's get started. They want us to enter into the same arrangement as before. But right now, we don't have enough food to feed ourselves.'

'What choice do we have?' Michelle asked. 'Believe me, I don't want to give them a damn thing. I know better than anyone how difficult it is to grow anything here. But the alternative...That doesn't bear thinking about.'

'So the whole cycle starts again,' Dale said. 'We never should have let those parasites live off us in the first place. Bug should have made a stand, not rolled over and then run away.'

'He was protecting the Colony,' Celine said. 'We were in a bad way. We weren't strong enough to fight.'

'Because he let them take our food!' Dale's roar silenced the hall. 'I'm sorry, I shouldn't have raised my voice. But I think it's time we fought back. Now, before they take us for everything we have.'

Not one person responded.

'Come on!' Dale said. 'Doing nothing isn't an option.'

'There are children here.' It was Pearl's voice. 'Do we ask them to fight, too?'

'Of course not. Look, let's put it to a vote,' Dale said. 'No veiled midnight attacks. No hit and runs. We fight for what's ours out in the open. Hands up those who are with me.' I couldn't see to count, but in a few moments, Dale quenched my curiosity. 'Cowards.'

'So we try and eke out what extra we can from the greenhouses, increase the foraging expeditions...' Michelle let her sentence trail off.

'And slowly starve to death,' Dale added.

'I think you're forgetting that wasn't the only request they made,' Pearl said. 'What about the girl?'

Blood began to rush in my ears as I wondered how she knew.

'Who told you they asked for her?' Dale asked, echoing my thoughts.

'Because they were always going to, as soon as they found us,' Pearl said. 'Bug never should have let her stay.'

My chest tightened. How could Pearl talk as if I were so expendable?

'Well, he did, and now she's one of us,' Celine said.

'Is she?' Bev asked. 'She's been pretty vocal about wanting to leave this whole time. Maybe we should let them have her.'

The world spun, and I slid down the doorframe. Were they really discussing handing me over to the Pack?

'What's wrong, Dale?' Pearl asked. 'Not so keen to put this one to a vote? The truth is, Bug calls the shots around here, and we all know it. I, for one, can wait a few more hours for him to pull himself together.'

I didn't realise she was leaving until she burst through the door next to me. A trail of Colony members followed her.

'It's only going to get worse!' Dale stood at the door, shouting at the backs of the exiting people. 'Don't say I didn't warn you!' It was then he noticed me, my back pressed to the wall, pretending I was invisible. 'Do you enjoy sticking your nose where it doesn't belong?'

My jaw dropped. 'I think if anybody should have a say in this, it's me. Well, at least now I know the truth. Nobody here gives a damn about me.'

Ruth appeared behind him. 'Evie, I told you to go home.'

'And you,' I said, jabbing a finger towards her. 'I didn't hear you speaking up—' A high-pitched whistle brought my hands to my ears. 'What is that?'

'A warning,' Dale said. 'Get back to the cabin, both of you.'

Neither of us listened. I outran Ruth as we followed him to the main gate.

'What's happened?' he asked Celine.

'I came straight here for my shift. Look.' She pointed to the gate. A rock, lodged against the post, propped it open. A wheezing whir could be heard from the mechanism within as it repeatedly tried and failed to close.

Dale flew up the ladder to the watch tower. 'It's empty.' I heard a clunk and the gate began to open.

'Don't open it! That's what they want.' As much as I hated to sound like a frightened child, I couldn't help but imagine members of the Pack lurking in the darkness beyond.

Dale clamped his feet on either side of the ladder and slid to the bottom. 'We just need to clear that out of the way, or the motor will burn out.'

'Kayleigh wasn't up there?' Celine asked. 'She would never leave her post.'

'I'm more concerned about where this came from,' Dale said, heaving the rock from the floor. He froze, then dropped it back where it was. There was something slick and dark on its jagged edge. Blood.

'What is it?' Ruth asked.

Dale put up a hand to stop us from following and went through the gate.

'Get your butt back in here,' Celine said, scanning the horizon beyond. It was pointless; the sky was already pitch black.

A moment later, Dale backed through the gate, dragging a body by the feet.

'Oh my God.' Ruth turned away.

Other members of the Colony began to gather, and they echoed her horror.

'Is she…' Celine pulled the curtain of mousy hair from the woman's face. 'Oh, Kayleigh.'

'How did she get down there, on the other side of the fence?' I asked.

'Maybe she opened the gate for them,' Ruth said.

'No.' Celine's jaw jutted. 'She was with us from the beginning. She knew the rules. There is no way she would put the camp at risk by opening that gate.'

'Maybe she betrayed us,' I said.

Dale rolled Kayleigh over. 'Does she look like she was working with them?'

There was nothing I wanted to do less than look at her. Still, I focused on her broken form. One arm jutted at an odd angle as if she'd gained an extra elbow. Her temple was oddly flattened underneath the layer of congealed blood. I was thankful that at least her eyes looked away from me, staring out into the moonless night.

'Somebody pushed her,' Dale said. 'Then they opened the gate.'

I looked at the ladder leading at least ten metres up to the watch tower. Nobody could have scaled the other side without being noticed. 'And it had to be somebody from this side.'

Dale shot me a warning look and gave a near imperceptible shake of his head. 'You see. We have no choice but to fight back. And it has to be now.'

Chapter Twelve

Excerpt from *A Societal Analysis of the Bee Colony*

Bees – The Natural Vaccinators

It is clear that threats to the hive go beyond those from their natural predators. Disease could infect and wipe out a bustling colony.

However, the bee has evolved to guard against this by naturally vaccinating its population. Researchers Harwood, Salmela, Amdam and Freitak (2021) investigated this process. They found that worker bees collect pollen and bring it back to the colony along with any infecting pathogens.

The pollen is then used to make royal jelly for the Queen. After she ingests it, the bacteria binds to proteins in her blood and is subsequently passed to her eggs. This primes her eggs to create an immune response to pathogens in the environment. The Queen uses her own body as a vessel to vaccinate her offspring.

Wakefield, R. (2025) *A Societal Analysis of the Bee Colony*. Third edition. London: Feisty Scholar Publications.

The Book of Evelyn

I climbed into the cargo bed of the truck.

'And what do you think you're doing?' Dale asked.

'I'm coming with you.' I don't want you to think I said that lightly, like I wasn't terrified. The truth was I had spent a sleepless night agonising over it. What was worse, waiting in the Colony for them to come and get me or facing them and showing them that I wasn't some lamb to be led to the slaughter? Neither option appealed, but I was sick of being a victim.

'Not a chance,' Dale said. 'As much as I appreciate the offer, I can't be worrying about you.'

'You don't need to. Cerato will come for me; you know that. And then you can kill her.'

'I don't think she discriminates between potential meals all that much, kid. Besides, I intend to take a more direct approach than that. A shoot first, think later kind of deal. If you want to help, keep an eye on Bug for me.'

'I don't need babysitting.' It was the first time I had seen Bug since the hives were destroyed. I'm pretty sure he was wearing the same jeans and t-shirt I'd seen him in that day.

'I wondered when you'd show up,' Dale said.

'Michelle told me what you have planned. You're insane. They'll kill you all. Then they'll come here and finish off the rest of us.'

Hearing his words, I felt my courage leave me like a punctured tyre. Still, I tried to stand taller. 'You don't know that, Bug. Maybe Dale's right. Maybe we should make a stand.'

'Please, don't get involved.' Bug trailed after Dale as he

loaded his truck. 'No good can come of this. We must be smarter than them, not fall to their level.'

'Look where your way has got us so far. Look where it got Kayleigh.'

Bug stopped in his tracks. 'You think I don't feel bad about that? If I could change places with her, I would do it in a heartbeat.'

'Save the platitudes,' Dale said. 'When the Colony needed you, you hid in your cabin, mourning a bunch of stupid bees. And all the while, the Pack were waiting to strike.'

'We should negotiate.'

'No.' Dale swivelled on his heel and faced his brother. 'You aren't made for leadership, Bug. You never were.'

Bug deflated. 'I never asked for it.'

'You're right. You didn't. And you have done so well. It's down to you that we are all still alive. Now, let me take this burden from you.'

'I...'

'Just think about it.' Dale climbed into the seat of his truck. 'We'll be back as quickly as we can. For now, keep everybody inside the fences. Double the watchtower guards.' He closed the truck door, but at the last minute, he rolled down the window. 'Bug, I'm not trying to take away your accomplishments here, you know? For a time, you were exactly what this place needed. But that time has passed.'

Bug stared long after the gate closed behind Dale's truck. 'Evelyn, I need your help with something.'

'What?'

'You and I are going to visit a mutual friend in the Sanctuary. I need to talk to Doctor Wallace.'

'To Marney? Why?'

'Because she has access to samples of the virus, and we can use it as a weapon.'

'That's a stupid idea. Even if she does have it, you'd put the whole Colony in danger.'

'They're already in danger.'

I followed him to his unit. It smelt of unwashed flesh and abandoned meals. The trays piled by the door confirmed it wasn't in my mind.

Bug spied me looking. 'It's the housekeeper's week off.'

'I don't care what you say; I'm not going back there. You have no idea how they treated me.'

'I can guess.'

'No, you can't. They treated me like a criminal.'

'You're not a child any more, and they have no pow—'

Celine threw open the door. 'Bug, you need to get out here.'

'We're in the middle of something. Whatever it is can wait.'

'No,' I said. 'We're done. I told you, I can't go back there.'

'This isn't just about you, Ev—'

Celine cleared her throat. 'Whatever little domestic you two are having is going to have to wait.'

'What is it?' Bug asked.

'The world is on fire.'

We ran from the unit and stared open-mouthed. Plumes of smoke rose in every direction. Ash danced in the air around us.

'How close is it?' I asked.

'I don't know,' Celine said. 'But the wind will push it our way if the direction doesn't change soon.'

'What are we going to do?'

Bug didn't answer. He turned in a wide circle. Then he darted back to his unit. Celine and I followed.

Inside, Bug was flattening out a map. 'No. It can't be.'

'What's wrong?' I peered over his shoulder. 'That's the hive map. You don't think...'

His face was grim. 'I really hope not.' He rummaged in a drawer and pulled out a radio. It crackled and hissed into life. 'Anya, can you hear me?' No answer. 'Come in, Colony 4. Anya, can you hear me?'

'Maybe they're—'

The radio cut short Celine's sentence. 'Is that you, Bug?' a man asked.

'Yes, it's me. We can see smoke. Thank goodness you're okay.'

'We're not okay. The Pack attacked us. They set fire to our camp.'

'I feared as much,' Bug said. 'But you can rebuild. The people are what's important.'

Static garbled the man's response.

'You're breaking up,' Bug said. 'Say that again.'

'...terrified...killed Anya.'

'Anya's dead?' Bug dropped the radio onto the desk, but the answer still came through loud and clear.

'They burnt her alive.'

∼

Marney
Entering the Sanctuary

They'd spent the last hour waiting for the admission panel to see them. Marney's nerves grew with each passing second, made worse by the fact that Wakefield had gone in before them and not returned.

'He's been in there a long time. Don't you think?'

'Yeah. Richard is definitely the strong silent type, so I'm surprised they've found that much to talk about.' Ben chuckled at his joke. Nobody else did. 'Look, worrying won't change anything, so come and sit down.'

Marney fidgeted on the bench next to him, too distracted to tell the girls to stop racing up and down the corridor.

Ben spoke through gritted teeth to the strangers waiting with them. 'Sorry. They've had a long trip and have energy to burn.' Their silence, devoid of comforting reassurances, spoke volumes; hadn't they all?

When they were finally led into the chamber, all that worry seemed unnecessary. David and Aleksey met them with wide grins and firm handshakes.

David bent down to speak to the girls. 'And who are these young ladies?'

Ben nudged them forward. 'Jodie and Emma.' Jodie stuck out her hand for him to shake, whereas Emma snapped back as if on elastic and clutched onto Ben's leg.

'Pleased to meet you,' David said. 'Are you a betting girl, Jodie?'

She looked up at Marney, frowning, but before Marney could explain, David pulled out a lollipop.

'I'll play you for it. Rock, paper, scissors.'

Marney watched bemused as David made his choices a split second after Jodie made hers, letting her win. As much as she appreciated his kindness, Marney still wasn't sure what to make of him. He was easy on the eye if you liked the coiffed businessman look. Personally, she preferred bumbling librarian. Besides, something about him made her wish he had a dimmer switch. Skin a touch too bronzed, smile a little too white, laugh much too loud; he was intense. Marney thought it must be exhausting living as a caricature.

'Fire!' David shouted, wiggling his fingers under Jodie's paper.

'Hey!' Jodie shrieked with laughter. 'You can't do that!'

'Careful.' Aleksey didn't look up, shuffling through screens on his tablet. 'He cheats.'

But it was Marney who David winked at. 'My game, my rules.' He turned back to Jodie. 'I better get back to chatting with your mom. But for now, I declare you the victor.' He handed her the lollipop. Then he went up further in her estimation when he gave another to Emma, who had been quietly watching from Ben's lap. 'If it's okay with your mom.'

'Of course.'

The girls tore off the wrappers.

'Good. Just remember,' he said to Jodie, 'I will require a rematch at some point.'

That sounds promising, Marney thought, before chiding herself for reading into a throwaway comment made to a child over a game.

'You have a lovely family,' David said.

'Thank you.' Ben shifted Emma into a more comfortable position on his lap. 'Is there anything else we need to do, any more forms to fill in?'

For the first time, David's smile faltered. 'No, not for yourself and the girls. However, I will need to borrow your wife for a confidential chat about her position here. If that's okay with you?'

Ben bristled. 'She isn't mine to lend.'

'Of course not. Just a turn of phrase. I hear you've already met Caleb. He will show you to the waiting area.'

'I'll be fine,' Marney said as her family were shepherded out. Ben was still casting furtive looks back at her even as the door closed.

The space felt massive without the support of her family filling it. Marney wracked her brain for something to say so it didn't seem so empty. 'I thought Edmond Pearse would be here.'

'Sorry to disappoint.' David's tone was salty.

'I didn't mean—'

'Ignore him,' Aleksey said. 'David's used to being his own boss, not playing, how you say, second fiddle. Please be assured Edmond has proved to be a great cheerleader for your application.'

'So is this just a formality then?'

'Hmmm. Not exactly.'

'We still live in a democracy, after all,' David said. 'And we have to ensure the interests of all of our citizens, present and future, are considered.' Marney must have smirked, because David added, 'Is that funny?'

'No. It's just that Benjamin Franklin quote just popped into my head. You know the one. 'Democracy is two wolves and a lamb voting on what to have for lunch."

'Sinister,' David said. 'I like it.'

'I didn't mean to imply that your motives...Ignore me;

I'm exhausted. What other information do you need? I'm happy to supply it. Qualifications, experience; it should all be in my file.' She pointed towards the tablet in front of him.

'Oh, it isn't your suitability that we're questioning.'

'No?'

'Marney, for every person we let in, we have to send ten more away. Each potential citizen must demonstrate their worth, show us that they have skills to help us survive.'

'And?'

'Well, understanding the Dewey decimal system doesn't fall into that category.'

'Ben? You're questioning his admittance.'

'I wouldn't put it like that,' Aleksey said.

David leant back in his chair and steepled his fingers. 'It's a matter of what each person can bring to the table.'

'Ben offers plenty.'

'It's not as straightforward as my friend here suggests,' Aleksey said. 'We need skills, sure. But also, we need citizens with a certain, let's say, temperament.'

'What are you talking about? Ben is the calmest, most—'

David turned around the tablet. However, it wasn't Ben's picture grinning up at them, but the irritated scowl of Wakefield.

'Richard? You're questioning his admission, too?'

'We have to keep a balance,' David said. 'Ben may lack the scientific skills we'd prefer, but he is more likely to flourish in a subterranean setting. Doctor Wakefield, however, is renowned for being...unpredictable.'

'If you have a point, could you make it?'

Aleksey and David exchanged a brief look. 'I didn't

realise you had somewhere more important to be,' David said.

'No, I just don't like hearing my friends and family run down.'

'Richard Wakefield has a worrying medical history. In his teens, he suffered episodes of mania and psychosis. He's still under treatment for depression.'

'And? Plenty of people are. And I think you're forgetting that Richard helped create the vaccine.'

'Yes, but is there anything he contributed that you can't replicate?'

Marney kept tight-lipped.

'I didn't think so.'

'Are you asking me to choose between Ben and Richard?' There would be no competition, but Marney didn't want them to wriggle out of saying it.

'Not at all,' Aleksey said. 'Ben is your family. He has a place here because we want *you*. If you can accept the inevitable.'

'Which is?'

David swiped a finger across the screen, making Richard's file disappear with ease. Marney imagined he would do the same with the real man with as little thought. 'For this place to be a success, we can't accept everyone. It's a simple matter of mathematics. We are already being flexible in admitting Ben to make the Sanctuary an acceptable choice for you because we need your skills. But we have to draw the line somewhere.' David let his sentence hang in the air, appearing to be waiting for her to react. When she didn't, he added, 'You can rejoin your family. But Marney, keep this conversation between us.'

Even if she were allowed, what would she tell Richard? That she'd dragged him thousands of kilometres to leave him stranded? That they intended to use his mental health, a factor out of his control, against him? Their complete lack of empathy astounded her. Worse, she didn't think she had any choice but to accept their terms.

Wakefield and Ben were hunched together on a bench, exchanging furtive whispers.

'What's wrong?' she asked.

'Nothing, hopefully,' Ben said. His dark look told her otherwise. 'Richard has a worrying theory.'

'It's not a theory,' Richard said. 'I'm telling you, that man isn't who he says he is. Marney, do you remember I told you I thought I knew one of the men responsible for the virus? It was David Malone.'

Marney blinked silently at him for a moment. Then she felt suddenly furious. 'I don't want to know. Have you never heard the term ignorance is bliss?'

'No, you don't understand.'

'What do you want for me, Richard? Should I get my young children and march them back into that hell hole on principle?'

'Don't you think we should tell somebody? What if he's dangerous? Your girls may not be any safer here.'

Marney's anger deflated. 'Richard, are you feeling well?'

'Excuse me?'

'These allegations are a little...'

'Crazy?' Richard lowered his voice. 'Who have you been talking to?'

'What? Nobody.'

'Liar.'

Ben placed himself between them, facing Richard. 'I think we need to calm things down.'

'Clearly, she's been talking to somebody about me. Who was it?'

'Richard...I...Look, Paul Stuart mentioned you'd had some difficulties.' She suppressed a pang of guilt, deciding it would make no difference to Stuart any more if she sullied his name.

'How did he even know?'

'You know what those government facilities are like. They do background checks on everyone from the cleaners up. I am so sorry; I didn't mean to upset you. I was just concerned.'

'There's no need. I had a medical issue, and I dealt with it.'

'Absolutely. It's none of my business.'

'All I'm asking is that you hear me out. That isn't David Malone. There are similarities, sure. But that man is younger for a start.'

Marney sighed. 'Perhaps he had a good surgeon. But even if you're right, maybe that's a good thing. I wasn't thrilled about living near a mass murderer.'

'It's probably just a coincidence anyway,' Ben said. 'The name sounds pretty common.'

Richard shook his head. 'I questioned him on some of the facts. The company he ran. What he did there. It all checked out. But it's a different man.'

Marney's heart sank. She so wanted to explain Richard's accusations away, but her instincts were shrieking at her that there was truth to what he was saying. 'You questioned him? Do you think he knew why?' She mentally added, *And is that why he's determined not to let you stay?*

'I don't see how. Do you think it matters?'

'Maybe. Just keep all this to yourself, okay?'

'Surely we should let Pearse or the other guy know.'

'Richard!' Marney hissed. 'Just stop. If you're correct, let's not test how far this man, whoever he is, is willing to go to protect his secret.'

Jared

Sienna placed her tray on their table. 'Can I sit with you?'

Jared considered her question moot, as she pulled out a chair before they could answer.

'Actually,' Beth said, 'I was just leaving, but you two enjoy your meal.' She gave Jared a theatrical wink and whisked her tray from the table. 'I'll see you back in the chapel.'

'Your friend thinks something is going on between us,' Sienna said.

'Ignore her. She's desperate to live vicariously through me.'

'Well, if she's hanging her hopes on me in that regard, she'll be disappointed. I'm done with romance.' She spiked carrots onto her fork but let it clatter onto her plate uneaten. 'Did I thank you for finding my father? I'm not sure I did.'

'No, but there's no need.'

'Of course there is. He's the only family I have now that my mother's gone.' Her brow furrowed. 'But then she's been gone for years. All this time, I've been picturing her on the surface with my father, when actuall...You can't imagine what it's like.'

'No, but I get the feeling I'm in for a steep learning curve.'

Sienna's eyes widened. 'Oh, Jared, I'm so sorry. I wasn't thinking. Is there still no word about your mother?'

'Nothing. It's like she evaporated.' Jared pushed away memories of others in the Sanctuary who had appeared to do the same. Serena Durand's body was never found. The knowledge that she lay far beneath the platform of the entrance chamber belonged to Martin and him alone. They had only found Doctor Reed when his stench began to invade the Sanctuary. Countless others had vanished over the years. 'I didn't even get to speak to her properly before she disappeared. There were things I wanted to say.'

'Like what?'

'For a start that I forgave her, and I wanted her to be happy.'

Sienna nodded. 'Aleksey wants me to say that to Oliver in court for everybody to hear.'

'And are you going to?'

'I'm considering it. Do you think I'm a fool?'

'Not at all.'

'Then tell me what you *do* think. Please, I trust your judgement.'

Jared considered this for a moment. 'I believe he was forced into that life. But still, I'm not sure I could ever be an accomplice to the things that they did.'

'I need a straight answer. Do you think Ollie deserves to die?'

'No. Durand groomed him from an early age, and still, Oliver defied him.'

'Am I crazy to think that underneath that Durand veneer, he's a good person?'

'I don't know him well enough to comment.'

'I'm not convinced I do either. Who knows what made Victor Durand match us up? Perhaps he pulled our names out of a hat. Pure chance.'

Jared suspected he knew. Oliver's guilt over Stephanie Hiatt's death would keep him in the Sanctuary, protecting her daughter. Exactly where Durand wanted Oliver to stay.

'I guess we'll never know. But from what I saw, you cared for each other.'

'We were friends long before...what happened.'

'There we are. And you seem to have a knack for seeing the good in people.'

'It's a curse,' Sienna said. 'I want to hate him. But at the same time, I want him to tell me he's innocent.'

'If it helps, Martin said it was Luca's hand on the orb.'

Sienna shook her head. 'That boils down to geography. If Ollie had been closer...'

'But he wasn't. Besides, it might have made no difference. The portal might have closed at that point regardless of what Oliver and his brothers did or didn't do.'

'What do you mean?'

'My grandfather worried that the portals might weaken the fabric between the timelines. It was all theoretical, but he didn't want to risk them collapsing into one.'

'What would happen if they did?'

'Maybe nothing. Maybe the end of everything. My point is that he built in a fail-safe. If a portal wasn't closed manually within two minutes, it would do so automatically.'

'So she might have died anyway?'

'It's possible.'

Sienna grabbed his hand. 'Is there any way to tell?'

'I suppose. If I could access the computer again, I might be able to see whether the timer was overridden and closed early. But do you really want to know? It could just as easily bolster the case against them as weaken it.'

Sienna hesitated. 'I *need* to know. Jared, I've spent a chunk of my life imagining a future with a man who may have been an accomplice in my mother's murder.'

Jared took a deep breath. 'Then let's find out. The court is adjourned for lunch. We could take a look at the computer.'

'Thank you.'

They headed back to the chapel. But as they approached, Devon put his hand on the doorframe, barring their way. 'You can't go in.'

'Why not?' Jared asked. 'You know I've been granted access to the computer history.'

'Not today you haven't.'

Kristoff appeared behind him. 'Would you like me to double check with Doctor Wallace?'

Devon grimaced. 'That won't be necessary.' He twirled his arm in an exaggerated bow. 'Your Highness, do let me know if I can do anything else for you. A refreshing beverage? Foot massage?'

Jared ignored the sarcasm, but Sienna chose violence.

'Watch where you're stepping!' Devon yelped as he grabbed his toes.

'Terribly sorry,' Sienna said. 'We won't be long.'

Kristoff followed them in. 'That was a little unnecessary.'

Sienna marched on ahead. 'So was his attitude.'

'Yes. But that's just who he is. Besides, Felix was his best friend.'

A lump formed in Jared's throat. 'I didn't know.'

'There's no reason that you would,' Kristoff said. 'Just don't take it personally.'

'Yeah, well, like attracts like,' Sienna said. 'They've both been pretty vile to me over the years, so forgive me if I forgo the mourning period.'

'Whatever,' Kristoff said. 'It's not like I'm going to offer to do a eulogy for him or anything. I just...I don't know.'

'I get it,' Jared said. 'Don't think I don't feel bad. If there had been any other way.'

'I know. I was there, remember.' Kristoff unlocked the vestry that doubled as an office. 'Help yourself.'

It took Jared moments to pull up the list, but that was where he stopped.

'What's wrong?' Sienna asked. 'Earth calling Jared.'

'This isn't right.'

Sienna slumped. 'Thank you for looking. It didn't really make any difference anyway.'

'No, not that. I haven't checked yet.'

'Then what?'

'The orb has been used in the last few days.'

'Yes, when you came home,' Kristoff said.

Jared wrinkled his nose at the word 'home'. 'No, after that.'

Kristoff rubbed his chin. 'Not to my knowledge. It's been locked away back here.'

'It's logged right here,' Jared said. 'Somebody opened a portal to the eighteenth century on the night my mother disappeared.'

∼

Laura

They approached the courthouse long before twelve, but already people were filing out. 'What's going on?'

'Fion!' Helen sprinted towards the door.

He was already trying to scarper back inside but turned with a groan at the sound of his name. 'What now?'

'Where is everyone going?'

Fion wouldn't meet her eye. 'They've adjourned for the day. You'll have to come back tomorrow.'

'Tomorrow?' Confusion clouded Helen's face, followed by a stormy rage. 'You lied to me! You said midday!'

'I said no such—'

Helen shoved him, and he sprawled through the doorway behind him. 'You wicked...' A sob stole her words. 'How could you? She'll think I've abandoned her.'

Duncan appeared from inside and hauled Fion to his feet. Other than the damage to his pride, betrayed by the glow in his cheeks, he looked unhurt.

A man appeared. 'You are causing quite the commotion, young lady.' From his gleaming buttons to his starched uniform, he could not have stood out more.

Duncan spoke with his head bowed. 'This is the one I was telling you about, Captain Ross.'

'I see,' Ross said. 'It's Helen, isn't it?'

'Who I am is none of your business.'

'As the sheriff, I'd say it's very much my business.'

The fight seemed to leave Helen's body, and she fell to her knees before him. 'Please, sir. My mother is Janet Horne and—'

'I know who you are.' Ross eyed the crowd that gathered behind them. 'You're the witch's get.'

Laura flinched. 'You've found Janet guilty?'

'Well, not yet. But the evidence is compelling. I'm sure a confession will follow soon enough.' Ross looked Laura up and down. 'And you are?'

Laura hesitated. 'A friend of the family.'

'Then you should choose your company more wisely. Often the offspring of a witch will be damned along with them.' He leant down to peer closer at Helen. 'Is that right, girl? Are you a witch too?'

'No.' Helen got to her feet and stepped back. 'I swear I'm not.'

'But your mother is; is that right? You'll testify to that?'

'No! Neither of us are witches.'

Ross sniffed. 'That's exactly what a whore of Satan would say.'

'Actually,' Duncan said. 'Helen did ask me...No, ignore me; it was just silly talk. It doesn't matter.'

'Spit it out, man.'

'Well, Helen asked me if I expected her to get saddled up and gallop off with her mother.'

The sheriff's eyes sparkled. 'She's been shape-shifting. Just like her mother.' He seized Helen's wrist. 'Look at her hand. That's the mark of the devil if ever I saw it.'

Helen twisted away. 'I was only jesting with him. My hand has been like that from the day I was born.'

'No doubt. You didn't have a chance with a mother—'

'No.' Fion stepped between them. 'Helen is no witch.'

Laura saw the way Helen's fists balled. She knew her

friend would be torn between wanting Fion's help and telling him where he could shove his protection.

'Aren't you the one that accused the mother?' Ross asked.

'That's right. But not Helen. I've known her since we were children, and I have never seen any evidence of witchcraft.'

The sheriff glanced back at the crowd and huffed. 'I guess she should consider herself lucky then. Isn't that right, girl? We've intervened before your mother's poison could infect you.' He narrowed his eyes. 'Unless our friend here has it wrong. Maybe you are just very good at hiding what you are.' His eyes bored into Helen. 'Duncan, take her to the cells. Just as a precaution.'

'Please. Don't.' Laura snatched at the skirt of Helen's dress.

'Don't what? Do God's work? Free this village from Satan? Perhaps you are closer to the Horne women than you've let on.'

Laura's tongue felt fat and dry, and she struggled to force out her words. 'I just find it hard to believe.'

'Of course you do. That's what makes witches so cunning. Now, be on your way, unless you want to join them.'

Chapter Thirteen

Excerpt from *A Societal Analysis of the Bee Colony*

Cannibalism in Bees

One of the less palatable (to us, at least) habits of the honey bee is often referred to as hygienic cannibalism. If a larva becomes sick, a worker bee will locate it, open the cap on its brood cell, and eat it. Biologically, this makes sense, as it prevents fungal and bacterial diseases from spreading through the hive.

Beyond this, the cannibalism of sick larvae is a practical tactic to keep the hive clean. Removing the body by consuming it means it is not left within the hive to rot and spread further disease.

This behaviour is not limited to the consumption of larvae. Researchers have also noted instances in which worker bees will attack and eat their adult counterparts. The reasoning behind this behaviour is not obvious, but it is theorised that a sick or weak bee gives off a chemical signature identifying it as such. The strength of the hive depends on each and every individual. Weakness is not tolerated, and those found lacking are fated to contribute to the hive in a more nutritional sense.

Wakefield, R. (2025) *A Societal Analysis of the Bee Colony*. Third edition. London: Feisty Scholar Publications.

The Book of Evelyn

The Pack had left me no choice. As much as I hated the idea of asking the Sanctuary for help, I couldn't let anyone else die. Particularly not me.

'I'm coming, too,' Gabriela said as she jumped into the back of Michelle's truck and slumped next to me. 'Maybe I can persuade George that there's life outside the Sanctuary.' I know now how tragic that hope was. But at the time, I was glad not to face my demons alone.

Celine followed her. 'If you run into the Pack, you'll need backup.' She touched the gun stuffed into her waistband.

'I suppose there is safety in numbers,' Bug said. 'Would one of you like to trade for my seat upfront?' We all declined, claiming to prefer the open air. Really, we knew what a struggle leaving his unit had been, let alone the Colony. We didn't want to add to that.

Michelle clambered into the cab and turned the ignition. 'So, what's the plan? Are we going to ask the Sanctuary for weapons?'

Bug shot me a glare, warning me not to panic them with the details. I was still trying to process his plan myself.

Gabriela jumped in before I was forced to lie. 'You know the chances of them helping us are slim, Evelyn. Malone and his henchman aren't exactly the neighbourly type.'

'We can only ask.' It's not like I lied to them. I simply bent the truth until it fitted their perception. Still, I suppose such shades of grey are little comfort to them. Or you. Perhaps one day, you will all decide it was worth it. 'At least the wind has changed direction. The Colony should be safe.'

'For now.' Bug stared off towards Colonies 3 and 4. He didn't need to elaborate.

I'd been travelling on foot to the boundary of the Sanctuary for months to deliver my messages, so the drive felt like nothing. When we reached the chain link fence that encircled the Sanctuary, Michelle switched off the engine.

'That's it? It doesn't look all that impressive.' Her scepticism was understandable. But even after being away for so long, it was impossible not to picture the maze of tunnels winding below the unassuming black building.

'Well, they don't want to broadcast their position,' I said. 'They can't risk getting overrun by every survivor in the area.'

'Right,' Michelle said. 'So, what now?'

Bug looked at the smears of smoke still blotting the horizon. 'Ram them.'

'Sorry?'

'We don't have time to wait for a welcoming committee,' Bug said. 'Ram the gates.'

'Okay,' Michelle said. 'Let's do this.' She slammed the truck into reverse. 'Everybody hold on tight back there.'

That was easier said than done. We cowered on the truck bed floor as we smashed through the perimeter gates. I tumbled over, my kneecaps striking metal. Michelle brought the truck to a grinding halt at the door to the Sanctuary.

Gabriela helped me up. 'Are you okay?'

'I've been better.'

Michelle twisted around in her seat. 'All in one piece?'

'You know, we could have got out before you did that,' Celine said.

'Oh, yeah, I guess you could have done.'

'What now?' Celine asked. 'Do we knock?'

Gabriela sniffed. 'No need. They know we're here. They're just weighing up whether it's in their best interest to shoot us or not.'

The door to the Sanctuary swung open. A line of guardians poured out, each aiming a gun at us. 'Get out of the vehicle and put your hands up,' one of them shouted.

Bug raised his arms and slid from the truck. 'Let's hope they settle on 'not'.'

~

<u>Laura</u>

Laura fixed her eyes on the road ahead, frightened that if she turned around she'd manifest her fear and Ross' men would be chasing her. The crowd's murmur faded, but she didn't slow her pace. Where she was heading was unclear. The house, she supposed. Even if it wasn't the nearest place to where she'd entered this timeline, it wasn't as if she had any other options. The thought of watching that portal fizz into existence left Laura churning with mixed emotions. If by some miracle it appeared, how could she step through it and leave Janet and Helen to die?

The sounds of horse hooves penetrated her turmoil, and Laura was horrified to see Fion trotting behind her. 'Stop and talk a minute.'

Laura's heart thundered at the sight of Helen's attacker, and she ran. She cursed her dress as it caught around her knees, forcing her to hitch up the fabric.

'I just want to talk to you!' Fion steadied his horse next to her, the animal whinnying its protest at matching her slow pace.

'Yeah, I bet that's what you said to Helen.'

'Hear me out, will you? I want to help her.'

'And why would you do that?'

'If you stop, I'll tell you.'

Laura had no intention of stopping but said, 'Go on.'

Fion jumped down from his horse. He clasped the reins and mirrored Laura's step. 'I loved Helen. Really, I did.'

'Do you think that makes what you did all right? If anything, that's worse. You don't attack people you love.'

'That's not what that was.'

'And I guess she gave herself those bruises.'

'Look, are you just intending to keep slicing me with that sharp tongue of yours, or do you want to listen to my plan?'

Laura pretended to consider this. 'I'm excellent at multi-tasking.'

'It's my job to watch over Janet,' Fion said. 'I've spent more hours than I can count holding onto that damn chain. If she closes her eyes for even a second, I've got to jerk her awake by tugging on it.'

'But...why? That's barbaric. Didn't you notice how confused she was even before you brought all of this on her? She's not well and needs to rest.'

Fion massaged the bridge of his nose, and for the first time Laura noticed the dark rings around them and the ashen grey of his face. 'I know how she feels.'

'My heart bleeds for you.'

'Do you think I want to spend my night torturing some mean old goat of a woman? It's Ross' orders. He wants a confession. If he's going to convict the first witch in years, he wants to make sure there's no doubt that she's guilty.'

'And that's where you come in. Deny her sleep until she puts her name to a lie.'

'It's not a lie. Janet has confessed to witchcraft a thousand times. And my cattle—'

'Got sick. A coincidence. You didn't need to lay the blame at Janet's feet.'

'She did that herself.'

Arguing in circles was making Laura's head throb. 'So while you were torturing my friend, you devised a plan to free her.'

'No. Not her. Helen.'

'So you are happy to let Janet rot in jail?'

'Aye. She's guilty. But if she confesses, then they don't both have to suffer. They'll have to let Helen go.'

'That's it? That's your big plan? Pathetic. Besides, Helen would never leave her mother behind.'

'Even if the alternative is death?'

'You're all sick.' Laura felt the heat of threatening tears flush her face. 'Let me get this straight. Your plan is for me to persuade them that Janet should confess so Helen is set free?'

'Do you have a better suggestion?'

'Yes. Open the cell door and let them both leave. It's the least you can do after the lies you've told.'

'They weren't—'

'I don't want to hear it.'

'I'm a busy man. Are you in or not?'

'You haven't left me much choice, have you?'

'All right then. I'll pick you up before my shift starts this evening, and we'll ride in together on my buggy.'

Laura added up the hours she had to come up with a plan. Whatever it was, she prayed it wouldn't involve sacrificing one of her friends.

Marney
Entering the Sanctuary

All the applicants were herded into the dining hall while they awaited their outcome. It felt like they'd been waiting for an age, and the girls' incessant questions were beginning to grate.

'Will we have to go to school here?' Jodie asked.

'I don't know,' Marney said. 'I guess so.'

'I miss school. Will they have a uniform? Mom? Are you listening?' She wasn't. No matter how she tried to stay present, Marney's eyes kept wandering towards the door, praying for someone to walk through and bring her anxiety to an end.

'Mom's tired,' Ben said. 'Give her some peace. And no, I doubt they'd use precious resources on something as trivial as a school uniform.'

'No?' Richard said. 'I don't think their flashy blue uniforms are standard army issue.'

'I hope there will be a class pet in our new school,' Emma said. 'My old class had a hamster.'

'Oh yeah? What was he called?' Richard asked.

'Bandit. He used to be called Hammy, but he got into our lunches one day and ate someone's sandwiches. So we changed it.'

Richard laughed. 'That's a much better name, anyway.'

Marney wondered if they would be expected to sleep in the dining hall when Caleb finally walked towards them.

'I've been asked to show you to your unit.' A ghost of a smile played on his lips.

'I really can't thank you enough,' Marney said. 'If it weren't for you, we'd be wandering up there, lost and afraid.'

'No problem. I was happy to...Oh, I'm sorry, but it's just Doctor Wallace and her family.'

'Oh.' Richard plopped back into his chair. 'That makes sense. Your family won't be wanting a lodger, I'm sure.'

'They're probably settling the families first. Then they'll sort the single people.' Ben looked at Caleb. 'That's right, isn't it?'

'I'm sorry; I don't know.'

Marney began to scoop up their belongings. 'It makes sense. That will be it. Come on, girls, gather your things.'

Richard picked up one of their bags. 'At least let me help you.'

'You must stay in the dining area, I'm afraid.' Caleb took the bag from him.

'Of course. Yes. I just...'

'We'll see you tomorrow,' Marney said, patting his hand.

Marney could feel Richard's eyes burning into her as they followed Caleb out of the dining room. As they neared the end of the tunnel, a clatter of furniture and muffled voices trailed them.

Emma stopped. 'What's that noise?'

'It's none of our business.' Ben tugged her along. 'Keep walking.'

The echo of Richard's panicked run reached them before his cry. 'Marney! Ben! Wait!' Two guardians barrelled into him, sending him sprawling onto the ground.

Marney exchanged a fleeting look with Ben and realised they were contemplating the same thing; walking on and not looking back.

Jodie rejected that choice for them. 'Are you hurt?' She slipped her hand from Marney's and ran towards him.

Reluctantly, Marney followed, pulling Jodie back towards her. 'Caleb, would you mind going ahead with the girls? They don't need to see this.'

Caleb nodded. 'I'll take them to the unit and come back for you.'

'Let Richard come with us!' They could still hear Jodie protesting after she was led out of sight.

The guardians dragged Richard to his feet, each holding one of his arms behind his back. 'My application has been denied,' he said. 'They're tossing me out like garbage.' He tried to twist from their grip, but they only clung on tighter.

'Is that necessary?' Marney asked.

'We're just following orders,' one of them said.

'Oh yes, and I bet I know whose.' Richard's tone was strained, somewhere between laughing and crying. 'Well, you can tell Malone from me that he has lost a valuable asset today. We'll find somewhere that recognises the good we can do.'

We. That tiny word struck Marney like a slap, making her realise that he thought they'd leave with him. 'Richard, I'm...' *Sorry. Staying.* Neither option would pass her lips.

'But if we both go, the vaccine goes with us. Don't you see?'

She did. If they threatened to leave together, David and Aleksey might be forced to relent and let all of them stay. Maybe. But Marney just wasn't prepared to gamble her children's lives.

'I'm sorry,' Ben said. 'If it weren't for the girls...'

'Oh. I see. It doesn't matter. I doubt I'd have stayed long anyway.'

Marney felt guilt pawing at her guts. 'No?'

'I've never been great at following orders. I don't imagine I'd be much good as one of their drones.'

'I'm so sorry. If there were any other way.'

Richard's face hardened. 'You don't need another way; Paul Stuart chose you.'

'I have no idea why he picked me to take his place. I know it's not fair. You put so much more time into the vaccine than me.'

'I do. You're a survivor, Marney. He knew that. And you'll do what it takes to protect yourself and your family. I think you're going to need that strength here.'

'What will you do?' Marney wondered how she'd live with herself. She'd dragged him to a strange country, where he didn't know a soul, and now she was letting them cast him out.

'Don't worry about me,' Richard said, covering the tremor in his voice with a veneer of positivity. 'I'm an easy man to underestimate, but I have a habit of proving people wrong.' He looked over his shoulder at one of the guardians. 'If you don't mind, I'll walk out of here unaided.' After a slight hesitation, they released his arms. 'Thank you.'

'Richard, maybe I could try talking to Edmond Pearse again. I could explain again how important you are to our work.'

'This is nothing to do with me or our work, and you know it.' Richard walked back towards the dining room. When he got to the end of the tunnel, he paused. 'Goodbye,

Doctor Wallace. And good luck. I think you're going to need it.'

Jared

Jared could hear Beth's voice, but it was as if she were calling to him from above the surface of a murky pool, despair weighing him down.

'Talk to me,' she said.

'I've tried,' Sienna said. 'But he's barely spoken since we found out about his mother. He said he had to go but only got this far.'

'What about his mother?' Aaron asked. 'They haven't... Did they find...'

'Nothing like that. It seems the orb was used the night she disappeared. Come and see for yourself. Maybe you can help me look something up while we're there.'

Jared was relieved to hear them walk away.

Beth stayed with him though, crouched next to him on the floor of Saint Kinga's chapel. 'I'll just sit with you a while.'

'Misery loves company.'

'Ah, he speaks. Well, lucky for me, you're better company on your worst day than most are on their best. Are you ready to talk about it?'

'There's not much to add to what Sienna said. They opened a portal on the night she disappeared.'

'Okay. And you think they sent her through?'

'It would make sense.'

'Where?'

'Scotland in 1727. Which is strange in itself.'

'How so?'

'I don't know. It just seems that of all the places they

could have sent her, a sleepy little town like Dornoch wouldn't have been their usual style.'

'I can tell you there was plenty of trauma occurring around that time.'

'Sorry, I forgot you're the expert on that era.'

'You say expert; I say survivor.'

'Was it really that bad?' The panic that he'd just quelled began to rise again.

Beth must have sensed this because she shuffled closer. 'By then, the main threats were under control. Plague, famine, drought...fire. People are the trickier factor to account for. I'll need to do a little research. Leave it with me. I think they're expecting you back at the trial anyway.'

'I can't. Not while she is back there, lost and alone.'

'Jared, trust me. Please. Let me look into it, and then we'll go back and find her together. Prepared.'

'Okay.'

Aaron returned from the office, Sienna in tow. 'They definitely opened a portal. But have you considered that it could be a decoy?'

'What do you mean?' Beth asked.

'Maybe nothing. But wouldn't it be convenient for them if we went charging back to the eighteenth century looking for her? They'd get rid of us and be free to do whatever they like with the Sanctuary.'

'I wish I knew who *they* were,' Jared said. 'It's difficult to fight an enemy when they're anonymous.'

'Okay. So, what shall we do?' Sienna stared at him, and Jared realised she thought he had a plan.

'I have no idea. Just give me some time to think.'

Voices echoed from the chamber beyond. 'It sounds like we're all out of that.'

Aleksey's face fell when he saw the four of them standing there. 'What's going on?'

'You speak to him,' Beth whispered. 'I'm going to see what I can find out. And Jared, remember how strong you are.' She shot Aleksey an icy stare as she passed.

'Well?' Aleksey kept his voice to an irritated rumble, clearly aware of the citizens leading in behind him. 'What are you doing here?'

Marney followed him in. 'I'd be interested to hear that story myself.'

'I...I've decided I want to give evidence,' Sienna said. 'The citizens should hear my story in my own words.'

'But you were so adamant that you didn't want to,' Marney said.

'I guess I've had a change of heart. 'Please, after all I've been through, shouldn't I have my say?'

'I can't argue with that.' Marney motioned towards the chair Jared had been so grateful to escape from after his testimony.

'Then I guess we have another witness,' Aleksey said. 'Guardians, lead in the defendants.' His eyebrows bobbed as he regarded Jared and Aaron. 'You two had better sit down.'

Oliver's eyes looked impossibly large when he saw Sienna. 'No! What is this?'

'Just shut up, Ollie. You might be able to pretend I don't exist, but it was my life that was ruined, and I won't be ignored. My opinion matters.' Sienna's voice cracked as she addressed the citizens. For the first time during the trial, Jared realised they were silent of their own accord. 'I guess you've heard the news about my father by now. The years apart from him are just another item on the list of things they took from me. The Durands robbed me of so much. My childhood, my free will, and my parents, just for starters.

'But that loss wasn't just mine. All of the children conscripted into the Guardian Elite experienced this to some degree, few more so than Oliver Sawyer. I know this because before he was my boss or my fiancé, he was my friend.

'Ollie's a year younger than me. That's nothing really. But I used to feel so grown up compared to him. He'd trail after me, refusing to let me shake him off. Until one day, I realised I missed him when he wasn't there. I used to tell him he grew on me like mould.' Her smile was fleeting. 'It's hard for me to link my image of that kid to what happened to my mother. But I have to. The reality is inescapable. Although not for the reasons you might be thinking. That child who acted like my shadow was a victim, too. Like me, he was kidnapped, tortured and groomed. All so we could embody the Guardian Elite, Victor Durand's legacy.'

'As generous as all of this is,' Marney said, 'we've already heard this argument. Do you have anything new to add?'

'Yes, thanks to Jared and his friends. We've looked at the records for the orb. The portal closed automatically.' Sienna spoke directly to Oliver. 'You didn't kill her. Not on purpose anyway.' Sienna faltered as she fought back tears. 'That may not change the fact she's gone, but it makes it a little easier to forgive. So I've decided that the only part of the Durand legacy I want to be involved in is shattering it. Empathy and forgiveness, that's what we should take forward from Durand's reign, if only to spite him.

'Oliver's death will accomplish nothing and will avenge

nobody. If there are still those among you who demand action, then let him work to bring back some of the light they took from us. Misguided revenge won't bring back—'

Behind them, Seb sprang to his feet and jabbed a finger towards her. 'Speak for yourself. If you want to forgive your boyfriend, that's between the two of you. But you don't get to give him a pass on what he did to mine.'

'I'm not saying that.'

'Then you need to explain, because it seems you want him free so the two of you can live happily ever after.'

'No, Seb, please listen. I could never, would never, be with Ollie now.' She turned her gaze to Oliver, but he stared at his shoes. 'He betrayed me in the worst way imaginable. But killing him won't change that. Aleksey says we need to keep the mine open if we're going to survive. But not through the labour of innocent people like my father. Let Ollie and Martin work off their sins there.'

Behind her, Aleksey perked up at the mention of his name. 'You will all soon see how integral the mine is for our survival. That sounds like a sensible plan.'

'Of course, you would think that,' Marney said. 'Credibility for your slave camp has to appeal.'

'You'd rather we suffocate? Or that these boys are put to death?'

'Well, no.'

'Then maybe you shouldn't dismiss the idea out of hand. Sienna, your plan is both practical and generous. Personally, I'm happy to make that call now unless you have a better idea, Marney?'

Marney opened her mouth, but no words escaped.

'I thought not. Oliver and Martin will be sentenced to the mining camp.'

'This court is a joke,' Seb said. 'They deserve to suffer for what they did.' He slammed through the chamber doors, leaving the chapel in a cacophony of debate.

'Quiet!' Aleksey hammered his gavel. 'We all know Seb is grieving and deserves our compassion right now. But we cannot let sentiment run the Sanctuary. Unless there is any objection from Doctor Wallace, my judgement stands.'

Marney's lips disappeared into a thin white line. 'No.'

'There we are. Oliver and Martin Durand will work for the remainder of their lives in the mines. Guardians, escort the Durand brothers to their cells until arrangements for their transfer can be made. The court is dismissed.'

Martin allowed Emma Wallace to tug him along by his cuffs. But Oliver struggled to look back at Sienna as he was led away. 'I didn't ask for mercy.'

'You didn't get it. Death would be the coward's way out. You still have time to do some good in this world.' Sienna stared at the tunnel long after he'd disappeared down it.

'Are you okay?' Jared asked her.

'I suppose. Although I'm still not convinced I've done the right thing. Ollie might be harmless. But Martin? Can we trust him?'

'I doubt it. But if he's lying about having changed, this will allow us to see his true colours. Come on, let's see what Aleksey has to say about the orb.' He was already at the chapel door when they caught up to him. 'Can we talk to you for a minute?'

Aleksey's jaw clenched so hard that Jared could see a muscle tic. 'I have preparations to make.'

'It's important,' Jared said.

'It always is. Everybody in this place thinks their drama is more pressing than their neighbour's.'

'Somebody used the orb the night of my mother's disappearance.'

'I know nothing about that,' Aleksey said, puffing out his chest. 'To my knowledge, you were the last person to use it.'

'And ours, until very recently,' Sienna said. 'Yet there it was in the log.'

'I'll start an investigation, see if the guardians saw anything.'

'That will take too long,' Jared said. 'Let us go back and see what we can find.'

'If you must.' Aleksey's Adam's apple bobbed as he swallowed. 'But if she was sent back, what hope is there of finding her alive?'

'We're a resourceful family. She would have found a way to survive. And if she's back there waiting for me, I can't let her dow—'

A piercing siren cut Jared off. He watched as Devon muttered into his radio, his words drowned out by the wail slicing through the air. With a few frantic hand motions, he sent every guardian darting for the door.

Marney hooked a finger into Kristoff's jacket as he passed. 'What's happening?'

'I have to go.' Kristoff tugged himself free. 'There are survivors up on the surface, and they're ramming the gates.'

The only guardian left was Devon, who spoke in a frantic whisper, his mouth close to Aleksey's ear. Then he shoved past before Marney could ask what was happening.

Aleksey strolled towards them, his hands in his pockets.

'So?' Marney asked, barely containing her irritation. 'What's going on?'

'It seems Jared isn't the only prodigal child to return to us. The group of survivors that bashed their way through our gates.' Aleksey's lip twitched in a snarl as he jerked his head towards the surface. 'Evie is with them.'

'Evie?' Jared's pulse raced, through excitement or fear, he wasn't sure. 'Maybe she needs our help.'

'You're so naive,' Aleksey said. 'You witnessed how she left us. She clearly has a vendetta against us and has brought her friends along to settle it. Well, if she wants to bring trouble to our door, we will give it to her.'

'No! She wouldn't do that!' Jared turned to Aaron. 'Help Beth prepare for the trip. I need to find out what's going on.'

The Book of Evelyn

It wasn't just the guns pointed at us that tied my stomach in knots. I'd sworn to myself that I'd never again walk through that door, feel the thinning of the air as we descended that dark staircase, or the rising panic as the salt rock walls entombed us. Gabriela walked so close behind me that occasionally she stepped on the backs of my shoes, making me lurch into the back of Celine. The cackling mob, clad in yale blue, hemming us in on either side didn't help. The thought that plagued me often during my time in the Sanctuary now played on repeat in my head. *There's no escape.*

The guardians all looked around my age, but there was a clear pecking order, with one barking commands at the others. He pointed to the tunnels leading from the platform, assigning a guard to each.

'We need to speak to Doctor Marney Wallace,' Bug said.

'You don't get to make demands.' The lead guardian squeezed the shoulder of his colleague. 'You see him?' he asked. 'If you move, he's got orders to shoot you.'

Our guard's eyes widened, and he raised his gun a little higher. It wavered, so he clasped his wrist to offset his shaking hand. I almost felt sorry for him.

But I had problems of my own. The trauma of my old life threatened to overwhelm me, and I took long, rasping breaths in an effort to calm myself. The last time I'd stood on that platform, the crowd gossiped about me in barely contained whispers. Victim or murderer, which I was labelled as depended on who you asked. Either way, none of them could look at me. Heads would dip or swivel, avoiding my eye.

No, that's not fair; there were two exceptions. David

Malone, of course. I think he revelled in the impact of his actions. As always in the Sanctuary, he'd set up the dominoes and took great pleasure in knocking them down.

And then there was you, Jared. You may not even remember it. But when you held up your palm, mirroring mine, it wasn't just a farewell. It told me you were there for me, not as some malicious spectator. Someone cared. If it weren't for that life raft amongst the horrors, my memories might have pulled me under.

I wasn't the only one struggling. Bug shifted feet, the creaking of the wooden floor amplified in the cavernous space. 'Can you at least tell us if he's gone to fetch Marney?'

To give him credit, the guardian looked apologetic. 'Devon doesn't tell me anything.'

'Then can we sit?' Bug asked.

The guardian looked around at the men behind him before saying, 'Sure. I don't think that can hurt.'

Bug flopped down onto the floor, and the rest of us followed suit.

At first, the guardian shadowed us with the barrel of his gun, but I guess he felt foolish, because he dropped it by his side. 'I'm sorry. Believe me, I hate this as much as you do.'

'I doubt that,' I said. 'You aren't the one being held at gunpoint.'

'Well, you did ram our gates.'

'Fair point.'

He smirked. 'You don't remember me, do you?'

'Should I?'

'My name's Kristoff.' He must have read my blank look because he added, 'I was friends with Jared.'

'Was?' That one word prickled my nerves.

'Oh, of course. You have an awful lot to catch up on.'

Footsteps echoed around the cavern, making it impossible to say which tunnel they came from until Marney burst into view. We jumped to our feet. When she saw us, she stopped dead in her tracks. 'My God. You made it.' She could have been talking to Gabriela or me, but her attention was locked on Bug.

Aleksey pushed past her. 'Who are these people?'

'You don't recognise me?' I asked.

Aleksey's lips were pinched. 'Evie? We thought...'

'I was dead?' I don't know what it was about his manner, but I didn't trust him. Not that I think I ever had.

'I don't know what we thought. But here you are, alive and well. Thank the Lord.'

'I doubt he had anything to do with it.'

Marney took a step towards Bug. 'Richard, I'm so sorry. I should have...I don't know what I should have done. But you deserved better.'

'Yes, I did.'

The air was rife with tension, as if I could drag my fingers through it and watch sparks weave between them. 'You know each other?'

'He didn't tell you?' Marney said. 'Richard and I are old friends.'

Bug's upper lip twitched. 'Colleagues might be a better description.'

'We were on the team that created the vaccine.'

'That was a lifetime ago,' Bug said. 'I'm a different man.'

'But clearly not one to be underestimated. How have you managed to survive up there all this time?'

'It's not been easy,' Bug said. 'But we've built a community. We are more than surviving; we're thriving.'

'Then why are you here?' Aleksey crossed his arms over his chest. 'If you're doing so well, why come crashing in here ruining our peace?'

'Because we are facing a new danger—'

'Oh, here we go.'

'One that has nothing to do with the conditions up there.'

'What is it?' Marney asked.

'Another group of survivors called the Pack. They have attacked and killed members of our community.'

'Worse than that,' I said. 'They're eating people.'

'Yes,' Bug said. 'There have been reports of them turning to cannibalism.'

How sanitised he made it sound, as though the circumstances dictated such depravity. But I'd seen first-hand the glee on their faces as they'd explained their plans for me. I doubted they lost a minute of sleep over what they did.

'It doesn't come as a surprise,' Aleksey said. 'Our teams have stumbled across the mess they left behind on a few occasions.'

I opened my mouth to point out that the mess he referred to was the remains of human beings, but Bug jumped in first.

'So you know how dangerous they are,' he said. 'You'll help us.'

Aleksey huffed. 'On the contrary, we will be staying as far away from them as possible.'

'And what if we tell them where you are?' I hadn't planned on saying it, but when I saw Aleksey's face darken, I knew I'd scared him. That power gave me momentum. 'Maybe a trade will satisfy them; the safety of our group for the location of a much healthier, better resourced one.'

'You wouldn't.'

'We would, and we have.' I have to admit, watching him squirm was satisfying. 'Or at least, I've planned for it. If we don't return, our people have instructions to tell the Pack exactly where you are. So don't get any ideas.'

'I don't believe it.' Aleksey's jowls wobbled as he shook his head.

'No? Then you don't know me at all.'

Marney reached for me. 'Evie, this isn't you.'

'It's Evelyn now.' I turned back to Aleksey. 'And I don't owe any of you a thing. Loyalty is earned.'

Aleksey sniffed. 'Blame us all you want, but—'

'Oh, I will.'

'Enough,' Marney said. 'It doesn't have to be like this. What exactly is it you want from us? Weapons? Supplies? We will give you what we can.'

Aleksey flushed with anger. I couldn't help a smile creeping across my lips.

'The virus,' Bug said. 'We want a sample of the virus.'

Aleksey snorted. 'Ridiculous. Why would we keep something so dangerous here?'

Bug ignored him and kept his eyes trained on Marney.

'What do you want with it?' she asked.

'To weaponise it.'

'Are you insane? I can't let you do that.'

Aleksey cleared his throat. 'Why are we even talking as if it's a possibility? We don't have a sample to give them. Do we?'

Marney didn't answer.

'No,' Aleksey said. 'Please tell me you were not stupid enough to bring it down here.'

'Will you just stop talking for one minute so I can think?'

'I...How dare you?'

'It's safely contained,' Marney said. 'We need it in case we ever have to alter the vaccine. Pearse and Malone both knew it was here.'

'Reckless,' Aleksey said. 'You're completely reckless. You risked every person here.'

'No,' Marney said. 'Richard and I saved every life here. We owe him.' She turned to Bug. '*I owe you.*'

Aleksey scowled at her. 'On your head be it.'

Marney headed for the exit but stopped. 'Evelyn, somebody here would like to see you before you go.'

Gabriela beamed. 'Is it Geor...Is it Luca?'

By contrast, Marney's smile flickered and vanished. 'I'm afraid not. Let me show Evelyn the way, then you and I can talk.'

I knew instantly that she meant you, Jared. In my imagination, we were living parallel lives, you below the ground and me above it. I assumed you'd reached adulthood flanked by your mother and grandfather, cloistered within the suffocating rule of the Sanctuary. I knew nothing of the worlds you'd visited, the adventures you'd had, the losses you'd suffered.

My instincts are telling me to leave this part out, that it makes no difference any more. However, you asked me to give the whole truth, that the details would matter to those who would one day read this. And I believe context matters here, not to justify why I did what I did, but to explain why it was such a difficult decision. So if you rip this page from the book, tear it into confetti or burn it to ashes, I will understand.

'I'll leave you here,' Marney said as we stood outside your grandfather's old unit. 'He's expecting you.'

I blinked numbly at the door. 'Maybe this isn't a good idea.'

'Why?'

'Everybody lets me down eventually. I've got so few happy memories. I'm not sure I want to taint the ones I have of him.'

'If you don't take the risk, you won't get the chance to make new ones.'

'I guess you're right.' I took a deep breath and went inside. And there you were, Jared, older but otherwise just as I remembered you. I fought the urge to wrap you in my arms, assuming you wouldn't want that. So when you threw your own around me, it meant that much more.

'Marney wouldn't let me meet you at the gate. She said it was too dangerous until we knew who the people with you were.'

'They aren't dangerous.' I looked you up and down, drinking in the familiarity of you. 'Jared, is it really you? I didn't think we'd ever see each other again.'

'It's me. I'm sorry, Evie. I should have followed you. Or at least come looking for you later.'

'Don't apologise. I found a new home with people who care for me.'

'Oh.' The muscle by your mouth ticced.

'What is it?'

'Nothing. I'm happy for you. It's just I care for you, too.'

'I know that, silly. And you? Have you been happy here in the Sanctuary?'

You smirked. 'I've been off on adventures of my own.'

And so you gave me the highlights. My head spun with the images you painted, the destruction you'd witnessed. If I ever earn back your trust, I'd love to read *your* book, by the way.

'What brought you back here?' I asked. 'If I could go anywhere in time, the Sanctuary wouldn't even make the top million.'

A shadow passed over your features, and you turned away. 'I had no choice. Luca Durand made it clear they'd hunt us forever unless I stopped them.'

'Luca? No, he wouldn't.'

'He killed my friend. Maybe not with his own hands, but his actions led to her death.'

My mind reeled. Luca and I were once so close. I couldn't imagine a reality when you and he were enemies.

'Evie, he's dead.'

'What? No.'

'Victor Durand shot him. It was an accident, but only because he was aiming for Aaron instead. I'm sorry. I know there was a time when you and Luca were friends. But I can't say I'm sad he's gone.'

I had to sit down. 'All that time while I was on the surface, I'd imagined the two of you going through the motions in this claustrophobic life. I never imagined...'

'You don't have to imagine. You could come with me. Together we'll see such amazing places.'

Your words made hope flutter in my chest. 'Where would we go?'

'Wherever you want.' You took my hand. 'We could build a life together.'

I thought about Bug and the colonists. 'Or you could stay. Jared, you could do such good in this world. You and Bug together, you could save it.'

You pulled your hand back. 'No. This isn't my home. And I don't think it's been much of one to you either.'

Bubbles of anger rose to the surface and burst. 'What happened to you? The friend I knew had integrity. He'd have helped me rebuild our home instead of wasting his time watching other people's burn.'

Your face fell, making me wish I could swallow my words back down. 'That's not fair.'

'I know; I'm sorry.'

'I have to go. Just give my offer some thought.'

'Go where? I just got here. Please, I said I was sorry.'

'It's not that. I wish I had more time. But my mother's missing. I think they used the orb to send her back in time. I have to find her.'

'I'm so sorry, Jared.' You looked terrified, with good reason. We both knew that people who went missing in the Sanctuary were rarely found alive. I cupped my hands over your elbows and pulled you close. 'Don't go back. What if you get hurt? I don't want to lose my friend again. Just open a portal and let her make her own way back.'

'That's not possible. My grandfather thought leaving a portal open could be dangerous, that the fabric between the worlds could weaken, so they close automatically.'

'Are you telling me that the biggest genius I know couldn't make a few adjustments?'

'I'm telling you I wouldn't dare try.'

'Okay. I guess you're right.'

'When all of this is over, please think about coming with me,' you said. 'Think about everything I could show you.'

'I appreciate the offer, but people make a home. And you and your friends could have one with me in the Colony. We'll give Marney our location. You can come to us whenever you are ready.'

I had such a clear image of what we could be, and all we could do. Together we would find a way to breathe life back into this world. As a team. As a family. I guess I was naive, because the picture I painted is a million miles away from what we've become.

∼

Marney

Marney had no idea why she led Susan towards the empty cafeteria. She'd picked a direction and started walking, wracking her brain about how to break the news to her. It was only when she motioned for Susan to sit that she justified her choice. 'You probably remember what it's like trying to find privacy here.'

'I try to think about this place as little as possible.'

'Right. Well, we should be safe here for the moment.' Marney took a deep breath. 'I don't know how to say this.' Marney knew she was about to blow Susan's life apart. She'd experienced her share of moments that she'd forever now think of as 'before' and 'after'. Now she would be forced to inflict that on someone else.

'Well, dragging it out isn't helping,' Susan said.

'I know, it's just...'

'He's dead, isn't he?' Susan's voice was hollow. Marney remembered only too well that numbness.

'Yes. I'm so sorry.' Marney placed a hand on Susan's shoulder, but she flinched away. 'How did you know?'

'I didn't. Not really. But I couldn't picture him any more, could never imagine the day we'd be reunited.' Susan gnawed on her lip. 'I'm alone now.'

'I wish I could say something to make you feel better.'

'How did it happen?'

'An accident, of sorts. There was a fight, and Luca was shot. But he wasn't supposed to be the target.'

'Who did it?'

'Victor Durand.'

'Oh, God.' Susan stifled a sob. 'Why did we leave him here?'

'You couldn't have known.'

'But we did know. Believe me. I found out first-hand just how dangerous Durand and Malone were. Yet I still left my child here with them.'

'The way I remember it, you had no choice. I wanted to keep him safe for you. But in the end, I couldn't even protect my own family.'

'Your girls?'

'Jodie died a couple of years ago. A building collapsed when they were up on the surface scouting for resources. Ben died of a heart attack last year.' If they were to talk one-upmanship, there was no doubt Ben had won. Dying of a broken heart, there was no competing with that. Never mind that he'd left her alone to protect their remaining daughter.

'That's awful.'

'Please, no, I wasn't expecting your sympathy. I just wanted you to know I understand a little of how you're feeling.'

'Thank you. If you'll excuse me, it's time I got back to the others. They'll want to get back to the Colony. If I'm honest, I do too. This place doesn't exactly have fond memories for me.'

'I can relate. Are you sure you're going to be okay?' Marney knew it was a stupid question.

'No. But I'm just going to keep putting one foot in front of the other, like every day in the years since I left him. Can I ask you one last question?'

'Of course.'

'Did he make me proud?'

Marney's mouth was suddenly dry, and her swallow sounded infeasibly loud to her ears. 'He looked out for his adopted family, and the other guardians respected him.'

Susan frowned. 'I suppose that's close enough. I hope he found at least a little happiness here.'

'He did. Of that I'm certain.'

'Good. Hold on tight to Emma, and never let her go, no matter what. If I've learnt anything, it's that family is all that matters.' Her eyes glistened. 'There's so much I'd do differently, given the chance.'

Chapter Fourteen

Excerpt from *A Societal Analysis of the Bee Colony*

Worker Sacrifice

Worker bees play many integral roles both inside and outside the hive. From foraging for pollen and nectar to feeding the Queen, larvae and drones, the colony could not survive without them.

A colony is far more than a group of individuals working together. Some scientists have gone as far as to label honey bee colonies as 'super organisms'. There is no behaviour more illustrative of this concept than altruistic suicide. When a worker bee suspects that she is sick, rather than risking the infection of the hive, she will go off by herself and wait to die.

Defence is another example where individual sacrifice is embraced for the greater good of the colony. The barbs of a worker bee's stinger attach it to its opponent's skin and it is subsequently torn from the bee's abdomen, resulting in a fatal haemorrhage. There is no denying that loyalty to the colony comes at a considerable price.

Wakefield, R. (2025) *A Societal Analysis of the Bee Colony*. Third edition. London: Feisty Scholar Publications.

The Book of Evelyn

Marney agreed to help us. Still, her hands shook as she handed over the metal suitcase containing the samples. 'Don't make me regret this. Please.'

'I won't,' Bug promised.

She waved us off with what little resources they could spare.

'Let's keep this between us,' Bug told us as we loaded the truck. 'We don't want to start a panic.'

'Okay.' I tried not to look at the case as we bumped our way back to the Colony. Fate had granted me few mercies in my short life up until then, but I was grateful that I'd been spared from witnessing the worst effects of the virus. I had no desire to change that.

Once we were home, there was nothing to do but wait. Finally, Dale and the others returned amongst cheers and whoops, mainly their own. The gate clunked shut behind them, and Dale headed straight for Bug and me, where we stood outside his cabin.

'We did it,' Dale said as he clambered from the truck. Neither Bug nor I asked what, but he told us anyway. 'We killed at least three of their members. They will think twice about messing with us again.'

I think he was expecting congratulations, but Bug stared at him, stony-faced.

'Aren't you going to say something?' Dale asked.

'I don't think death is ever worth celebrating,' Bug said. 'Lest you forget, some of the Pack were colonists once.'

'They were?' I asked. 'Who? When?'

'It doesn't matter,' Bug said.

Dale and I both followed him towards the cabin, where minutes before, we'd been discussing his plan.

I put my hand on the frame, stopping Dale before he entered. 'Was Cerato one of the people you killed?'

'No. I'm sorry. I looked for her, but…'

'It doesn't matter.' But it did. Despair washed over me. Despite the years that had passed since that night in the abandoned house, Cerato still haunted my nightmares.

'I really wanted to get her for you, kid.'

Bug was already laying bits of paper on the table, his scrawled handwriting all over them. 'Damage control. That's what we need now.'

'Bug has a plan,' I said.

'So do I,' Dale said. 'We hit them again and again until there's nobody left.'

Michelle appeared at the door. 'Bug, you better get out here. Cerato's back.' We followed Michelle to the gate.

Cerato casually ran her knife along the bars of the gate. 'I didn't expect to have to visit again so soon.'

Bug stopped in his tracks.

Dale, however, didn't miss a beat and stormed towards her.

'Evelyn,' Bug said, 'go back to my cabin and wait.'

'No way. I won't let her think I'm scared of her. I mean, I am…'

'Then you are very sensible.' Bug strode towards the gate. Michelle and I followed.

Dale stood, hands on hips. 'I asked what you want?'

Cerato smiled. 'I've come to thank you, of course.'

'Thank us for what?'

'Hmmm...motivation, I suppose, to get our situation sorted.'

'Do you want to call a truce?' I asked, although I knew even then there was no chance.

'Of course not.' Cerato's laugh was filled with scorn. 'I'm here to tell you what happens next.'

I didn't hear the gunshot, just a soggy slap of flesh. But that may have been Michelle's hand on her own neck as she tried to stop the bleeding.

Dale reached for the gun at his hip.

'I wouldn't if I were you,' Cerato said. 'My friends are still watching, and if you harm a hair on my head, they'll kill you all.'

I scoured the landscape but couldn't see where the shot had come from. So, I tried not to think about the gun trained on us and focused on helping my friend. Michelle fell to her knees, her white shirt turning crimson.

I put my hand over hers and tried to apply pressure. 'God. Michelle, hold on.'

'There's no point, Princess. She's dead already.'

Michelle looked into my eyes, pleading, terrified. Then she collapsed forwards.

'See,' Cerato said. 'Inevitable.'

'You're a monster,' I said, my palm still pressed to Michelle's neck.

'Sticks and stones, Princess. Besides, I didn't shoot her. That's just how life works sometimes; the innocent end up paying the price.'

'What do you want from us?' Dale asked, all of his previous confidence gone.

'Justice,' Cerato said. 'You killed three of our people last night. I want three of yours in return.'

'What for?'

'Whatever I like.'

'You can't be serious.' Bug's voice quivered.

'Oh, I'm deadly serious.'

'Please,' Dale said. 'From now on, we'll submit to your terms. Just leave the colonists alone.'

'If you are so keen to save your people, you are free to take one of the places.'

Dale took a step back.

'I didn't think so,' Cerato said. 'I'm a fair woman. I'll even count your friend down there as one of the three.'

Michelle's chest still heaved, and I hated to think of these being the last words that she heard.

'You're sick,' I said.

'Yes, yes, you already covered that. I'm a monster. But you have no idea what these people took from me. Which brings me to my next demand. I want the girl.'

My stomach flipped. 'Why can't you just leave me alone?'

Cerato sneered at me. 'It's always been the way with you little rich kids. But you may be surprised to learn that the world doesn't revolve around you, Princess. However, if you want to offer yourself as one of the three, I wouldn't say no.'

'Then who...'

Bug stepped forward and grasped the gate. 'Please, Rhiannon, you're better than this.'

That name echoed in my brain. 'Rhiannon? You can't be. It's not possible.'

'You're right about that one, Princess. Rhiannon died

when Bug forced me to swarm, tearing me away from the only family I had left. That day, I decided to do whatever was necessary to survive. It's just good luck that I ended up enjoying it.'

I tried to piece her words together, but I couldn't make them fit. It didn't seem possible that my best friend could be the sister of the demon that stalked my nightmares.

'You have until sunrise. Then I'll be back for what's mine.'

∾

Jared

'We need to talk.' Beth motioned towards the sofa.

The leather still squeaked, just like when he was a child, probably a testament to how little time Edmond had spent relaxing on it.

'Have you found out more about where they sent her?'

Beth nodded. 'I think I know how it was possible. There is one major event recorded traumatic enough to have caused the DNA coding that signposted that place and time. The Dornoch witch trial. It was the last of its kind in the British Isles.'

Jared swallowed down the stone that formed in his throat. 'Did any of the reports mention my mother?

'No. But...'

'Go on.'

'Something, or someone, is changing things. The details differ depending on which version of the timeline you examine.'

'There must be a branching point.'

'I agree. But I've not seen one alter the course so significantly. Not unless...'

'We get involved. Like we did with Aaron. Which details are changing between the timelines?'

'Every article I've read agrees on one thing. A local woman named Janet Horne was accused of being a witch and burnt alive. From what I read, she probably had some form of dementia, and they used her confusion against her.'

'That's barbaric.'

'It gets worse. In a few timelines, they killed her daughter, too. Another even reported that Janet's niece was murdered alongside them.'

'Such massive differences don't occur through chance.'

'Exactly. I think, whether she knows it or not, your mother is changing things, Jared. And not necessarily for the better.' A rush of colour flared in Beth's cheeks. 'When is this world ever going to change?'

'They have, haven't they? It's not like people go around burning *witches* any more.'

'Maybe. But it was only days ago we were being chased through time because some backward religious nut decided the science we were using was evil. That sounds like a witch hunt to me.'

'You have a point. You know I can't let my mother be another victim. Not of the witch hunters of Dornoch or the Durands.'

'I know.'

'So you won't try and stop me from going back?'

Beth raised her hands. 'I wouldn't dare. As long as you realise that I'm going with you.'

Jared couldn't suppress his smile. 'Of course you are.'

They made their way to the vestry of Saint Kinga's chapel, where Aaron was already setting up the equipment.

'What's with the audience?' Jared asked, nodding towards Aleksey and Marney.

'I guess they trust us as much as we trust them,' Aaron said, barely glancing up from the computer screen.

Jared had to agree about Aleksey. But there was still some part of him, perhaps misplaced, that hoped Marney was the good person he'd believed her to be when he'd been a child.

'Scoot over.' Jared traced a finger along the computer screen, making the odd adjustment to the coordinates Aaron had entered.

'I don't want to sound negative,' Aaron said, 'but just how much do you know about eighteenth-century Scotland? Usually, we'd spend weeks researching, surveying and—'

'I'm going with him,' Beth said. 'My original timeline wasn't much before that.'

'Yeah,' Aaron said. 'In London.'

'Close enough. I'm going.'

'Great. You two go off and leave me with Thing 1 and Thing 2 over there.'

Jared locked in the coordinates. 'I'm still not convinced it's a good idea.'

'You seem to have me confused with someone who needs your permission,' Beth said, then turned to Aaron. 'We won't be long. Just make sure the portal is open at the same time tomorrow.'

'Sure. If they haven't fed me to the tunnel goblins or dropped me off a ledge.'

'Don't even joke about it,' Jared said.

'Why? Because it's a ridiculous idea or too close to the truth?'

Seb burst into the chamber before Jared could answer.

'Jared! I need your help.'

Devon followed. 'I warned him that he didn't have permission to be in here.'

'Yes, well, it's urgent; a matter of life and death.'

'Let him talk,' Aleksey said.

Seb eyed Aleksey with suspicion, then turned his back on him and spoke directly to Jared. 'I've done a stupid thing.

After they transferred Martin and Oliver to the mines, I went to the resistance.'

Aleksey's face flushed red. 'Who? I want names.'

'It doesn't matter who. She's low-level, just a messenger, really. But I told her I wanted to join, to get my revenge.'

'What then?' Marney asked.

'She said I needn't worry, that there was already a plan in motion to kill them.'

'Isn't that what you had in mind?' Beth asked. 'I hate to sound heartless, but that sounds like exactly the outcome you were going for.'

'Yes. Or at least I thought so. But it isn't what Isaac would have wanted.' Seb ran his fingers through his hair. 'You have to understand, I never actually thought they'd go that far. Insulting fliers and carved names, that's what I thought the resistance was. Not killers.'

'So what's the plan?' Aleksey clicked his fingers, and Devon moved closer. 'I'll ensure the Durand brothers have an armed guard with them at all times.'

'I have no idea,' Seb said. 'She wouldn't give me specifics, just that it would happen soon.'

'Oh, God.' Marney cupped her hand over her mouth. 'Emma was assigned to oversee their transfer. I have to warn her.' She sprinted for the door.

'Hang on,' Aleksey said. 'Let's stop and think. I will send—'

'You will not cause me to lose another child!' The heat of Marney's rage silenced him.

'Do what you want then. I only meant to keep you safe.'

'I will.' Marney stormed from the chamber.

'Why come to us?' Jared asked. 'If the situation was as

dire as you feared, why not go straight to the mine and warn them there?'

Seb hesitated. 'I wasn't sure where you stood on their plan.'

'What do you mean?'

'Don't make me say it.' Seb chewed on his lower lip.

'You must,' Aleksey said, taking a step towards him.

'Everyone is talking about it. The citizens are saying Laura Pearse is the head of the resistance and that she's hiding because they're about to make their move.'

Jared's eyes widened. 'No, that can't be right. She wouldn't put me through all of this.'

'I don't know about that,' Seb said. In truth, Jared didn't either. He knew so little about her. 'But it makes sense for it to be someone on the inside, doesn't it?'

Jared glanced at the orb, torn between following his plan to go back looking for her or seeing if there was any truth to the rumours.

'It's okay,' Beth said. 'You go and investigate. I'll go back. If she's there, I promise I'll bring her home.'

'I can't let you do that. Not alone.'

'You saved me once. Let me do this for you.'

Jared's tongue was so dry he could barely force his words out. 'I can't lose you, too.'

Beth hugged him close. 'You won't. I promise.' She ran her hand over the orb, and the portal sparked into life.

～

Laura

The dilapidated house was made eerier by the silence. At first, Helen's and Janet's synchronised snores and random snuffles had grated on her. Now Laura was surprised to realise that she missed them.

Abandoning hope of sleep, Laura threw back the blanket and headed outside. The bite of the night air left her skin pocked with goosebumps. She looked up at the stars, wondering how many would blink out of existence before this Earth caught up with her own time. If there had been any silver lining from the Levelling, seeing the stars again would have been it. When she was a child, the heavens were so marred by dust and pollution that it had taken the apocalypse to wipe them clean. Only when humans were all but exterminated had the atmosphere begun to clear. It was a shame the surface was too dangerous for them to enjoy it.

An explosion of colour in the distance brought Laura back to her senses. Blues and purples danced across the horizon in waves.

'It...No, it can't be.' Laura raced towards the pulsing lights. 'Wait! Please!' She puffed out clouds of cold air. Although she knew her chances of making it were slim, she couldn't stop.

Laura was only meters away when the portal began to shrink. 'Jared! I'm here!' She pulled up sharp in front of it. Peering through, she strained to see the other side. Shadows drifted amongst the sparks of electricity.

It wasn't the unknown that stopped her from stepping through. It wasn't even the fear that she might be caught in the closing portal. No matter how she squinted, the shadows drifting amongst the sparks of electricity combined to make one image: Helen and Janet huddled in their cell. 'I'll come back! Please don't forget me!' The portal snapped shut, and Laura crumpled to the floor. 'What have I done?'

The snap of a breaking twig caught her attention. 'Who's there? Come out!' Laura scanned the ground around her for something she could use as a weapon. Scooping up a rock, she held it aloft. 'I'm not alone. My family are just over that hill, and if you even think about trying to hurt me...'

A shadow darted from the bushes. Without thinking, Laura gave chase, launching herself at the figure. They both tumbled into the dirt, and Laura rolled so she was on top. 'Why are you following me?' She held the rock poised high over her head. But before she brought it down, the moon cast enough light for Laura to see that it wasn't one of the villagers, set on beating a false confession from her, who she held pinned. It was a woman with waves of auburn hair. 'I know you.'

Instead of answering, the woman reached up to Laura's cheek and raked her nails across it. 'Get off me!'

Laura screeched with pain and clambered off. 'Tell me who you are.'

Panting, the woman crouched as though ready to pounce. 'The death of you, that's who I'll be if you try and come at me with that thing again.'

Laura realised she was still grasping the rock and dropped it to the ground. 'I'm sorry. I didn't mean to frighten you.'

'I should hope not. Or do you treat everybody who tries to help you like this?'

'I do know you, don't I?'

'I'm Beth. Jared's friend. He sent me to look for you. Although by the looks of it, you're more than capable of looking after yourself.'

Laura's eyes prickled with tears. 'Why didn't he come himself?'

'Because we didn't know for sure if you were here. He's searching for you back in your own time.'

'He didn't give up on me.'

Beth kept one eye on Laura as she dusted herself off. 'Of course not. Your son is nothing if not determined.'

'And you? You risked your life to come back and look for me?'

'No. I risked it for him. He needs to know you're safe, and that's the least I owe him. Although, I'm beginning to regret the decision now.'

'I'm sorry. I thought you were one of the villagers. They haven't exactly been welcoming.'

'That I can believe. The portal will open again in twenty-four hours. We just need to keep out of their way until then.'

Laura wrung her hands as she stared at the spot where the portal had been. 'I might not be able to leave with you.'

'Why not?'

'My friends are in trouble. I need to go to the village and see if I can help them.'

'That's crazy. We need to hide and wait for—'

'You don't understand.'

'I know better than most the dangers of living in a place like this. Which is why we need to leave.'

'I'd be dead if it weren't for Janet and Helen. I can't just abandon them.'

'You know, Jared and I had a friend called Helen. Although, we called her Nell.' Beth's brow knotted. 'We didn't manage to save her.'

'I'm so sorry. What happened?'

'She was murdered.' Beth pulled in a sharp breath. 'But that's a story for another time.'

'Well, time is something my Helen doesn't have. She's to be tried for witchcraft. Do you have any idea what they will do to her?'

'I have a fair idea,' Beth said. 'But no matter how much we want to save her, it doesn't mean we can. And we might end up getting ourselves killed along the way.'

'I've let too many people down to add them to the list,' Laura said. 'They helped me when I had nothing and nobody. I have to at least try to return the favour.'

Beth turned in a circle, grumbling. 'We have twenty-four hours until Jared opens the portal again. I'll do what I can to help you in that time. But Laura, believe me when I tell you, I will drag you through that portal back to him if I have to.'

Laura's eyebrows shot up. 'I guess we have a deal.'

The Book of Evelyn

I found Riley sitting in the destroyed apiary, picking pieces of yellow grass while she looked over the splintered frames.

'You know, don't you?' she asked.

'That Cerato is Rhiannon?' Even saying it out loud seemed crazy. 'Yes.'

'I didn't realise either. Not at first. You have to believe that.'

'Okay.'

'It was them, wasn't it?' she said. 'They destroyed the hives.'

'Probably.'

'I guess I owe Dale an apology.'

'Nah, I wouldn't bother.'

'I had no idea they would do that.' She hesitated. 'When I let her in.'

'You let Rhiannon in?' My head swam. 'Did you...did you push Kayleigh?'

'No! I got Rhiannon in the same way we'd sneak in and out. I swear!'

'All right, I believe you.'

Riley's shoulders slumped. 'But it's still my fault. It must have been one of the Pack who killed her. Maybe even Rhiannon.'

'Once you realised, why didn't you tell me who she was? All this time, I've been telling you how terrified of Cerato I am, and she's your big sister.'

'I didn't know until she came to the fence that day and said she wanted me back. When I saw how terrified you were, I didn't know how to break it to you.'

'How about, 'Hey, Evelyn, you know that psychopath who's been stalking you? Well, funny coincidence but..."

'Oh, shut up. If you are going to be like that, then just leave me alone.'

'Okay, I'm sorry. I know it's not your fault.' I thought back to that day at the fence. 'It makes sense now. It wasn't me she wanted. It was you.'

'Exactly! They aren't as bad as they pretend to be. Rhiannon told me that they play up to the stories so that—'

'So that what? Best case scenario, they act like monsters so they can steal from innocent people. But we know that's not true. Gabriela told us what happened to her.'

'I don't want to talk about this any more.'

'Well, you have to, because I need to know what you plan to do.'

'What do you mean?'

'Are you going to tell her to stay away and leave us alone?'

'I...I don't know.'

'You've got to tell her yourself that you don't want to go with her,' I said. 'If it comes from you, then she might back off.'

'Who says I don't want to go with her?'

I spluttered. 'You can't be serious? She's a cannibal!'

Riley sprang to her feet. 'I'm not listening to this. She told me that Bug has been twisting the truth about the Pack for years, turning everyone against them.'

I grabbed her hand. 'In your heart, you know the stories are true.'

'I can help them change. I'll set up an apiary, show them—'

'I don't want you to go.'

'You'd miss me?' she asked. 'Despite who I share blood with?'

'You know I would. You're my best friend.'

She forced a smile. 'I'll give it some thought. But it might be easier for everyone if I just do what she wants.'

'Not for you.'

'Maybe. But staying in the Colony isn't an option either. Do you think anybody here will ever let me forget that I'm Cerato's sister?'

Chapter Fifteen

Excerpt from _A Societal Analysis of the Bee Colony_

A Question of Loyalty

Worker bees are renowned for their loyalty. They dedicate their lives to keeping the hive safe at all costs, even death. This is one of the positive traits that most often attracts people to beekeeping.

However, a sceptic might suggest that a hive is closer to a dictatorship than a democratic monarchy. The Queen controls the hive by releasing pheromones, preventing her worker sisters and offspring from reproducing.

It could also be debated whether the Queen is actually the all-powerful force in the hive that we assume. It is well documented that if a Queen bee begins producing drones or her pheromone levels drop, loyalty is forgotten, and the worker bees will kill her. They achieve this by balling around her to raise her body temperature to a level at which she will overheat and die. Although this may sound brutal, a productive Queen is essential if the hive is to keep thriving.

Novice beekeepers will likely confuse balling with a similar shielding manoeuvre deployed by worker bees to protect the Queen when she is under attack. This is understandable as, in the bee world, protection and aggression look alarmingly similar.

Wakefield, R. (2025) *A Societal Analysis of the Bee Colony*. Third edition. London: Feisty Scholar Publications.

The Book of Evelyn

I could see the scratches on the lenses of Pearl's sunglasses. It took nothing away from her look. That is the way I will always remember her – pristine and irritated.

'Why are you sitting here?'

Pearl pulled the glasses down her nose and peered over the top. 'What does it look like? I'm getting some sun.'

'Yes, but I mean, why *here*?' My eyes drifted towards the stacks of vegetables the gardening group had piled by the gate. But that wasn't what I was looking at, not really. It was the wooden crate hidden behind, Michelle's body secured within. I knew it was there because I'd laid a handful of daisies on her chest before they'd nailed on the top. Roses would have been more appropriate. Or lilies, I suppose. But the pickings were slim on the surface.

Pearl replaced her sunglasses and turned her face to the sky. 'I'm waiting.'

'For what?' Call me stupid for asking, but I don't think any of it had sunk in at that point.

'You, my girl, are a joy and irritation in almost equal measure.' She heaved a huge sigh. 'For the Pack. They're late.'

'What? No. You can't mean...'

She took off her glasses and looked at me. 'Oh, stop it. It's a simple matter of mathematics, Evelyn. I'm one of the oldest here.'

'What difference does that make?'

'A huge one. Out of all the people in the Colony, I will likely be useful for the least time.'

'No, I won't let this happen. I will go and speak to Bug and tell him—'

'The same thing that I did: 'Stop your whining; this isn't your choice'.'

I stared at my friend, trying to form words through my rising panic. 'You can't leave me.'

She waved a hand in my direction. 'Nonsense. Of course I can. You'll be fine. This place will go on just as it always has, thanks to me. Let those gossiping harpies in the kitchen say a bad word about me now.' She winked at me, her eyes as playful as ever. 'They'll have to talk about me like I'm a saint. Saint Pearl, I like the sound of that.'

'You...you know what the Pack are planning, right?'

She wrinkled her nose at me. 'Don't insult my intelligence, young lady. Besides, despite a lifetime of trying to pickle myself with a diet of champagne and gin, I can't deny I may have become a tad gristly over the years. I can only hope that I choke them on the way down.'

'Can I change your mind?'

'No, dear. Menopause hasn't left a flexible bone in my bod—'

'Please stop.' I'd given up on the idea that my words had power. So when she did as I asked, I wasn't sure what to say to fill the silence. Finally, I settled on, 'You're my friend. You matter.'

She smiled. 'Yes. And after years of telling myself that, it took a sarcastic, wonderful, infuriating girl who reminded me so much of myself to truly believe it.' She took my hand. 'I wish I had something deep and meaningful to add, but unless we're talking bitchy comebacks, I've never really been that good with words.'

'It doesn't matter. You don't need to say anything.'

'I do. But forgive me for stealing your words. Evelyn, you matter.'

I swiped away a traitor tear. Not because I was ashamed of it but because I knew that it was not what she needed to see.

She put her glasses back on and turned her face back to the sun. 'Now, if you'll excuse me.'

'Goodbye.' It was a whisper, so tiny, I doubt she heard. But then, I said it for me, not her. I'd been robbed of so many goodbyes.

I headed towards the cabin. Bug was slumped on the floor, leaning against a cupboard.

'Are you okay?' I asked. A stupid question, I suppose.

He didn't answer.

A box of vegetables sat on his workbench. 'Are you still thinking about covering these with the virus?'

He shook his head. 'Even if we had enough, it wouldn't work. There are too many members of the Pack.'

'Then...then what was the point of going *there* for it?'

Dale strode into the cabin before he could answer. 'It's nearly time.'

I imagined the withering look Bug gave him matched my own; as if we'd done anything but watch the clock over the last ten hours.

'What will we say to them when they realise they don't have...don't have a third?'

Dale didn't question my arithmetic, so clearly he knew about Pearl's sacrifice. 'We tell them no more...'

'...and pray they accept it,' I added.

'Yes,' Dale said. 'We pray.'

'We still have the virus,' I said. 'Maybe we could put it into the darts somehow...'

'It's too risky.' Bug snatched the vial from the side.

'But it was your idea.'

'To infect them, yes. But as a Trojan horse, hidden amongst the supplies. Not fired all over our home.'

'It's better to go down fighting.' I couldn't comprehend any other reality. The thought of allowing the Pack to control the Colony was too horrifying to imagine.

'No,' Bug said. 'Not if we take the people we're trying to protect down with us. Besides, we have one vial of the virus. Your idea wouldn't work.'

'And what about when they see it's just Pearl? Do you allow them to come in and select the third person?'

'That won't be necessary,' Bug said. 'We have a third volunteer.'

'They'd better make themselves known fast,' I said. 'The Pack will be here any minute.'

Bug ignored me and rummaged in his supplies, looking for something. I assumed he was just preoccupied.

The waver in Dale's voice told me he knew his brother far better than I did. 'Bug, tell us the name of the third volunteer.'

'It doesn't matter.'

'Of course it—' Dale gasped. 'What the hell are you doing?'

Bug unscrewed the top of the vial and extracted the contents using a syringe. Then he positioned the needle over his thigh. 'What is necessary. I told you, we need a Trojan horse.'

I grabbed for the syringe. 'You're insane. You'll die.'

Bug held it aloft, out of my reach. 'Almost certainly. But I have no other choice.'

A crescendo of horns came from outside. Dale cracked the door and peeked through. 'They're here.'

'Let's just take a minute to think,' I said. 'They can wait a minute.'

'We're just delaying the inevitable,' Bug said, the syringe still held high.

Dale plucked it from his hand. 'He's right. We're out of time.' He plunged the syringe into his own leg.

'What have you done?' I asked.

'Gone some way to making up for my mistake, I hope.' Dale pulled himself up onto a nearby stool. 'Just give me a moment, and I'll go.'

Bug stared at the syringe that Dale had dropped to the floor. 'Wh...why?'

'Because the Colony needs you far more than me.' Dale stood up. 'I was wrong, Bug; you are a leader. You're exactly what this place needs.'

'Not without you,' Bug said. 'I don't want to be in charge. I never have. How will I keep this place going on my own?'

'You're not alone,' I said. 'I'm here.'

'But I can't...'

'You don't get to do that.' Dale's words were as steely as the look he gave his brother. 'You don't get to use me as an excuse to give up. Do you understand me?'

'I...'

'And no disappearing into your cabin for days on end. Or I'll come back and haunt you.'

Bug said nothing.

'Promise me, Bug.'

He nodded.

'Right.' Dale got to his feet. 'You make this my legacy, too. I'll die knowing that together we gave this world a chance.'

A sob jerked Bug's chest. 'I'll try.'

'Evelyn will help you. Won't you, kid?'

'Of course.'

'How long before I'm contagious?' Dale asked. 'Do I at least get to hug you goodbye?'

Bug heaved in a calming breath. 'Of course you do.' He wrapped his arms around him.

'Okay,' Dale said, cupping Bug's face. 'You know, of all the whiny little brothers out there, you were the best.' He slapped Bug on the back. 'You are stronger than you know.' Dale turned to me. 'Promise me you'll stay with him.'

I hesitated, thinking about Marney's offer. 'Bug will always be my friend, wherever I am. He knows that.'

'I guess that will have to do. And Evelyn, tell your mother I love her.'

'I will.'

Dale walked from the cabin.

As soon as they saw him, the Pack upped the frantic tooting, adding whoops and cheers to the mix.

Covering her ears, Pearl stepped backwards towards the cabin.

Dale put his arm out to her, and his face cracked into a grin. 'Let's do this together. Are you ready?'

'You know, I think I am.' Pearl straightened her pantsuit and looped her arm through his.

'There must be something else we can do,' I said, my eyes

flitting from my friends to Cerato, who stood waiting at the gate.

'Well, I'm certainly open to ideas,' Pearl said.

But I had nothing.

'I thought not. Then we'd best get this over and done with.'

'Really?' Dale asked. 'You don't have any last-minute barbs for me? Maybe a light tongue lashing to mark the occasion?'

'Don't take it personally,' Pearl said. 'It's how I show affection.'

'Wow. You must love me.'

'I wouldn't go that far.'

Their forced joviality made me want to cry. I knew, at least in part, that it was for my benefit.

The gate began to open. I stayed, rooted to the spot, praying that one or both of them would change their minds. Neither of them did. Rex pointed towards his truck, and they headed towards it, cattle to the slaughter. Dale helped Pearl up, and she carefully arranged her outfit as she took a seat in the dirty cargo bed. Then she stared ahead, deadpan.

Cerato nodded. 'Their sacrifice is appreciated, and I assure you they will be treated with respect.'

'After what they did?' Rex spat on the floor next to the truck. 'Three good men are dead.'

'And soon we'll be even,' Cerato said. 'With Bug's own brother making up the numbers.' Dale took the seat opposite Pearl. If he heard her words, he ignored them.

'You have what you want,' Bug said. 'You can leave us alone now.'

'Not quite,' Cerato said. 'Where's my sister?'

'She's practically a child,' Bug said. 'Just lea—'

'I'm not a child.' Riley stormed along the path from the dorm room, her boots kicking up a cloud of dust. 'And you don't speak for me.'

I gawped at her. 'Riley, you promised me.'

'I promised I'd give it some thought, and I did. Rhiannon is my family.'

Rex grinned. 'We all are now.'

'You were just going to leave without even saying good-bye?' I spat the accusation at her, knowing there was nothing she could say to change that fact.

'What choice did I have? You will never understand why I have to do this.'

'Choose me!' Rage bubbled, and I tried to push it back below the surface.

Riley's face crumpled. 'I can't.' I remember thinking she looked genuinely sorry, genuinely pained. *Good*, I thought. It could not have been a fraction of what I felt. She tugged up the straps of her backpack. 'This is bigger than us. You have your mother. I have nobody.' Riley hesitated. 'Come with us.'

I looked at Cerato.

'Always room for one more, Princess,' she said. 'I know you think I'm a monster, but most of it is for effect. If you come with us, I promise you'll be safe.'

Leaning closer to Bug, I said, 'I belong here.'

Riley's eyes glistened. 'But I don't. This doesn't change how I feel. Please believe that. But I can't stay.' She reached a hand towards me, and I flinched away. 'You never have to be scared of me, Evelyn. Not ever.' She walked towards the truck, slinging her bag in before clambering up. Pearl didn't even look at her.

That left just Cerato. 'You know this isn't over,' she said in her most saccharine tone.

'I know,' Bug said. 'I didn't dare hope that it would be.'

She turned to me. 'The offer's still there if you change your mind, Princess.'

'Never.'

'Suit yourself.' Then she walked towards the truck. The door opened, and a child jumped out. Cerato draped an arm around him. She pulled him close and pressed a kiss onto the top of his head. Then she turned back to me and smirked.

'That's Cory. He's alive.' Relief swept over me, followed by a sinking realisation. 'He was with them all along, wasn't he? They were just baiting us.'

'So it seems,' Bug said. 'They knew you wouldn't willingly let a child die.'

I couldn't watch them leave, so I ran to Bug's cabin and slammed the door. Blood rushed in my ears, but I could still hear the throaty roar of their engines. When they finally disappeared, the silence was just as consuming.

The door creaked open. 'We're safe for now,' Bug said.

'I'm beginning to wonder if all this is worth it.'

'All what?'

'The Colony, the Sanctuary, all of it. Maybe humanity doesn't deserve to be saved.'

Bug sighed. 'I decided that as long as I still found glimmers of hope out there, like you, and Pearl and so many others here, I would do what I could. But yes, I can't deny, more and more I have been wondering that myself.'

~

Jared

Jared caught up with Marney and they sprinted towards the mine.

'Are you sure it's this one they were sent to?' Jared asked.

'Yes.' Marney was grim faced. 'I swear to God, if they put my daughter in danger...'

Jared skidded to a halt as they reached the staircase. 'I can see Oliver. Where's Martin?'

'I don't know. There must be fifty people down there.' Marney craned her neck as she searched the crowd. 'Where is she?'

Jared made his way down the stairs. 'They won't hear us over the machines. Over by the bell – there's the flag they use to signal for work to stop.'

Jared picked it up and waved it high over his head as he shouted to the workers. 'Move. Get out of here. Go back to the dorm room.'

Marney tugged at the rope of the bell. 'Everyone out.'

Emma appeared from one of the side tunnels. 'What are you doing?'

Marney stopped ringing. 'Emma, thank goodness. Lead the miners back to the dorm.'

'They're in the middle of a shift.'

'Just do as you are told!'

The side of Emma's mouth tugged up in an incredulous smile. 'I'm not a child any more. I'm staying here.'

Jared stepped between them. 'Emma, please. We think there will be an assassination attempt on the Durand brothers. If it's anything like what they did to Millicent, then we need to get the miners to safety.'

Emma sighed before taking her mother's position by the bell. She gave it a few sharp tugs, but most of the workers had already stopped and were whispering amongst themselves. 'You're getting a half day. Now start leading back.' The miners began to file into the tunnels.

'Not you, Oliver,' Marney called.

Oliver stopped mid-step and turned to face them. 'What's going on?'

A crack, so loud that it sucked the air from Jared's eardrums, bounced around the mine. He cupped his hands over the side of his head but couldn't dull the ringing. 'What was that?'

Before anybody could answer, the platform on which they stood began to tilt.

'It's going to fall,' Marney said, shoving Emma towards the stairs.

Jared's eyes darted left and right, trying to determine if he'd be better running for the tunnel or the stairs. The floor jerked downwards, making his decision for him. As wood became dirt and salt rock, he plunged the flag pole he still held into the ground and hoisted himself up the steep incline.

'That was close.' Martin stood in the mouth of the tunnel.

Jared dropped to his knees, panting. 'Did the others—'

The mine echoed with a sickening thud. Martin rushed past. 'I'm coming. Hold on!'

The platform was almost vertical, and hanging from it a metre down was Oliver. Martin lay on his belly. 'Give me your hand.'

Oliver reached up, and their fingertips brushed. 'I can't

reach you.'

Martin looked back at Jared. 'I'm going to climb over and try and reach him. Hold onto me.'

Jared clasped Martin's forearm as he shifted his body over the edge.

'Reach up for my hand!'

'It's too far.' Resignation tainted Oliver's words.

'Can you reach my feet?' Martin asked. 'Climb up me.'

The weight doubled, and the flesh on Jared's knees burnt as he inched closer to the edge.

'Don't you let go, Morgan,' Martin said.

Jared tightened his grip.

Pale fingers hooked over Martin's shoulders. 'You're nearly there,' Martin said. 'Jared, grab him.'

Jared let go of one of Martin's arms. Using his free hand, he tried to haul Oliver up. 'I'm not strong enough!'

A rumble shook through the tunnel floor. Martin left fingernail scrapes in the dirt as he struggled to stop himself from falling. 'I'm losing my grip!'

The momentum of the scrambling men dragged Jared millimetres from the edge. In his left hand, he held Oliver, in his right Martin. But he knew he couldn't keep it up for long. Their fingers, slick with sweat, were slipping from his grasp.

Jared stared into the pleading faces of the Durand brothers. 'What shall I do?'

Oliver's voice was a croak. 'Let go, or we'll pull you over with us.'

'No.' Martin glanced at the drop below. 'We don't both need to die. Ollie, I'm sorry I wasn't a better brother to you.' Then he let go.

Jared tried to keep hold of him, but it was no use. Martin

locked his eyes on Jared as he fell. There was a crunch as he hit a ledge about twenty metres down. The darkness was merciful, sparing them detail beyond the odd angles of his limbs.

'No!' Oliver wailed. 'Martin, say something!'

Jared heaved him upwards. 'Stop struggling, or we'll lose you, too.'

Oliver threw a leg over the ledge and dragged himself to safety. He crawled to the tunnel wall and sobbed into his folded arms.

The sniffling of a woman's cry caught Jared's attention. Emma Wallace crouched on the stairs that now led to nothing but a lethal drop. 'I'm so sorry, Mom. I should have listened to you.' She stared at Martin's body before clasping her palm over her mouth to contain a wretch. 'I didn't think it would be like this.'

Marney rubbed her back, but it was to Jared she spoke. 'I told them no, that we'd find a better way. I had no idea they would do it anyway.'

'It's you, isn't it? You're the leader of the resistance.'

Marney pressed her lips together into a hard line. 'If I am, I'm doing a poor job of it.'

'That's not a denial, then.' Jared was startled as the wooden frame the women sat on creaked. 'You'd better go. That staircase can't be safe.'

Marney pulled Emma to her feet. 'I'll send help, I promise.'

It hadn't occurred to Jared until then, but they were cut off from not only the Sanctuary but the world above too. 'I know you will.' Although, if he was honest with himself, he wasn't sure he believed that.

The two women tip-toed up the stairs. Marney's hands hovered behind Emma as if she thought she might be able to catch her should they plummet into the cavern below. Jared wondered how she still assumed she had control over anything. None of them did.

'Oliver, are you hurt?' Jared asked.

'I'm fine. Just give me a moment, please.'

That's when Jared noticed the flag he'd hastily planted in the ground. That sheet of red material brought Martin's words flooding back to him.

My mother haunts me. Each night she visits, still dressed in her crimson gown. She stands at the foot of my bed. And she waits. And she watches. And she judges.

Maybe she just wants to be found. It must be lonely down there in those unmapped tunnels. Perhaps she still wants me to join her, the question she asked me that night still fresh on her lips: 'Are you coming with me?'

I think that would be the honourable thing to do. But not just yet. First, I have some wrongs to right.

Jared peered over the edge at Martin's body. 'Oliver is safe now, thanks to you.' Then he tore the red cloth from the flag. 'Neither you nor your mother has to be alone any more.' He dropped the fabric and watched as it ballooned and hung in the air for a heartbeat before fluttering down towards Martin. He liked to think Serena Durand guided it as it landed, draped over Martin's body, tucking him in for the final time.

～

Marney

Jared was slouched near the mouth of the tunnel, exactly where she'd left him. He raised his palm in greeting when he saw her. Otherwise, he was silent as the guardians constructed a makeshift bridge across the cavern to reach him.

'It's safe,' Kristoff called. 'Make your way over slowly. Actually, it might be best if you crawl.'

Marney offered her hand on the other side, hauling him to his feet.

'You came back.'

'I told you I would.' Marney glanced around to make sure the guardians were preoccupied with Oliver. 'But I don't blame you for doubting me. If I'm honest, it crossed my mind that my secret would be trapped over there with you.'

'Then I'm even more grateful that you didn't abandon me.'

Devon walked towards them.

'Please, Jared.' Marney's lips barely moved as she whispered her plea. 'Give me a chance to explain before you tell anyone.'

Devon smiled at him. 'Jared Morgan, you need to come with me.'

'No.' Marney stepped between them.

'But, Aleksey said to detain him.'

'Jared will be with me. I'll keep an eye on him.'

Devon ran a hand through his hair and turned but quickly changed his mind. 'I'm confused about who I'm taking orders from nowadays.'

'I guess that depends on who you ask,' Marney said. 'But choosing wisely now could make your life much easier later.'

Devon screwed his mouth into an angry knot. 'Yes, mam.' Then he stomped back towards the bridge.

'Don't worry about him,' Marney said.

'By the sounds of it, he's the least of my problems. Aleksey wanted me arrested?'

'Not exactly. He said it was a precaution until we know what's happening with your mother.'

Jared gasped. 'Beth! With everything that's happened, I didn't even think.'

'I was told she went through fine. As planned, they will open up the portal at the same time every day until she's back.'

'Or I'll go looking for them both.'

'Well,' Marney said, 'hopefully, that won't be necessary.'

'What now?'

'Now, I have some explaining to do. Let's go to your unit and talk. The guardians have things under control here.'

As they headed towards Edmond's old home, Marney churned over the details in her mind. But words escaped her when the first thing Jared did when he entered was pick up a pen and paper.

'You don't seriously think I'm going to let you write this down.'

'I'm a historian. It's what I do. I try to write an entry for anybody I encounter who I think may have shaped life as we know it. I call them my 'books'. Besides, nobody here will read it. Not until it's safe anyway.'

'I'm not convinced it ever will be.'

'You have to believe it will, or what's the point of all this?

And one day, the people of the new world will want to know how we shaped their lives.'

'The new world, I like the sound of that.'

'I won't use your name if that helps?' Jared put the tip of the pen to the paper but paused. 'Usually, I name them after the person the story belongs to, but it can't be 'The Book of Marney'. What shall we call it? 'The Book of Resistance'? 'The Book of Rebellion'?'

'No,' Marney said. 'It should be called 'The Book of Hope'.'

The Book of Evelyn

Ruth howled when I told her. I didn't think it was possible for a sound like that to come out of a human being, let alone my prim and proper mother. 'No! He wouldn't do that to me. Dale wouldn't leave me!'

I tried to wrap my arms around her, but she wriggled away. 'He did it for you. For all of us. To save us. Dale's a hero.'

She gulped in lungfuls of air between sobs. 'Like that's any good to me. I wanted someone to grow old with, not a martyr. Who will keep us safe?'

'We'll keep each other safe.'

'Because I've been so good at doing that before?'

'That wasn't your—'

'Don't, Evie. Just don't.' She slowed her breathing and looked me in the eye. 'That is my failing to live with. You don't need to take away my guilt. I want it as a reminder to do better.'

'You have.'

She let me hug her then. The weight of her grief pulled us to the floor. I sat with her until the grain of the wood bit at my bare legs.

Eventually, her whimpers subsided, and she let me lead her to her bedroom. I waited until I thought she was asleep, but when I went to pull the door closed, she said, 'He was a good man.'

'He was.' And I meant it. Years before, when we'd arrived at the Colony, I'd made Dale into a caricature of a wicked stepfather. But he was just doing his best, like all of us.

That night it was impossible to focus on anything beyond what might be happening to Dale and Pearl. And Riley, of course. I wasn't sure which fate was worse, the virus or the Pack. The possibilities shuffled through my mind like playing cards. So when someone knocked on our cabin door, I was happy for a distraction.

Bug pushed past me. 'We need to go back to the Sanctuary.'

'Why? Because they were all so thrilled to see us the last time?'

I'm very aware that you know the rest. But as you keep telling me, this story isn't for my benefit, or yours; it's for the future, for the people who come after us to know how things transpired as they did. I think I owe them honesty. Besides, I own my decisions.

'Do you think Jared would help us?' he asked.

'Possibly. But he hates the Sanctuary and has no intention of staying. What makes you think he has any power there?'

'It's not the Sanctuary that interests me. I want him to make us one of his orbs.'

On the way back from our visit, I'd relayed in minute detail your discovery. It wasn't just awe that left me babbling about the portal and the places you'd visited. It was pride. Because, although you may not feel like it right now, you always have been and always will be my friend.

'You want to travel back in time?' I asked. 'Why? Have you given up on the Colony?'

'Far from it. We need to think bigger.' There was a sparkle in his eye that I hadn't seen in such a long time. 'With an orb, imagine what we can achieve in this world. We won't have to start again repopulating the bees if we can travel to when they were flourishing and bring them back with us. The same with other pollinators.'

'But look around. What is there to pollinate?' My words might have suggested resistance, but I felt hope blossoming in my chest.

'We'll make it work, Evelyn. If we can save even just a part of our world, make some kind of oasis in this desert, shouldn't we try?'

'Of course.'

'So you'll talk to him for me?'

'He's a good guy. I don't think he'll take much persuading once he realises that it could save us.'

And I was right, wasn't I? Eventually, you were happy to help. But then, you didn't know that our actions would cost you your freedom.

❧

Laura

The plan, if it could be called that, was simple. Once inside the prison, Laura would somehow incapacitate Fion and sneak out with Helen and Janet.

'Perhaps he'll just let us go?'

'It's possible,' Beth said. 'But from what you've told me, he doesn't sound like the charitable type.'

'Yes. Wishful thinking, I guess. Am I mad? The chances we will get them out, let alone away from this place, are pretty slim.'

'Maybe,' Beth said. 'But I wouldn't leave a friend behind either. Nor would your son.'

'I wish I could say he got that from me...'

'Hush now. I speak as I see things, and you stayed to help your friends. Jared would be proud of you. *Will* be proud of you, once we get you home.'

'Thank you. You better get going. Remember—'

'I know.' Beth draped one of Janet's moth-eaten shawls over her head. 'Wait until Fion is inside, and then untie the horse and wagon.'

'What's with the shawl?'

'From what you've said, the townspeople are about ready to boil over. They won't react well to a stranger walking around. And a red-headed one at that.'

It felt like an age since Beth had left to walk into town. Still, the clip-clop of hooves and the crunching of stones under wheels as Fion pulled up outside the house took Laura by surprise.

'Have you thought about how you will talk some sense into them?' he asked as she clambered into his wagon.

'Hello to you, too.'

They travelled in silence, each lost in their thoughts. Laura would have liked to keep it that way, but Fion said, 'I've known Helen my whole life. I wasn't lying when I said I had feelings for her.'

Laura forced herself to keep the scorn from her voice. 'Do you always attack women you care about?'

'That was a mistake.'

'A mistake is knocking over her drink or standing on her toe. What you did was unforgivable, and nothing you say will convince me otherwise.'

'I know. But maybe doing this will show how sorry I am.'

'And you think they'll just let us in?'

'Of course. I'm the watchman for tonight.'

'Just you?'

'Aye. Duncan will be watching over Janet, ensuring she doesn't fall asleep.'

Laura shook her head in disgust.

'You know, there are worse ways to force a confession from a witch. Would you prefer they use the thumbscrews on them? Would you see them whipped?'

Being near him made Laura's skin crawl, so she focused on the sun ducking behind the horizon. It felt wrong for such beauty to be suspended above a world capable of such ugliness. As if in agreement, the warm light faded to nothing, leaving the silver moon to stalk their route. 'If there is evil in Dornoch, it isn't inside Janet or Helen.'

When they eventually pulled up to the prison, Laura couldn't wait to jump down. 'Let's get this over with.' She followed Fion inside.

All was peaceful when they reached Janet's cell. Her

head lolled to one side, and she snorted in her sleep. Duncan mirrored her on his stool outside the cell.

'The lazy little...' But instead of grabbing the chain and yanking Janet awake, Fion booted the bottom of Duncan's stool, sending him lurching to his feet in a sleep-deprived panic.

'What? Has she escaped?'

'No thanks to you.'

Duncan stretched, and Laura could hear the cracking of his joints. 'I'm just so tired.'

'Imagine how she feels.' Laura nodded towards Janet, who had somehow slept through the commotion.

'You can go, Duncan.'

'But the next watch isn't here yet. Are you assigned to Helen?'

'Aye. But this lady here will try to talk some sense into Janet, get her to confess.'

'Then I should stay for that.'

'No,' Laura said. 'She'll never talk with both of you here. She's too proud for that.'

'You'll get no argument from me.' Duncan passed Fion his keys. 'I don't want to be here a minute more than I have to.'

Once they heard the front door close, Laura went to Janet and rubbed the top of her arm. Her flesh was stony cold through the nightgown she still wore. 'Wake up.'

'Helen?'

'No, it's Laura.'

Janet peered through unfocused eyes. 'Am I going home?'

'Not just yet. Janet, they want you to confess.'

'To what?'

Fion grumbled behind her. 'You know what you did to my cattle.'

Janet's fingers pressed into Laura's wrists. 'What's he talking about? I never hurt any cattle, his or anyone else's. I just want my house, my bed, and my daughter.'

'Well, maybe we could do something about the last one.' Laura got up and whispered to Fion. 'Why don't you bring Helen in here?'

'Not a chance.'

'Listen to me. The last thing she'll want is her daughter to be treated like this. When Janet sees—'

'All right, I'll fetch her.'

When he was out of earshot, Laura knelt next to Janet. She rattled the chain around her ankle, but it wouldn't budge. 'I'm going to get you out of here. Somehow.'

'You're a good girl, Helen.'

Laura cupped her face. 'I'm not your daughter. But you'll see her soon.'

'Why won't they let me leave?'

Laura squeezed her hand. 'You said some things about being a witch and having powers. They think you made Fion's cattle sick.'

Janet shook her head as if trying to jumble the facts into order. 'I did?'

'Ma!' Helen tried to reach for Janet, but Fion tugged her back by the chain on her ankle. 'Ma, are you well?'

'My poor girl, what have they done to you?' Janet said as though she, too, hadn't shrunk to a shadow of herself.

'We can sort all of this out.' Fion paced forward. 'Helen can go free if you just confess.'

Laura dropped back behind him, looking for something she might be able to use as a weapon.

'She's sick, not wicked,' Helen said. 'I'll not have her confessing to something she hasn't done.'

Fion snarled through gritted teeth. 'Then you'll burn with her, you stupid girl!'

'Burn? Over some cattle?' As Helen edged towards her mother, the jangle of her chain gave Laura an idea.

'No, she'll burn because she's a wit—'

Laura snatched the chain from the floor and looped it around Fion's throat. Helen grabbed the other side, and they tugged.

Fion flailed his arms, trying to bat away the two women. Then, as his face turned a dark plum, he tried to wedge his fingers below the chain. It was useless, and he soon fell to his knees. As he lost consciousness, Laura let go.

'Helen, he's out. You can stop.'

But Helen kept tugging, her face set in a grimace.

'Listen to me. You aren't a killer. Let go.'

With a growl, Helen dropped the chain, and Fion slumped to the floor.

Chapter Sixteen

Excerpt from *A Societal Analysis of the Bee Colony*

Deformed Wing Virus

Regardless of potential benefits, cannibalism between bees is not without consequence. A growing threat to the already declining bee population comes in the form of a Trojan virus. Much like the fabled Trojan horse that led to the sacking of Troy, the victim bee may contain a nasty surprise. But instead of a group of Greek soldiers, ready to attack, it contains the deformed wing virus, which is just as deadly to the colony. When the infected bee is eaten, the virus is passed on, turning hygienic cannibalism from a means of protecting the hive into a vector for infection.

Trophallaxis, the function of regurgitating and sharing food with other worker bees, allows the virus to spread further. Hence, the beneficial social behaviour of sharing a meal can become the path to a colony's destruction.

Wakefield, R. (2025) *A Societal Analysis of the Bee Colony*. Third edition. London: Feisty Scholar Publications.

The Book of Evelyn

I was bumped and jostled in the back of the truck. Ruth rode up front with Bug, staring stony faced at the road ahead. I hadn't wanted her to come, but leaving without her hadn't been an option. 'You're all I have left,' she'd said. 'I'm not letting you out of my sight.'

We hadn't been travelling long when Bug slammed on the brakes.

I was propelled forward, my shoulder slamming against the window. 'Could you take it easy?' I yelled, rubbing at my bruised arm.

It was then I noticed the vehicles lining the side of the road like a parade of ants.

I slid the window open. 'It's them. That's Rex's truck.'

'I guess they didn't make it too far,' Bug said.

Ruth clambered from the cab.

'Where are you going?' I asked.

'I have to know for sure. If Dale's still alive, I can't leave him.'

Bug jumped out the other side. 'Either way, he'll be contagious, Ruth. He wouldn't want you to put yourself at risk.'

Ignoring him, she rushed towards Rex's truck. Drawing up short, she stared into the back. 'They aren't here.' She walked up and down the line of vehicles, peering inside. 'None of them are.'

'They must be.' As much as I shared her hope that somehow our friends had survived, the thought of the Pack still lurking around, unscathed by the virus, filled me with dread.

Bug looked over the railing at the side of the road. 'They're down there.' A circle of tents marked the site of the Pack's camp.

'They wouldn't have left their vehicles here unguarded,' I said.

'Probably not,' Bug said. 'Unless there was nobody left.'

Ruth climbed over the barrier. 'Let's find out.'

I grabbed her arm. 'Are you insane? It could be a trap.'

'Yes. And Dale could be down there, hurting and alone.' She made her way down the slope.

I followed. You may think me foolish, but that's just what we did, how we worked. She called the shots, and I paid the consequences. But not this time, not directly at least. Ruth paid a far greater price. I wonder if she'd still have gone if she'd known she'd die there.

Behind me, Bug cussed as he slid, regained his footing, and slid again.

A tiny avalanche of rocks pinged at the back of my legs. 'Are you okay back there?'

'Fantastic.'

Ruth picked up her pace. When she hit level ground, she sprinted towards the heart of the camp.

'She's going to get us killed,' Bug said.

'Ruth! Ruth, wait for us,' I called after her.

She ignored me, tearing aside the flap to each tent before moving on to the next. I left her to it. There was nothing inside that I wanted to see.

Instead, I waited by the long dead fire in the centre of the camp. An image of the Pack huddled around the flames made me shiver. I picked up a stick, its end charred from stoking the fire, and poked amongst the ashes. When I uncovered something white, I sprang back in horror. A pebble, I reasoned, or fragment of pottery. My treacherous brain laughed at these suggestions and reeled off its own: skin, bone, a tooth.

I dropped the stick when Ruth let out a strangled whimper. She held a tent flap aloft and stared inside.

Bug was at her elbow in seconds. 'Come away.' He glanced inside and then away just as quickly. 'We can't help them.'

'Get off—'

I don't know if Ruth's sentence was cut short or if the ringing in my head, as it slammed into the ground, blocked it out. Under my palms, I felt the rough scratch of the ashes that had disgusted me moments before. The pain spreading across my shoulder blades was too intense for me to care. Stretching my arm over my shoulder, I patted at the searing spot from where the pain radiated. When I pulled my hand back, my fingers were coated in blood. My blood.

I rolled onto my back. 'Ruth...'

But she wasn't looking at me. Nor was Bug. They both glared at Cerato, who stood with her gun trained on them.

'Sorry about that, Princess.' Twin crimson trails smeared her cheeks. 'I'd wanted to finish this with a more personal touch. But as you can see, I'm feeling a little under the weather.'

Despair and pain wrung a wail from me. 'Riley! Please don't let her do this.'

My tears made Cerato snarl. As her top lip twitched in disgust, I saw blood staining her teeth.

She jabbed her gun towards the tent Ruth stood by.

'She's in there. Your friends were the first to go, and her soon after. But then you know that, don't you?'

'This is nothing to do with her,' Bug said.

'No? Then why was she so desperate for Riley to stay? And what about the virus? I guess you want me to believe that, after nearly a decade, it rose again to strike down my family and me?'

'Maybe it's karma,' Ruth said.

Blood bubbled into Cerato's mouth, and she spat it to the floor, gasping for breath. 'And maybe you're murdering scum,' she said, between pants.

'Us?' Ruth asked. 'You call us that, after all you've done?'

'Out of necessity! To survive.' Cerato pointed the gun towards Bug. 'If he hadn't forced me to leave, taken the last person who mattered to me, things might have been very different.'

'I'm sorry,' Bug said. 'Even back then, you had something missing, Rhiannon. I had no choice.'

Cerato shook with the effort but stood tall. 'Neither do I.' Then she turned the gun towards me.

If future generations will read this, then I should probably make myself sound good. But it was no clash of Titans, no grand standoff. I was terrified, and I closed my eyes.

The shot rang out, but I didn't feel it strike. Still, I only risked looking when I heard Ruth's furious sobs. She straddled Cerato's torso, smashing her head, over and over, against the parched earth.

Cerato put a clawed hand to Ruth's face and drew her nails over her skin.

Ruth yelped and pinned Cerato's wrists above her head. 'Why won't you die?'

'Oh, I will.' Cerato grinned. 'But so will you.' She rammed her knees into Ruth's stomach, knocking the wind from her.

That was when I realised that while there was a single breath in Cerato's body, she would never let us be free. I pulled myself onto my hands and knees and crawled towards the gun by their feet.

Cerato laughed. 'Are you going to shoot me?'

'That's right.'

'You don't have it—'

I fired. Cerato's temple exploded, splattering the tents in chunks of brain. She didn't fall straight away. Her body wobbled as she raised a hand to her destroyed forehead. There was no anger, just confusion, as she uttered her last word. 'Princess?' Then she fell.

'Don't look,' Bug said. 'She left you with no option. Besides, she'd have been dead in an hour anyway.'

He was worried about me; I could see that. Perhaps he thought my actions, that memory, would haunt me. But that was far from the first, or the last, dead body I had seen. There was none of the horror that came with Michelle's passing or the self-loathing that consumed me when I killed my stepfather. I felt relieved. Justified.

Still, stars blotted my vision, and I lacked the energy to explain that.

'Keep pressure on your wound.' Bug pulled me into a sitting position so he could assess my condition.

'Is she going to be okay?' Ruth asked.

'We need to get her to the Sanctuary. But it doesn't look too bad. I think it went in and out.'

I probed my shoulder, trying to assess the damage, and whimpered. 'It hurts.'

Ruth got to her feet. 'You will be okay, Evie...sorry, Evelyn.' She beamed at me, but her smile faltered. 'I promise. You will be just fine.' Ruth took a step backwards towards the tent.

'Where are you going?' I asked, but if I am honest, I knew.

'I have to leave you now. If she infected me, I won't risk giving it to you.'

'But...no! What am I supposed to do all alone?'

Bug clasped my hand. 'You aren't alone.'

'You go back to the truck now,' Ruth said, turning to the tent. 'I'm going to rest a while.'

'Stop. You can't just leave me. Mum.'

Her smile returned. 'Thank you. It's so lovely to hear you say that, even if I know you deserved a far better one than me.'

'Don't say that. I love you, Mum.'

'I love you, too. Now, I'm going to sit with Dale for a while. You go with Bug, and you be happy.' Ruth ducked into the tent and let the flap fall behind her.

~

The Book of Hope

I'm a magician. I bet you didn't know that about me. For years, I cut myself into two. But unlike a glamorous magician's assistant, wiggling her severed toes, I pretended both of my halves were complete. While at work when my children were young, I fooled my colleagues into believing there was no child-shaped hole in me. The trick at home was not letting on that my mind was elsewhere. To be fair, I'm not sure I ever really pulled that one off. Yet, despite all the guilt I heaped on myself, our family thrived and was filled with love.

My daughters adored one another. They were also chalk and cheese. The younger one believed in the system, adamant that if the citizens just followed the rules and did the right thing, then all would be well. I envied her naivety.

The older saw injustice and strived to fix it. It was her that pushed me into the resistance. She was nine at the time.

'But if I'm not allowed to go to school, how will I become a doctor like you?'

'You *will* go to school. Just not yet. Until then, I'll teach you.'

'What about the other kids?'

She was right, of course. The universe didn't begin and end with my family. So I began to meet with other concerned parents, mainly from the trade sector. We had no idea our disorganised little group would become the foundations of the resistance. And believe me, if I'd known the path they'd lead my daughter down, I'd have barred the doors to keep them out and chained her in her room to keep her safe.

But I know that wouldn't have been right. People like her are meant to change the world, not hide from it.

The day I accepted that we were the resistance and not some powerless parent association, I learnt to cut myself three ways. I couldn't let my family know what I was up to. It was far too dangerous to get them involved. And it goes without saying that the rest of the Sanctuary couldn't know. My family's place there depended on me maintaining a zombie facade, following the orders of David and his cronies. It didn't come naturally to me, but after my stay in prison, I got good and fast. I watched as my comrades disappeared and learnt to live with the gnawing dread that I might be next. But I don't think I knew genuine fear until they came for my children.

At first, the Guardian Elite was voluntary. In the early days, you needed to demonstrate through trials that you'd earned your place. Once Durand seized power, that all changed. Every youth was expected to join. Any sign of reluctance from the child or the family would see them dragged from their homes and assigned to a dorm. Sometimes their parents accepted the situation. And sometimes they vanished.

Maybe this was why both girls faced their conscription with smiles. They told us the same thing. 'Don't worry about me. It's a chance to make a difference.' Their words may have been the same, but I know now that they had very different meanings.

The younger became a model soldier for the Durands. She was slipping away from me. I don't like to admit it, but I became guarded about what I said around her. My opinions were no longer my own.

It was quite another story with my older daughter. The first time she appeared at one of our clandestine meetings, I was furious. 'My child is off limits,' I raged at the group. 'You will not drag her into this.'

'I am in it, Mom. While we live here, neither of us has any choice over that.'

While we live here, that's what she said. I should have scooped the three of them up and found somewhere else. Especially now that I know there were other options on the surface. But the unknown was more terrifying than the Sanctuary.

'I'll be careful,' she said. 'Consider me your eyes and ears inside the Guardian Elite.' I was so proud. And so stupid. The Durands knew, probably from the start.

Foraging is a way of life for us. Plans for the Sanctuary to be self-sustaining didn't pan out. We all knew it was dangerous to go to the surface, knew people who had been lost up there. But you never imagine it will be a member of your own family. I guess such delusion is a form of self-preservation.

Luca made the selections. I don't know what criteria he used, but both of my girls were chosen to accompany him to the surface. Only one came back.

They told me it was an accident, that the earthquake damaged the hospital and Luca warned her not to go inside, but she knew how valuable the medicines would be.

'She died a hero,' Aleksey said as he patted my hand.

I stared back at him, too shocked to even cry. 'Do you expect me to take solace in that? She was fourteen.'

At least he had the decency to look embarrassed. 'I'm sorry for your loss.' But he wasn't. Not really. I think Aleksey realised early on that he wouldn't survive on the surface, and he intended to sacrifice whatever or whoever he needed to make the Sanctuary work. Millicent knew that, which is why she accepted the risks when she accompanied him into that tunnel. She wasn't supposed to die.

The night my daughter was killed, I held her sister as she sobbed. 'They're lying! Luca sent her into that building knowing it wasn't safe. Mom, I think he wanted her to die. Why else would he do that?'

Like that, one daughter was snatched away from me, and the other was returned. I tried to keep her out of the resistance. Maybe I was being selfish, but I couldn't lose another child. Not that it made a difference. I was both blessed and cursed with wilful children.

When I heard about the planned assassination of the Durand brothers, I went straight to her. 'You can't do this?'

She all but patted me on the head. 'I'm not a kid any more, Mom.'

'You are. You're my child. And that isn't my point. Two wrongs don't make a right.'

'No, but it does even the score.'

'Is that what this is? Don't you see that revenge and justice are not the same things?'

I thought I'd persuaded her to call off the attack. She swore on Jodie's soul that it wasn't going ahead. Let's hope she had her fingers crossed, because you know how that ended. As I led her away from the mine, from Martin's body, I hoped some part of her thought it was worth it. Guilt is cancer to the soul.

So there it is. Could I have done more? Probably. Evil

sprouted roots and grew here because people, including me, let it. But if you keep my secret, if you trust me to lead, I promise I won't let that happen again. I can bring hope back to the Sanctuary.

The Book of Evelyn

I kept my eyes trained on the little piece of sky I could see outside the truck windscreen. Every bump brought fresh pain, and I tried not to scream.

Bug's rising panic was clear. In my periphery I could see him casting furtive looks at me. Still, he told me over and over it was just a flesh wound. Perhaps to reassure himself as much as me. 'We're nearly there,' he said.

'Dale will be mad that I ruined his seats.' I don't know if my error in tense was the blood loss or habit.

Either way, Bug let it slide. 'He'll understand.'

I must have blacked out, because the next time I looked up, the patch of blue I'd focused on was torn in two by the jagged angles of barbed wire.

My body tensed at the sight of it, despite knowing that my only hope for survival lay inside.

Bug smashed his fist down on the horn again and again. The gate swung open. At first, the truck's back wheels whirred impotently as he pressed the accelerator. Bug cursed, changed gear and tried again.

'It's been a long time since I drove,' he said. 'The last time we came here was the first I'd left the boundary of the Colony in...well, goodness knows how long.'

'I wish we'd never left at all.'

'I understand that. Your mother would still be with us, and there is nothing I can ever do to make up for that. But, Evelyn, I really think their sacrifice will be worth it. In the end.

A wave of sorrow overwhelmed me. 'Nothing could be worth losing them. Nothing.'

'Of course; you're right. But they've given us a chance to save this world. We'll make sure they're remembered for that. He pulled up outside the entrance and tooted again.

'Back so soon.' It was Kristoff's voice. 'Aleksey isn't going to like...Evie, what happened to you?'

The pity in his voice bough my grief bubbling to the surface. 'She killed my mother.'

'Evelyn has been shot,' Bug said before I could reveal something best left between us. 'Now, would you be kind enough to let us inside before she bleeds to death?'

'I ...Okay.' Kristoff opened the passenger door before hesitating over where to put his hands to lift me.

I spared his blushes and pushed myself from the seat, anchoring my arm over his shoulders. Moments later, Bug was on my other side, supporting me between the two of them.

The stairs were trickier. Too narrow for us to walk three abreast, I pushed up close to Kristoff. Bug trailed behind us. Each time I stumbled, I felt his fingers clamp on my shoulders, steadying me.

When we reached the bottom, I was propped against the wooden barrier. Drops of blood marked my path and were sucked into the salt rock, a perfect metaphor for how this place sucked the life from me all those years ago.

'Wait here,' Kristoff told us, as though I had any choice.

He returned with Marney. 'Evelyn, what happened?'

'That psycho Cerato shot me.'

Marney examined my wound. 'I think the bullet went through. Still, I'd like to get you to the infirmary to take a proper look.'

'Can't you just use the medilaser to close it up?'

'Not if the bullet is still inside.'

The rest is a bit of a blur. Marney gave me something to ease the pain, but it softened the edges of my reality, too. I kept losing time. One moment Bug and Marney stood with their foreheads millimetres apart, their hushed tones confirming that the conversation was about Ruth and Dale and all the other people we'd lost. Then they were gone, and the lights all around me dimmed. When my world regained its angles and edges, you were next to me, Jared.

'You're awake.'

'Apparently so. What time is it?'

'Early.' You looked so serious. I mean, you always do, but more so than usual. 'I was worried about you.'

'You didn't think a little bullet wound would take me down, did you? I'm far too stubborn to die that easily.' I propped myself up on the pillows. 'Where's Bug?'

'Still sleeping, I imagine. With all you've both been through, you must be exhausted.'

'He filled you in then.'

'I'm so sorry about your mother.'

Tears pooled in my eyes, and I blinked them away. 'Me too.'

'I wish I knew what to say to make you feel better.'

'There is nothing. Except...Did Bug speak to you about the orb?'

'Yes, but Evie...sorry, Evelyn. That's going to take a bit of getting used to.'

'You know, from you, I don't mind Evie so much.'

'Evelyn.' You sounded it out so carefully. 'As much as I want to help, it isn't as simple as that. What's happened here since we left is nothing short of evil. The Durands twisted my grandfather's technology into something vicious. I can't let his legacy be tainted any further.'

'Bug isn't like that! He's a good man.'

'I'm sure he is, but it's not a risk I can take.'

'What risk? If anything, if Edmond were here, he would be working with Bug on this. You know he would.'

'I...Let me give it some thought.'

I remember how you couldn't meet my eye when I grasped your hand. 'Get some rest,' you said.

In that bed, drifting in and out of consciousness, was when I realised that we had to do more. The Pack were gone, but another evil would arise to take their place. We had been left to argue over the scraps in a dying world, and there would always be those who refused to fight fairly. Not when survival was at stake. It was time to stack the odds in our favour.

～

Jared

Jared didn't know why he'd expected the lab to look the same, like a fly caught in amber. In his mind, it was still littered with discarded components and half-finished projects. In reality, he knew they'd have ripped it apart after his grandfather's escape. They'd sought answers at any cost, stripping it of anything of use and leaving it sterile and heartless.

There was no point asking who was knocking as Jared headed for the door. He'd sent for Bug. Jared didn't even bother with a 'hello' as he stepped aside and let him in. 'Evelyn says I can trust you.'

Bug considered this. 'You can trust I will always put the greater good ahead of my own interests.'

'Is that the same thing?' Jared asked.

'I think so. I've had to make tough decisions. But they've got the Colony this far.'

Jared frowned. 'You talk in riddles.'

'Only because what we are discussing isn't a straightforward issue. But I promise that the orb will be used as we discussed, to bring pollinators back to Earth.'

'I've never shown anybody how to make one before,' Jared said. 'I've shown them how to use it, sure. I had to so we could travel between timelines. But never how to replicate it.'

'I'll use the knowledge wisely. You have my word.'

Jared spent the next couple of hours talking Bug through the process of making an orb. When it was finished, he held it out.

Bug reached for the orb. 'Thank you.' However, before he touched it, Jared closed his hand.

'I'm sorry. It's just, my grandfather trusted me with it. I guess this feels kind of like a betrayal.'

'Jared, this will be a whole new legacy for him. We will renew the insect population, and our Earth can thrive again. All because of him. That's pretty special.'

'Evelyn trusts you.' Jared knew he was repeating himself, but saying the words made him feel better. 'So does Marney.'

Bug smiled. 'I always knew smart women would save the world.'

'Then here.' Jared placed the orb in Bug's palm. 'When will you use it?'

'Tomorrow at sunrise. The sooner we get started, the better. Now, I have preparations to make.' Bug got up to leave but stopped before he reached the door. 'Thank you, Jared. It takes courage to put your faith in another's vision. Especially when you can't see it yourself yet. But I promise it will be worth it.'

The following day, Jared hurried up the stairs and towards the exit of the Sanctuary. Kristoff helped him turn the metal circle that disengaged the lock to the Sanctuary, and before he knew it, he was outside.

The last time he'd stepped foot on the surface of his Earth, it was in the middle of a sandstorm. Now, everything was so bright, the edges too sharp. Jared had seen many time-lines, yet it struck him that none looked as real as this one.

Evelyn and Bug were already waiting at the arranged point on the perimeter of the Sanctuary. They'd picked it because it was close enough to move the equipment there easily but was shielded by the back of the building should prying eyes be watching them. 'I'm sorry I'm late. It doesn't look like you need my help, anyway.'

Bug was all set to power up the orb. 'You gave good instructions.'

'I'm glad you made it,' Evelyn said. 'We wanted to explain our plans to you first-hand.'

'What date have you decided on?' Jared asked. He'd given them thousands of possibilities taken not just from his list but also the DNA the Durands had collected since his departure. Their options seemed endless.

'The middle of the Palaeolithic period,' Bug said. 'I'm opening a portal in Asia almost 300,000 years ago.'

Jared frowned. 'Why so long ago?'

'Homo sapiens were just evolving, so they shouldn't be too much of a threat,' Bug said.

'You're probably worrying too much,' Jared said. 'The chances that you'll have any trouble in the short time the portal is open is small.'

Bug didn't meet his eye. 'During this period, honey bees were prolific, spreading right across Europe and Africa.'

'Okay,' Jared said. 'So you think that will make them easier to locate?'

The sun peeped up over the horizon, stretching out their shadows. 'Time to get started.' Bug reached out his hand towards the orb.

'Can I do it?' Evelyn asked. 'It should be me.'

Bug nodded, and she ran a finger around the top of the orb. It crackled and popped.

Jared grinned at her. 'Your first portal.'

Bright green bolts cut through the air. 'It's beautiful,' Evelyn said. 'I see trees!'

Jared breathed in the heady perfume of the foliage. Full and lush, they were nothing like the lifeless shells of their world. The three of them stood together, staring.

Bug reached his hand towards it. 'It certainly is a marvel.'

The joy didn't last. A sudden tearing sound made the hairs on Jared's arms stand up. 'That doesn't sound right.' The portal widened, its edges blackening. 'What's happening?'

Evelyn took a step towards him, her arms outstretched. 'Jared, stay calm. It's going to be okay. Bug knows what he's doing.'

'And what is it he's doing?' The scorched air filled Jared's nostrils.

'I'm opening a permanent doorway,' Bug said. 'Life from the other side will be able to move freely between the two worlds.'

'No,' Jared said. 'Are you insane? What if it doesn't stop? What if you tear the fabric between the two worlds away completely, and they collide?'

'It will stop,' Evelyn said.

'How can you possibly know that?'

She took a step towards him. 'Because this isn't the first doorway we've opened today. It's already happening, Jared. Life is spreading from their world to ours.'

Jared cupped his hand over his mouth. 'You have no idea what you've done.'

'Just breathe.' Evelyn looped an arm over his shoulders.

Jared shrugged her away. 'How many doorways? Where are they?'

'We can't tell you that,' Bug said. 'You'll just try and close them.'

'I have to! If they collapse, we could all die.'

'I don't think they will. But either way, the gamble is worth it.' Bug walked towards the portal and peered into its depths. 'Don't you see? Humanity had its chance. Now it's all about saving this planet. Pollinators will be free to inhabit our Earth.'

'So could anything else.' Jared stretched out each word. 'Mammoths, mastodons—'

'Bees, butterflies, moths, wasps...' Bug said. 'Jared, I'm not some crazy megalomaniac. I just want this world, *our* world, to have a chance. Don't you see the amazing opportunity you've given us?'

'And what about your Colony?' Jared asked.

'Just like you, they will have a choice to make. Are they the dregs of humanity destined to go extinct? Or the Adams and Eves, ready to lead us into a new era?'

A terrifying realisation overwhelmed Jared. 'You've trapped me here. We can't open another portal, not when it's so unstable.'

Evelyn took Jared's hand. 'You have friends here. Family. You could be happy.'

'You didn't need to do this,' Jared said. 'You could have set up your Colony anywhere you liked in time. I'd have helped.'

Bug shook his head. '*This* is our world. *This* is our time. We have a responsibility that we can't, or at least we shouldn't, be allowed to escape from. I hope you make the right choice and join us, Jared. But I promise you this; I will ensure this world survives either way. For me, there is no cost too high.'

Laura

The lock to Helen's cuff clicked, and Laura moved on to Janet's. 'It's stuck.'

'Leave me,' Janet said. 'You girls get away from here while you can.'

'That's not happening.' Helen plucked the key from Laura's hand. 'Let me try.' But nothing happened as she turned the key again and again. 'Come on, you stupid thing!'

'Be careful; you'll break it. She will have to keep it on for now. Once we're safe, we'll find someone to cut it off.'

'You don't think people will notice this?' Helen jangled the length of chain.

'We're getting straight into Fion's wagon. My friend will be waiting outside to drive us.'

'What friend? You don't know anyone in Dornoch.'

'It's a long story, and I promise I'll explain.' Laura helped Janet down from the stool and looped the chain over her arm. 'Let's go.' But when they got to the front door, the handle rattled. 'Who is that? Fion sent Duncan home.'

'I don't know, do I?' Helen pulled her mother closer. 'Maybe the other watchman is early.'

'This can't be happening.'

The door swung open, and Captain Ross stepped through. Seeing the three women, he beamed. 'What do we have here?'

Laura's heart sank, and she cursed her stupidity. *This is it*, she thought. *This is how it ends. I'll never see Jared again.*

'They're with me.' Fion's voice was hoarse from behind them.

'Really? Because it looks like they were heading for the door.'

Malcolm pushed past Ross. 'What's going on?' He peered closer at Fion, who had flicked up his collar to hide the angry welts on his neck. 'Are you feeling well? You look a little flushed.'

'I'm fine. Just excited to tell you the news. Janet here has confessed that she, and only she, cursed my cattle.'

'Did she?' Ross' eyes narrowed. 'And what inspired this little change of heart, Janet?'

Janet crossed her arms over her chest, perhaps embarrassed to be standing in her nightgown in front of the three men. 'If I say I did it, will you let my girl go?'

'Quiet, Ma,' Helen said. 'Don't you say another word.'

'You're the one who needs to hush,' Fion said. 'Your mother knows what needs to be done.'

'I hope by that, you mean telling the truth?' Ross asked. 'Because I don't believe this for a second.'

'And what would you prefer?' Malcolm asked. 'The townspeople are already pointing fingers at their neighbours, their kin. Would you prefer the crown question your judgement in allowing a plague of accusations?'

Ross bristled. 'They wouldn't dare.'

'Let them leave,' Fion said. 'I was the accuser, and I say justice will be done with Janet's confession.'

In one stride, Ross stood directly in front of Janet. 'Then let's hear it, Mistress Horne. Did you sign your name in the devil's book? Are you a witch?'

'Get away from my mother.' Helen wrapped her arms tightly around Janet. 'Don't answer him, Ma.'

Janet shrugged from her embrace and clasped Helen's

face. 'Precious girl. You were the blessing of my life.' Then to Laura, she said. 'Take her where they'll never find you.'

'If they're innocent, as Fion says, then they have nothing to fear,' Malcolm said. 'You have my word on that.'

Janet ignored him and kept her eyes trained on Laura.

'I promise.'

'All right then. I'm guilty. Me and only me.' Janet grinned and stood straighter. 'I'm powerful. I've seen things, been places, that the likes of you can only dream of.'

'No, Ma!' Helen fell to her knees, clutching at the cloth of her mother's nightdress. 'Don't you understand, they'll kill you?'

'I'm ready to rest now. Take me back to my cell.'

'No!' Helen sobbed. 'Please don't do this! She's just a barmy old woman. Don't take her from me.'

Fion caught Laura's eye. He didn't say a word, but she read his look as clearly as if he'd bellowed at her. *We're even now.* Clasping Helen's upper arm, he pulled her to her feet. 'It's done. Now, go, save yourself.'

But Helen still struggled. 'I won't leave her!'

'Come now, Helen. It's time to go.' Laura forced her words through the tears stinging her throat and clutched Helen's other arm.

'Say your goodbyes,' Ross said as he led Janet back towards her cell.

Her voice was tiny as she looked over her shoulder. 'Be happy, my love.'

Chapter Seventeen

<u>Excerpt from *A Societal Analysis of the Bee Colony*</u>

<u>A World Without Bees</u>

The U.S. Department for Agriculture found that approximately two-thirds of beekeepers have suffered unsustainable losses in their colonies. In short, without enough bees to keep their hives going, they will fail and die.

So, what implications does that have for us? Around nine out of ten flowering plants rely on pollinators. It has been estimated that bees alone are responsible for pollinating around a third of our crops. But the devastation would not end with plants. It would quickly filter along the food chain until it inevitably reached us. With a human population of over eight billion, food would soon become scarce.

The cause of honey bee decline is likely a mixture of factors. However, man-made issues such as pesticides and climate change are certainly on the list. The pertinent question repeated in the media is, 'Could the human race survive without bees?' Let's hope we never have to find out.

Wakefield, R. (2025) *A Societal Analysis of the Bee Colony*. Third edition. London: Feisty Scholar Publications.

Laura

Beth helped bundle Helen into the back of the wagon. 'You stay back here with her.'

'Do you know how to drive this thing?' Laura asked.

'It's a bit late to go asking me that now. But yes, I have a fair idea.'

Laura climbed up next to Helen, hemming her in.

'Let me go! I need to get back to my mother.'

'Please,' Laura said. 'There's nothing we can do. Janet knows that. Don't let her sacrifice be for nothing.'

'You expect me to let them kill her?'

'You haven't let them do anything. This will be a mark on their souls, not yours.'

Helen's tears faded into a shocked silence. Laura couldn't think of anything beyond false hope or hollow platitudes to fill it, so she let it hang between them.

'We're nearly there,' Beth called over her shoulder.

'Where?' Helen asked.

'Not far from your house.' She left it at that. Anything else seemed impossible to explain.

'No. We can't go there. Mark my words; they won't be satisfied with my ma. They'll get a taste for killing and come after us.'

'No, that's not where we're going. Please, trust me.'

Helen settled back into the bed of the wagon. 'I do.'

When Beth brought the wagon to a halt a few minutes later, Laura was first out. Once Helen joined her, Beth slapped the horse on the rump, sending it into a gallop. 'He'll find his way home.'

'That's more than Fion deserves.' Laura stared into the night air. 'Did we miss it?'

'I don't think so. Besides, Jared said if I wasn't here, he was coming through after me.'

'Missed wh—' Helen recoiled in horror as the portal burst into life before them, the flashes of light mirrored in her wide eyes. 'What is that?'

'Please don't be scared,' Beth said. 'Think of it like a doorway.'

'To where?' Helen's face contorted with anger. 'I'm so stupid. It goes to hell, doesn't it? The two of you are witches. You would let my poor mother die in your place.'

'No!' As Laura stepped towards her, Helen stepped back. 'This isn't magic or witchcraft or anything else to fear.'

'I'm not a fool.'

'I know you're not,' Beth said. 'Tell me, if we were witches, would you care? We tried to save your mother from those barbarians, didn't we?'

Helen hesitated. 'Yes.'

'Exactly. All we want is for the three of us to get somewhere safe.'

Helen looked at the road behind as if she were debating whether to run. 'You're white witches then?'

'If it makes you feel better to think of us like that, then that's fine,' Laura said. 'Please, we need to step through the portal to a place we'll be safe. We don't have long before it closes, and we'll be stuck here.'

'What's on the other side?'

'Opportunity,' Beth said. 'We can take you anywhere in the world.'

Helen's face crumpled. 'Back to my mother?'

'No,' Laura said. 'But how about to some of those places she dreamt of going? You can see them for her, make her proud.'

Helen swallowed her tears. 'Tell me, was my mother like you? Was she a white witch, too?'

'I don't know about that.' Laura took Helen's hand. 'But what I do know is that your mother was strong and brave and far too good for a place like this. Your mother was exactly like you.'

'All right,' Helen said. 'I'm ready.'

The three of them stepped through the portal together.

Jared

Aleksey had been pacing the length of the chapel since Jared broke the news to them. 'First things first; we are going to send a group of guardians and arrest that maniac.'

'On what authority?' Marney asked. 'We have no control over the Colony. Besides, we supplied him with the orb. It's not like Richard stole it.'

'No.' Aleksey jabbed a finger at Jared. 'He gave it to him.'

Aaron slapped his palms on the table. 'Back off. Don't you think he feels bad enough?'

Aaron was correct. Guilt pooled in Jared's chest, and he willed himself to breathe. 'I'm sorry. I didn't know what he'd do.'

'You handed some of the most advanced technology this world has ever seen to a stranger, and that's your excuse; you didn't know?'

'Evie isn't a stranger.'

'No,' Marney said. 'But Evelyn is. She is very different from the girl we knew.'

Jared added grief for the friend he'd lost to his itinerary of emotions. 'Aleksey's right. This is all my fault. Aaron, I'm so sorry. I've trapped us here.'

Aleksey sniffed. 'Worse than that.'

'What do you mean?'

'You've trapped your mother back there.'

'No.' The world around Jared span.

'And your friend. You can't expect us to open up another portal when—'

'Shut up, Aleksey,' Marney snapped. 'Let me give this some thought. We need to be smart about this.' She cupped her hands over her mouth for so long that Jared suspected she'd given up. 'Okay,' she said finally. 'We are monitoring the portal behind the Sanctuary, and so far, it seems stable?'

'That's correct,' Jared said.

'But for all we know, Bug and Evelyn could be opening more portals as we speak, right?'

Aaron gave Jared a weary look. 'It's a possibility.'

'And even if they are, we only have a theory from Edmond to tell us that their actions could cause issues?'

'Cause issues?' Aleksey gaped at her. 'I think cataclysmic consequences might be a more apt description.'

'But we can't know that,' Marney said. 'Neither could Edmond. He disappeared long before he could test the true potential of his creation.'

'What are you suggesting?' Jared asked.

'I'm saying that I don't see that one more portal will make a difference either way. I'm saying I think we should proceed with our plans to bring Laura home.'

'You're insane,' Aleksey said. 'It's too dangerous. And I'd like to remind you exactly who is in charge here.'

'Oh yes. I'm well aware that you are the last remaining committee member, Aleksey. On this side of the portal, at least. Would you like to hold an election? Your popularity rating must be soaring with all that mine business.'

Aleksey mumbled something inaudible under his breath. 'On your head be it. I'm going to brief the guardians. The sooner we track down Bug, the better.'

'There's no need,' Marney said.

'What do you mean?' Aleksey froze halfway to the door.

'Richard gave me his location before he left.'

'And you've been sitting there with it, saying nothing, all this time? Give it to me so we can have him arrested.'

'What good would that do? We don't want to start a war with the Colony. We need to make an alliance with them.'

'After what he did?'

'Especially after that. Richard is an extremely clever man, and I can't imagine he did this lightly.' Marney took a deep breath as if steadying her nerves. 'So we will work with him to make his plan successful. Once he trusts us, we get them to come back and close the portal closest to the Sanctuary and agree not to open any more. Eventually, when he's got all he needs from the other timelines, we might get him to close them all.'

Jared felt the weight of his mistake lifting from him. 'Do you think they'll agree?'

'I think they want to survive, just like us. It wouldn't make sense for them to reject a truce.'

'What benefit could an alliance possibly be to us?' Aleksey asked.

Marney frowned. 'Maybe it could save everything. Have you considered that his plan might actually work?'

Aleksey didn't answer.

'No, I didn't think so. At least Richard's trying something. He's not cowering under the ground, waiting to die.' Marney patted Jared's hand. 'However, that is a problem for tomorrow. For now, let's see if we can get Laura home.'

'You're insane.' Aleksey hissed. 'But if you're going to open another portal, I will be there to shut it at the first sign of trouble.'

They waited in silence as Aaron set up the orb. Jared couldn't bear to do it himself. He knew it was illogical, but he felt cursed. He'd lost more friends of late than he cared to count.

'Ready?' Aaron said.

Jared didn't know how to answer that. At least with the portal closed, there was a chance his mother and Beth were waiting on the other side. Once it opened, he'd know for certain either way. It didn't help that this might be their only chance. He couldn't imagine Aleksey letting them repeat it. But still, Jared nodded.

'Then let's do this.' Aaron swiped his finger around the orb, and it burst into life.

Jared was still blinking the light from his eyes when he found himself in a tangle of embraces. He pulled away to see Beth and Laura both beaming at him. 'You made it,' he said. 'You're really here.'

'Thanks to you,' Laura said, folding him back into her arms. 'And Beth, of course.'

'Can I get one of those?' Aaron asked, hoisting Beth onto her tiptoes with the ferocity of his hug.

It was then that Jared noticed a third woman staring around the chamber, backing away from them. Her cheeks were streaked with dirt and tears.

'Helen,' Laura said. 'It's okay. This is my son, Jared.'

'What is this place?'

Aleksey stepped towards her. 'I think who *you* are would be the more pertinent question.'

'Get away from me.' Helen dipped her head, and Jared was sure she'd fly at Aleksey, given the slightest provocation.

Aleksey sneered. 'You aren't in any position to be giving orders.'

'Leave her alone.' Laura held a hand out to her. 'Helen, I promise you're safe.'

'I want to go home.' Helen's eyes darted for the door, and her feet quickly followed.

'Please, wait!' Laura called after her. 'Let's talk about this.'

The whole group trailed after her, but Helen didn't get far. She stood slack-jawed in the middle of Saint Kinga's chapel. 'This is a tomb. Are we dead?'

'It's not a tomb,' Beth said. 'It used to be some kind of church.'

'Then let me go outside. When I have the moon above me again, we'll talk.'

Aleksey sniggered. 'It's not that simple. We're hundreds of metres below the ground. We can't exactly throw open a window.'

Helen gasped. 'You lied to me, Laura. All we showed you was kindness, and you've damned me to hell!'

'I swear—'

But Helen had already broken into a run towards the stairs. She scrambled up them and out into the tunnels beyond.

'She won't get far,' Aleksey said. 'I'll alert the guardians. They'll soon round her up.'

Laura shoved him. 'No, you won't. You will leave her be. Do you understand me?'

'How dare you?'

'Easily. Felix isn't here to do your dirty work now, is he? If you want to take me on, I'm right here.'

Aleksey's jowls wobbled. 'I have no idea what you mean.'

'You would say that.'

'Mum.' The word felt strange in Jared's mouth, but it silenced Laura instantly. 'Forget him. Let's go and find your friend.'

They peered into every tunnel they passed, calling her name. 'Helen! Please come out! You're safe!'

'Will you be quiet,' Aleksey hissed. 'You'll wake the citizens.'

'Maybe it's time they woke up,' Marney said. And they did. Bleary-eyed and confused, they began to appear, asking questions and offering help.

Aleksey flapped them away. 'There's nothing to see here. Go back to bed.' They didn't listen.

'She's never going to come out to a huge group like this,' Laura said.

Beth nodded. 'Then let's split up.'

It didn't take long for Jared to find her scrunched into one of the alcoves. 'We aren't going to hurt you.'

Even in the gloom, her eyes blazed. 'Oh, I know you're not. But I won't promise the same.'

Jared slid down the wall opposite her. 'I used to think this place was hell, too. Then I realised I was giving it more importance than it deserved. I've met some evil people here, sure. But we've got rid of them now, I think.'

'Then what is it?'

'A hiding place. There was trouble up there, in the real world. Storms, famine, sickness; they saw it all.'

'I lived through those things and more, and I'd still rather be up there.'

'Me too. But they're scared.'

'I'm not.'

'Then come out of there, and I'll take you to the surface so you can see the moon, just as you asked.'

'Really?'

'Of course.' Jared held out his hand, and Helen took it. Then together, they walked to the entrance cavern.

'How long have you lived down here?'

'Me? I don't. I escaped as soon as I had the opportunity.'

'I felt the same way about Dornoch. Although, I never managed it.'

'Well, you have now.'

Helen kept her eyes trained on the floor, so she didn't give the gasp Jared expected as they reached the cavern. 'We're here,' he said.

Helen looked around. 'It's big.'

Jared laughed. 'It usually gets a bit more of a reaction than that.'

'I'm not easily impressed.'

'Jared?' Kristoff appeared from one of the tunnels. 'What are you doing here?' He clocked Helen but perhaps decided it was best not to ask who the strange woman was.

'We're going to the surface.'

'Do you have permission?'

'No.'

Kristoff hesitated before saying, 'All right then. Be safe.'

'We will. Thank you.' Jared turned back to Helen. 'There's a lot of steps. Are you sure you're up to it?'

'I'm not afraid of hard work.'

They started their ascent, Jared glancing back occasionally at Helen. She cursed the material of her dress, which seemed to make the climb harder.

When they reached the top, Jared turned the heavy lock. 'Are you ready?'

'Yes.' They stepped outside. The tension seemed to leave Helen's body as she stared at the moon. 'In the cells where they were keeping us, there were little windows. Barred, of course, but we could still see out. If my ma is looking at the moon now, is it the same as this one?'

Jared's brain began to sift and process the layers of information that fully answering that question would require. But to Helen, he just settled on, 'It is.'

'Good.'

Voices behind them caught Jared's attention. He'd expected to see his mother and the rest of the search party. Instead, Kristoff stood at the door, encouraging somebody to step outside.

'Who's there?' Jared asked.

'The citizens followed you,' Kristoff said. 'I didn't see what harm it could do to let them come up.

Jared smiled at his old friend. 'It is a lovely night.' He joined him back at the stairwell and peered inside. Pale round faces, like reflections of the moon above, stared from the gloom. 'It's safe. You can come out now.'

They were still trailing from the darkness when he went back to Helen. 'They haven't seen the stars in a long time,' Jared said. 'Some of the younger ones never have.'

'They won't be happy going back down there once they see this beauty.'

'No, I don't imagine they will be. Helen, what would you say if I told you there was another place for you to live up here?'

'If it means I don't have to stay down there, I'd say yes.'

'Alright then. I'll see what I can do.'

The next day he spoke to Marney. 'I think it's a good idea,' she said. 'It could be the start of a partnership with the Colony.'

'Then you'll talk to Bug?'

'No. It should be you.' Marney wasn't asking, she was telling him; that much was clear.

'Why? They both know that I have no power here.'

Marney held his shoulders, so he was square to her, looking him directly in the eye. He tried to slope away, but she wouldn't let him. 'Don't sell yourself short. The people here trust you. *I* trust you. You can persuade Bug and Evie to work with us; I know you can. Please, Jared. I can't go myself. Not when things are so volatile.'

On that point, at least, she was right. From the moment he'd opened the door to the Sanctuary, and the citizens realised the world wasn't as hostile as they'd been led to believe, the community fractured in two. Half wanted to disappear over the horizon. The rest wanted to return to the refuge below. Aleksey was holding the two halves together by his fingernails.

Despite his protests, Jared knew he couldn't deny Marney's demand. How could he when the fault for their current predicament could be placed so logically at his feet? That was how Jared, Beth, Aaron and Helen came to be bouncing along a deserted road towards the Colony. Aaron looked at ease behind the wheel of one of the Sanctuary trucks.

'Let me have a turn.' Helen reached a hand towards the wheel. They'd expected her to be terrified of her first experience in a motor vehicle, but she'd taken it in her stride, demanding to ride up front.

'Not a chance,' Aaron said.

'Who made you king of the road?' Beth asked.

'Well, you two ladies are from a time before cars were invented, and Jared moved to the Sanctuary before he was old enough to learn. So in answer to your question, my dear Beth, experience puts me in charge here.'

'Yes,' Jared said. 'But *I* experienced watching you crash your aunt's car over and over for what felt like an eternity.'

Beth chuckled and jabbed Aaron in the upper arm. 'Now he mentions it, I have a distinct memory of that happening, too.'

Aaron stared daggers at them both. 'Well, I don't remember that. If some other versions of me can't handle themselves, that's on them. Just be grateful that you got the best of the bunch.'

Watching his friends tease one another, Jared's muscles eased. Maybe they could be happy there. Perhaps they could somehow build a life together in the wasteland of his Earth.

'Are you sure this place will even take me?' Helen asked.

'I think so,' Jared said. 'You have skills they need. Farming, beekeeping; I think you will be an asset to the Colony, Helen.'

She blushed. 'I hope so.'

In the days since she'd crossed over, Jared had developed a soft spot for Helen. Feisty and independent, she didn't want any of them to see how fragile she was after what happened. He hoped she would let somebody in eventually. They weren't the kind of wounds that you could heal alone.

One day, he'd caught her crying by the lake, although

she'd tried to wipe her tears once she saw him. 'I miss my ma every second of the day,' she'd said. 'I can't stop wondering what happened to her.'

'Do you want to know?'

After a little thought, she said, 'Right now, the answer could be anything. And I am pretty sure any of the options I dream up for her will be better than the truth. So thank you, but no, I don't.'

Jared was relieved. In reality, Janet's death was brutal, earning her a little corner of the history books as the last woman in Scotland to be convicted of witchcraft and burnt alive. There was no gentle way of breaking that to her daughter.

They reached a forest, or at least the remnants of one. The shells of dead trees blocked their view of the path beyond, and they all got out to get a better look.

'Cheery,' Helen said. 'Not a leaf to share amongst the lot of them.'

'And we're going in there? On foot?' Aaron asked. 'Can't we, I don't know, go round or something?'

Jared pulled Marney's map from the truck. 'No. The Colony is somewhere in the middle.'

Beth linked her arm through Aaron's. 'I'll protect you.'

'We'd better get going or we could get lost in the dark.' Jared took a last look at the world behind them, bathed in sunlight, before stepping beneath the decaying canopy of tangled branches.

An anxious silence fell over them as they each navigated the forest floor, made dangerous by twisted tree roots and blanketed with shadows.

'Ow!' Aaron sprawled on the path in front of them. 'Stupid branches!'

'Yes,' Beth said. 'How dare they be lying there just waiting for a clumsy oaf like you to fall over them.'

Aaron dusted himself off. 'No, honestly guys, don't worry about me. I'm okay.'

Helen clutched Jared's arm. 'Did you hear that?'

'I didn't—' The snap of hollow twigs truncated Jared's sentence, and the four of them froze. 'Hello?' No answer. 'Maybe it was an animal.'

'With Bug's portals everywhere,' Aaron said, 'that doesn't make me feel any better. Let's keep moving.' But Beth was right in front of him, blocking his path. 'Beth? Are you okay?'

'I think something stung me.' She clutched her neck. From between her fingers protruded a feathered dart. 'I feel...'

Jared caught her before she could fall. 'Aaron, get her other arm!'

But Aaron dropped to his knees, followed by Helen.

'Please!' Jared yelled into the forest. 'Don't hurt my friends!' There was a sharp pinch as the dart hit him in the chest. Jared pulled it from his flesh and stared at it. It was the last thing he saw before the world went black.

When he awoke, Evelyn's face was millimetres from his. 'Thank God you're okay.'

'I'm not sure he has much to do with it.' Jared swung his legs over the side of the bed he lay on, but the world began to swim in front of his eyes.

'Bev!' Evelyn's shout hurt his head. 'I think something's wrong.'

'Nah, he's just got a hangover. It'll pass. Make him drink some water.'

'Here.' Evelyn pressed a cup to his lips. 'Drink this.'

Jared did as instructed but showered the floor before him in coughs and splutters. 'I'm sorry.'

'Don't apologise. I swear, Jared, if we'd known it was you, there's no way the lookouts would have fired. I guess tensions are high after what happened with the Pack. We can't be sure there aren't more of them out there.'

'Where are my friends?'

'Look.' Evelyn pointed towards a row of nearby beds where they slept soundly. Jared laughed when Helen snorted, told herself to shut up, and drifted off again. 'They're fine.'

'Let them sleep it off,' Bev said. 'They'll feel better for it.'

Jared massaged his temple. 'No doubt.'

'Can I get you anything?' Evelyn asked.

'Just some fresh air.'

'Okay. Let's take a quick walk.' Jared noted how she hovered her hand near his elbow as if caught between being afraid to touch him and letting him go. 'Do you feel steady?'

'I'm fine.' They stepped out of what Jared assumed was the infirmary, and he cringed away from the sunlight. When his vision cleared, he saw the greenest field he'd seen in years, dotted with thousands of daisies. 'That's amazing. All of this in a matter of days. How can that be possible?'

'It's not. This has taken Bug and the other Colonists years. Since before you and I even entered the Sanctuary, apparently.'

'It's beautiful.'

Evelyn smirked.

'What's so funny?'

"Beautiful' is pretty useless nowadays. You have to be strong to survive.'

You're both, he wanted to say but swallowed the words down. 'Well, I'm still impressed.'

'Good.' She beamed at him. 'Let me show you around.' They walked silently for a few minutes before she asked, 'Why are you here?'

'You invited me.'

'True. But I didn't think you'd accept.'

'Sorry.'

'I didn't mean it like that. What I meant was, I didn't think you'd be able to forgive us for what we did.'

'It's not your fault. Bug—'

'Don't do that. I didn't ask for a pass. I own my actions and choices. I'm not some little girl manipulated by some evil genius.'

'Calm down. I didn't say you were.'

'Good. Because I don't think I deserve your forgiveness.' Evelyn's resolve seemed to disappear.

'Tell me what happened.'

'I can't. Not yet.'

'Then at least make amends.'

'How?'

'Close the portal closest to the Sanctuary.'

'Bug would never agree to—'

'And then work with us to police the others.'

She turned to face him. 'Not to close them?'

'No. Marney has agreed that we will try Bug's plan.'

'Is she running things now? Aleksey must be thrilled.'

Evelyn gnawed at her lower lip. 'I'll talk to Bug, see what he thinks.'

'Thank you.' Jared hesitated, afraid to undo the progress they'd made. 'I'm not sure there is anything you could say to make me hate you.'

'Don't be so sure.'

'But I think I have the right to decide that for myself.'

'I know. I just don't know how to say it.'

'Could you write it?'

'Sorry?'

'We're creating history. The Sanctuary, the Colony, even the Pack; all of their journeys should be recorded so that one day, when we've saved this world, they'll know how it came about. I'd like it to be in your words if you're willing. The Book of Evelyn. Tell me your story?'

'What if you don't like what you read?'

'All I ask is that you tell the truth. Can you do that?'

Evelyn nodded. 'It's the least you deserve.'

~

The Book of Evelyn

Bug agreed to your truce. I had a feeling he would. He'd never craved confrontation or war. He'd say he'd never even wanted leadership. That I can relate to. Fate seems to enjoy dealing these things to the unwilling and unprepared.

We made our third trip back to the Sanctuary at your invitation. 'It's nice not to have to ram the gates this time,' Bug said.

'Or to be bleeding out in the back,' I added.

'Silver linings. Are you ready?'

'No.'

'Me neither.'

Discontent had continued to rumble through the Sanctuary in our absence. I think it was a kind of grief for the life they thought they'd have, isolated but safe, cocooned beneath the earth. As denial and anger gave way to acceptance and curiosity, some citizens decided they wanted to explore the emerging new world.

Aleksey called a meeting in the Grand Chamber. Returning, however briefly, made my skin crawl. Echoes of trauma assaulted me every second I was there. But I endured it for the greater good. You see, I've been making sacrifices, too. Please try to remember that.

Aleksey stood in front of the citizens, palms outstretched and pleading. 'Don't throw your lives away. I can't bear to think of our community being decimated by such recklessness.'

The citizens murmured between themselves, arguing the merits of going or staying.

'It's too dangerous,' Aleksey said. 'Earthquakes, famine,

not to mention the possibility that some God-forsaken creature has wandered through one of those portals. There are hundreds of ways to die up there.'

Emma Wallace gave the most fitting reply. 'Yeah, but I know boredom will definitely kill me down here. This isn't living.'

'Smart woman,' Bug said from the back of the hall. 'In fact, I see a lot of intelligent, capable people here. I think they deserve to know the truth. Tell them what you are really afraid of, Aleksey.'

'I have. I'm afraid they will all perish up there.'

'Aren't you a thoughtful leader. I suppose there are no selfish motives involved.'

'What are you talking about?' Aleksey asked.

'The way I see it, the Sanctuary is a closed ecosystem. If anything changes, like half of your workforce disappearing, it will collapse.'

Aleksey glared at him. 'Not everyone thinks like that. What is it you call your people? Workers? Or is it drones? How many of them have you allowed to perish in pursuit of some misguided dream?'

'Aleksey, you know so much but understand so little. Survival isn't about keeping your heart beating as long as possible. It's about knowing that we, as a society, have a future.'

'That's what I want, too.' He spread his arms wide. 'That's what all of this has been about.'

'Is that right? Every member of the Colony works for the greater good. Me included. Can you say the same?' He turned to the citizens. 'When was the last time you saw Aleksey get his hands dirty?'

'I do my fair share.'

'I doubt that. But either way, what if there were a better way for your people? Why aren't you willing to explore the possibility?'

'I am.' Aleksey hesitated. 'I'll go.'

'Excuse me?'

'I'll travel to the Colony. With the proviso that we close the portal behind the Sanctuary on the way so I know the citizens will be safe.' He beamed at his audience. 'Then I'll report back to you all so you can make an informed decision about your future.'

I couldn't suppress my laugh of disdain. So I was surprised when Bug nodded. 'That sounds like a start.'

I don't know for sure what happened that day, so I've used my imagination a little to fill in the gaps. However, I think you'd tell me that's all the history books are, somebody's interpretation of half-remembered or second-hand events.

Of course, I only have Bug's word for any of it. But he told me this was the truth, and I choose to believe him. You probably think me naive. Still, you've told me to include here anything that might be relevant to future generations, so that's what I'm doing.

The morning Bug and Aleksey left, I was helping fill the truck with rations gifted by the Sanctuary. Marney told us to view them as a symbol of our future alliance.

'Let me come back with you,' I said.

'Soon. For now, this is where I need you, ensuring poison isn't dripped into these people's ears.'

'I hate this place.'

'I know. It won't be for long.'

A question was plaguing me. 'What happens if they all want to join us?'

Bug didn't sugarcoat his answer. 'Then part of the Colony will have to break off and swarm.'

'No. That's not fair. I, for one, won't sacrifice my home for them.'

'It will be as it is meant to be. There is no 'I' or 'me' any more, not if the human race is going to survive. There can be only 'we' and 'us'.'

I knew there was no point arguing.

'If it comes to that, they'll need a Queen,' he said.

'I won't be volunteering.'

'Don't discount it yet. You're more than capable. You've only just begun to discover your potential, Evelyn.'

That was how Bug and Aleksey came to be driving along one of the deteriorating roads between the two camps.

'Aren't you forgetting something?' Aleksey asked.

'What?'

'The portal.'

'Oh. Jared told us that's what you wanted so we closed it before we arrived.'

'Why didn't you say anything?'

Bug smirked. 'You seemed to be enjoying your moment in the spotlight.'

Apparently the conversation was sparse. In fact, Aleksey spent much of the journey dozing. Perhaps that's why Bug didn't notice it at first. Not until Aleksey began to flap and yelp. 'Get it off me.' A creature the size of a rat rested on his chest. The force of Aleksey's slap as he swiped it away sent it hurtling into the car's footwell.

'Will you keep still, you are going to cause—' One

wheel of the truck mounted the bank. Bug told me it all happened so fast that he didn't have time to correct his course. The next thing he knew, they were nose first on the other side.

'You idiot!' Aleksey snarled.

'That's not helpful.'

'Neither is driving us into a ditch.'

'I wasn't the one flipping out over...' He crouched down in the footwell and scooped up the insect. 'Wow, it's beautiful.' It was as big as his fist and covered with red and black fuzz.

'Get it away from me!' Aleksey squirmed to the other side of the cab.

'Relax, you killed it, the poor thing.' Bug held it out on his palm in front of Aleksey's face. Stretched out, it was so long that it hung over the end of his fingers, its abdomen curling around them.

'Is it an ant?'

'In a way. It's called a velvet ant, but it's actually a type of wasp. But this one is not like any I've seen before.'

'How so?'

'It's about five times bigger than it should be. And look at that stinger!'

'I'd prefer not to,' Aleksey said.

'It shouldn't exist.'

'Agreed.' Aleksey kept his eyes locked on the forest of dead trees outside.

'No, I mean literally. The males have wings. The females have stingers. They can't have both. At least not in our world and our time. Yet this one does.'

'What are you saying?'

'That it's working. The animals are coming through the portal.'

Aleksey sat bolt upright. 'You mean one of those portals is close by.'

'Maybe. Or perhaps this little guy has been on an adventure.' Right on cue, the velvet ant jerked into life. It lifted from Bug's hand and hit the roof of the truck.

'Kill it!' Aleksey grabbed for the door handle and tugged over and over. 'Why isn't it opening?' The velvet ant bashed against the windscreen, each time making an audible thud.

'Just keep still,' Bug said, pressing the button for the electric windows. 'Don't make it any angrier.'

'I thought I was supposed to 'relax' because it wouldn't hurt me,' Aleksey said, pinning his body against his seat.

'That's when I thought it was dead. They used to call regular size velvet ants 'Cow Killers'.'

Aleksey's whimper turned into a cry as the ant whizzed towards his face before disappearing out of the window.

The two men slumped while they caught their breath. Eventually, Bug said, 'Let's get moving.' He turned the key again and again, but the engine choked. 'I guess we're walking.'

'Are you joking? There might be more of those things out there.'

'No. They're solitary creatures.'

'Or maybe we'll meet something worse.'

'The Colony is just over that hill.' Bug pointed to a spot in the distance, between the trees. 'Either we leave now on foot and get there by nightfall, or we wait here and hope that by some means of telepathy, they send help.'

'They'll come looking for us.'

'Aleksey, the Sanctuary thinks we've gone to stay at the Colony, and the Colony has no idea we're coming.'

Aleksey stared into the distance. 'I won't make it. You should go and send back help. I'll wait here.' Aleksey clambered back into the cab of the truck. He was still sitting, looking defiantly ahead, when Bug left him.

Bug didn't get far before he heard the noises. Rustling in the decaying trees became a crash as something went hurtling past him. Then there was a growl, a smash, a scream.

I asked why Bug didn't go back. He just shrugged and said, 'Adapt or die.' And he did send help. After he reached the Colony, a group went back looking for Aleksey. They found Dale's truck but nothing more. No blood. No tracks.

Of course, as I said, I don't know if any of that is true. For all I know, Bug took Aleksey into the desert and left him there. Or shot him. Or both.

Bug left the ant out of the version of the story he told the others. 'Best not to scare them,' he'd said. The Sanctuary sent out search parties, but eventually they gave up. The possibilities ahead of them were too much of a distraction to let them dwell for too long. Besides, making their peace with the disappearance of those around them had become a way of life.

It might surprise you, but that made me a little sad for Aleksey. For all his hot air and bluster, he did help keep the citizens alive. But when it came down to it, he was assigned to a footnote in a history they wanted to forget.

So here we are, at the beginning of the end. Or of a fresh start. I guess which you believe is a matter of perspective.

This is the part I have been dreading. It will hurt you to

listen to my side of the story. I realise that. But there's no way around it; you must go through it. And I am truly sorry.

I know I am going back over old ground, but I left out some key information. That was cowardly of me. If we are going to build a life here, I want you to know the whole truth. What you choose to do with it is up to you.

The afternoon that we left you in the Sanctuary, after you gave us the orb, my mind was already racing. 'It's not enough, Bug. It will take years to get enough pollinators here to make any difference.'

'I know. But maybe we'll be able to save our little piece of the world.'

'We could do more.'

He stopped the car. 'What are you suggesting?'

I took a deep breath, knowing there would be no turning back. 'You plan to take what we need from another timeline, shut the door behind us and hope for the best.'

'That's right.'

'What if we opened a permanent gate between the worlds and joined the two together?'

'Is that even possible?'

'Jared thought it might be. When he sent his friend back to save his mother, he said the portal needed to be closed because it might weaken the fabric between the realities. Not that it wasn't possible to keep it open.'

'He told me the same thing; leaving it open could be dangerous.'

'Only because that's what Edmond believed. That's why he designed it with a timer that would close it automatically. But what do we have to lose?'

'The two worlds could collide.'

'Or ours could be saved.'

There it is. It was my idea. I know you don't want to hear that, and it would be easy to let Bug take the fall. But I own my decisions. This is me taking back control of my life. Although, it pains me to know that by doing so I've taken away some of yours. If it helps, I really do think we can flourish in this new world. That's probably not much consolation to you when you've lost your gateway to countless others. I know that if they find out, the Sanctuary will want to put me on trial for what I've done, and I don't expect you to stop them. Why would you? Still, I pray you can forgive me, Jared; because, of all the labels placed on me over the years, one of the few I fear losing is 'your friend'.

I've asked you before, but you never gave me an answer. What do you see when you look at me? I've been so many things to so many people that, somewhere along the way, I lost my sense of who I am. A thief, a victim, a murderer. A leader, a princess, a Queen. Evie, Evelyn, Eve. I've been called all of these things and more. Now I know that it doesn't matter what others think of me. I know who I am now, and I'm content with the person I've become. After all, light and dark, good and evil: aren't we all a mixture of these things?

~

Jared
<u>Three Months Later</u>

I thought my book was closed. But here I am again, telling you this is not the end. It's just a new chapter. Granted, not one I anticipated.

Then, my life so far has been anything but predictable.

The portal is holding strong, and already we are seeing flourishes of life in the most unexpected places. With the odd flower poking from between paving slabs and weeds invading abandoned buildings, nature is finding a way.

My fears over what else might travel through the portals haven't disappeared. The guardians have a new purpose now, protecting the old Earth from the inhabitants of the new.

As the residents of the Sanctuary and the Colony brave the wider world, they look to us for leadership. Evie, Bug and I didn't ask for that job. After all, what type of leaders could a chameleon, a misfit and a deserter make? But each of us played a part in shaping this new world, and now we have a responsibility to its inhabitants.

Besides, I am beginning to think that maybe Bug is right. Perhaps we are exactly what they need. I know that one day I will find a way to explore the past again. But for now, home is where my future lies.

A Note From Cher

I hope you enjoyed reading The Book of Evelyn as much as I enjoyed writing it. Leaving a review is a great way to help other readers find my books. I don't have the advertising budget of some of the bigger name authors, so a review on Amazon, Goodreads or any other online platforms that you use would be really helpful. I would be very grateful for your support.

Please review The Book of Evelyn on Amazon by scanning the QR code at the top of the page.

The Book Of Beth

Free Ebook

I have received so many comments about how sad my lovely readers are to see the Escaping Sanctuary series end that I decided to write another 'book'. Despite being one of the most enigmatic characters, there just wasn't enough space to include Beth's back story in the main novels. If you would like to learn more about her life before she met Jared, then please join my mailing list to receive a free digital copy of her story. Just scan the QR code at the top of the page.